To Peg:

Follow Your Dream
&
find where it takes you...

Anna Gill

Rave Reviews from the Readers

~"Enchanting, mesmerizing. Anna Gill brings the readers from the halls of Harvard to stand on equal footing with the watermen of the Chesapeake. One is drawn to take a closer look into the complexities of conservation and preservation of our historic cultures."

> N. Stevenson, Corporate Finance Accountant, Rhode Island

~"A fun and fast read on issues of importance to all of us."

> B. Rinebold, Legal Guardian Consultant, Ret., Rochester, NY

~"Anna Gill hooks you, at first, with her humor and then holds your attention with her characters until you are seduced into the story. You feel her passion for the Eastern Shore as she paints a canvass of the area in your mind. The Tale of Dickie Short is an important book of our time. It hits right to the heart of the matter."

> K. Zois, Artist, Maine

~"Great Read. A fascinating story of the Chesapeake you just can't put down."

> C. Harper, Interior Designer, Saddle River, NJ

The Tale of Dickie Short

Anna Gill

authorHOUSE®

AuthorHouse™
1663 Liberty Drive, Suite 200
Bloomington, IN 47403
www.authorhouse.com
Phone: 1-800-839-8640

First published by AuthorHouse 4/2/2010

ISBN: 978-1-4389-1579-1 (sc)

Library of Congress Control Number: 2008908770

Printed in the United States of America
Bloomington, Indiana

This book is printed on acid-free paper.

This book is dedicated to the mighty watermen of the Chesapeake and to my dear friend, CR Hook, who can spin a yarn about these men better than anyone I know.

Acknowledgments

HITTING ON A STORYLINE THAT works is a rare and wondrous thing. Dickie Short's tale has been a project in the making for a number of years and without the assistance of so many wonderful people, he would never have been able to spring to life and tell his story.

So, to those folks who have made this possible, I give a huge round of applause.

Many thanks and appreciation to CR Hook, whose extraordinary knowledge of life and history on the Eastern Shore of Maryland encouraged me day by day to keep on going. A very special thanks to Christy Davis, my wonderful editor with the keen eye and loving heart to do the tough job of making sense of this story and assuring that the fun abounds. To Stanley Bennett, who fascinated me with his knowledge of muskrats and what really goes on down on the marsh in wintertime. To the gang on the shore who welcome me back each winter and give me my space to write my heart out. And a rousing round of applause to Scott Levy, my "IT" guy who teaches me new things all the time in this fast-paced world of all things technical.

A most special salute of gratitude and appreciation from me goes out to the tough and rugged watermen. Their stories of how they came to make their livings on the water will forever be emblazoned in my heart. You are all part of this wondrous tapestry we call American history and you make this world a better place.

I most certainly could never write a word if it weren't for the love and support of my husband Alan and all those daughters, sons, grand babies, and friends who keep rooting me on in times of stress. Thanks to you all. You give me the courage to keep my dream alive.

It is my hope that through humor, this book will shed new light on the difficult and serious challenges that are confronting not only the mighty Chesapeake, but all coastal and water areas throughout America.

Enjoy!

"To know who you are you must have a place to come from…"

CARSON McCULLERS

Preface

A YEAR HAS PASSED AND I am still right here at The Baltimore Sun. I still love being a reporter. And I still am waiting for the big story that will make me rise to the top of my game.

I have some lofty ambitions, don't I? I mean I am a fledgling pisser compared to some of these old dogs who have all the fun getting the big assignments. Did I really expect to graduate from Harvard and knock them all dead the first year? Well maybe I did, but I see now it takes a whole lot more than that. It was easy breezy when I was a kid, writing all those adventure stories about pirates and scallywags who roamed the seas looking for adventure. I always won first prize in class for those. But this is the big time and all adventure I ever seem to get are inane stories of cats stuck in trees or big fires set in old warehouses by winos who had better lives once upon a time. I keep telling myself it will come if I have the patience in me to shut up and do my job...and wait.

At least my Mom is proud. Dad is still sore I didn't follow in his footsteps at the Boston Globe. He just couldn't understand how an Alston man, Harvard all the way, could decide to go anywhere else. Well I wasn't at all Alston- I had my Mom's Irish and more sensitive side raging inside of me more times than not. He would just have to settle for being the best sport's editor the Globe had ever had and leave me to find my claim to fame on my own. I have to admit to myself sometimes that it didn't hurt that his closest friend from Harvard was the Managing Editor of the Sun down here in Baltimore. And, as it turned out, apparently old Max had been a fan of mine all the years I was growing up and when Dad spoke to him he didn't hesitate to talk to me about coming on board with his paper. Hey, today it's all about who you know, isn't it?

However, with my first year under my belt, I really have to try to get some bigger and better assignments. I know that whole story of how you have to pay your dues, but I mean really, the stories I am covering are enough to make you run out of the building with your hair on fire.

He can't be partial, but I know Max is pleased with my work. How do I know that? I see that little wink he gives me as we pass in the halls. Maybe that's lame, but I have known him forever and I know that wink. I don't want to take advantage, but I mean I really have to make some kind of a break for it soon or I will go crazy. Being a newbie puts you down at the bottom of the food chain waiting for that one break. That one certain story that has your name on it. I have to admit that there are days the sport's desk at the Globe might look pretty appealing, but no, I am here and here is where I will stay. Even if it means I have to continue a while longer covering asinine stories like the last one that had me interviewing an old woman who had bagged some pretty handsome lobsters at a ritzy-titsy grocery store in the burbs. I couldn't believe it. Nobody could believe it. Come to think of it, I am going crazy and I really have to make my case soon or else, or else I will do what? When I think of it, it was a pretty funny story and I did bring the paper a lot of attention. I still laugh thinking of that day and how I raced off to the police station, I could hardly believe that the honchos at the grocery store were actually going to arrest granny. I mean this was hardly grand larceny. I arrived just after they had taken her in. I dashed inside and flashed my creds. That's the really great thing about working for a paper- you get the cards that let you in just about anywhere. Finding where she was and after they questioned her, I got the go ahead to go on in and talk to her.

I could tell the officers handling this inquisition weren't really into arresting a woman the age of all their grandmothers. These guys were my age and I automatically felt a kindred spirit. They were looking for a better assignment too.

When I opened the door, I understood exactly what those looks meant. Sitting in front of me was *Aunt Bea*, clutching one of those outdated pocket books that only your grandma would have. She smiled up at me, looking as if she were going to reach up and lay one on my cheek.

Trying to look very official, I said, "Hi. I am Tug Alston from The Sun. May I ask you a few questions?"

Her voice was sweet and shockingly sincere. "I would love that, dear." She acted like she was at a tea party and I was her guest.

"But before you ask me anything, could you be a sweetheart and get me a small glass of water? It's very warm in here."

Without thinking twice, I got up and went to fetch the water. Returning, I noticed that she was sitting in the exact same pose and waiting for me with that exact same smile on her face. How *do* I get these sterling assignments?

Taking a few sips, she said, "Ah, that's better. Thank you so much." Then she leaned toward me and lowered her voice, suckering me in all the way. "I really did it this time, didn't I? I took one too many of the fish."

Was I hearing right- *This* time? My eyebrows flew up and my eyes bugged out. "What do you mean, this time?"

This hip, old clever granny, who was somewhere in the neighborhood of eighty, was telling me that she was an absolute pro at this kind of thing and that there was absolutely nothing wrong with stealing her supper.

"Oh yes," she went on quite sincerely, "I usually take two, but tonight I am having a third for dinner. Now, two just wasn't going to make it around, you know."

I was speechless. She had completely thrown me for a loop. This was a lulu of an old woman; and I instantly liked her.

Trying not to scare her too much, I said, "They are aiming to keep you here for the night you know."

Without a moment's hesitation she interrupted, "Oh no, they won't. They will just tell me what a bad girl I was and when I offer to pay for the lobsters, they will let me go.

"Been through this before, have we?" I could hardly contain myself. This granny had spirit and I loved her.

Whispering to me, as if the FBI were listening in, she said, "Well, yes I have but that doesn't matter much. This time they must have felt I was important enough to send me a nice young reporter who will tell my story and not make me out to be a common thief. Isn't that true dearie?"

That did it. I broke out with hoots of laughter. This was a game to her. With my head shaking side to side, I asked, "Why do you do this?"

"For fun, my dear," she giggled. "At my age what's left for excitement? I rather fancy myself as a late bloomer. A *Bonnie Parker* type, don't you know."

I had it all down on tape as well as on paper. I was still laughing when I stood up and gave her a hug. I knew exactly how I was going to write this story and I was definitely going to make her into the sweetest old lady robber Baltimore ever knew.

Returning to my humble cubicle, I wrote the piece for the next day's paper, I never dreamed that it would cause such a stir. People began writing letters to the editor in her defense and they picketed the grocery store. I have to admit I really laid it on a little thick, but hey, she was delightful and I was certainly writing it tongue and cheek. Could I help it if I suggested that if she were left to her own devices, she could throw the biggest lobster fest Baltimore had ever seen? And at taxpayer's expense? Hell, even crusty old Max loved it.

Of course having that edition of the paper sell like hotcakes' didn't hurt either.

That sweet old lady will never know that her larceny was going to help me make the leap into the bigger leagues. I just had to wait for his call. Max was going to give me that chance I was waiting for. I could feel it. The little boy who wrote adventure stories has grown up. He is a hero now, at least to that nice, old lady. But, hey, he writes the stories and he always ends up the hero. Right?

The Assignment

Driving into work, I went over the million things I had waiting for me. It was going to be a pretty hectic schedule and I had to attend a meeting at five. No drinks for me with the gang today, I thought.

I pulled into my usual space on the third floor of the ramp and trudged on in. I decided to grab a cup of "Joe" and a bagel before heading up. You just can't face the day without a good, stiff jolt from an over caffeinated cup of coffee from this place. They seem to leave it in the pot until I arrive so I can have the pleasure of drinking the dregs.

As the elevator door opened on my floor, I saw my old buddy Roger standing there.

"Where have you been? I have been waiting for you for a half an hour?"

"What do you mean, Roger? The last time I checked my watch, I wasn't late."

"Well, forget about it. That pretty, young assistant for Max Pierson has been down here looking for you. When I asked her what had her panties in a bunch, she smiled that sweet smile only she can flash and said to have you call her the minute you came in."

"Why would Beth be looking for me? Did she say?"

"No. She just said to call her immediately upon your arrival."

"Okay, Roger, I have arrived, and if you would get out of my way, I will call her."

"God, Tug, you don't seem to be too nervous about it."

"Should I be? What's with you, Roger? She works here just like the rest of us."

"Works here just like the rest of us? Shit, Tug, she can make or break someone around here if she says the right thing to Max."

"Afraid of her are we?"

"Call her Tug and then let me know what she wants."

Shooting his buddy a stiff salute, Tug said, "Yes sir, Roger Brown. I will take that as an order."

Roger patted his friend on the shoulder and laughed. "I don't mean to be so intense, but she seemed to be intent on talking with you."

"Then get out of here and let me make the call. That is unless you want to stand over me and hear for yourself."

Waving his hand in the air, Roger stalked off back to his cubicle down the hall.

Plunking his briefcase on the desk and swallowing two gulps of the God-awful coffee, Tug Alston dialed Beth's extension.

"Beth? It's Tug. I hear you wanted me to call you."

In the most syrupy-sweet voice, Beth answered, "Why yes, Tug, I did. I am glad your friend Roger could remember to tell you."

Ouch! She could be stinging, that was for sure. I guessed she didn't appreciate Roger's overactive sense of humor sometimes.

"What's up Beth?"

"Mr. Pierson wants to see you at ten sharp this morning. I hope you don't have anything else on your agenda because if you do; cancel it."

I caught her drift. This was important and apparently very important although I couldn't think of one reason for Maxwell Pierson wanting to speak to him.

"I am free Beth and I will be there in one hour. Could you tell me if you know what this is about?"

2

With a slight giggle in her throat, Beth answered me as if she knew, but wasn't about to tell me. "No, not really Tug. You know he doesn't tell me…everything."

I bit my lip. She lied like a champ. Beth Andrews knew everything that went on in Max's office. I'll let her keep playing her little game.

"Okay then, I'll see you in a little while."

"I can't wait Tug."

Why did she say that? I thought. I picked up on something in her voice. She was a fox alright. Oh well, I will find out soon enough.

I heard a light, and annoying tapping behind me. It was Roger who had come back to get the scoop.

"Well?"

"Well nothing, Roger. I am to see the man at ten sharp according to our gal Beth."

"She didn't say anything about why he wants to see you?"

"Is there something about the word nothing you don't understand?"

Pissed off and frustrated, Roger turned away and I could hear him mumbling to himself all the way down the hall.

BETH WAS SITTING WITH HER back to the door when I entered the office. I gave a slight knock, so I didn't scare her.

Twirling around, Beth looked up at me with those killer blue eyes she flashes all the time. "Hi Tug. Glad you are on time. He is in a bit of a cranky mood this morning."

"Swell," I mumbled. "Anything else I should know before I enter the lion's den?"

Beth laughed and brushed aside her long blonde hair out of her gorgeous face. "No, not that I know of. He just seems a might more aggravated today for some reason."

"I hope I don't have anything to do with that." I was still trying to pry some info out of her, but it didn't work.

"I see he is off the phone now, so it's your turn up at bat. Good luck."

Now I knew she knew something. Why else would she say 'good luck.'?"

As I walked through the door, Max stood up to greet me. Or maybe he just wanted to stretch for a minute. Beckoning me with his hand to take a seat, he said, "Glad you could come, Tug."

Was there a choice? "Yes, I am too Mr. Pierson." I was still more than a little nervous not knowing why he wanted to see me. He wasn't a man who spent idle time with the underlings.

"I thought I told you when I welcomed you aboard that I am Max around here to all you employees."

"Sorry sir, I guess it's old habits, you know."

"Your dad is an old and dear friend, Tug. As a matter of fact he called the other day and asked how things were going with you?"

I swallowed hard. My father had a way about him. He was always checking to see if his disobedient son, who wouldn't write for the Boston Globe, could possibly make it on his own. I decided to hit his comment head on. "And what did you tell him…Max?"

"Why I told him you were becoming one damned good reporter. I told him about the story concerning the old woman. I think he must have pulled it up online while we spoke because I heard him chuckle on the other end. I told him you sold more papers with that story then we had sold in a long time. He did make one rather interesting comment though."

Here it comes, I can't wait. "What was that?"

"He said he never knew you could be so funny."

Zap! Right where it hurts. But that's always the way it is with him. He never lets you win at anything. He always has to be the one who triumphs. Hell, that's how I got this stupid nickname Tug. It started when I could barely walk and he would draw a line on the kitchen floor and then get a rope and tell me we were going to play tug of war. Yeah, some game, he never let me win. I was never strong enough to pull him over that line. I wasn't the athlete he had hoped for. Not like my brother Mikey, who yanked him over at the age of ten. Now he was the athlete. But he was never going to be Harvard material.

"Sorry, sir, what were you saying?"

"I was saying he never knew you could be so funny. Well, I didn't either. That article about the old woman was not only well written, but it hit the nail on the head in a very humorous way. I think you have found your niche in writing stories Tug. That's why I asked you to come here this morning."

Here it comes. I have captured his attention and he is going to give me a new assignment. I can feel it. My time is at hand.

"I want you to take the weekend and go to the Eastern Shore."

I was hearing the words but nothing registered. Was he giving me a vacation?

"There is an old geezer over there who keeps writing me letters about murder or murders or…or I don't know what all."

Sitting there, trying to figure this out, I finally said, "Murder sir? Are there murders taking place over there that we don't report on?" I was wondering where over there was exactly.

"To tell you the truth, Tug, I don't know what the hell he is talking about. But what I do know is that this witless fool writes me a letter every day and has been for a full month and a half. I mean *every* day. I read some of the first ones, but then I had Beth read the rest and start keeping them in a file. I mean I have a few better things to do than to read one of his crazy letters every day. But, they keep coming and I don't think he aims to stop. It is costing him a small fortune in stamps and paper. He uses nice paper too. Not scraps or cheap stuff. I know his kind and he will keep this up until he grabs my attention; or annoys me to death. So now he has my attention and that's where you come in."

"I see, Max. Or I think I do. What do you have in mind?"

"Well, I've been thinking it's time to advance you a bit and send you out of the city on assignment. I have decided to stop this fool's letter-writing literary campaign and send you down there to look the place over and see what has him so fired up. I mean this man has no intention of ceasing his little siege with me until I do something. I don't know what he is talking about, but he has himself so aggravated, agitated, and motivated; that he is making me nauseated."

I couldn't help it. It was the way he said it. I laughed out loud. "I don't mean to be disrespectful, Max, but you sure do have a way to turn a phrase."

Max moved forward in his big leather chair. I could see he was not at all amused by this man's antics. He shoved a file across his desk. It sailed at light-speed on the highly polished surface and almost flew into my lap. I caught it just in time. I gave it a quick glance and then said, "What's this?"

"That, my dear boy, is your new assignment. All the letters are inside. I want you to leave this afternoon and go there for the weekend. Then, on Monday morning, you can tell me what in tarnation this old bastard is so upset about."

My mind whirled around. I had a very important meeting later today and I couldn't miss it. The city council was redistricting parts of Baltimore and if I wanted to get ahead of the story, I had to be there.

"I do have a slight problem. I am supposed to be at a meeting this afternoon. I am covering the upcoming redistricting of some very controversial sections of Baltimore. I was told it was a must attend kind of thing."

"Don't worry, Tug, I will reassign it to someone else. I want you to get going and take care of this matter. You might think I am overreacting about this, but I remember when this happened once before. Those plucky Eastern Shore men got themselves in a real dust up years ago when they added the second span to that bridge. Now, that turned ugly. I don't know what is going on over there now, but something is and we better cut it off at the pass. They can make life a living hell for us folks over here. A lot of them are still fighting the war for God's sake."

I swallowed hard. Just where was I being sent? "I don't understand Max. They are still fighting the war? What war?"

"The Civil War, damn it Tug. They consider themselves part southern, part pole cat, and more stubborn than any mule you will ever run into. They are a dying breed of Americans. I admire them a whole bunch, but when something sparks them off, it can get mean in a hurry. By the way, have you visited our beautiful Eastern Shore since you came down from Boston? It isn't your Cape, but it is about the prettiest part of this country you will ever lay eyes on."

"No, I haven't Max. Roger Brown goes there every summer. His folks have a summer place in a town called Berlin."

Max sighed showing a bit of delight. The first I had seen since he started talking about my new assignment. "It's a lovely place. Changed a lot in recent years, but it's still so very lovely. You better get going. It will take you about 4 hours to get down there and settled in."

"Just where is it I am going, Max?"

"Somerville. It's a small town at the lower end of the peninsula. I went there once a long time ago when my granddad took me out crabbing. I had the time of my life.

Don't worry about directions though; Beth put a map inside the folder along with those damned letters. She also made a reservation for you at a nice little motel."

"How thoughtful of her. I will thank her on the way out."

"I am counting on you to get to the bottom of this, Tug. Let me know how it goes. We'll talk on Monday. Have a safe trip."

"Thank you sir. I'll do my best. And please don't forget about that meeting, Max. I will be in hot soup if someone doesn't show up."

"I'm on it, Tug." With a broad grin on his face, Max smiled at me as I looked down and picked up the file. My eyes did a quick scan down the front where Beth, ever playful, had drawn one of those stupid smiley faces that had crabs for eyes and ocean waves for a mouth. Written across the bottom of the file, in child-like letters, she wrote: The Tale of Dickie Short.

NEEDLESS TO SAY, I WASN'T as amused at this as she must have been when she drew her little caricature. Shaking Max's hand, I retreated through his office door, determined to make a stop at the lovely Beth's desk.

She was sitting, filing her nails when I interrupted her little beauty routine.

"You think this is funny, don't you, Beth?"

"Why Tug Alston, I have no idea what you are talking about."

"Like hell you don't, Beth. I must say you are quite an accomplished artist." The smirk was dripping on my face.

"Have a good trip, Tug. I see the weather is going to be lovely straight through the weekend. You are going to love our Eastern Shore. It's where we all go to play in the summer."

Deciding to end the sparring match with her, I said, "I am looking forward to it, Beth. I want to read some of these letters before I leave, so I had better get on my way. Thank you for being so efficient and enclosing a highlighted map of where I am going."

"Anything to help you, Tug," she answered in the most sarcastic tone.

As the elevator door was closing, she shot me a wink and waved one of those little finger waves good bye. I could have smacked her.

Roger was pacing the floor, waiting for me when I got back down to my desk.

"So, what did the old man want?"

"Roger, do you never do any work? Or do you just stalk the halls trying to find out the latest gossip?"

"Come on, good buddy; give. What did he say to you?"

"I see you aren't going to go away until I tell you, so here it is. He wants me to go on assignment over to your Eastern Shore. It seems some old man over there has launched a writing campaign to him about murders taking place and no one doing anything about it. I don't know. I didn't get it all, but he gave me this file and told me to go and find out what this man is talking about. The guy has really gotten to him. I mean he was pretty steamed up about him."

"Is that the file in your hand? Let me look at it."

Shoving it in his hands, I began to clear my desk.

I heard Roger laugh out loud while reading one of the letters, so I turned around and asked, "What's so damned funny?"

"This man is funny, that's what. He writes in that dialectic jargon that the old timers over there speak."

"What *are* you talking about?"

"Come on, Tug, haven't you taken a ribbing for saying *Baahston*, or *pak* your car instead of park? We all pick up twangs from the areas we come from. Well, the Eastern Shore folks have their own way of talking. It's like Martian to some of us. If you don't catch on to it quickly, you aren't going to know a word they say."

"Great. Just what I need. Going to some backwater place with people who don't speak the King's English."

Roger laughed again and said, "That's kind of funny, as a lot of them *do* speak the King's English."

"Okay, I'll bite. Care to explain that one."

"There is an island about a thirty minute boat ride off of this town where the families date back to the sixteen hundreds and they still speak in that language."

I was confused by this whole matter. "Have you ever been to this place, Roger?"

"Yes, a long time ago. I went fishing with my dad and then we ate some of the best crabs that ever came out of the water. You'll get the hang of it too if you stay for a while."

"I am staying there over the weekend, and that's all. I am to find out what this old bloke is trying to tell us, and then I will report back to Max on Monday."

"See, you are already getting into it. Bloke is an English word. You will make out fine over there, just be careful going over that bridge. I hope you don't mind bridges."

"Bloke is actually an Irish word, Roger, but then again, I guess you could stretch that out to be somewhat English." I shook my head and then thought of what else he had said.

"Why did you ask me if I minded bridges? Is there something you aren't telling me?"

From the look on my face when I asked the question, Roger's keen intuition told him I might have issues with bridges that he didn't know of. Before making a hasty retreat, he answered quickly, "No reason, Tug. Just be careful on your way over and back and I'll see you on Monday. I am sure you will have a story like no other."

Shutting down my computer for the rest of the week, I was beginning to wonder what I was about to encounter.

Everyone I had spoken to this morning seemed to be kind of ...well...kind of vague in their answers and reactions to me about this whole assignment. I guess I will have to show them that I can return with a class A piece. Or at least find out what goes with this Dickie Short. Even his name conjures up some pretty wild visions in my mind. Who calls a grown man Dickie? But then again, who calls a grown man Tug?

The Bridge

I RACED THROUGH MID DAY TRAFFIC and arrived at my townhouse in Fells Point around noon. I had to pack and I thought it might be a good idea to sit down and actually read some of the letters this old man had sent to Max. That way, I would have some idea of what I was heading into. I also thought it might be smart to try to contact Dickie Short and let him know I was coming over there. That way, I might be able to ward off any more of his letters that seemed to be driving Max up the wall.

I love my townhouse. I bought it just after I landed the job. It's a completely renovated and restored old building down by the harbor. It has a lot of history, which I am into big time. I guess you would have to be an idiot to be from Boston and not have a real appreciation of American history. This place is loaded with it. I used part of my trust fund from my grandfather to get a mortgage and I haven't regretted one minute of that decision. While it is very narrow, and I do mean narrow, it has four floors. The basement is pretty well off limits as it's pretty rustic down there, but the other three floors are simply divine. But I have to say it was the third floor that really clinched the deal for me. It has a full bath and a large room that I use for an office. I did buy a pull out sofa for the nights I worked especially late and just wanted to crash right then and there. There are three windows at one end of the room that let the sunlight in, but it's the door that leads to the prize of the whole place. There is my refuge from a tough day. A roof-top paradise. A lot of the lofts and townhouses have them down here and mine is simply perfect for me. I have installed an electric awning and have classed the place up with a wicker table and chairs I found at Pier 1. I spend most every night up here writing in my journal or sprucing up whatever story I have covered for the day. I love it and it lets me dream of that one story I will find that will put me on the map as far as news journalists. That once in a lifetime piece that will find its way to me, Tug Alston, and then I will know what it is that burns inside of me and tells me that there is some great adventure that awaits me, if only I can find it.

I threw a couple of pairs of slacks and some freshly pressed shirts into a weekend bag. Those along with the essential socks, underwear, and toiletries, I was good to go. I headed on up to my office and popped a cold can of Coors from my small office fridge. Now, out to the roof I go and sit down to read some of these letters.

As I picked up the file, I smiled quietly looking, once again, at the cover design by Beth. If the letters were half as good as her artwork, I was in for something... The file was neatly arranged by date. One thing you could say in Beth's favor was that she was organized. Apparently old Dickie had started his little crusade the first of April. How appropriate. April Fool's Day. At least this man had a sense of humor.

April 1, 2004

Dear Mr. Maxwell Pierson,

Allow me to introduce myself. My name is Richard Short, but you will get to know me as just plain Dickie. That's what everyone calls me. I am known some around these parts as my family has lived here as long as anyone can remember. I am an Eastern Shore waterman through and through. That's what we Shorts have done forever and then some. I am soon to be going on my eightieth year and am right smart

13

upset at the goings on down here. The murders have been taking place now for quite some time, but it hasn't been 'til recent that we here in Somerville have felt the mighty blow of them bastards. No one in your fancy city paper seems to take count of it all, so I elected myself to tell you. It is a bad thing when you can't wake up in the morning and feel like you or your home is safe. We need help and I reasoned that you might just be the man to do it. I know you are real busy, but we are desperate in these regions. Please write and let me know if you can come on down here and give us a hand in dealing with this matter and stop these here murders.

If I don't hear from you, I will keep on writing 'til you come here and see for yerself.

Dickie Short
Somerville, Md.

Wow! This man is like a character straight out of central casting for a western. I like him already. He is to the point and even though he doesn't use the best of English, he is sincere in what he is saying. I wonder just how many murders have gone unnoticed down there. How can this be? I mean it may be somewhere at the end of the earth, but there must be a policeman or two around.

I skimmed through the rest of the file, stopping to read a bit from each letter. I saw that they were mostly the same content; just put a bit differently. This Dickie Short was a colorful man indeed and it came through loud and clear that he was a kind of community spokes person. Someone everyone looked up to. He spoke of his friends and how their lives were being affected by all this crime. He also spoke of a place where time had almost stood still, until all this started. These men made their livings on the water and fishing was how they did that. These kinds of men are usually pretty tough guys. What is going on that has them so spooked? Well, I wouldn't know anything until I went down there myself and scouted around and it was abundantly clear that if Max hadn't called me in to go on down there, this man was in no mood to stop his literary siege.

There is no real address on the letters other than Somerville, Maryland, so I will take that to mean that I won't have a very hard time finding Dickie Short. I'll just ask around a bit and surely someone will know where to direct me.

God, what has Max gotten me into? For sure there was no way he was ever going to respond to this guy. Looking at my watch, I could see it was almost 2:30. I better get my ass going if I want to get down to this place by dark. Glad that sexy Beth stuck this map in here. And she even highlighted the whole route. Now, isn't she something? Up and at it boy, I moaned not really wanting to leave the peace and serenity of my rooftop. One never knows that destiny may be awaiting me right around the corner. Perhaps it's on this place called the Eastern Shore of Maryland. Wouldn't it be something if I returned with a real *killer* story to hand Max?

I THREW MY BAGS AND cameras inside my Jeep Cherokee and then jumped in to get to the beltway before the traffic got too bad, or I would be spending the rest of the afternoon crawling along at a snail's pace just to connect to Route 50.

Twenty minutes into the drive, I could see that I was in luck. The cars were moving along at a good clip and as I headed around the beltway, I had my tunes blaring, and I had to admit; I was jacked pretty high.

My year old Jeep is my favorite possession; even more than my townhouse in Fells Point. As I recall now, my mother couldn't get over how she had been able to completely surprise me for my graduation from Harvard. It was at the end of the day and I was getting ready to go out with some of my friends. My mom appeared at my bedroom door and told me that there was something she wanted to show me before I dashed off. Having no clue what she was talking about I said I would meet her down stairs in a few minutes. When I came bounding down the stairs, she was standing jangling a set of keys in her hand. I stopped right in front of her and said, "What gives with those?" She smiled and pointed toward the door. "Why don't you go on out and see for yourself." As I walked out the front door, there, standing in the circular driveway was what she wanted me to look at. A brand new white Jeep Cherokee. I swallowed hard and turned and looked back at her. She was smiling at me, with tears in her eyes. "I knew you wanted one of these so badly that I just couldn't resist. I am so proud of you."

I will remember that day forever. The look that passed between us, without saying a word, was enough for both of us to understand that I was making my passage to a new life; and she was so very proud. I have no idea what her father would have said if he had been alive to see his daughter spend part of her inheritance on such a luxurious gift, but I was certainly glad that she did.

Making excellent time around the beltway, the Route 50 exit was in front of me. Ah, this is great. I am making even better time than I thought I would.

Tug's cell phone rang and he let it go into voice mail. He would stop and check his messages and his map before crossing the bridge that Roger told him about.

So far, so good. I was sailing along and when I saw a sign for a McDonalds up ahead, I decided that was as good a place as any to use the bathroom, grab something to eat, and answer any messages that sounded like they might need my attention.

I clicked onto my voice mails and most of them were from friends, who could certainly wait until I had more time. The only message that grabbed my attention was from Beth and being I had just left the paper a short time ago, I thought it might be something important and that I had better answer that one.

Two rings in, the friendly voice of Beth answered, "Maxwell Pierson's office."

"Hi Beth. It's Tug. I see you called. What's up?"

"Oh hi Tug. I was just thinking about you and wondered how your trip was going so far?"

I mean didn't she have anything more pressing to think about? "The trip is going just fine, thank you Beth. I was just looking at the map you included in the file. It's a big help. Thanks for highlighting it, but the route doesn't look to be all that difficult. It looks pretty straight forward, as far as I can see."

A bit hesitantly she asked, "Have you crossed the bridge yet?"

"No. As a matter of fact I am about three or four miles from it. Is there something I should know about this bridge? Roger mentioned it a couple of times before I left, and now you are asking about it."

Beth paused a moment before answering. "You haven't ever been over there before, have you?"

"No, I have not. But I am beginning to wish I had taken the time this past year. It's pretty country around here. Slightly impatient with her avoidance of his question, he asked again. "Is there something special I should know about this bridge?"

"Well, not really, Tug. I just hope you aren't nervous about heights."

I could feel a slight twinge in my stomach because the truth was I didn't like heights very much, but there was no way I would ever admit to it. Particularly to a girl. It was one of those guy things, I guess.

"No, they don't bother me much," I lied.

"Well then, you won't have any problems. All I will say is that it is a pretty big bridge. It bothers some people. I'm glad you won't be one of them. I guess you are alright then so I wish you a safe and enjoyable time over there. If you need anything, just call me."

"I will be sure to do that, Beth. Once I find this Dickie Short things should move along pretty fast. By the way, I read some of his letters. They are entertaining, to say the least. He sounds like quite a character. And by the way, your cover artwork amused me. You are quite a little artist."

Laughing into the phone, Beth said, "I couldn't help myself. Max has been handing those letters over to me for more than a month. You have to hand it to the guy; he is tenacious."

"Well, tenacious or whatever, I aim to find out what on earth he is talking about."

"You just do that, Tug. Good luck and we'll see you on Monday."

"You hold that thought, Beth; unless Dickie Short kidnaps me."

I could hear Beth laughing as she hung up the phone. She sure was a sweetie.

Time to hit the road again. Between Beth and Roger, I sure was anxious to see what all this bridge talk was about.

It didn't take long and a few bends in the road later; there it stood. Right smack in front of me was the biggest, and highest, expanse of bridge I had ever seen. I felt my palms get a little sticky, and then I told myself that this was nonsense. I had to get to this Eastern Shore and this was the way, so I paid my toll and then drove on.

The assent up the bridge was breathtaking. I had heard about the mighty Chesapeake for years, and had studied it some in school, but any pictures I had ever seen of it just didn't do it justice. Huge tankers were in the bay heading north, I figured to the ports of Baltimore, Wilmington or Philly. Dozens of sail boats were gliding in the warm breezes of the bay. The scene was magnificent. As I reached the top of the bridge, I could see everything on the other side. Land stretched north and south. I tried to remember my history of this area, which wasn't too great, but I did reflect on how badly the British wanted to control the Chesapeake during the Revolution, and now I could understand why. I have often wondered why they don't teach history in the field. I mean when you are in grade school and even high school, you would be better served to take trips to all the places they tell you about. That way, you can put yourself into the action, rather than trying to imagine it.

All of a sudden, that odd feeling swept over me. I was definitely feeling the height of this bridge, but on the other hand, I was exhilarated by the majesty of this engineering feat. I was half-way over and I had to keep going. There was no place to stop on this baby, so I did the only thing that I knew would get me the rest of the way. I said a little prayer, pushed down on the accelerator, and raced the hell out of my Cherokee until I was down and the bridge was a sight in my rear view mirror.

Take that Roger and Beth, I thought. I did it without incident. The truth of the matter was that I truly loved it and was already looking forward to my return trip. Yet, there was something inside of me that felt a sort of kinship with this place. I didn't know why, but it was as if I had been destined to come here.

I was now on the shore and the sign said I was in an area called Kent Island. This too was beautiful, except for the fact that it was built up all over the place. I thought back to how it was when I was a kid and my family went to Cape Cod. Now the development sprawl was everywhere. I assumed that was the case here too. It must have been so natural at one time. Most likely only islanders lived there and now this bridge brought the world to their shores. Progress is nice for those who come and enjoy their vacations, but it can bring with it the dreadful course of overcrowding and take away all that once was.

I spotted a graceful heron descending to the water to find its next meal. Its wingspan was enormous but its flight was light and delicate. Oh, how I love sea birds. They are survivors, but none survive better than the gulls. I have loved them since I was a kid. I was the one in my family, who would troop off in the early morning to feed them. My Mom was scared of them, as most people are. I would laugh at her when we sat on the beach and she would duck her head when they would swoop down to grab a piece of my hamburger bun or French fry. They are birds with an attitude and maybe that's why I feel a kindred spirit with them. I was a kid with a quiet and determined attitude. I was careful not to show it most of the time. I respected the fact that my father was a very different kind of man than I was turning out to be. But couldn't he ever accept that? I guess not. But then, he had Mikey to push around. I love my kid brother more than I can say, but I wish he would stand up to him and do what makes him happy rather than follow in the exact footsteps Dad has planned for him. Oh well, each to his own.

Route 50 was a terrific highway. I passed by a town named Easton and the sign said it was once the colonial capital of Maryland. I would have to check that out sometime. I loved the landscape. It was all things shore. There was sand for soil and small houses along the way that reflected back to another time and place. I was taken with grand plantation homes that stood way off the road. I had never thought of this as a plantation state, but then again, I was just learning.

Cambridge was my next landmark on my journey to this town at the ends of the earth. Another long, but flatter bridge led me across the Choptank River. I was impressed at the size of this waterway. Lots of fast-food places and gas stations along the roadside told me that once again, development may have grown this area a lot faster than the town folks may have wanted. But it meant money and taxes to these areas. That's why they let it happen and then they regret it all when they see what actually happens.

Finally, I was to the center of the peninsula. The sign read- Welcome to Salisbury- the hub of Delmarva. Now what the hell was a Delmarva. I thought about it for a minute and then it struck me that while I was looking over the map, this part of Maryland was touched by Delaware to the north and Virginia to the south. Yeah, brilliant Tug, get it? Delmarva.

It sure was a hub. It was past five o'clock and the traffic was pretty rough going. I guess it didn't matter where you lived; people trying to get home after work caused backups all over the place.

I saw one of those green signs that told you a college was in the area and where to exit to get there. Then I remembered my brother, Mikey, talking about a Salisbury College that had a pretty fair athletic department. I wondered if this was the one. He said they played damn good ball. Good, god, I thought, wouldn't it really frost the old man if Mikey came to a college on Delmarva? If he had two sons who went overboard and left the mother ship of Boston?

However, he always secretly knew that his mother, while Boston bred and part of the "old guard," preferred the quieter life she rarely achieved with Ted Alston. She had graduated from Simmons College with a major in music and a minor in English and she was far more introspective than her husband. She loved nothing more than to curl up with a good book while listening to classical music. That is, until dad came home and the house turned upside down. It was those private desires she kept to herself that drew me so close to her. Mikey, on the other hand, was a whole different kid and loved the rough and tumble world of our dad.

I decided to make a stop just outside of Salisbury. I thought it would be a good idea to gas up and grab a sandwich and chips. I had no idea if I would be able to find a place to eat once I got to my final destination. For that matter, I had no idea what I was headed into at all.

The break felt good and I was back on Route 50 and shortly turned onto Route 13 in no time. This main highway took you south all the way down and over the Bay Bridge Tunnel. I can remember reading about that and how they built two tunnels under it so the big ships could still get through. I would love to see that but that would have to be another trip. It had to be something fantastic as it was the north south way to go and I had heard from family friends who took that route from Boston on down how astounded they were at the length of it. Right now, I was on assignment and had to pay attention so I didn't miss the cut off that led me on in to this place. Thankfully, that would be my last leg of this rather interesting journey. I was seeing places I had never seen before and I still had the dubious pleasure of meeting this old character named Dickie Short and finding out what all this hubbub was about. The thought swept over me that maybe I should be more careful if this place was so dangerous. You can't be too careful, my mom always said. Come what may, I was getting close and I had to admit the reporter side of me was dying to get this story.

First Impressions

A T LAST, I SPOTTED THE turn off. Almost instantly, I was out in the middle of absolutely nowhere. Aside from some scattered houses here and there, not much else was to be seen. I thought about what Max had told me regarding the people who lived here. "They are a different kind of people down there. Nice, but very independent." They would have to be to live in these outer regions of the peninsula. I didn't see many stores and figured that they must have to travel a good distance to get their groceries and other supplies. I just couldn't imagine living in such a place. It might be fun for a while, but it would get old real quick.

I passed by small towns named Marion and Hopewell. I wondered what they were like years ago or was it always like this down here? The first thing I noticed was a geographic change. The tall pine trees that lined the road were disappearing and I knew from the sign at the turn off that I must be getting real close to Somerville. The maps told me that the water was out there, but I was damned if I could find it. This sure looked to me like a place where one could murder people and then stash the bodies just about anywhere. If that's what was happening, Dickie might have a point in making such a big deal of what was going on. Bodies could disappear into thin air, and not be found until the Messiah came. Now how the hell was our paper, or Max, supposed to know that?

A zillion thoughts ran through my imagination. All of a sudden I was that young boy again, thinking up a ghoulish ghost story placing it in these dense woods and side roads leading to God knows where. But before I could go any further with those thoughts, a sign in front of me said "Welcome to Somerville- Where Crabs are King." I had arrived.

THIS IS WHERE THE REPORTER in me has to stay alert. I wanted to make sure not to miss one detail of this incredible little town. A huge water tower hovered overhead with the most enormous picture of a Maryland crab right on the front. It appeared like a sentinel to all who came to town. It wasn't very hard for me to see that its message was loud and clear. I was now in crab country. I slowed my Cherokee down to a crawl as I drove down the main street. I had the distinct feeling I was back in time. It was a little strange, but I can't say unappealing. There was something nice about this town. The hardware store on my right was like the old ones I remembered from when I was a kid. I was thrilled to see that one still existed like that. It had all its shiny wares sitting out front that said come on in and take a look.

To the side of the road as I ventured further down, was a huge fenced lot with what looked like hundreds and hundreds of some kind of wire traps. Then it hit me, they are crab pots, dummy. Remember, you used to see them on the Cape when you would go there for the summer.

A sign pointed to a packing house, which I would check out some time over the weekend. My job right now was to get the lay of the land and then get some information of how to get to my motel for the night.

The sun wouldn't be setting for a while yet, and I was determined to follow this street to the end. I could tell it would lead me to the water which is what I wanted to see right now. That strong pull to be near water was calling to me again and I couldn't ignore it. That thought wasn't completely out of my head when I saw the dock ahead. I pulled into one of the parking spaces and jumped out.

The minute I was up on the pier, my heart stood still. Cape Cod was beautiful, but there was something about this place that pulled at me immediately. I looked out and as far as I could see, there was water. I could see small islands dotting the horizon and for no reason I can explain, I felt like I was home.

I dashed back to my Jeep and pulled out a pair of binoculars that were always at my side. These were, I discovered soon after arriving at the paper, one of the essential tools of the trade. I focused them on those strips of land straight ahead of me and saw the pristine beauty of them.

I was so intently into what I was doing that I never heard a man come up and stand beside me. And, with a booming kind of voice, he said, "Kin I help you with anything there, son?"

I jumped a little and then turned my head to see this old man looking at me with a kind of peculiar look on his face. His eyes made me feel immediately like I was an outsider.

"I was just taking in all the beauty of this place. Too bad more people don't know about it. It's really special."

"More people?" he shouted out. "We have too many people down here now. That's what's changed it so much."

Boy, did I say the wrong thing. He definitely didn't like my comment so I figured it was time to change directions.

I held out my hand and said, "I am Tug Alston, sir. I assume you are a citizen of this fine town. I am a reporter from The Baltimore Sun and I am down here on assignment."

He stood and took the full measure of me. My hand was still hanging out there. I could tell he wasn't ready to shake it until he had studied every inch of me. I was feeling like an idiot but I was determined to get a shake from this guy.

He was an extraordinary looking man. His face showed his life had been a hard one, probably outside, but there was a grace about it. He reminded me of *Santa Claus* with that same grin that said that life was full of happy expectations. His body was sturdy and his hands were rough but steady. However it was abundantly clear he didn't much trust strangers in his town.

I refused to withdraw my hand and finally he gave in and shook with me. It was the tightest grip I had ever felt. Yes, he was an outdoorsman all right.

Not mentioning his name, he skirted the issue by saying, "Glad to meet ya. What's your assignment a way down here in Somerville?"

I needed to be careful with my answer. I didn't want to insult this *Curious George* because my business was with Dickie Short. I was here to see and find out if there was any validity to what his cockamamie letters said. I didn't need to have this one running and telling anyone I was here and possibly messing up any chance I had at making a good impression with the main man.

"I am down here to explore some interesting facts about this part of the Eastern Shore."

"Is that so?" he quickly responded. "Well, you research away, son, but please don't make it sound too good. We are about overrun right now with 'come heres.'"

My eyebrows bowed upward as I asked, "Come heres? I don't think I understand."

"You know 'come heres.' Folks who aren't from these parts. They come here and love it so much that they stay. That wouldn't be too bad, but lately, there are just too many comin' here."

Now I understood completely. Remembering another piece of wisdom that Max imparted to me, I realized he knew something about this place. They really do speak differently. I made a mental note that I was going to have to pay close attention in order to get this story.

I didn't want to belabor the point with this man any longer. I could see that this subject was upsetting to him. "By any chance, sir, could you tell me how I can find the Evergreen Motel?"

"Why sure I kin. You jist go back the way you come, and you'll see a sign to yer right that'll tell ya how she goes."

"Right," I said with a grateful smile on my lips and a vague look on my face. "Thank you very much." I said good bye and walked back to my car, I determined right then and there that I was definitely in trouble and would need to begin to make a brief dictionary of the words and phrases I was now going to be exposed to. I knew that journal was going to be my lifeline down here.

HE WAS EXACTLY RIGHT; NOT that I doubted him for one minute. This is that old man's home and I am the interloper. As I turned into the driveway of the Evergreen Motel, I realized I truly was back in time. The Cape wasn't the only place left in this country with the old "Mom and Pop" motels. I breathed easier because I loved these motels. They always had an old fashioned bottle opener in the bathroom and I could park right outside my door.

No one was in the office. I even peered around a tiny corner of the room and no one was there either. Maybe they had gone to bed. After all it was seven thirty and folks down here didn't seem to stay up very late cause they are all early morning types. Then I saw a bell on the counter that had a sign scotch-taped to it : "Ring for service."

One slap and the bell brought forth an older man who walked slowly through another door in the back.

"What can I hep ya with?"

"I need a room for a couple of nights, if you have one, sir." I kept a straight face even though I wanted to laugh. There wasn't another car in sight so I guessed I could have my pick. But it's always good to be nice to the people who would be my hosts for the weekend.

"I think I kin do that. You said you need a room fer how long?"

"Until Sunday morning, sir," I answered while my eyes took in the stuffed wild life on his walls. Obviously he was a hunter and obviously he was proud of these trophies of fox, birds of prey, and some really ugly little sort of animal that looked like an over-sized ferret.

"If you'll jist sign here, I kin get you all straightened around. You must be tired. I see yer plates are from Maryland. Where did ya come in from?"

"Baltimore, sir. I work there." I could see this man had a thousand questions rolling around in that head of his, but he must have thought discretion was the better part of valor; and didn't say another word.

I took the key from his hand and left promptly without any further discussion. By now, I was beginning to feel exhaustion coming on. Not three minutes out of the office, and parked in front of room number 2, I remembered that I didn't ask him the most important thing of all. So, I lugged myself back out my room door, and back down to the office, praying he would still be in there. He was.

"You know, sir, I did forget to ask you something. I wonder if you could tell me if you know a man named Dickie Short. I am down here to see him, and I am afraid he didn't give me an address or phone number where I could reach him."

His host broke into laughter. "That's old Dickie for you. Sounds jist like 'em. What do you need from him? I don't mean to pry, but jist thought I'd ask."

I was beginning to like this man, and I was beginning to see that the folks down here were more a part of that old south that I had read about long ago. There was a genuine hospitality and truth about them, even their speech was somewhat similar. Somewhat.

Deciding I better give him what he asked for if I wanted him to tell me where to find Dickie Short, I said, "I am a reporter, sir. I work for The Baltimore Sun and it seems that this Mr. Short has himself some kind of story he wants us to cover. So, that's why I am down here and that's why I need to meet him. Do you know where he lives?"

He was sizing me up all right. His eyes bored into me like a drill into wood. After making me stand there for a few minutes, he said, "I kin tell ya where to find Dickie, but it won't be at his house. Your best bet to find him will be tomorrow morning- down to Virgil's. He goes there every morning. Hell, for that fact, he is there on and off, most of the day. That's where you'll find Dickie Short."

"Virgil's? How do I find Virgil's and what is it?"

I know I was stretching his patience, but I could feel he liked me. "Virgil's is where we all go to eat and talk things over. It's where all the watermen go afore they go out on the water crabbing. Dickie don't go fishing no more, but he still meets with the guys. You'll like it. That's the best place to find 'em. But keep in mind, boy, you'll have to be there by four in the morning, if you want to meet old Dickie."

Four in the morning? I thought. This is way beyond the call of duty.

"Yes, sir. I'll do that very thing. Four in the morning, huh?"

I walked back to my room, stripped my clothes off and slid into the bed. How can people live like this? What time do they get up to be at this Virgil's by four AM? I picked up my travel alarm and set it for three. I can't go unshaved to meet this man, but this will cost Max a little extra.

I tried to reread a few letters but my eyelids closed for the last time of this very interesting day.

Not Quite Breakfast at Tiffany's

THE ALARM BLASTED AT PRECISELY three and I jumped out of bed. I wanted to be sure I got there by four. What an ungodly time of the day. But it is when all the action takes place on the water. No wonder old sailors always said "early to bed; early to rise." I dragged my sorry ass to the shower to wake up and get ready for what I was sure was going to be a day like no other. The only problem was that the shower wasn't exactly what I was hoping for.

This baby was definitely a left over from earlier centuries. The thin stream of water trickling down told me that this was not going to be the powerful surge that I needed to rouse my body. In point of fact, I was lucky to get five droplets of cold water on me at all. I grabbed a washcloth that was so stiff that that should surely get me moving. Suddenly my mind flashed back to that classic movie- *Planes, Trains, and Automobiles*. That scene with Steve Martin in the bathroom, taking a shower, will never be forgotten. Now, I felt as if I were living that scene with the single exception that I didn't have a side-kick named Dell Griffith. But then again, I had no idea what was ahead of me when I met Dickie Short.

Shower accomplished (somewhat), clothes on my back, I headed out the door in the pitch dark, and drove off to find Virgil's.

The directions from my new found friend in the office turned out to be, thankfully, right. Virgil's was practically just around the corner from the motel. To my complete astonishment, the parking lot was bustling at this hour of the morning and there was only one parking space left, so I gently squeezed my baby right in.

As I stepped from the car, I realized how nervous I had become. I had no idea why. I was used to going into strange environments all the time with my news assignments, but for some odd reason, this situation had me feeling tense and unnerved. I knew I wasn't the most outgoing guy in the world, but this mix of emotions running wild inside of me, was ridiculous. I always envied Mikey for his ability to be able to walk into just about any situation and just get right into it. I suddenly wished he was here with me. He would know just the right thing to say to these folks.

I stood out front for a few minutes, getting my nerve up to walk in. Thankfully, nobody came along while I stood there, feeling like the biggest idiot on the planet. This restaurant was like something back in time. An old Hershey's ice cream sign hung in one of the front windows. I hadn't seen one of them since I was a kid, and even then, they weren't very common. I mostly used to see them on the old drug stores on the Cape. Time's up- I have to go in, like it or not. A deep breath later, I was inside and my deepest fears all came true. Every eye ball turned to look straight at me.

I did the one thing I knew best. I panicked. And I am certain every man in there knew it. I tried not to make eye contact as my eyes darted around the room looking for someone who just might fit the description of Dickie Short.

I was sinking and no one was going to save me. They seemed to enjoy having some fun with the "outsider." I knew my face was beet red, and my stomach kept growling like I hadn't eaten for weeks. Well, come to think of it, just what time was it that I last ate?

The smell of home cooking was beginning to drive me crazy. Finding this man or not, I wanted to sit down at the counter as inconspicuously as I could and order everything on the menu. Inconspicuously was out of the question now with everyone quietly whispering about me and my face the color of scarlet. If only I could see one kind face in the room, I would feel better. Dear God, will someone help me, Please?

I decided to give up on the idea of sitting at the counter and moved on toward the back of the room. I can't even begin to tell you what it's like to be the main attraction in a roomful of men who are all suited up to go outside and take on the seas. I felt like a real wimp and I knew they knew it too. Now the smell of fresh coffee, eggs and bacon frying on the griddle had overcome me. I had to eat no matter what.

Thankfully I spied a place at one of the old wooden booths. I was in luck. Just as I got my feet to move and proceed on over there as nonchalantly as possible, I heard a loud voice yell in my direction. "Come on over here, son."

Naturally my instincts told me to look at the person who was yelling and when I did, I was in disbelief to see it was the same old man I met the day before on the pier. I was so relieved to see a familiar face. Not a best buddy; but he was someone I *sort* of knew.

"What in tarnation are you doing here at this hour of the day, son?"

He motioned for me to sit next to him so I slid in. "I am trying to find someone. The man at the motel said he would be here. But with this crowd, I don't have a clue how I am going to find him."

I was somewhat drawn to the fact that this old man seemed to be amused with me. "What's his name, son? I'll yell 'er out fer ya."

"Dickie Short, sir. I am looking for a man named Dickie Short. And by the way, when I introduced myself to you yesterday, I don't recall getting your name."

The craggy lines on the old man's face crinkled up. His eyes danced with a kind of light that comes with age and a good life. He was laughing so hard, he had to wipe a tear from the corner of his eyes with his hand.

The hilarity had escaped me and I couldn't understand what the hell was so funny. Finally I said, "What's got you laughing so hard?"

He ignored my question and threw his hands up, yelling, "One more coffee over here Lindy. Make it from the 'here's to mud in yer eye' pot."

No sooner had he finished yelling to the young, and very pretty waitress, than he grabbed my hand and shook it. "Son, you have found who you are lookin' fer. I'm, Dickie Short."

As I shook his hand I wondered why the heck he couldn't tell me that when I met him yesterday? He knew I was down here on assignment and he had to know it was him I would be looking for. This sly old fox is really something.

Half annoyed, I said, "Why didn't you say something yesterday when I told you who I was and why I was here?"

"Calm down there son. It was plain fer me to see you was doin' some detective work, and I didn't want to bother you none. You was studying everything that sits around that pier. Come to any conclusions yet? I mean, about the murders and all."

I didn't know what to think. My head was swimming. Here I was in this old time lunch room surrounded by the largest bunch of fishermen I had ever been with. It kind of looked like that bar scene in *A Perfect Storm*. The only thing missing was the bar. Virgil's had to be one of the last restaurants of its kind left anywhere in the United States. It was truly incredible. Actually kind of neat.

"Well, no, I have not come to any conclusions whatsoever. But if you are Dickie Short, then you and I need to talk and you need to tell me about these murders. I am down here for the weekend and Mr. Pierson, who you should know pretty well by now, is back in Baltimore waiting for some answers."

Waving his hands around, he said, "Everything in good time, son. You and I will git to talkin', but here comes cute little Lindy with your food."

"Food? I didn't get the chance to order any food."

"Ah, she jist knows what to bring. I give her the look and she jist bring it, so you may as well suit yourself and eat up. Then, we kin talk."

This Lindy leaned in to the booth and placed down some of the best smelling food I have ever seen. When she backed up, I took a good look at her face. She was a stunner and I figured her to be maybe in her early twenties. I was instantly attracted to her. And that is no small thing as not one gal had been able to catch my attention since I had moved away from home. It kind of unnerved me for a minute. Apparently Dickie didn't miss the sheepish grin on my face when I looked at her because after she had left, he leaned across the table and whispered to me. "She don't have no regular guy, so she is free as a bird." For the second time in less than thirty minutes; I blushed.

"Yes, well thank you for that information, but I am down here to find out what all you and your letters are about. I have to tell you, Dickie, you sure have a way with words. I am a bit confused though. You must have a police department down here, so what's happening that they can't handle? And what exactly is that you want our paper to do?"

Dickie shot me one of those slow growing smiles that begins at one corner of your mouth and then spreads to the other. "Finish your breakfast, son, and then we'll take a walk."

I wasn't sure I wanted to go off walking with this man. I had no idea who he was or much about him. Or didn't I? I realized that reading through his letters to Max, that I did know him. He was speaking right to me as if he knew I would be the one to come down here. The whole thing unnerved me like this was some weird ghost story and he and I were in the starring roles. And yet, I was drawn to him. "Just where are you taking me?"

"The pier. You know, where I met you last night. I love to go down there every morning and watch the guys go out on their boats. I miss it so much, but the doctor says I am done with those days. I can't hardly stand it. It's all I ever knew. Fishin' or crabbin' or arsterin' on those waters out there. Now that's the real life.

A sad shadow crossed his face that hadn't been there moments before and I could feel it just as if I had known him for years.

"And you go back in the evening? To watch the sunset?"

"You got that right. My whole life has been spent down at that pier in one way or another. Until now, that is. Now, with all this blasted murder going on; it's changed things. It's changed the whole town."

"I'm almost done eating, Dickie. We can go in a minute. This is the best coffee I have ever tasted. And as for this food, well, all I can say is that I thought my mother was the best cook anywhere, but I have found her competition."

"Best food for miles around. You want to know their secret ingredient for the coffee?

I shook my head nervously. Maybe I didn't want to know.

"It's because they have used that same old pot for as long back as this place has been here. If they's ever got to buyin' a new pot, it be all over. The coffee jist wouldn't taste good."

Lindy appeared out of nowhere and began to clear the plates. I felt like I was going to get all tongue-tied the way I usually get around good looking gals. I prayed I would not do that. The Lord must have heard me because before I knew it I was babbling like a fool to her.

I looked straight up said, "That food was the best ever. Really. I know why all these fishermen come down here every day."

Her gorgeous blue eyes flew open to the size of quarters. I could see I had said something terribly wrong. But how could making a compliment be wrong? What gives with these people?

She turned her head and looked at Dickie who instantly corrected me in a booming voice that I knew God could hear.

"Sweet Jesus, son. Don't ever call these men fishermen. They are the watermen of the Eastern Shore and they are proud as hell of it. Fishermen are their distant cousins a way up north. These here are watermen."

I blushed for the third time and was now feeling like a complete idiot. Lindy looked down at me with a sympathetic eye because she could easily see I wanted to crawl under the table and curl up and die right then and there.

Consoling me like I was a child, she whispered, "You'll get used to the way we talk down here. I hope you come back. We really are good people." She then shot me a wink from those irresistible eyes, and walked away.

I felt like the weight of the world had just been lifted off my shoulders. The prettiest young woman around had just told me to come back. She liked me. I knew it.

Dickie smirked as he picked up the check. I noticed at once you didn't argue with this man. You just went along.

I followed behind him to the register where he picked up a toothpick from out of a small glass container that looked like it had sat on that counter since Noah's flood. He grabbed inside his pants for money and asked, "How did you like yer breakfast? I'll bet you never ate Scrapple before."

"Scrapple? Was that what that was? What is scrapple? I have never heard of it."

A man standing in back of me, waiting to pay his bill, quietly chuckled and mumbled, "Here we go."

"It's from the pig, son. Or sort of."

My face went blank and I said, "Sort of?"

"Yeah, son. It's all of the rest of the pig that don't get used fer anything else. They say it's got a little bit of everything 'ceptin' the squeal."

My stomach immediately danced a turn or two. "Well, isn't that something special? I have to say, Dickie, it wasn't exactly breakfast at Tiffanys, but I have to tell you, it sure was delicious."

Dickie Fesses Up

AFTER PAYING, DICKIE YELLED BACK, "Have a good day on the water" to some of the guys and then we walked out. It wasn't yet day break but I was fully awake at this point. I was ready for anything come what may. Breakfast gave me renewed energy and after being with Dickie and surrounded by the watermen of these waters, I felt remarkably as if I was beginning to fit into Somerville.

Dickie tapped on my shoulder and said, "Come on, let's jump into my truck here."

"But I thought we were going to take a walk and talk some things out."

"We are going to walk, but first we are going to drive down to the pier and then I can show you what I have been writing about in all those interesting letters you said you have been reading." Damned if he didn't look like a proud papa.

Taking one look at his old, beaten up truck, I turned and shot a desperate look at my Cherokee, thinking sorry boy, I hope it all works out for you sitting in this lonely and vulnerable lot. That old man was reading my mind. "Don't go worrying about your vehicle none, Tug. This isn't like the city. No one here will bother that fancy car of yours. When we are done walking and talking, and I bring you back, your car will still have all its wheels in place."

I know he must have seen the embarrassment on my face, but I still hesitated for a moment before pulling myself away and then I followed him to his junked up truck parked in front of Virgil's. I hopped in the passenger seat without saying a word. I felt it best to keep my mouth shut at this point.

Running his weathered hands along the dashboard, Dickie said, "She's a beauty, ain't she? I have been driving this truck since she first came out and she still drives like a virgin girl on her maiden voyage."

I hardly knew what to say. The man simply took my breath away. The only time I had ever seen a truck like this was in the old movies I used to watch when I was writing my adventure stories. I liked it though. It was an old, original Chevy truck, with chrome all over the front that wasn't in such bad shape. Dickie surely had taken good care of his little pet here.

"Not bad, Dickie. I can see you two have been together a long time." They were like a matched set and I was about to find out which one held up better through all the years.

"You can say that again. This old truck has driven me in and out of more scrapes than I would care to tell you. And the back part of her has carried tons of crabs and arsters in our day."

I assumed he meant oysters and, for him, that was pretty close. These folks made sure you paid close attention when they spoke or you would be lost in a hurry. I would be sure to add arster to my journal along with all the other little phrases he and his friends used. I might need them to write my story, if indeed there really was one down here.

Once we got her started, Dickie's truck kind of coughed its way down the main drag. His window open, and the soft morning breezes billowing inside, he suddenly leaned half his body out of the truck and yelled to a man walking down the sidewalk.

"Mornin' Poke. How's she comin? You all take care now." With a wave and a smile on his face, he returned to sit straight behind the wheel.

I stared blankly at him because I knew that Dickie Short was going to go down this street at five miles and hour and yell from his car window at every living person on the streets in Somerville. I was entering the "Twilight Zone" and it was only going to get more bizarre.

"That guy's name is Poke? I suppose there's a story behind that name?"

"Son, there's a story behind everyone that lives down here. Most all of us have nicknames of some sort. It's the way of things. I jist happen to be plain old Dickie. Now surely that's not my Christian name. I was born Richard D. Short, but I never was called that. What I can't figure out is why my Dad jist didn't call me Dickie from the start. I haven't ever been called Richard. Not even when my Mama got to fussing at me."

As I listened to his jargon, a permanent smile became affixed to my face. He was a character and I remember what Max had told me, that these folks were different down here. Oh Max, how right you are.

"Well, what's Poke's story then? Please tell me."

"Aw, he is one of them flibbertigibbet kind of guys. You know, half not there and the other half may as well not be. But he is genuine. He makes his way down to the packing house. You'll see it in a minute. Old Poke; now he's a good man. Stays out of trouble and he has been on those docks for more years than I can count now. He doesn't work no more, but he still goes down and talks to the guys on their way out in the morning and then goes back to welcome them in around mid day or so when they bring their catches back in."

Just listening to Dickie was an exercise in some kind of wild rhetoric from god knows where. Max was not going to believe this. Even if there wasn't one word of truth to his letters, he was going to get a kick out of all the tales I would have to tell him and the guys next week.

"By the way, son, I wouldn't be goin laughin it up at us and our names. Tug isn't exactly a Christian- born name now is it? Care to tell me *your* story?"

The fact was that at the rate Dickie was driving I could tell him my story, recite the *Declaration of Independence*, and throw in the *Gettysburg Address* for good measure and we might just be arriving at the dock.

"I guess you're right, Dickie. I told you yesterday, when I introduced myself to you at the pier, my name was Ted. However, my father took great joy in beating me every night at his little game of tug of war, so from the time I was a toddler, I became Tug. That's it. No more or less to the story. However, I guess you could say that that little game turned into a lifetime of the two of us pushing and pulling one another until one of us permanently wins. At least, that's how it seems." Why did I feel so comfortable with this old man? And in such a short time?

"Well then, there is a story. I bet you I can tell you just what it is."

"I'll bet you that you could, Dickie. I'll just bet you that you could."

"Well, lucky for you, that will have to keep. We're here already."

Here already? It seemed to me this one and a half mile drive took an eternity. I was relieved. I really didn't want to get into my relationship with my father with this strange, old coot. I was here to find a story and not be analyzed.

AT THIS EARLY HOUR, THE pier was alive with men and a few women hustling and bustling all over the place. The sky was just beginning to lighten in that magic time moments before the sun's first rays hit the horizon. Some were handing bait and coolers over the side to the waiting boats that would be taking off shortly, while others were gathering their gear to join them on the small fishing crafts. I felt my heart race with excitement. Unexplainably, I was feeling somewhat proud, and a bit awed, to be in the presence of these watermen of the Eastern Shore. Their anxiousness to get out on the choppy, morning waters was palpable. It was plain for any fool to see they loved what they were doing.

My thoughts and impressions were suddenly interrupted when Dickie yelled over to me. "Don't dawdle, Tug. We have a lot to do this morning."

I shut the door of his truck and walked toward him. I could see he was already entertaining the men with stories and as I approached, his voice lowered, but not enough so I didn't hear him telling them who I was and why I was here.

Everyone knew this old character and it was plain to see that they loved and respected him. I felt as if I was in the company of water royalty, if there is such a thing.

Dickie's introduction was short and *very* loud. I guessed he wanted to do this only once. "This here is Tug Alston. He is going to write about us and make us all famous."

The men all waved to me and saluted with their hands like they all knew what was going on here and that it was some secret that only I didn't know. I didn't mind though. I got the distinct impression that whatever was going on here was soon to unfold after the watermen left the docks.

As each boat pulled away, I felt a rush of something stir inside of me. I was being pulled toward something. What that was, I didn't know yet. I have never had so many strange feelings in such a short time in my life and yet I wasn't afraid of any of it. I leaned over to Dickie and said quietly, "They really love what they do, don't they?"

"Indeed they do, Tug. I only wish I had my years back and was going out with them again. I miss it more than I can say. That's why I come down here all the time." It's all I ever knew and now that Shirley is gone…well everything has gone to hell."

The first bit of personal information about Dickie Short was finally out in the open. I didn't have to ask, I automatically knew who this woman Shirley was. It was all over his face.

"She was a good one, she was. Shirley put up with more of my antics than a gal ought to have. "

Hmm, ought to have. Another one I will add to my journal.

"I'll bet you loved her a lot, Dickie."

"Loved her? Old Shirley was a woman that any man could love and why she picked me and said she'd marry me, I have no idea. We were together 58 years when she passed. It hit me like a ton of bricks, even though she had been sick for quite a spell."

I could see the hurt was still there and would be for the rest of his life. He was like one of the native geese down here, mated for life. "I'm really sorry, Dickie. That's a long time. I guess I never really thought of how lonely it can be when someone you love for that long, dies."

He desperately wanted to change the subject and patted my arm. "Yes, well anyway, we have to get walking."

"We will walk in a minute, Dickie, but first you have something to tell me. I have gotten up at the crack of dawn to find you and I have sat through breakfast and a drive down Main Street. Now, I believe you owe me an explanation. I am on assignment down here and it's time for you to talk."

Dickie nodded his head slowly, looking me up and down. " You liked her, didn't you? I could see it in yer eyes."

What planet did that comment come from? I was completely taken off guard. What the hell…? He is crazy and has forgotten why I am here.

"What are you talking about?"

"Lindy. I saw the way you looked at her and I kin tell you; she looked back at you the same way."

What did that girl have to do with the price of beans? And why did it matter what I thought of her, and why now? A good ploy, old man, but it won't work on me.

"She seemed a pleasant girl, but that's not what I asked you, Dickie."

He planted his feet and the look on his face was down right resolute. We were going nowhere until I answered his question the way he wanted me to. "But it's what I asked you, son. You liked her."

Figuring that a quick answer might hasten this along, I said, "Yes, I liked her. Now, can we get to the matter at hand?"

"She's a keeper that one. A real special young gal and I wouldn't want anyone or anything to hurt her."

My polite patience had run out. "Dickie? I met a gal who served me my breakfast. She was real nice and that's all there is to it. Now, please, let's get on with why I am here."

Dickie stood his ground like a bull before he charges. "Nope. I ain't goin' nowhere until you tell me exactly what you felt when you first laid eyes on her."

No use. The old man was as stubborn as my father when he got to thinking about something. I tried staring him down until I couldn't do it any longer. I broke out laughing. You just couldn't stay mad or annoyed with this man.

"You know, you are embarrassing me, don't you, Dickie? I am not used to telling anyone how I feel about those kinds of things. It's personal. But, if you insist, and I see you do, I think if I ever come back here I wouldn't mind seeing her again. Now there. I have said all I am going to. Besides, what's with you and this girl? Is she your grand daughter or something?"

Dickie's head slumped down to his chest. I had wounded him and didn't know why. Then I realized what I had asked. I should have known better. I had learned from a past experience that it's not always good to ask about people's children. You never knew what was in their past. But as quick as I had the last word out of my mouth and was feeling guiltier than hell, a huge smile broke out all over his face.

"You're almost right, son. She isn't my grand daughter. I am too old for her being that anyway, but I would have been proud as day to have her be, but she is related to me. She is my brother 'GD's' little great grand daughter and I love her jist as if she was my own. I guess you could say we have a kind of special thing goin' on between us."

After a quick repeating of what he said to me, I figured it all out and who was who in this puzzle. "Ah, I see, so you do have a vested interest in her."

"I'm not sure what you jist said, but I think I get the drift. Those three dollar words aren't easy on me, you know. Jist speak plain around me, if you could."

I laughed so hard I thought I would wet my pants. Here this man was asking me to use plain English when he spoke in some dialect from another world.

"Yes sir," I said as if taking orders. "No use trying to schnooker you. You are way ahead of me on that score."

We both enjoyed a good laugh this time. "Well, I knew what was goin' on in there this morning. She gave me that wink when we left which means I better bring you around soon and often. She has brought more joy to me and my Shirley than I can ever tell you. That damned brother of mine never really appreciated her and how wonderful she was."

"And that would be 'GD'? I don't' think I will even ask what that stands for."

"You can and you should. No one around here will answer you if you don't get their names right. And their nicknames *are* their names, remember? The GD is for gonna do. That man has more gonna do things in his life then I can tell you. He was always saying he was gonna do this and gonna do that. Get it? And he never did a damned one of 'em."

This man was his own circus act. I simply was going to have to get myself under control here, but it wouldn't be easy. So, to try to get us back on track, I gave it one more try. "Now, can you tell me about the murders Dickie?"

DICKIE TOOK OFF AND WALKED ahead of me. I didn't know what to make of all this. He didn't say a word. I knew I had to wait on him. These people seemed to be like that. You waited until they were ready.

The silence was getting to me, but I had to be patient. A trait I didn't excel in. Then, suddenly he stopped and turned around and stared at me.

"I want you to take a long look around this pier and tell me what you see."

"Is this where one or more of the murders happened?"

"Just tell me what you see, son."

I did what he asked. I took my time and did a panoramic swing around. I wanted to take in every detail. This place was beautiful and for as far as the eye could see, there were the magnificent waters of this cove.

"Okay, I am looking Dickie. Is there something in particular you want me to see?"

"Jist keep on looking. Do you see that big tall building right smack dab in the middle of this pretty place? Up until a short time ago, that was a restaurant called The Mate's Galley. Served the best crab cakes anywhere around. The seafood and fish was beyond good eatin'. Folks from all over came here in the summer and fall to eat there. Now it's a condominium. I kin tell you that caused more than a dustup around these parts. People went nuts trying to block them from building her. But the developers and bankers won in the end and down came the restaurant and away went the beautiful view of the water."

"It's happening all over these days Dickie. There isn't much you can do about it. Its change and progress. It brings money down here. Don't you want that?"

Dickie looked as if he wanted to kill me, but if he did; he kept it to himself for the moment.

"Keep on lookin' round son. I spect you will see some more of that *progress* you are talkin' about."

I scanned all around and saw an old crab packing house along the water's edge and then in the background I saw another group of condos and building going on. I thought it was kind of strange that down here, in the middle of nowhere

45

really, so much developing was going on. But still, I didn't see anything out of the ordinary yet and I couldn't quite see what it was he was trying to get me to see. When I finished my visual tour of the area, I said, "It sure is beautiful, Dickie. What are those islands out there?"

"Oh, one is just a strip of land and beyond that is the sound. Over there, a way out, is James Island. She is something magnificent. You and I will go over there before you head back. We can take the mail boat over in the afternoon."

My head was churning out thoughts as he spoke. But he still hadn't said one word about murders.

"Dickie? I am going to leave today if you don't get to the point. I have come a long way down here to talk to you and I have surprised myself at how much I like your town, but I have a job to do and that job is to report stories of interest to the people who buy our paper. Now I am going to give you one more chance to spit it out."

I noticed the old man fidgeting with things in his pant's pocket. That was always a sign of nervousness. What in hell was he so nervous about? I began to get the feeling that whatever it was; I was in for a pretty good story and one that might make me want to commit murder myself.

"Well, son, you see I had to git yer attention. I had to git someone down here and see fer themselves. I had to make it sound real bad."

I knew it. I knew it the minute I forced the point with him that he was avoiding telling me what this whole thing was about. I genuinely liked him, but now was the moment of truth, and God knows what was going to come out of his mouth. I decided to be patient and listen…and then walk back and get into my Cherokee and head on out of this town.

"Go on, Dickie. I am listening."

"Well, yer here aren't you? So you must have thought it was important…"

"Dickie," I interrupted, I want the truth. What the hell gives here?"

"When you looked around jist then, didn't you see it? Didn't you see what they have done? And they will keep doin' if someone doesn't stop them. You have to stop them, Tug. You are our destiny. I saw it last night the minute you told me who you were."

I stared in disbelief. I just couldn't take my eyes off of him. My first instinct was to belt the man, but that wouldn't be too well received in Baltimore. Besides, my mother would kill me for just having that thought. I sincerely was trying to grasp what this man was saying. My entire mindset had been on murders taking place down here, while he obviously had a different take on the situation. But what was going on? He was riled up about something pretty bad and he was trying to get me to figure it out on my own. I had to admit to myself that I wasn't connecting with where his mind was at and for that, I was sort of thankful.

Then, out of the blue, something occurred to me. Dickie had just said he had to get our attention somehow and that somehow was painting a picture of dastardly deeds being committed. However, the dastardly deeds weren't actually people being snuffed out but that his home and town were being snuffed out by over development of the waterfront. Good God! Could I be right? Could Max have gone mad with this man and sent me all this way to come back with a story about over development? Even this crazy old man wouldn't have gone that far...or would he? I had a bad feeling.

In the calmest voice I could muster up I looked him straight in his eyes and said, "Tell me if I get this right Dickie. You have written a letter a day for over a month to the man at the top of one of this country's premier newspapers and told him a made up story to get his attention?"

Dickie flashed me a sheepish grin and said, "Want to keep on going Tug. You are doin' pretty good so far."

Could I really bludgeon him and get away with it? I mean I used to do it in my adventure stories and being I was in a real life adventure story now with this crazy old man, could I get away with murder and stash his body in the pine forests?

"You really consider this building of condos murder, don't you? Is that what all this is about? And all that talk in your daily tirades (that's every day discussions for you Dickie) is all about a few condos being built down here?"

Dickie's eyes narrowed. Steam was coming out of his nostrils. I was in for a real tongue lashing, Eastern Shore style now.

"Is that what all this is about?" he yelled. "Do you think that this isn't murder, son? This is murder of the highest order. Did you ever read anything about the Indians, for God sakes? That's what's going on down here. It's the same mess. It's another come and take our land from us and promise us that everything will work out fine line of bullshit. Well, this might not be so big to you, young reporter, but to us down here on the shore; this is murder pure and simple."

He finally took a breath. I was glad of that. He was beginning to turn purple and I could tell he was more than a little agitated with me for not instantly understanding. Or maybe he was just agitated at what was happening to the home he loved so much.

I had to calm him down. If something happened to him, I would be the next one to disappear in those woods I passed coming down here.

"I didn't mean to say that this doesn't affect you, Dickie. It's just that we thought you were talking about people getting murdered and no one doing anything about it. I really didn't mean to offend you. I know how over development is making a lot of people everywhere crazy, but what can you do about it? I mean they have a right."

"They have a right? Hell they do," he shot back. "They may have a permit to do so, but they will never have a right to do. It's not just the land they are tearing up. It's the water too. The arster beds are about done and the crabbin' is going to be a thing of the past soon too. Watermen all up and down these parts are up in arms. Their *right to do* is killing our way of life and our folks have been here since this country was first settled. You just go over there to James Island and talk to those people about who has a right to do."

Clearly Dickie was exercised and I was afraid he would have a heart attack if we kept up at one another. So I did the one thing I had learned well from my father. I retreated.

"I can see you are upset about this. I understand it now and can see how you could write this to Max as if they were murdering, but us shouting at one another isn't going to solve a damn thing. I tell you what. Let's get in your truck and if you would, please drive me around this whole area. I really would like to see it. I haven't ever been with someone who knew so much about the water and the land that surrounds it. You can teach me and then we can talk about it some more and that way I can, at least, return to Baltimore with an explanation of what you were trying to tell Max."

Dickie got off his soapbox. He pulled in his horns because he saw an opportunity here. If he could take Tug around then maybe he could still have his cake and eat it to. The young reporter was sharp and he was sincere. He could use those traits to see if he could still enlist him in his cause. Every young person loved a cause and God knows; this was as good a cause as any.

The Water Sings to Me

GRATEFUL THAT I HAD BEEN able to calm the storm, we climbed back into his truck and began his tour de force of Somerville. It was not particularly a large town but it sure had a lot of twists and turns that led down streets that rambled off to dead ends. Dickie told the history of each old building with such vivid description that, for a moment, I would have believed he was the real story teller. For him, time meant nothing. Why should it? He had nothing much he had to do anymore. So, I was going to learn everything there was to learn about Somerville and the lives of the watermen of the Eastern Shore. I was being drawn into their world down here and I was enjoying every minute of it.

We were out for quite a while, stopping to look here and stopping to look there when Dickie said, "We'll go back to Virgil's directly and we kin have some lunch. I know all this trekking around and me, runnin' off at the mouth must be makin' you hungry, son."

I looked down at my watch and couldn't believe it was going on eleven o'clock already. Unbelievably we had been out here farting around for hours. Incredible. Time seemed to fly by.

"Morning passed like piss water around here. It goes even faster when you are out on that water. We all start so early that round about this time, some of the boats will start comin' back in and those men will be starved. As you might have picked up, Virgil's is the place we all go most times. You will not believe the cheeseburgers. Best anywhere. And you kin meet up with Lindy girl again. She usually works breakfast and lunch."

This Lindy thing made me so uncomfortable. Not because I didn't like her. Hell, I didn't know her enough to like her or not like her, but Dickie was pushing me and that I didn't like at all. "I hope we aren't going to get into that conversation again, Dickie. I don't think I have the energy and besides, I was up so early today that I am ready for a nap. So, I'll take the offer on a quick lunch but then I am heading back to the motel for a quick rest and then I can start up again."

Dickie leaned toward the door, grabbing his sides he was laughing so hard. "A nap, you say son? I don't think that is going to happen. I only have you down here for a short while and I have to show you everything and make you see why we need your help. A nap is definitely not going to happen."

He meant what he said and I realized I was trapped. He was right, of course. There wasn't a whole lot of time to sort this mess out and I was acting like I was on vacation, but could I go the distance?

"I see. Maybe you would like to tell me just what all is on our itinerary today."

"I haven't got no schedule son. We are jist goin' to mosey around and I believe it may be the best day you have ever had in your young life. To my way of thinkin', a reporter such as yerself will pick up a lot just by observing our lives down here."

From the way he said it, I almost believed him; if only I could stay awake and make it until he let me go for the day. He might prove to be correct on all counts; I might have the best day of my life. Yawning slightly, I said, "Well, I can't do anything about it anyway, so lead on, great one."

I STUDIED EVERY LITTLE DETAIL of the houses and the buildings. They were fairly old and had obviously been there a long time. They weren't anything special but they said solid Americans lived here. Fairly similar in construction, they were mostly two-story frame homes with front porches where you could imagine nightly conversations being exchanged as people walked by. It was definitely a place where time had stood still and was more like the yesteryears of this country when our social lives were in the front of the house and not the back, on fancy decks with built-in luxuries that were once considered only for the rich. Even though my home in Boston was pretty upscale and in the ritzy, historical district, I still remember the fun my brother and I had on our big front porch when we were kids. Mikey and I would play endless games of Monopoly on an old, antique wooden table for hours and then Mom would bring us cold lemonade and peanut butter sandwiches. I was beginning to feel uncomfortably nostalgic as I rode slowly around this town with Dickie.

As we drove on, I couldn't help but think of what a shame it was that our lives had changed so much over the years. When urban sprawl hit big time, developers built homes differently and they plunked relaxation time in the backyard. Maybe that's why we all became a little less friendly towards our fellow neighbors. Funny, how being here seemed to give me a clearer picture of how much and how quickly our lives were changing in this country.

"Where do you live, Dickie? I'll bet you live close to town."

"I sure do and I will take you there after we have done our little tour of this side of the town."

"I can't wait." Inwardly I was wondering just what his house would look like. He was a character and now that his wife was gone, I shuddered to think of what he was going to show me. Dickie wasn't the most put together man I had ever known, but he, at least, smelled like he took a shower and washed his hair once in a while. The mismatched pants and shirts were a whole other subject.

"Now don't you go thinkin' things you oughtn't. I kin see it on yer face. You think I live like a slob. Well, maybe it isn't quite the way Shirley kept it, but it ain't so bad neither. You will see."

You couldn't help but laugh at him. Dickie Short seemed to perceive things that you just didn't think he could. He was no dummy and it wouldn't surprise me to find out he had more education than most; even if it wasn't in a formal academic environment. I may have graduated Harvard, but I was fast learning that this man was hard to stay ahead of.

We poked along streets as Dickie made comments about every house and who lived there now or who had lived there once. He was a telephone book of information. Almost without exception, everyone worked on the water and if they didn't; they worked in something related to it. I was fascinated at the stories he told about everyone. A lot of the families in Somerville had been there for generations and had their own ways of doing things. I had already discovered they had their own way of talking. That part of my journal was going to be a killer when I shared it with Max. Funny, that was the first time all day I had let my mind go back to Baltimore or where I lived. I wasn't missing it at all.

"Hey Dickie. Is there somewhere we can grab a quick cup of coffee? I would really appreciate that."

"Up ahead, son, we will stop by the Glendale Packing House and visit a while. They always have coffee going in there, so you kin hep yourself then. It's only a few minutes down here."

We wound around this curvy little road that was more like a lane actually. Straight ahead of us was the marsh. Dickie stopped and shut down his truck.

"Stick yer head out the window and take a whiff."

I did as I was told and he was right. The heavy scent of salt was everywhere. I closed my eyes and pretended to be up at the Cape.

"Smell that salt, son. Isn't it good? That gets right into yer soul. I couldn't ever live anywhere where there weren't no salt in the air. That jist wouldn't be right fer me."

I stared at his marvelous face while he kept breathing in the salt. He was amazing. The simplest things brought him such immense pleasure. I envied that because as young as I was to this man, he enjoyed life more than I possibly could. I began to realize that if I paid close attention I might learn the secret to real happiness from him. Now wouldn't that be a kicker?

"I love that smell too Dickie. It reminds me of my summers on Cape Cod. Have you ever heard of Cape Cod?"

Dickie snapped his head back through the window and grumbled, "What do you take me fer, Tug, an idiot? Of course I have heard of Cape Cod. As a matter of fact, back years ago I used to drive the crabmeat up to New York City to sell in the restaurants. I even went as far up as yer precious Boston and her beloved *Cape*. Some of those fancy restaurants like to buy our Maryland Blues. It was a hell of a long haul, but I made good money. Down here, son, you got to do what you got to do to make money. It isn't an easy life, but we wouldn't know what else to do. That's why all this infernal building is making us madder than hornets. It's disturbing everything."

He started his beauty back up and we went down a little farther where he stopped to show me yet another new high-rise project of townhouses that were being built. The setting stole my breath away. They were being built on some of the prettiest land I had ever seen. The view was panoramic. From the windows you could see out to the islands on one side and the entire, picturesque scene of Somerville. I could understand why developers would want this parcel, but at the same time,

I was getting angry about how this land was being swallowed up for concrete condos.

Apparently my thoughts were showing on my face. "You are beginning to see the murders now, aren't you?"

I didn't say anything. I was taking it all in and I leaned down to my canvas bag and grabbed out my binoculars. I scanned the entire horizon and then saw another cluster of condos back in on the side of the cove.

"Good God, Dickie. They are building up this whole waterfront, aren't they?"

"And they won't stop, son," he said disgustingly. They are murdering everything down here. It may not be human bodies, but the toll it is taking is pretty bad. It's rape of the land and they don't give a damn what we think. We have been up in arms for a good long time now, and somehow, almost under cover of darkness, things get decided and the bulldozers come in and there you have it. New buildings covering up the water views. It's murder to us, and it's killing the waters and the wetlands."

"I'd like to get out here and walk a while. Would you mind?"

"Mind? Not at all. I'll tell ya what you are looking out on."

As we jumped out of the truck, I grabbed my camera. I wanted to get a lot of pictures. Something was going off in my head and I wanted to get it all in photos.

"Out there, to the left side, heads you out to old Bingham Island. There's nothing but watermen who live out there and a few places to do business. The arsterin' is still good out there. However, we all know that that could change in a heartbeat if rich people decide they want some of that land fer themselves. You know, I told you it's not easy to make a livin' down here and a whole lot of money, waved in someone's face, could talk pretty loud."

While I snapped away with my camera, I poked fun at him and the way he talked. "Your language down here is a jumble of dialects. It's kind of neat but it would take me quite a while to get it all."

This time Dickie snorted he was laughing so hard. "I hate to tell you this son, but there are some who have lived down here fer years, and they still don't get some of it. So, good luck on a weekend visit."

I shook my head and snapped some more pictures. Dickie wanted to go and when he wanted to go, you left.

By now, the truck seemed to drive like it knew all about these day trips of her master. In my mind I began to think of the magical car, Herbie. The one in that movie that thought it was a human. I was waiting for it to begin talking to Dickie. Who knows? Maybe it did when no one was looking. They had been together for a long time now. Surely if this truck could talk, it would have tales of its own to tell you.

As we rolled on down the road, a huge sign greeted us saying that yet another large parcel of land was for sale. I felt a twinge in my stomach. I was really beginning to resent what was going on down here.

At the dead end we reached our destination…and, I was hoping, my cup of coffee. Refrigeration trucks were parked to the side with their owners name on it.

"See those trucks, son? Many an afternoon I hauled crabmeat out of here and took off to some of those fancy restaurants I told you about in far off places. Crabs is running pritty good this year I hear, so this afternoon, those trucks will be leaving and flying up that road you come in on. Let's go in. I want you to meet some of the men and see the place. You can git yer coffee in there too."

Ah, music to my ears.

Dickie went on and I waved to him that I would be following shortly. I was observing yet another world down here. It was a world where we get our beloved seafood. I had met some good men this morning at the restaurant and was sure to meet some more here. They were simple folks who wanted to be left alone to do what they had been doing for generations. Now, it was all being taken from them and they were smart enough to know that when the condos came, the pleasure boats came. When the pleasure boats came; the fish left, and when the fish left, they left too. I watched Dickie shake a man's hand and they laughed together. There was a symbiotic feeling between these men. They had grown up together and they had worked out on those magnificent waters together and no doubt, they had looked out for one another in case there was trouble. This was a good place and you could feel it deep down to your soul.

Their contentment was contagious. I was being sucked into their world and I was feeling that happiness that Dickie said I might. They all loved it here and I discovered that it must have taken a lot of courage for this old man to write those letters that represented all of them and how they felt about what was happening in their part of this world. Up until this moment, I had not ever understood one real thing of how the Native Americans must have felt when their land was being invaded and their culture was about to change. Outside people wanted what they had and didn't give a wit what they did to get it. Wasn't this how Dickie and the rest of these people were feeling right now? They had a chief who was willing to try to do something about this and even if they could not stop it totally, they could preserve some of it.

Once again, my mind flashed back to the stories of my youth where the real heroes were the unexpected ones. Perhaps, just perhaps, I had found my story after all.

The Crab's Shack

THE NEXT THING I KNEW, a cup of steaming coffee was being handed to me by a woman whose smile could have brightened the darkest day.

"Dickie says to give you this. He went to the men's room and will be back in a few minutes. You can drink it out there if you like. Good view of the pier. By the way, I'm Jean. Dickie says you are a reporter come down here to take a story for your paper."

"Yes I am. You have a real nice town here. The people are all so friendly."

"Well, we ought to be that way. Most of us have grown up together and our parents before us and their parents before them."

"Do you ever leave Somerville?"

Jean belted out a laugh like a sailor and looked at me straight on. "Sure we do. We go up to Salisbury to shop and stuff like that. Sometimes, we even take our boats and go around the bay to other towns. We aren't loners you know. Maybe it just seems that way to you. We know what's going on."

I thought I had offended her and wanted to quickly erase that notion. "Oh, I don't mean it that way, Jean. It just seemed to me that most of you may not travel around a lot. Please, I didn't mean to imply…"

"Imply what, son?" Dickie's voice bellowed out. "I haven't been gone from you fer ten minutes and have you gone and gotten yerself in trouble?"

I hated to admit it, but I was sure glad Dickie was back on the scene. I liked these people, but wasn't exactly sure how to take their brand of humor. The one thing I didn't want to do is start any bad feelings about me being here. After all I was an outsider, even if I was making up my mind to write a story in their defense. I would keep that fact under my hat for a while until I had made my final decision.

"I don't think I am in trouble, am I Jean?"

"Aw, go on Dickie. The boy is nice. He was just asking questions. Isn't that what reporters do?" Then turning back to her work at the switchboard, she commented, "He just thinks we don't go anywhere. That we stay right here in Discovery Cove all our lives. You might want to straighten him out on that point."

His strong arm slid over my shoulder and we walked outside to the dock.

"I can see this is where the action is."

"Always is, Son. Here sit down for a spell." He turned me around to sit on the oldest, most worn out recliner I have ever seen. No doubt it had been on this dock since the day it was bought- which had to be a generation ago. I got a little queasy thinking of my putting my clean clothes down on this sucker, but that really might piss the old man off.

"You can get a real good dose of what goes on here from sittin' a spell."

When I sat down, gently, in this beast, I sank to China. I mean my ass was so buried in this chair that it might take me the rest of the weekend to get it out. It was hard to keep any balance doing this trick and I lost some of my coffee on the way down, but what was saved tasted divine.

"It's pretty comfy for being so worn out, isn't it son?"

No answer was required at this point. I smiled the smile of a simpleton because I think my face said it all.

"You kin git a good look at those condos from here. What makes it all really bad is the height of them. They jist tear the whole thing apart." I looked where he was pointing. He was absolutely right. If the builders had been thinking at all, they would have stopped at a few floors instead of heading to the sky. But then that wouldn't have fetched as much income from the property.

"We fought like the devil over them, but, as you kin see, we didn't win."

"I'll bet you were all pretty sick about that. I know we have been through this before, Dickie, but they do have a right to build even if a lot of people hate it."

Dickie looked down at his feet, thinking. "You are right, but no one seems to understand what all this is doing. It's really ruining this area you know."

"I saw all the building on my way down here. It seems to be everywhere on the shore."

"Everywhere is right. You ought to take a drive up to the Delaware end of the peninsula. It's so bad up there that there's nothing left of what was. They are even building on the wetlands and even you must know that's not good."

"How do you know so much about Delaware?"

"Well, for one thing, your own paper has run stories about all the development up there and all the problems they have run into. Don't you read your own paper son?"

I could feel my face redden as I answered. "I have to tell you, I only read the stories I write and the sport's section, Dickie. But now that you mention it, I did hear something about all this from a friend of mine at the paper. I just had no idea. I mean before this weekend, I didn't even know there was an Eastern Shore. I am beginning to regret that now."

"Hmm, well, that don't say much fer yer taste? Where do you go for vacation?"

"I don't. I have only been on the job for a year now, so I haven't even gone back home to Boston yet. I am supposed to go in a couple of weeks though. My dad wants me to continue our tradition of our annual trek to a Red Sox game."

Dickie stared almost longingly at me. I could see he was thinking he might have liked to do that if he and Shirley had had kids. "He really won't take no for an answer on that one."

"He shouldn't. It's something you have been sharing together for a lifetime. You ought to bring him down here and the two of you could go out and crab some."

"That's a nice thought, Dickie, but that wouldn't interest my dad in the least. He is a rough and tumble kind of guy and I never fit that description. My brother was the sportsman I could never be."

Not one word came out of his mouth. I could see that he had caught the drift of the whole relationship between me and my father. We loved each other but there was a definite divide between us. I was truly my mother's son, quiet, shy, and introspective. I wasn't a sissy, but I wasn't an Alston athlete either.

"I guess all that doesn't really matter much anyway. It's hard to be a son and sometimes no matter what you do, it doesn't seem to fit the picture of what some fathers have in mind. Personally, I think you're a pretty good kid just the way you are."

His eyes sparkled in a devilish sort of way. I was kind of shocked to hear this crusty old man get kind of sentimental with me. He almost sounded sweet, and that didn't appear to be the kind of man I had been with for the last umpteen hours. To tell you that I didn't need his kind of support would be lying. There was a lot I didn't know about Dickie Short, but I had a profound feeling I was going to learn.

SEEMINGLY OUT OF NOWHERE, a man approached us. I guess I had been in a zone and hadn't much attention to anything else other than what Dickie had just said to me.

"Mornin' Dickie. Who you got with you this fine mornin'?"

"Well, I'll be. Look what the cat dragged out here. Come on and sit a spell. I want you to meet a nice, young man down from Baltimore."

I stood and shook the man's hand as he grabbed for a chair sitting on the edge of the dock. His head turned a little to keep me in his view. He looked at me in a suspicious way and then said, "You look like one of them fancy young fellows; right out of college." After making that little statement, he shook my hand and said, "Right nice to meet you. I am Alvin Crockett."

Dickie about fell off the dock laughing. I mean the man almost dropped right into the water. "Who the hell are you? I don't believe I have heard your Christian name since we was kids."

I just sat and watched them go on at one another. It was high entertainment to listen to the two men and I didn't understand more than a few words now and then.

"Well, he looks like a fancy man, so I thought I would jist show him I'm not no dummy from the sticks."

"Okay, I am just going to take a guess here. You have a nickname. I would love to hear it. You might say I am doing research on names of the Eastern Shore."

Dickie knew right there and then that Tug could play with the best of them. The kid had a good sense of humor.

"Aw, he won't tell ya. But I will. His name is 'Hawkeye.' And if you want to know where he come by that, he will have to tell ya."

"It's a nice name, care to give me the story behind it?"

Alvin's face reddened some and he said, "It's no big deal, but if you really want to know, then here you go. I have worked on these docks heping bring in crabs and arsters since I was a kid. I worked the water some too in my younger days, but now I jist stay out here. The boats come in, hand up the bushels of crabs or arsters, dependin' on the weather, and I never miss a trick as to what is goin' on in their boats and in the baskets. So, from the time I worked out here, I was called Hawkeye or sometimes Hawks. That's all there to it."

There was a story for everything. This area was a virtual tour de force of Americana the way it once was. Good God, it still is. That still is if expansion doesn't overrun the area. Then, in a generation it will all be much different.

"Would you mind answering some questions for me, as long as we are sitting together on this fine day?"

Hawkeye turned to Dickie with that look that asked; what should I do? "Talk to him, Hawks."

"Go ahead. Ask away."

"Tell me how you feel about all this new building. I mean you obviously have grown up with Dickie and you must have some strong thoughts on what's going on down here."

Hawkeye stared out on the water for, what seemed like, a long time. I could tell he was having a tough time with this. I couldn't imagine why until he began to speak.

"Well, son, you see it's good and it's bad. I know Dickie hates it all because he is a stubborn old man and he won't see anything but bad in it."

With that, the gloves came off. I stood there in shock that this man had a different view of things and by God, now he was going to get it. These two old men loved each other as much as two men could, but they also loved to go at one another like booming thunder. It was like the two old guys in *Grumpy Old Men*. Loved to hate and hated to love.

"Why you old bastard," Dickie shouted to him. "You know you hate all that's goin' on down here. You're jist puttin' on airs in front of our Harvard boy here."

Hawkeye's rotund stomach started to bounce around with laughter at his old friend as he leaned in to me." Harvard huh? I heard of that school. You must be pritty danged smart."

I decided I would try to get into the fray with these guys. I loved it. "Smart enough to know when not to say anything, sir."

They caught on. I was into their game. "Oh, so now it's sir, is it? Well we'll jist see about that."

"Please continue Mr. Hawkeye. What's yes and no mean, and do you mind if I write this down?"

Dickie looked over at Hawkeye and saw his friend was staring at Tug's pad like it was a cobra. "He's a reporter, you idiot. He's down here to help us stop this mess."

"I guess it's a mess but it might be good too. It's hard to tell. I jist wish they hadn't built the danged things so high. And now that they have gone and done it, some of them ain't doin' so good neither."

"What do you mean by that?"

"Well, they is sinking some and now they have to fix that little problem."

Sinking some didn't sound good to me, even if I was a Harvard boy. I caught his drift though and that, perhaps, is what was more disturbing to me than anything.

"Would you care to tell me what the yes part of this might be?"

"Well I do feel mostly like Dickie and a whole mess of town's people. We didn't want this to happen. We have heard what's going on north of us. Delaware is gone already. I have a brother-in-law who had to move up there to live closer to the hospital on account of his wife. I visit him once in a while and then I get so peeved I could scream. They don't even have proper ambulance coverage in some of those towns; they have grown so fast. All of them 'come here' people' come here to have the life we have had all our lives and when they do that the developers make money, the banks make money, the contractors make money and a whole lot of other people make money and so that's not so bad. So, you see it's good and bad."

I didn't know where to start with this. Good God, once this guy got started, his mouth flowed like the Ganges.

"Come heres? Could you please explain that expression? The way you said that almost sounded like a not very nice name for the people who are retiring here." "It's just a name we give them long ago. It's for all of the outsiders, you know, not born and bred here. We call 'em 'come heres. You see they all come here from someplace else. Most of us here have families that go way back to the beginning when the British sailed up the coastline."

"Ah, I see. But I probably think it isn't such a nice name?"

"Think of it as you want. It's how we call them."

It was beginning to get late in the morning and a few boats were starting to come into the cove. Hawkeye stretched his arms and said, "I have to get back to work. Them boats won't wait and the pickers are jumpin' ready to get started."

"Thanks for what you shared," I answered. "I hope we can talk again before I leave."

"Oh, I spect you will. If that old bastard takes you to Virgil's for lunch, I will see you then."

The very thought of lunch was more than a little appealing at the moment, but I had the feeling I was far from done out here at the packing house.

"What are pickers, Dickie?"

"Lord, son; come on inside with me."

Following like a puppy dog, the next thing I saw was a whole other world. It was a world of people sitting around tables with all kinds of instruments. Dickie pointed to the mostly women, and said, "This is where they pull the crab meat out of their shells and then send that meat all over the place to restaurants and some go to roadside stands that sell crabs in the summertime. Remember I told you I drove the trucks to market sometimes. Well, this is where it begins. There a few places around the wharf here that do this. Used to be our wives did all this work in the summertime, with our kids in tow while they worked. We men were out on the water. Now, it's not the wives so much, but people who come here jist to do this. Immigrant types. You see, the boats go out early and come back in starting about now and that goes on 'til early afternoon. Some of the men go on home and eat a big meal. Some of us go back to Virgil's and exchange stories from the day."

"I could remember seeing lobstermen off the Cape bringing back their catch for the day. I guess at that age I didn't have any idea how early so many of these folks go out on the water. I was still in my neat little bed fast asleep when they were up and cracking."

"They are nice childhood memories you have there, son…" he said as his voice trailed off.

"Yes, they are. I don't mean to change the subject but can you tell me if everyone down here is going to call me son? I notice they like to use that word a lot."

"I guess it's our way of giving you a name without giving you a name. Understand?"

At this point, I did understand, and now I was down right disturbed at what I was morphing into.

Dickie drifted back outside and talked some more to Hawkeye, who was now hauling bushel upon bushel of crabs out of the waterman's boats. In a stage whisper he leaned over to Hawkeye's ear and yelled, "I sure am getting a huger up. I'll bet, you that young man wouldn't disagree with me one bit."

He must have spotted that desperate look on my face. He was a man. He knew that look. It was the look of a man in pursuit of food.

"How could you tell?" I said. "I thought I have been pretty good about not telling you I am starved out of my mind."

"Are you now? Well, if you jist wait another minute or so, I will take care of that for you."

With that, Dickie leaned down and grabbed a bushel up from the man on the boat. I couldn't take my eyes off of the crabs. They were big, huge ones with the blue claws. Dickie pointed out that the ones that had tips that looked like were painted like nail polish were the females or they called them sooks. The males were jimmys. I was in another land altogether.

"Look at them move around, Hawkeye. They look fine today. I'll go in and ask to take me some for dinner tonight. I'll bet our young friend here has never had steamed crabs the way we do 'em."

I said nothing, but noticed that Dickie was speaking about me like I was already an adopted member of this unique shore family.

While Dickie got his crabs, I said good bye to my new friend, Hawkeye or Hawks to me. I told him I hope I would see him later on at Virgil's. He would become another character for my journal who was part of this rich tapestry of life on these waters.

"Well, son, I see you said good bye to the old man there. He'll catch up to us later on, no doubt. What do you think of the crab's shack? It's some place, huh? I just love it. If I didn't have these places to go everyday, I don't know what I would do."

My eyes flew open in complete shock. It was a little weird that they would call this house of death for the glorious Maryland Blue Crab; the crab's shack. "Well, Dickie, that's one way of saying it, but I don't think those crabs would agree with you."

When we got back to the truck, Dickie placed the crabs on the open back of his truck. They were iced and wrapped with newspaper. I was imagining how good they were going to taste when this veteran of the sea was finished steaming them.

As the truck slowly tooled around again, Dickie turned onto a narrow little street. He suddenly pulled into the driveway of a white, two-story house adorned with red shutters and a bright red door, and then got out.

"Come on out here, son. Help me get these crabs into refrigeration."

This had to be his house, but nothing like I had envisioned. It didn't have dirt piled up all around outside. And it was immaculate and even had beautiful flowers all around the house. It had been painted not long ago. This was the house of a man who loved his late wife enough to keep it the way she had it.

Dickie shoved the bushel basket into my arms and said, "Surprised, aren't ya? I'll bet you thought I lived in some run-down old trailer..."

He was kind of right.

"Aw, forget it. I know what you was thinkin'. I don't talk too good, but that doesn't mean I don't know things. And I don't dress too spiffy, but that don't mean I don't know how to put on a good suit on Sundays and go to church right and proper. And I don't spend a lot of time at home anymore because I can't stand to be here alone, but that doesn't mean I don't take care of Shirley's flowers jist like she were still here."

Coming up for air from his little tirade, he added, "But I am glad you like it. I kin see that as plain as day all over yer face."

"I did like it. It was a real home. It wasn't one of those castles with all the amenities that were being built today. This was a place where true love was shared, lived, and then separated until they met again. Dickie missed her so much, but in the meantime, he would take care of all she loved.

"Follow me into the garage. I have a refrigerator in there and we kin put these babies right in. Don't want 'em to spoil up on us."

I really had to start remembering to log these expressions down. They might be worth something someday. At the least, they were worth something to me right now.

"Please, Dickie, give me a tour of your house. I would love to see it, if you don't mind."

"Oh, you'll see it alright. After I feed you, we are going to go down to The Evergreen Motel and get all yer stuff. You are going to stay with me for the rest of your visit…and I won't take no for an answer."

He meant every word of what he had just said and the answer no would not be an option. I had no choice and right now that seemed good to me. I sensed the adventure of it all. I would be living with a real Eastern Shore waterman and he would tell me stories right up the kazoo. Does it get any better than this?

"I wouldn't complain if you did that, Dickie. It *would* give us more time to talk about things and see what we can do about all this. Besides, for all I know, you can cook too."

Once the crabs were inside of the garage refrigerator, we got back into the truck. "I know how hungry you are. I am too and after lunch we can get you all settled in at the Short motel, and then take off again. Oh, by the way, I kin cook up a storm. You jist wait 'til you taste those crabs tonight."

The truck lurched forward and away we went. As we got back on Main Street, the road had filled with a lot more traffic than I would have imagined would be down here.

"Where did all this traffic come from, Dickie?"

Tourists," he shot back. They come every summer through fall. They come to take the excursion boats over to James Island and out to Bingham Island. They do spend a lot of money here though, so I can't complain about that. They have been coming for years. I'll take you out there before you go. I think it would help you to understand a whole bunch."

"You're probably right." As I looked inside the cars, I saw kids of all ages, dressed in shorts and tee shirts. They were ready for a day on the beautiful water. Actually, I envied them. I was glad when Dickie said he would take me out to the islands. I was ready to explore it all, but not until I had eaten something.

I was thanking God when Dickie's truck finally came to a stop and we were parked in the same spot where we headed out that morning. It seemed an eternity ago. Yes, the world was round and Virgil's front door was feet from me. Food was finally at hand. He was an amazing man. He didn't seem tired at all while I felt like death warmed over.

With everywhere we had been that morning, I had completely forgotten *my* precious baby. I snuck a look to the side parking lot. I was trying not to be conspicuous, but he caught me anyway.

"See, your fancy vehicle is still there and she has all her wheels on her."

I was mortified; and busted. He knew exactly what I was thinking. I quickly added, "Yes, Dickie, my car is still here, just like you said it would be."

He opened the door to the restaurant and waved me through. I saw a smile go across his face. We were becoming friends and I was glad of that.

The Divine Cheeseburger

THIS PLACE NEVER SEEMED TO rest. It was just after noon and already all the counter seats were filled. The fryer was doing overtime and the smell of grease was everywhere. I wanted food and I wanted it right now. My stomach let out a roar that could be heard all over the room.

Dickie was doing his entertainment thing and they were all asking, "How's it comin' Dickie?" Down to the last man, they all spoke in that same twang and by now, having been with Dickie the entire morning, I was actually catching on fast. Imagine that? When I stopped to think of it, we kind of spoke weird from Boston too. Maybe it had something to do with living by the water.

I got the feeling that the same booth we were in hours before was usually saved for Dickie Short. It's like that here. Everyone has their own spot, a place they belong. I wondered how many years he had been coming here and exchanging stories about each other's lives. I was beginning to feel the rhythms of this town and it was only day one.

I slid in and grabbed a menu. Everything looked good and maybe everything would be what I would order. Dickie joined me and he didn't even have to look to see what looked good to him. It was probably the same thing he had been eating for years.

I was so intent on ordering my food that I didn't notice the very large man heading our way, but when he arrived, you couldn't ever miss that voice. It was loud and full of mischief.

Dickie looked across and said, "You remember old Burger Boy, don't you, Tug? You ran into him this morning, or didn't you notice him?"

I heard a great hoot and as I turned around, a behemoth of a man stood there; his belly bouncing up and down. "How could anyone miss me, Dickie?" he snorted.

I didn't know how I could miss a human this large, except I was so nervous coming in here alone. It was four in the morning, for God's sake.

That old thing about discretion, you know. "Nice to see you again," I said with a smile on my face.

Thank the stars, the very pretty Lindy came to rescue me and take my order. It was as if she could sense I was trying to fake my way through this introduction. She appeared even more attractive this time of the day. I quickly observed that she had brushed out her hair that had been plopped on top of her head in the early morning hours. I supposed maybe she didn't like getting up at that hour either. While she had pulled it away from her face, her very long and gorgeous locks cascaded down her back. She had a ton of streaks running through her blonde hair. Very attractive; and very sexy, I thought. When she asked what I wanted for lunch, her deep emerald eyes danced with excitement. This girl was alive. I couldn't help but be attracted to her, even if she was related to my host for the weekend. I prayed she might be old enough for me to at least have a passing fancy with her. There was no doubt she and I were exchanging vibes.

It was obvious she adored her Uncle Dickie, as she called him. I guess she was right. Sort of. He was a great uncle and no one called anyone great uncle unless they were from another generation in China.

They both teased each other as I sat and watched from the sidelines. All of these friends had such special friendships forged from birth and then passed down to the next generation. Virgil's was the central place in this town that they met each day and shared their hopes and dreams- and sometimes their disappointments.

"Hi Uncle Dickie," she said as a smile crossed her lovely face. Actually her smile pulled me in. I was smitten. Honest. I had never felt like this before. She even made me forget my hunger pains for a minute.

"Hi Lindy. Well, I have dragged this poor boy all over our fair town and he is about as hungry as a bear comin' out of hibernation. Let's get him fixed up fast."

Looking down at me sitting there, her sweet voice said, "You don't have to read what you want. You will want the cheeseburger platter. It's one of our main lunch specialties."

"Oh really," I answered. I wanted to have some fun with her even if I was two breaths away from starvation. I wanted to see if she had a sense of humor. I wasn't disappointed.

"Yes, really, Tug, I believe that was your name, wasn't it? It's simply to die for and I can't imagine you having anything else. "

I shot her a droll smile and knew she was into the game with me. Oh, is that so well okay, Lindy. Make it the cheeseburger platter, rare and with a slice of onion, if you don't mind. That way it won't take so long to cook and I won't die here." I was instantly finding myself less shy and very comfortable with her. That wasn't the typical me but nothing about this trip so far, had been typical.

Before he knew it, she yelled over her shoulder, "CB platter, rare and hoppin'."

Well now that was special. Rare and hoppin, she could speak a second language. Very interesting.

"I don't have to ask you other fellows what you want. It's always the same. Chowder and grilled cheese for you, Uncle Dickie, and another cheeseburger plate for Burger Boy here."

Burger Boy, who everyone doubted even had a last name, smiled at Lindy and said, "You have my number there, little girl. I don't know what I would do if I couldn't eat one of them greasy messes everyday. I would probably drop dead."

My eyes shot sideways, nearly out of their sockets. The man didn't say that, did he? Oh please tell me he didn't say that.

Dickie to the rescue. He heard my silent calls for help. "I have dragged this boy all over here this mornin' I showed him our *deelema*."

"Pritty nasty, huh boy? This here has got ole Dickie up in arms. That's good though. He is the one to do somethin' about it."

"He is a tiger, I'll give you that."

I couldn't believe when Lindy brought over the food. "Wow, that didn't take long."

"You ordered it rare, didn't you?"

"Does rare mean raw down here?"

"Try it and see. I think you will love it."

When she returned with the other's food, I was already in seventh heaven and half my cheeseburger had been consumed.

"Well, I see you approved," she shot at me.

"Excellent. My compliments to the chef." Now what did I say that for? Compliments to the chef? Oh my God!

I immediately turned to my new, large friend and said, I don't think I have to ask you how you got your nickname."

Burger Boy stared at me a minute and then said, "You're catchin', boy. You is learnin' about us down here, aren't you? We may be a bit standoffish to strangers but once we git to know ya, you will find us the nicest group of bastards anywhere in these parts."

Dickie almost spit the coke out of his mouth. "I told you to be nice to this boy. He is learnin' just fine. I am teachin' him. By the way, what story do you have for me today? You always seem to pick one up and let me hear it at lunchtime."

Leaning his full weight back so the chair tilted, and I thought would split in two, he stretched his body. "I don't really have one for ya today, Dickie. Seems everyone in this town behaved themselves last night. But I do think I should tell our young friend here what folks long ago thought of us. It might git him to thinkin'"

"What the heck are you talking about, Burger Boy? You don't know history worth a lick."

"Hell I don't," he snorted, as his chair landed back on the floor with such a thud, it shook.

Burger Boy shook his head and mumbled, "You old bastard. Why someday…"

"Someday what, Burger Boy? Someday you'll do something about me?"

Burger Boy put his hand up and gestured Dickie to stop already. It was their way of having a good time with each other.

"Now, where was I, son? Oh yes, I was goin' to tell you what one of our esteemed ancestors from the King's court, no less, had to say about us folks over here on the Eastern Shore. You see, he was sent here to report on the people who lived in these parts. Well, story goes that he didn't get much farther than Kent Island. You passed that way on your trip down here. I reckon he stayed just long enough to get the drift of what we were like 'cause when he returned, he made this report: My Dear Sir, these are the fightingest, drinkingest, fornicatingest people I have ever seen."

OMG! This one finished me off. I laughed out loud so hard that I thought we would all see my cheeseburger again. It took me more than a minute to gain control and by now, everyone in Virgil's was laughing and carrying on. I ripped out my pen and a small pad and said, "Now, tell me that again. This is a must have for my journal."

"Take it easy, son," Dickie yelled out at me. "You'll have plenty more stories like that one before your visit is over."

As Burger Boy repeated what he just said, I wrote it as fast as I could. I was still howling at this outsider's impression of the people who lived in this region long ago. And who knows if it wouldn't still apply today? I was almost afraid to ask.

Lindy saw that we were totally out of control and walked over to the booth. Was every lunch time like this? Oh God, I hoped so. I wouldn't want to miss one minute of this fun while I was here.

"What in the world are you men going on about here? You've got the whole place going now. Uncle Dickie?"

Dickie took her arm gently and said, "Why don't you sit a spell, darlin'. We was jist tellin' Tug what we are really like down here."

"Good Lord, Uncle Dickie. Can't you see you have to ease someone in slowly to our ways?"

"Come on, Lindy. Set a spell."

Lindy looked behind her and saw that she really could take a short break and she was secretly glad he asked her to. She decided instantly who she was going to slide in next to, even if she risked scaring him off.

I must have blushed again because she remarked, "I don't bite. This way I can stare into that old, wonderful face of Uncle Dickie's."

I moved over slightly so our bodies weren't touching, although that wouldn't be so bad either.

Once again I decided to have fun with her and the best way to do that was to tease Dickie. Facing her, I said, "Dickie told me that you are part of his family. It's hard to believe because you seem so different from this wily old man."

Lindy smiled as if she understood why I was doing this. Her face lit up when she answered me. "He is a wily customer, for sure, but he is also the most loving man I have ever known."

This time Dickie blushed, but it was the blush of pride for this beloved young grand niece.

"You go on now, the two of you. You jist make fun of old Dickie." I tell you what, Lindy. Why don't you come around for dinner tonight? I jist got a mess of crabs and I aim to steam 'em up with some fresh corn. Maybe I'll even let you have some of that beer you like so much."

I prayed she said yes, but I didn't say a word to encourage her. She had to make the first move.

"Why, Uncle Dickie, that sounds wonderful. I'll buy the beer and be there around five. I really have to get back to work now." With that, she darted out of the booth and this time, disappointed; she didn't look back at me.

I wondered what kind of beer she would buy. That was a sure way of telling if we were going to get along.

Dickie bolted from the booth and leaned down to Burger Boy. He patted his back and said, "Well, old buddy, Tug and I have places to go and things to do. It's been fun."

I didn't have to say another word. Dickie was finished and he when he was done; he was done. I shot out of the booth and said good bye to Burger Boy and thanked him for a most entertaining lunch. This time, I would pay the bill. And I wouldn't take no for an answer. I lost.

"Dickie, you have to stop doing that. I can pay my way. The paper does give me an expense account, you know, plus you are being nice enough to take me all over the place and you and your friends have been giving me some of the *history* of the shore, so the next time is on me, okay?"

"Oh hell, Tug. Don't be such a pain in the ass. I have the money so let me do what I want. Besides, I haven't had this much fun in a long time."

I shrugged him off and then said, "And I assume Lindy is part of that fun?"

"You read me like a book, son. I can see when love's a foot."

"Love?" I shouted out. "Are you crazy? I just met her this morning."

"It's love jist the same. I kin see it everytime."

I didn't respond. He was an old man and I needed him while I was here. Another few days and I would have my story and be out of here.

Dickie motioned for me to jump into the truck again. I can't tell you how much I wanted to climb into my Cherokee and take off for a few hours. However, one didn't argue with Dickie. And my baby hadn't been touched, so I was trapped. At least, it might give me time to do a few sketches on my pad. I wasn't a great artist, but I sure wanted to rough in some of those faces I saw at Virgil's. They were wonderful faces of watermen who had just been out on the water and loved every minute of what they were doing.

Dickie looked over and saw me sketching. He couldn't resist asking me what that was all about. I would have preferred he kept his eyes on the street, but there was no use telling him anything.

"I just want to draw some pictures of some of those men, Dickie. They have fantastic faces. You can see who they are."

Thankfully he returned to look at the road. I went to say something to him and saw that he had a look of disappointment on his face.

"Is something wrong, Dickie?"

"How about me? Don't I have an interesting face?"

"Are you jealous? Don't be. All in good time, Dickie. All in good time."

"I'll bet you're going to sketch that old weasel, Burger Boy. Now that burns me up some."

"Calm down there, Dickie, I shot back. Of course I am going to sketch Burger Boy. Wouldn't anybody sketch that man's personality? He is quite a character; just like the others. The story of their lives is carved all their faces. To be truthful, I have never seen more interesting people in my life. Most of them love what they do and it shows. They have a great deal of character. I think I will make up a title for each one."

Eyes narrowing a bit, he added, "Character isn't the only word I would use for that snake. Why he probably knew he could get somethin' out of you. What title will you give him?"

I thought quickly of some names for his friend and then it came to me. "Well, I think there is only one name that truly fits him. I will call him 'The Divine Cheeseburger.'"

Dickie snorted. "That's jist perfect for him, son. He's divine all right. Yes sir, he is one son of a bitchin' divine soul."

I HAD TO SAY SOMETHING. I was exhausted and had been up since the beginning of time. I desperately needed a nap whether this man did or not. If I kept at this pace, I could easily be dead and buried by dinner time.

"Dickie? I know you want to take me around the world in eighty days, but I really am pooped. Would you mind taking me back to my car after you show me this one, last place?"

"I kin see you were never cut out to be on the water, son. Why, this is the way we live our lives every day."

I shook my head. "That's why I am a reporter. God knows who to put where."

Dickie chuckled. "You know, son, right then, you sounded jist like one of us. Better be careful or you will go back to your fancy office and they won't know a word that's comin' from your mouth."

He was right. Within this first full day here, I was beginning to slide into the zone with them. Frightening as that may be. "I'll have to be more careful then, won't I Dickie?"

Dickie slowed the truck to a stop and pointed out the window. "This here is the shucking house. Now here is where they shuck all them lovely 'arsters' in the winter and send them on their way."

I no longer had to guess what an arster was. I couldn't wait to try it out on Roger...or Max.

"Well anyway, Tug, this here place is busy as thunder on a winter day when them 'arsters' get to comin' in. You'll have to come back and see that for yerself."

"I will indeed, Dickie." I couldn't believe that I meant that statement but I did want to come back. Underneath it all, I knew I would. It wasn't just the town and the people; it was something else I couldn't quite put my finger on. Could it be the girl?

Patting me on the shoulder, Dickie said," I have to say, you have been a pretty good sport today, son. I'll take you back so you can go and git yer things and then move it all in with me. I think you'll like it in my house. I'll let you sleep in a little tomorrow morning. That ought to make you happy as one of our homegrown clams."

To say I loved his little sayings would be an understatement. To the outsider's listening in, they were down right hysterical. I didn't bother to ask him what sleeping in meant to him, but I figured it had to be better than three in the morning.

At last, I was back in my Cherokee. Dickie's truck didn't come equipped with the luxury of air conditioning so I turned that on and ran it full blast. The cool air swooshing out and onto my face let me know that I would make it. I had been in doubt about that a few times this day. Feeling a bit more revived, I decided to take a spin around the pier before going back to the motel and explaining to the man who ran it just why I was leaving one day after I got there when I said I would be there for four nights. He seemed pleasant enough, however, I'll bet my stay was one of his biggest reservations this season so I suspected that his nice disposition was about to go south and became one of "get the hell out now."

The pier was still busy and the vision of the sun dancing on the water, I felt immediately calmer. Thank heavens for that. People were waiting to board a large, summer tourist boat to go to James Island. I felt such a part of this town already. I even knew what times that boat went out and when they would be back. I was beginning to understand what drew the old watermen down here, long after they could no longer go out on the water.

Grabbing the last parking spot, I got out and walked away from the water and to the end of the docking area. I studied the new condos that had been built and started imagining how upset the people of this town must really be if they were still so angry after the condos had been up for a while. For some it was the height of them, for some it was the loss of the view, but I suspected for all of them these buildings represented a loss of freedom and open spaces. They felt closed in by them and would a developer ever care about that? No wonder they felt like they were being murdered. In a way; that's just what was going on.

No matter how pretty it was down here, I had to get going. Dickie had mentioned dinner was at six and that he was doing that for me so I could catch a rest. As a matter of fact, he didn't call it dinner, did he? He called it supper. I remembered that he had used the term dinner to tell me that that's what some of the men ate around the noon hour. They would come home after a long morning on the water fishing, and their wives would serve up cooked meat, potatoes, a couple of hot vegetables, and a dessert. It's what I was used to at night, but these men were hungry when they returned from being out on the water. This was another wonderful custom that was dying off everywhere in this great land of ours.

I really had to get to my journal and write this all down before my memory lost it. I grabbed out my recorder and now that Dickie wasn't permanently affixed to my hip, I could recall all I had seen. I didn't want to forget one thing, one face, and for heaven's sake, I sure didn't want to forget one, outlandish expression. Perhaps some day I could write a book about this place and dedicate it to them.

Expect the Unexpected

I COULDN'T PUT IT OFF ANY longer. I was nervous but it had to be done. I kept trying to tell myself I wasn't the first person to cancel out after a day or two. Please?

I could hear a TV blaring in the back room as I rang that damned bell again. I prayed I wasn't interrupting him from his all time favorite TV show. Now that could really make this tough. Any moment I could be looking down the barrel of a twelve gauge shot gun. It was my luck and nobody came out and I had to bang that bell again. He finally walked into the office, I saw immediately I was in heap big trouble *Tonto*. He was yawning. Yes, I picked his nap time to stop by and piss him off.

Staring at me like he had never seen me before, it was obvious I was the one who had to make the first move. I silently began to say a Hail Mary.

"Ah, hi there," I stammered. "I am sorry to interrupt you, but I have something to tell you."

He just kept on staring and didn't utter a word. The silence was deafening. Girding myself up for the task, I blurted out, "I have had a slight change of plans. Thanks to your good directions, I found Virgil's this morning and I found Dickie Short."

Still no comment. I thought a compliment might evoke some retort, but I was definitely wrong. So I pressed on. "You see, he has invited me to his home for dinner…I mean supper and then has asked me to stay on there with him until I go back to Baltimore."

Now the look on his face was changing by the second. His brow was knitting together and that was never good body language. Out with it, I said to myself. "I will need to check out and move on tonight. I am sorry for any inconvenience this may have caused you, but I think actually living with Mr. Short will help me to get a better picture of what is going on down here." Hell, Tug, he doesn't give a damn about you getting a better idea of things down here. He wants you to stay put, damn it, and show him the money.

Finally, he said something. The *Hail Mary* worked at warp speed. Thanks!

"Well, I can't say I am totally surprised. Dickie Short has a mighty persuasive way about him. He must have liked you a whole lot to ask you to come on over and stay in that house with him. He hasn't had many visitors since old Shirley passed and you being a stranger and all… Sounds pretty odd to me but it ain't none of my affairs."

Dickie Short had clout down here and right now I was damned glad of that. "I will be more than happy to pay you for tonight, as well, being I am leaving on such short notice. I would be relieved to do it because I sure could use a quick nap before I go over to Dickie's home."

He studied me up and down like a roadmap. His stare was unnerving. "Well, that would be fair, I guess. I have had a call or two about rooms being this is my busy time of the year. This way I can accommodate folks if they want it for the weekend."

Thank God, he was a reasonable man.

I fell on the bed about as physically tired as I had ever felt, but this strange mental resurgence had come over me. I grabbed my journal and began to sketch out some of the places I had seen and some of the faces that had left an impressionable memory with me. I couldn't stop. My pencil moved almost without me thinking ahead of it. It was like I had been here before and I was sketching places that were as familiar to me as if I had lived here all my life. Page after page the sketching continued and I was writing stories beside them that were snapshots of what I had seen and heard and felt. What was going on here? Was some strange mission calling to me and begging me to do something. What something could that possibly be?

I wanted, no make that needed to talk with my mother. She had always understood what was inside my soul. Even when my father would brush my adventure stories aside and tell me to grow up and stop writing stupid things and concentrate on the real world; she encouraged me and fed my creative side. I speed-dialed her and was relieved when I heard her voice on the other end.

"Tug? Is that you? This is so odd, I was just thinking about you dear. What's going on?"

"I should have known you were tuning in. We have always had that special something. You'll never guess where I am?"

"I give up, tell me. I hope it's where you want to be and that you are writing a fantastic story."

"Well, I'm not sure it's a fantastic story yet, but I am on the Eastern Shore of Maryland."

"Where is that exactly? Are you taking some vacation time? After all, you have been at the paper a year now. Isn't this your anniversary week?"

"You really don't forget anything, do you Mom? I am not on vacation. I am down here on assignment. Max Pierson, himself, sent me down here. This place is like stepping back in time."

I heard her laugh- that gentle, lilting laugh and I suddenly missed her so much. "Max must think you are pretty special if he sent you to cover a story way down…where was it?"

"It's a town named Somerville. It's at the very southern tip of the Maryland shore. It's truly a special place."

"I see. It sounds a lot like the Cape. Is it magical?"

She and I always had that spark of imagination going on between us. It was so natural for her to ask if it was magical or not. She would want magical rather than just plain old special.

"I guess it is; kind of. I hadn't though about this place in that way but I think magical would be one way of putting it. I think I like it. I think I like it a lot."

"What is it, Tug? You sound as if something is on your mind. Can I help?"

"I think so. I have met a very unusual old man. He's unique, kind of like grandpa was, but even more so. He's like no one I have ever met before. He reminds me of the *Old Man and the Sea*. He was a Maryland waterman until he couldn't go out anymore. He lives his life in a much simpler way than we will ever know and now his world is being torn apart. His small town is being overdeveloped with condos. He is furious and so are most of the people who live here. It's like what happened on the Cape and everywhere else that has water. He is simply crazy about it. That's how I got here. He wrote really wild letters to Max and Max has me down here trying to put the pieces together. It's a complicated story, Mom, but I see his point and understand what he is fighting for."

"And naturally that makes you sad, doesn't it? Life changes, Tug, whether we like it or not. Our yesterdays aren't our tomorrows." She sighed into the phone and then added wistfully, "they call it progress. You and I have always had kindred spirits about things like this, Tug. It's not easy to feel so deeply, is it? We love the natural state of things. That's why you and your father always get into things. He is a take charge man who doesn't have time for flights of fancy."

She was right. As usual, she cut right to the chase and pinned it down for me. I was a dreamer and so was she. We were given to literary genius and that isn't always a blessing. I still could not understand what held her together with my father. They were so totally different souls and yet she adored him and he adored her. Some things are not meant to be understood by children. It was between the partners and not to be dissected by those who would never understand.

"Is there something else you aren't telling me, Tug?"

"She hit the mark again. "Well, yes, but I don't know how to put it. I mean it's something, but then again, it may be nothing."

"You've met a girl, haven't you? And you don't know where it will lead you. Well the best advice I can give you is to give it time and then you will know for sure if she is the one. Love is like corn. You plant and water it but it isn't until it shoots up, that you can pick it."

"Gee Mom, I have never thought of love in those terms. It's a whole new approach. I will never look at corn on the cob the same way again."

Laughing out loud, she said, "I guess I have been reading too many stories lately and I am waxing poetic. I just mean to let it be and if there is something there; you will know. You will feel it like you have never felt it before."

I fell back on the bed, clutching my cell. I was in seventh heaven to be talking to the one person in the world who truly understood me. But before I could hang up, I had to ask the question. She would be hurt if I didn't. "Is everything okay with Dad?

I could feel her face breaking into a relieved smile when I asked. That's why I did it "Oh yes, he is happier than ever. He is working harder than ever too. I tell him all the time that he should retire so we can run off to our home at the Cape, but you know that isn't going to happen. He is a worker bee and I am a home bee. I know you don't understand how we jive together but I can tell you, Tug, I love him as much today as I did the day I met him."

And the fact was; she did.

"God, Mom, I am glad I called. You have done it again. You seemed to have answered life's questions in five or so minutes of conversation. I miss you."

"I miss you too, Tug, but it's your time now. Your intelligence and sensitivity is what will make you a darned good reporter. Or maybe you will end up a great writer of fiction. I think you have many destinies."

"Well, one of them is for me to get going right now. I have had an invitation to stay with Mr. Dickie Short. He is a book onto himself. I can't wait. I am heading back to Baltimore on Sunday. Don't worry about me. I'll call you again soon. And thanks Mom, thanks for everything."

Saying quick good byes, we both hung up. I knew tears would be in her eyes. When I left for Baltimore a year ago, she kissed me on the cheek, gave me a hug, and ran into the house so I wouldn't see her cry. She didn't know that when I got into my new Cherokee and drove a few feet down the long driveway, I had those same tears in my own eyes. Even though I have been gone for a year now, and am on my own, inside I knew I would always need her wit and wisdom in times of uncertainty. She always came through like the thoroughbred she is.

Where my life is headed, only God knows, but for now, I still had a bazillion things to get done before moving my camp to Dickie's home. I am already questioning my judgment about accepting his offer to stay with him, but he didn't give me much of a choice. Well, it will be an experience if nothing else, so here I go, ready or not.

MY MANNERS WOULDN'T ALLOW ME to go empty handed, so I ducked into a small convenience store and grabbed some chips and nuts. I knew those items were always a hit. Then, I picked up the beer I said I would bring. Corona was my choice. I hoped they wouldn't mind. Naturally, you can't have that without limes, so I threw some of them in the basket too. With no more errands to do, I made my way over to the house we had stopped at that afternoon. My body was now in overdrive and I was in my umpteenth wind. Glad that I had an excellent sense of direction, I found it on my first attempt.

I knocked on the door as I juggled the grocery bag. I don't know why I bothered to do that as I heard Dickie yelling to me to just come on in. Gee, I thought everyone opened their own door. Apparently not down here.

"Dickie? It's me, Tug."

"I know that, son. Who else would it be? Come on out here. Lindy's got a good steam going' on for the crabs and I am up to my eyeballs shucking this corn."

I was surprised as I walked through his living room on the way back to his kitchen. I had expected to see newspapers scattered all over the floor and old, worn out furniture sitting against a backdrop of dingy worn out wallpaper. It was just the opposite. The place was really clean and neat for a man living by himself. The mental picture I had made for myself was all wrong. As a matter of fact, his home was cozy and inviting. It was the kind of space that called out to me and said "take your shoes off and sit a while." I quickly scolded myself for not remembering my mantra as a reporter, Expect the unexpected. Here I was; right in the middle of that creed.

Dickie looked up from his corn-shucking duty and shot me an odd look. He was reading my mind again; something that was becoming a habit with him. "You look like you seen a ghost, son. Did you think my home would be a dump inside?"

I had to learn to disguise my expressions better. He was way too sharp and didn't miss a trick. I decided not to answer because I would surely get myself into big trouble if I did. I wasn't a very good politician at these things.

"Here, I brought you some things to go with dinner."

Lindy bounced through the screen door. She was beaming and she looked pretty nice too. "I hope you brought the beer. I am dying for one. Beer always tastes so good on a hot, summer evening, especially with crabs."

I handed over the bag to her. She wasted no time pulling the beer out and, startled, she shouted out, "I love Corona. How did you know? Oh, Tug, this is just perfect."

I had scored with the pretty gal and I felt pretty good about myself. I had a hard time taking my eyes off of her. She had a great body. Tall, but not as tall as me, with that gorgeous hair of hers tied back with a colorful ribbon. And she had on a fairly tight tee shirt that displayed her other attributes very nicely. I knew I was blushing all over the place. I frankly didn't know what to do with the feelings running up and down inside of me.

"I took a shot. It's my favorite, so I hoped you and Dickie would be pleased."

"Uncle Dickie? He never touches the stuff. Now he likes his Pepsi Colas."

"You two go on out back and tend to those crabs and get to know one another. I will be out directly after I finish with this corn and put on some potatoes. Did you bring me some of your mother's tomatoes, Lindy? Can't not have those home-grown tomatoes, you know."

"Yes, Uncle Dickie," she sighed. "You know I wouldn't dare come around here if I didn't bring those. They're over yonder there on that counter."

"Shoo now. You two go on and git out of here."

Lindy shot a wink at Dickie and then turned to Tug and said, "Come on, Tug. He can get pretty *ornery* about things."

I followed her through the screen door and out to a back porch that had a big old picnic table in the middle. Chairs of various shapes and sizes were placed all around the edge. This was definitely the center of activity. The crabs were steaming away on a huge pot over an open fire in the back yard. I felt like I was a kid again and at our cottage at the Cape.

While Lindy popped the caps off our beer and squeezed the limes on into them, I was immersed in looking all around.

"It's a nice house, isn't it, Tug? Uncle Dickie has lived here almost his whole life. Aunt Shirley said something about leaving some years back when he couldn't work the water anymore. She thought this house might be too much for him to handle. But he said he wouldn't go and secretly I know she was relieved. She loved this old house as much as he did. They were quite a couple. They loved one another so much. He misses her like nothing I have ever seen."

I stared at her for a minute. She spoke with the same accent as the rest of them, but somehow she was completely different. Maybe it was that she didn't use so many of those quaint little sayings and her grammar was nearly perfect. But then, all I saw in her was perfect.

"You folks down here sure do have a way of putting things. I am getting so I like it."

"When outlanders stay down here for a while, they catch on, and sooner or later, they start to picking it up. It's natural, you know."

I swallowed a long swig of the beer. It tasted wonderful. I wanted to know more about her without sounding like an inquisition. I would start off slow and discussing education was always a good jumping off point. "Do you go to school?"

Lindy instantly looked away. I had offended her. I thought the question was harmless and she saw it as me saying "you're not educated, are you?" I was a complete thoughtless jerk. Before I could correct myself, she said, "I...I started to go to college up to Salisbury. That was a few years back, but when Aunt Shirley took sick, I couldn't stay away so I dropped out and came back here to look out for Uncle Dickie."

Was there a hole I could drop into? I mean the look on her face told me she might have liked me too if I hadn't been such an asshole. I had to make this right. "That's so nice. I mean that's really nice, Lindy. Not many people would have done that."

She looked shocked. "Wouldn't you do that if it were some one you loved?"

"I guess so. I never thought about it, but that's because I never had to. Still, it had to be a very difficult decision."

"We all do what we think is right."

The conversation came to an abrupt halt when Dickie came bustling out the door with an armful of plates and newspapers in his hands. "Let's get this party started. Here Tug; put these papers all over the table. I spect we'll make a real mess of things directly."

Not knowing what he was talking about, I figured I would just go with the flow. I took the papers out of his hands and stood there looking like a fool.

Recognizing the confused look on my face, Lindy came to my rescue. "Here, I'll do it, Tug. Why don't you get us another beer?" Gladly I obliged.

"Those crabs ought to be about ready, don't you think, Lindy?"

"I'll go and see to them, Uncle Dickie. I dumped plenty of Old Bay seasoning onto them so they ought to be about the best batch we have had in a while."

The two of them worked so well together. It was obvious to see that they had done this a thousand times before and I felt honored to be a part of it all.

Sitting down at the long table, I waited as they plopped a few dozen of the aromatic crustaceans in front of me. They sure smelled out of this world. Dickie brought out the corn that was dripping with butter and then hot salt potatoes that were covered in a pound of salt. All of a sudden, I was starved.

Lindy picked up a crab and said, "Have you ever cracked and picked open crabs before, Tug?"

Before I could answer, Dickie snorted a little and quickly added, "I'll bet not. Show him how your Uncle Dickie showed you how to do it years ago." He winked at her and then said, "She's the best little picker anywhere around these parts, son."

"Stop it, Uncle Dickie. For sure now I'll screw it all up."

In all the times I had eaten lobster, I had never seen so many utensils as they had to attack this project. Lindy went to it with a gusto that could match anyone. First, she tore off the legs and then proceeded to demonstrate the assault on the main body. It was like watching Picasso working on a masterpiece.

In seconds, she had the tender meat out and handed it to me to take the first bite. I complied without hesitation. "This is really good. I mean really good, Lindy."

"Sure is. There is nothing like our Maryland Blues."

With huge pieces of crabmeat dangling from his mouth, Dickie chewed away and said, "There won't be none left if these outlanders don't stop their murderin ways."

Beginning to pick away at my crabs I decided not to get into that conversation again today. I hoped he would just let it go. But he did not. "Did ya git yer fill of what I have been sendin' those letters about, son?"

I was trapped. I had to answer. Especially with Lindy staring me right in the face waiting for my answer. "Yes sir, I did. I took a lot of pictures and a lot of notes. My journal is filling up with all kinds of information. However, Mr. Pierson may not be as hot for this storyline as you are. He might even be mad that he sent me here for a whole different story than the one I'm bringing back to him."

"You will take it back, won't you son?"

"I am thinking seriously about it, Dickie. I have to handle it carefully with him or we might lose any chance of having it seen in print."

Dickie almost fell off his seat he got so excited. "Then you *are* thinking of writing this story. You will help us, won't you?"

Lindy burst into the conversation with as much enthusiasm as her uncle. "You just have to Tug. You just have to make people understand what is happening to us down here."

I was now wrestling with these little beasts so much that I stabbed my finger with one of the edges of the shell. "Damn it! This hurts."

"You betcha," he grinned. "They are tellin' you it serves ya right for killin' 'em."

I shook my head and laughed. "I guess I would do the same thing if someone cracked me in half."

Lindy didn't give a damn about the crabs. She wanted to know about Tug. She felt drawn to him in a special way that she hadn't felt for any boy she had ever met and if her Uncle Dickie would shut up for two seconds, she could talk to this hunk.

"Where did you go to school, Tug?"

"I went to Harvard, Lindy. That's in Boston."

"I know where it is," she snapped. It's one of the best colleges in the world. I read you know. John Adams went there and so did a lot of our early leaders. I love to read about the colonial times. We have our own colonial history down here too, you know."

I thought I had strike two against me, but then I realized she wasn't as mad at me as I thought. And she liked history. This was a very good sign.

"I am beginning to learn that fact. I am sure you can teach me a great deal about it all. I would like that, Lindy."

Lindy wanted to get to know Tug better but she knew he would probably be tied up with her uncle, but she thought she would try to see if there would be any time at all for the two of them. "What are you two doing tomorrow, Uncle Dickie?"

"Well, I don't rightly know yet. Maybe I will take Tug around to meet some of the folks. He will get a better picture of things if he talks to the folks."

An idea popped into her head. If she could get her Uncle to agree to let go of Tug for a day, they could really get to know one another. She had to give it a try.

Putting on her most demure smile, she decided to try the feminine approach with her dear uncle. "Do you think it would be helpful if I took Tug on a day trip? I mean take him up north and show him what all the development has done up there?"

Dickie shot her a sly grin. He knew what his Lindy was up to. He didn't want to let the boy go, but if she had a sweet spot for him, well, he had to let her go with him.

"Well, I suppose it wouldn't do no harm. Yes, it might be just what he needs to see. Where will you take him?"

I was sitting in the middle of an auction and I would go to the highest bidder. My head went back and forth like a tennis match was being played.

"I was thinking of going up as far as Bethany and Rehoboth Beach. I would drive him in the back country. He could get a real look and would see how all our beautiful water property and marshes and farm land has been turned into retirement communities. Then, we would take some time around Salisbury. I am sure he didn't get too good a look at that just by driving through on his way here."

I was finally able to get in a few words before the two of them had my whole trip here planned. "I saw that area, Lindy. I know it wasn't as extensive a tour as you would give me, but it did strike me how much development was going on over here."

She looked a little hurt. I could see she thought I didn't want to make a full day of it and she was wrong. I wanted to be with her. I wanted to get to know her. If the feelings that were going on inside of me were anywhere close to being right; this would be the time to find out.

"I just meant that maybe you didn't want to take up your whole day with me. Don't you have to work?"

Dickie was enjoying this immensely. He was watching young love begin to sprout. But now the two nit wits had to stop this fussin' and git on with it.

"I will take the day off," Lindy insisted. "I don't have to be there every day. Besides, I haven't taken a day off in a long time."

Finally Dickie stepped in to save the day. "You two go on off around nine in the morning and make a day of it. I will talk to some of the men around town and then on Saturday Tug, you and I can sit on down with them and they can tell you their thoughts. How's that?"

"Sounds great to me, Dickie. Is nine o'clock good for you, Lindy?"

Smiling contentedly, she said, "It is more than fine. I will be here then. Now, I better clean this mess up and call over to Virgil's and tell them I'm not coming in tomorrow."

Lindy started to collect the huge pile of crab shells and corn cobs that had now soaked into the newspaper. "You two go on and take a walk. I'll clean this mess up and I will call Virgil's for you, Lindy. Just go have a nice time. Why don't you walk down to the pier and see the sunset. It's pretty special."

Lindy leaped up and ran over to him. "You are the best, Uncle Dickie. Ready to go Tug?"

"Do I have a choice?" I said smiling.

"No, actually, you don't."

As we walked away from the house, I felt warm and comfortable as if we had done this all before. I was as tired as I had ever been, but, as we walked toward the water, I never even felt my feet touch the ground.

Cruisin' the Beach

I WAS SHOWERED AND READY TO go by eight o'clock. Now, for eating whatever was cooking in the kitchen. The smells were making my stomach do flips.

My mind kept replaying the lovely walk I had gone on with Lindy the night before. There was definitely something going on between us, but for me, the more important thing was that I really liked this girl. I really didn't want to say too much to Dickie, although I knew that he was going to bombard me to death with a thousand questions. It was his little Lindy and I had better be a good boy.

He must have heard me walking around upstairs because by the time I hit the kitchen, my coffee was already poured and waiting for me.

"How'd ya sleep son?"

"Very well, Dickie," I said as I took the first swallow of this heavenly brew. "I was kind of surprised, to tell you the truth. When I get that tired it normally takes me forever to get off to sleep. But not last night. That bed is really something."

"I knew'd you'd like it. That used to be Lindy's bed when she came to stay with us."

Dickie put down a huge stack of his pancakes in front of me as I decided to let that comment pass. He had a way of bringing Lindy into every conversation.

"You have a good walk last night, son?"

There it was; right on cue. He wasn't going to stop. If I was going to get fed, I could see I was going to have to talk. "We had a real good time, Dickie. She is quite a nice girl."

Dickie plopped the syrup down. "She's a whole lot more than just nice. She is the best, the blue ribbon of them all."

I lifted the syrup and poured. I was determined to get one bite in before carrying on with this. My mouth drooled with delight.

"God these are out of this world Dickie. How on earth do you make them like this? I have never tasted pancakes so good."

"First of all, they is flapjacks and not pancakes. Those in front of you is made from potatoes. It's a family secret and I'm not about to give it to you...unless you get with the conversation at hand."

How could I deny such a man? "Okay, Dickie, Lindy is a special gal and we talked a lot. There's nothing more to it. I think we became good friends. Is that enough? I didn't kiss her or anything, if that's what you wanted to know."

Dickie sat, drinking his coffee and when he put down his mug, he said incredulously, "Why not?"

I had had enough of this. "Because I didn't. The time wasn't right, so can we drop this?"

Chuckling to himself, old Dickie ended up our little session by adding, "Should have."

"Being you aren't going to talk about anything else this morning, I am going to take this last bite and then go get ready for Lindy."

I got up abruptly and put my dishes in the big white enamel sink that looked like it had been there since the beginning of time. It was in pretty good shape though considering. Dickie's home had all the same amenities that most houses had; except they were the original forerunners of what we have today.

As I turned around to leave the kitchen, Dickie looked down at my feet. "What's wrong?" I asked.

"Good Lordy, son," he let out slowly. "Those is the biggest ant mashers I have seen in a month of Sundays."

I immediately looked down to see what the hell he was talking about. "What? What in the world are ant mashers, Dickie?"

"Feet son- feet. Look at them critters. You may as well wear the boxes they come in."

He had really done it now. I have always been sensitive about my feet and now this old salt has called particular attention to them.

I had to be polite to my host. He might put something really odd in my bed.

"I know, Dickie. I have always had these dumbass, big feet. My mom says that it's good for a man to have big feet; that way they can run faster."

Laughing so much that his small belly shook, he added, "Or fall all over yerself."

"That's not funny. And what was that term you used for my feet?"

"Ant mashers, son. I'll jist bet you could take out a whole colony with them babies."

I threw my hands up in despair. As I walked out of the room and headed for the stairs, I could still hear him laughing his ass off. What a way to start the day.

TUG SAT ON THE FRONT porch with Dickie, waiting for Lindy to arrive. She was running late, but she had called and told her uncle that. It gave the two of them some time for Dickie to make amends for his comments at breakfast. He was growing quite fond of the boy and didn't want to piss him off in any way.

"I hope you know I was just funnin' with you in there, Tug. I am a morning kind of person and I hit the floor a runnin'. That comes from all my years on the water. If you ain't awake afore you go out there, you will be sorrier than a mule in a rabbit race."

What was this man saying? There just weren't going to be enough pages in my journal to get this all down. I didn't want to miss one thing. I decided to stop and buy another writing tablet when I was on the road with Lindy.

I thought I had caught his drift, and answered, "I guess you're right about that. By the way, did Lindy say why she was running late and how long she would be?"

"That sweet baby of mine didn't want to disappoint the folks at Virgil's so she got up at three this morning and went in until seven. Then she wanted to get on back home so she could pretty herself some for you. She'll be along directly."

No sooner had he gotten the words out of his mouth than Lindy's old car pulled into Dickie's dirt driveway.

The Cherokee was at the curb, waiting to go. Tug was determined not to spend another day riding around in an uncomfortable, and un air-conditioned car.

Hustling a little, Lindy yelled out, "Sorry I am late, Tug. I hope you aren't mad?"

"Not at all. Why it gave Dickie and I more time to chat."

Dickie knew I was being completely sarcastic. I wanted off of this porch and into my car so bad, I would have promised anything; except for staying a few more minutes. God only knew what might come out of this man's mouth at any minute.

"Shall we go, Lindy? I am anxious to get started."

After planting a big kiss on Dickie's cheek, Lindy kind of skipped to my car saying, "I have never been in one of these kinds of cars before. I can't wait to see how she goes."

I turned my baby on and gently stepped on the gas. We were off. I took off so quickly that Lindy's head lurched forward as she groped to buckle her seat belt.

"Boy, Tug, I see you are in a hurry to get out of here. Did my uncle drive you crazy this morning?"

"I wouldn't say crazy, but he sure was in rare form. He asked me a million questions that I wasn't in the mood to answer."

She knew her uncle so well that it didn't take a tree full of owls to know what those questions were about. "He's kind of protective when it comes to me. I'm sorry if he asked things that he shouldn't have."

How did she know he was giving me the third degree about what we did last night? I glanced over at her with a smile that said it all. I also noticed that her khaki skirt was way higher on her legs than when she got in. I was in trouble and it wasn't eleven o'clock in the morning. Her legs matched the rest of her, long and lean and my senses were definitely piqued. Pay attention to the road, boy.

"Where are you taking me today, Lindy?"

"Oh you'll see. I'll let you know when to turn off. Just keep on going up the highway for a while." She was a sharp lass. I could feel that she knew just where my brain was at that moment.

"Dickie sure does have himself all worked up about what's going on down here. Did you know what he has been doing for the past month or so?"

"No, why? Has he done something bad?"

"Not bad, exactly. He has been writing letters and sending them to the Editor of my paper. He got him so upset about it all that. That's how I got here."

"Well, whatever Uncle Dickie wrote, he must have had good reason. He is the kindest man I have ever known and he really wouldn't hurt a fly."

I rolled my eyes. "To you he may be the kindest man, but I can tell you I wouldn't want to get on the wrong side of him."

"He can get pretty mad sometimes, and all this commotion with building in town has him near twitterpated."

"I take that to mean crazy."

"I'm sorry, Tug. I guess we do use expressions that outlanders just can't understand."

"Do you really blame people for wanting to come to the shore and live? I mean it's so beautiful and people love being by the water."

Sighing deeply, she said, "It's not that I hate them. I just think all of us hate seeing our land all torn up and the destruction of the marshes that's going on. The development is taking away all we love. It's not pretty and there should be much more planning to it. If the people in control did that, I think it would be easier for us to accept."

"You do make a good case, Lindy. Your uncle sees it as murder and maybe, in one sense, he is right."

"Wait until you see all of what I am going to show you. Then you will know why we feel the way we do. Turn right up here."

Now we were traveling through the farmlands of Maryland. I was stunned at the beauty of it all. It was a hot, summer day. The skies were bright blue with an occasional fluffy cloud passing along in the gentle breeze. Big birds, that Lindy called turkey buzzards, circled high in the sky, looking for their next meal of a careless mouse or a snake on its way through the cornfields. This was a way of life that has been going on for eons and it was nice.

"Up ahead, turn left, Tug. This is where I will begin my tour."

As I turned right, we were coming into a small town named Berlin. I could already see the expansion of new houses and stores."

"This all wasn't here a few years back. Keep on looking and you will get a picture of how much is going on here."

She was right. Track after track, the houses were going up. The fields were being consumed at a staggering rate. "God, this is amazing, Lindy."

"I would say sickening would be the word. The only good from it is that our poor economies are prospering up here. However, once again, there is no planning."

We drove and drove and everywhere we went; it was the same. I expected this in a beach resort like Ocean City, but the towns nearby were all becoming part of the whole scene.

"This must have been so incredible years ago. I know kind of how you feel. My folks have a place on Cape Cod in Massachusetts. Over the years, it has grown like this too. It was much nicer when we were kids, but then people started to build all-year round homes and that was the beginning of the end."

Lindy stared out the window. At each turn we took, she seemed to grow quieter. When we crossed into Delaware, we drove a few miles along a protected stretch. It was primitive and natural. It was the first place that looked like that in quite a while.

"This is unbelievable. I can't believe that they have been able to hold on to this. I hope the state never gives it up."

"If they do, it's lost forever. You see, Tug, as you know, there is a lot of money going down in these places by the ocean and bay. Not everyone is honorable and there have even been rumblings that money has exchanged hands so that builders can build on the wetlands. I know what happens when they do that. In the course of nature, nature will always reclaim the land. It's pitiful that the buyers don't know that when they think they have found their dream."

I thought hard about what she was saying. This was a catastrophe waiting to happen. One well-placed hurricane and the whole place would go under and things would start to sink.

"Gee, Lindy, I never thought of it that way. I can hear how much you love this place. I don't blame you and your uncle for getting so upset."

Lindy turned and then did something completely unexpected. She took hold of my hand that was resting on the console. "You *do* see it, I know you do. You are beginning to fall in love with it."

I didn't believe she said those words. Yes, I was beginning to fall in love with this part of the country, but I was beginning to fall in love with her too.

I must have blushed because she giggled at me for no apparent reason other than she saw what I was thinking. I wanted to die. No, maybe I didn't. For the first time in my life I really felt something for a girl. There is no harm in that. As a matter of fact, it felt about as good as it gets.

The next turn off was an entrance to the seaside state park. I pulled in. When I shut the car off, I turned slightly and kissed her gently on the lips. I even shocked myself for such a bold action. Uncle Dickie would have been proud.

The kiss was almost innocent and she returned my emotions. When we separated, she suddenly jumped out of the car and ran up the dunes toward the ocean. Waving for me to join her; I obliged eagerly.

Cresting the top of the dunes I saw one of the prettiest stretches of ocean I have ever seen. The beach was packed with summer vacationers and children digging in the sand as they had done for centuries. The gulls swooped from the sky' cawing that familiar sound they make. Sea birds dove under the water to resurface further down. Lindy took my hand and we walked toward the water.

Squealing suddenly, she cried out, "Look, Tug. There are the dolphins."

Even with sunglasses I had to squint to see them. "Well. I'll be damned." A whole pod of them passed gently close to the shore while we all stood there gawking with glee.

"Aren't they beautiful, Tug? I love them so much." Lindy turned to watch me staring out to them and said, "You have to make sure they will always be here, Tug. Promise me, won't you?"

She was asking something of me that I couldn't do. How could I ever make that promise to this girl I now found myself falling for in a big way? "I don't know if I can promise that. Lindy. How in the world could I do that?"

"Go back and write our story, Tug. You can do that and maybe people will get to thinking that maybe all this building isn't such a good idea. You can do that, can't you?"

"I suppose I can, Lindy. But I don't think a lot of the folks who are making bazillions down here wouldn't think too kindly of that. I mean they are the ones who buy the ads that keep the paper in business."

I could tell she didn't like that answer one bit. "Well then, you have to make them like it. That's all there is to it."

I was falling for one, independent woman. I smiled at her, thinking of how much like my mother she is. While my mom is definitely the second string in the house, she always manages to let my father think he is the king. I am not sure the man has a clue of how he is being manipulated all the time. He is so stuck on himself that he would never believe a woman was outsmarting him.

Lindy poked me in the ribs and said, "Where are you, Tug? A million miles away?"

"For a moment, yes, but I am back. You know, you may have something here, Lindy. I will keep on writing it down and who knows how this story will turn out?"

Squeezing my hand tighter, she mumbled, "I hope the ending of the story is like I want it." There was no misunderstanding what she meant by that comment. I didn't answer her but I did give her another brief kiss.

Lunch was wonderful. We drove up a ways and stopped at a neat restaurant in Bethany Beach and afterwards walked their beach. It was far smaller, but absolutely delightful. Erosion had apparently swept most of it away but then they got the money they needed to get it fixed and fixed they got it. The corps of engineers buried the jetties and built dunes up so high that it made the view a bit difficult around the boardwalk, but one thing was for sure. If hurricanes came knocking at this town's door, they could handle it.

We drove inland again and for miles, it was the same picture. Thousands of homes dotted the landscape. Everywhere we drove, more and more developments going up. It was far worse here than anywhere else. Delaware was fast becoming the retirement capital of America. I began thinking of what that age curve was going to do to the area. I had noticed that on the Cape. It was going gray fast and younger people couldn't afford to live there anymore. I suspected the same was true here too. The low taxes were bringing everyone down there, but the penalty for living in paradise wasn't apparent yet. It would come. Taxes would have to be levied in order to build new roads and schools and water systems. The infrastructure couldn't take all this.

"God, Lindy, this makes me sick to see."

"I knew it would, Tug. I haven't been up here in a year or so, and I can't believe what's gone on in that short time. If they don't stop; there won't be anything left."

"It looks to me, that in some areas, that's already the case."

"I think you have seen enough. You get the picture. Let's go back home. I can't stand to look at anymore."

I could see she really meant it. Lindy was becoming physically sick looking at all the development. I realized how the Indians must have felt when the railroad was built.

"Let's go, Lindy. Which way back?"

It was after six when we reached home. Home? Isn't it funny that I just called it that? And yet that was exactly how I felt at this moment. I hadn't even given one thought to my gorgeous townhouse in Fells Point. I thought that was home and I could never love anyplace more than that. I wasn't sure about that now.

Lindy raced out of the car and up the steps. Dickie was waiting like a nervous father waiting for his daughter to come home from a date.

Planting a huge kiss on his cheeks, Dickie reeled backwards in his chair. "Hey, girlie. What's got you so happy?"

Lindy leaned down and whispered, "I think he is the one, uncle Dickie. He is the one I have been waiting for."

Dickie knew better than to say one word. Nature had to go its own course and he also knew Tug would be mortified.

Nodding his head slightly, she knew he understood. "Had a good day, did ya?"

"The best," Lindy yelled. "Tug saw it all. All the building and the taking of the land, and we saw the dolphins and we ate at a great hamburger place and we…"

"Slow down, Lindy. Dickie's head will come off with all you're telling him."

Dickie laughed out loud. "Aw go on now. She is excited. That's a woman fer ya."

I headed into the house to use the bathroom. I knew she would want to spill all the beans and frankly, I was glad. That way, Dickie would know everything and he wouldn't ask me one question. At least that's what I prayed.

When I returned, they stopped talking. Dickie sat there like the cat that had swallowed the canary. She obviously had spilled *all* the beans. I decided discretion was the better part of valor and asked if there were any other plans for that evening.

"Do the two of you have anything else on your agenda this evening, or can I spend some time writing tonight?"

Lindy looked up at me from the porch swing she was sitting on. Her expression told me she might be a little disappointed that I didn't want to go out someplace with her.

Dickie noticed it to, and quickly chimed in. "I made us a mess of beans and some fried chicken this afternoon, so I think the only thing I have planned is to go on in and eat it."

"That sounds great, Dickie," I said. "Can you stay for dinner, Lindy?"

Her face broke into a smile. I knew I said the right thing. "I would love to, Uncle Dickie. I know when you get to cooking, you make so much that half the town could join us."

"Well, I did make right smart of it, honey. Good, that's settled then. Come on in and we'll start fixin' for supper."

I really had to get to writing all this down. I had seen so much and taken dozens of pictures that I wanted to get developed as soon as possible. "Dickie? Where can I find a drug store that develops pictures?"

"Down yonder some. Lindy can take you after we eat."

Once again, we sat out back on the porch, and I ate Dickie's fried chicken and the best green beans I had ever had.

After supper, we talked for a while and then Lindy said good night. Dickie was going to take me to the drug store and she said she really had to get going, but that *maybe* she would see me tomorrow. What was all that about? I didn't think she wouldn't.

Dickie cleverly disappeared to the kitchen and I walked Lindy to her car.

"I really enjoyed being with you today, Tug."

"I did too, Lindy." My heart started beating fast again. I was definitely in trouble with this girl."

As she opened the car door, I couldn't resist. I leaned over and kissed her lightly on her lips. I was in heaven and I knew she felt the same.

"I really do have to go, Tug. I get up early and I am feeling tired all of a sudden. Thank you for sharing my shore with me."

Our time together was at an end. "It was my pleasure. You gave me a lot to think about Lindy...in more ways than one."

She got the message and I still have no idea how I got the courage up to say something like that to her.

Off she drove and I didn't have to turn around to know that Dickie had seen it all. He wasn't too good at disguising himself behind the curtains in his living room.

"Can I help you with anything, Dickie? You have been so generous to me. I want to pay you for the food, if you will let me."

Dickie looked like I had shot him through the heart. My polite gesture had insulted his southern style hospitality. "I only meant that you have been so kind and I don't want to take advantage of you."

Patting me on the back and leading me out the door, he said, "I wouldn't have asked you to stay with me if I didn't want to. You are my guest, son. Guests don't pay fer a thing."

As we climbed into his old truck, I said, "Thanks, Dickie. You are quite a man."

"You go back home to Baltimore and tell that to that big shot news man."

THAT NIGHT I WROTE FOR hours in my journal. I made sure to sequence everything…that is except for the kisses I shared with the lovely Lindy. That I would keep to myself. I still had to figure out just what was going on in that respect. I knew that she had struck me like no other girl I had ever dated, but how on God's good earth, could people from such opposite worlds ever hope to make a go of it.

I finished up around midnight and I was tired beyond belief. Before I retreated to my room, Dickie told me to rest up because we were going to have another big day ahead tomorrow. When I asked him what he had planned, all he would say was' "Son, we got to deliver the mail." I shuddered to speculate on that one.

Mail's A Comin'

I HEARD FOOTSTEPS PANDERING IN THE hallway around seven o'clock. I prayed it wasn't Dickie coming to get me up. I was relieved to hear them on the stairs, so I knew I could sleep in late. At least it would be late for me. It was Saturday and at home, Saturdays were fairly relaxed days. Not as relaxed as Sundays, but never the less, slower-paced from the rest of the week.

I guessed wrong. Ten minutes after I heard those footsteps go downstairs; I heard them coming back up. I was screwed.

My door swinging open, his voice yelled out as only he could. "Come on now, son. Time is a wastin'. The coffee is on and so is the breakfast. Git in the shower and then come on down and join old Dickie."

I couldn't say no. Aside from wanting to kill him; I knew he wanted company.

Fifteen minutes later I was showered and down in the kitchen. I skipped the shave and thought I might take a vacation from that nasty chore.

"Smells good, Dickie. What's cooking this morning… flapjacks?"

"You learn fast, don't you, son? No, today you is gettin' my famous French toast."

"And should I ask what makes it famous?"

"Because it's me that makes it," he said with that humorous glint in his eye.

"Ah, I should have known that. I have to tell you, Dickie, that your coffee is the best. It even beats out Starbucks. Do you know who they are?"

"I've read about them in the magazines. I know more than you think I do, you know," he mumbled. "That's the place where they charge you two arms and four legs for a cup of what costs me pennies to make."

He had definitely heard of Starbucks. "I guess you have their number, but millions of folks really love their coffee. They wouldn't go a day without it." I didn't think I would tell him I was one of those people.

"Dern fools, they is. Them city folk like to piss their money away and when you drink that much coffee, that's what you do, piss it all down the toilet."

By this time I had to put my coffee mug down, I was laughing so hard. He knew he was doing it so he peppered it up even more. This man was the essence of humor and lovability. He was, as they say down here, pure. He was pure all right. He was pure country, out spoken and absolutely the most outlandish character I had ever met.

"Stop, Dickie," I begged. "I can't stand anymore. I can hardly breathe."

"Okay, son; enough of my antics this morning. Eat your food now. Then you can go finish gettin' ready and we can get on our way."

"You aren't going to give me a clue, huh?"

"Nope." That's all he said and when I was done eating the best French toast in the world, I finished dressing. I heard him talking on the phone in his bedroom. That wasn't exactly eavesdropping because Dickie is partly deaf, so he shouted almost everything. He was talking to Lindy, and when I heard him tell her what time to be here, I shaved.

This time I won the war of what vehicle we would drive. There was no way I was going in Dickie's old truck. That would mean I would be the one hanging out in the open back end... There was no way I would do that while I watched Dickie and Lindy laughing at me like I was one of their hunting dogs, flailing in the wind.

110

Dickie automatically got in the back so Lindy could jump into the seat next to me. Now I knew he knew, but I have to hand it to the man, he never said a word about it.

"Where are we off to, Dickie?"

"Just hang a left up here at the corner and head back down to the pier."

"Do we have time for me to stop at the drug store so I can pick up my pictures? They should be done by now."

Dickie let out a whoop. "You be lucky if those pictures ever git done if old "Tadpole" Ames does 'em. He is the dumbest bastard anywhere around. He's what you might say is a rubber-nosed woodpecker in a petrified forest."

Where does he get these saying? My sides already ached from laughing at the man, but this one took the cake. Even Lindy convulsed over that saying. Obviously it was a newbie to her to.

"Uncle Dickie," she cried. That's not nice. Tadpole is a nice man."

"Nice, but dumb."

I ran in to the store with apprehension running all through me, but to my surprise the prints were ready. The man who gave them to me seemed pretty sharp so I figured Dickie was just busting on me. I decided I would find out for sure and as I thanked him for the pictures I asked, "By the way, are you Mr. Ames?" There was no way I was going to ask if he was Tadpole."

He shot me a polite look and said, "Why no I am not. If you're looking for old Tadpole, he won't be in until later today."

Well, that settled that. I took my pictures and walked out.

"Let me see them, Tug, please," Lindy squealed.

"Hold on there girl, I am barely in the car."

She grabbed them from my hands and ripped them open. "How do you like *my* pictures?"

As she tore through them making comments for each, she stopped at one and said, "Oh Tug, you caught the dolphins and it brings back such a nice memory of us on the beach."

Now I knew she wasn't talking about just the dolphins. Maybe it was the wink she shot me as I looked over to her. "I'm glad you like it. I will have prints made up and send them to you when I get back home."

She slumped down in her seat. I realized that she hadn't thought about me going home and now I said it and she knew that tomorrow I would be saying good bye to all of them. I would be headed back to my home and job.

She put them back in the envelope and got really quiet. I didn't know what to say. Maybe whatever we were going to do would make saying good bye easier. At least that was what I was trying to tell myself.

At the pier, Dickie jumped out of his Cherokee in a hurry, while Lindy proceeded to take the big cooler out of the back. When I asked her what she had in there, she laughed and said we would be gone all day and we did have to eat something.

Where were they taking me? I didn't have to wait long before I got my answer. Dickie yelled to both of us to come on over. We were going to go out in the mail boat. This was going to be one of the best experiences in my life. I was going to see, first hand, how the islanders got their mail.

"God, Dickie, this is great. I can't wait to get started."

"There's no use trying to persuade ya to write about us if ya don't see, first hand, where a lot of town's folk originally came from. I think then ya might understand completely why we aren't so shot up about what's happenin' down here."

He was absolutely right and I couldn't wait for the boat to take off. The captain was right out of the central casting and, naturally, he spoke the same as Dickie except he had a bit of a different dialect. His was more English, like in British. I heard him tell a man something about a house being put up "aback" his. I knew that meant behind his house. I remember reading an old book at the Harvard library where they used such words. I just didn't think anyone spoke like that anymore.

Dickie walked over to Lindy and me and introduced me to the rough and good looking man standing next to him. "This here's Nathan Tolliver. He lives over to James Island. He will take us out there with the mail and packages for today." Patting Nathan on the shoulder, Dickie added, "He's a right good captain. He don't mess around."

"Thanks, Dickie. That's something comin' from the likes of you. In your day, you surely knew how to float that boat of yours. "

Lindy watched as the two men teased one another. She loved to see her Uncle happy. Suddenly, she caught a twinge of nostalgia. She always wished she had been Dickie and Aunt Shirley's daughter. Her Uncle Dickie's brother wasn't anything like him. It's as if it all got put into him and when God was finished making Dickie, there was nothing left. She prayed every night and told God how blessed she was to have them in her life.

"Last call, Nathan yelled out." Not two minutes later, we were sailing out of the inlet and headed out to the island. The day was perfect. It wasn't too hot and the water was calm. For that, I was very grateful because I could still remember a time on the Cape when my family went sailing and I spent the day hanging my head over board, turning greener than grass.

Lindy read while we sailed and I was so enthralled to be out on this water with Dickie, that I really didn't mind that she preferred to do that rather than talk to me. I didn't feel the least bit sick and this time, here with Dickie and other local folks, I felt that feeling again, the feeling that I had been here before and this was my home. Maybe there is something to that notion of reincarnation. I was beginning to become a believer.

We spent the entire day on the island and we would return around four in the afternoon. We weren't alone. In the summer, the tourist boats come out here and vacationers can enjoy it for themselves. There is a small restaurant, but Lindy had hauled that cooler with us and we had a splendid picnic overlooking the water. It was shear heaven.

"I can't believe you had time to do all this, Lindy."

"I can't take all the credit, Tug. My mother helped with some of it. Uncle Dickie told me yesterday, when I was on the swing, that we were going to come out here today so it wasn't so hard to get it all ready."

"Just the same, this is wonderful." Was the food wonderful, or was it Lindy's beautiful face staring back at me that made the day so wonderful? Maybe it was a little of both.

Dickie struggled to get up from sitting on the ground. "The legs don't work as good as they used to, son. That's why I had to quit the water. When ya can't walk no more, you can't go out no more neither."

I knew this was his way of telling me that he was getting old and that he hated every minute of not being on the water. In every look he gave toward the water, I could see his yearning to be back on it, to be all alone, with his boat in his charge.

I didn't know if I should ask this question, but I did anyway. "Do you still have your boat, Dickie?"

His eyes lit up. "I sure do. It's restin' down in a boathouse of a friend. I'll show her to ya before ya go. I like to think she is waiting fer someone special to come and take her out again."

"Well, you never know, Dickie. That someone special will come along here one day. I am sure that will make you as happy as a clam." That was my feeble attempt at Eastern Shore humor. They caught my intent and laughed their damned fool heads off. I never did know whether they thought I was truly funny, or if they were being polite. One never knew with these folks.

By the time Nathan sounded the horn for everyone to get back to the ship, I felt as if I had been to paradise. I met a lot of people and most spoke in that same King's English. It was so wonderful that somewhere in this world, time had stood still. But not forever. They told me how a lot of folks were coming into Somerville now. They couldn't make enough money to stay on the outland, as they called it. Their children wanted a different way of life and being on the water wasn't part of it. I felt oddly very sad at this. I wanted this world to be put in a bubble for all time. I knew that was never going to happen.

"How'd ya like our little outing, son?"

"I loved it, Dickie. I truly thank you for bringing me out here. It is unbelievable and the people are so genuine." It was a wonderful day even if I didn't get a chance to kiss Lindy again. She didn't seem to mind. She knew why her uncle had brought me here. She knew that once I had seen this, I would write…and then write some more.

The wind and the air made me so sleepy when we got home that I thought I would pass out right on Dickie's porch. I had to take a nap. I wasn't at all surprised that Lindy felt that way to.

"I am taking off, Uncle Dickie. I am tired from the day and I know Tug must be, as well. Let him take a nap for a while."

What did she mean by that? Did she know I would be going somewhere else? God help me!

"Don't go fussin' over the boy, Lindy. He kin sleep if he wants to and then I'll take him out later."

I was right. This old man was going to haul my ass everywhere and I wasn't going to have one say in the matter.

"Good night, Tug. Have a nice rest. I hope to see you tomorrow before you leave."

There were those words again. Tomorrow, leaving. It hit my stomach with a powerful punch.

"I am sure I will. I mean I will, Lindy." Dickie stood there staring at me like the idiot I was. If only I could have been more like dad in these matters. He was always so debonair and engaging. Even my kid brother Mikey was good at this and for a jock; that's saying something. God, why can't I put things right when I am around women? Dickie could see I was panicking inside. "Go on, son, walk her to her car. I have things to do inside. I will call you later, Lindy darling."

Relieved to have a few moments alone with her, I smiled as Dickie walked away.

"Lindy? I am sorry I am so awkward at saying things. If you haven't noticed, I am kind of shy and things don't come popping out of my mouth."

Gently taking my hand and leading me over to a corner of the house, she looked up at me and said, "If you were one of those loud and obnoxious kinds of men, I wouldn't like you at all. I want you to listen to me, Tug. For all we know, this may be the last time I see you and I want to say this to you. From the first minute I saw you come into Virgil's I knew you were different. I wanted to get to know you and now that I have, I am scared like hell that you think I am backward and ignorant…"

I cut her off by taking her in my arms and kissing her like I hadn't kissed her before. When we came up for air, I whispered softly through her long hair. "I don't think anything like that, Lindy. Quite the opposite actually. Don't ever say that to me again. Do you understand?"

Tears quickly came to her eyes and she responded in the sweetest way to me. "I promise I won't say that again, Tug. It's just I am trying to tell you that I really like you."

I put my hand gently over her mouth before she said too much. We weren't ready for that yet. "Okay, Lindy. We have a deal then. I will see you tomorrow and say good bye then. You are a special person in my life and I will not forget you or any of the people I have met down here."

She cried out loud now. "I am a special person? That's what I am? You can have a special pet or a special house, but I don't want to be a special person to you. I want to be more than that."

"Shh, I begged. I just told you I am no good at saying those kinds of things and we don't have any idea where this is headed. I like you a lot, Lindy, but I am not ready to say anything more. We have had a few short days together. That's all. We would need more time to make that kind of commitment, don't you think?"

Wiping her tears away, she felt totally embarrassed. "You are so right, Tug. I must look like a fool to you. I must look like some schoolgirl who has her first crush on the school quarterback. I'm sorry. You are right. Absolutely right. I guess I am just trying to say that I want you to come back here soon."

"Lindy, I have a very good feeling this won't be my last trip down here. So, please don't cry anymore. I really get all tangled up inside when a woman does that."

We said good bye and then I went and collapsed on my bed. I was asleep before I could think one more thought.

Not even an hour had passed before Dickie was standing over me shouting in a loud roar to "Get Up.!" My one eye opened slowly and then the other caught up. I was now staring right into Dickie's face that was so close to me, I could feel his breath. This wasn't a dream. The man was definitely a sadist. He knew I was beyond exhaustion, but what did he care?

""Get up, son. It's Saturday night."

So? I thought, but I didn't dare say that one out loud. In a stupefied state, I automatically dragged my body upwards and then stopped dead in the middle of my room.

"I take it we are going out somewhere Dickie?"

Dickie advanced on me like a cannonball flying through the air to reach its target. "We sure are. Saturday nights, a whole mess of us men folk go down to the garage and have a good old time. So, go and splash some water on that dragin' face of yours and meet me downstairs in ten minutes."

I was his slave and there was no escape.

Ten minutes gave me the time to shower quickly and then change my clothes. Thank God I learned one thing at Harvard.

"You about done with yer primpin' son? No women will be within fifty miles of us tonight. You could have gone in yer underwear if you'd wanted to."

I shook my head to him and said, "Lead on, oh great master."

This time there was no arguing with him, we were taking his old truck. I had the feeling that was a better idea anyway as God knew where we were going.

Buckled in, I said, "Should I bother to ask you where we are headed?"

Dickie grinned ear to ear. "Why son, we are goin' to the garage."

I wasn't sure I heard him correctly, so I repeated what he just said. "We are going to a garage?"

"Not *a* garage. We are going to *the* garage. You have never been to a place this wonderful in yer life."

Driving slowly out of town, I had that sinking feeling that one gets when they know they are in big trouble.

Hangin' Out in the Garage

WHILE DICKIE'S TRUCK CHUGGED ALONG the highway, I tried hard to gain my second wind. It wasn't easy. My body felt as though it had been on a non-stop tour de force to some distant galaxy. Come to think of it; it had. Dickie seemed so excited about going to this "garage," that now I could only hold my breath in anticipation of just what I was in for.

About two miles down the road, he made a sharp turn into a dirt driveway. In front of me loomed an old, white farm house that looked like it could have been home to the Munsters. It hadn't been painted in a very long time and a few of the peeling green shutters had come unhinged on one side and hung lopsided as if that was the way they were supposed to be.

Where in the world was he taking me now?

Dickie looked at me wearing his usual grin. "I'll jist bet you have no idea of what is going on here, do you, son?"

"No, no, I don't Dickie. However, I might stagger a guess that it's going to be something quite special." I didn't want to hurt his feelings, and tell him what I was really thinking, so I thought that this approach might be the best.

"You know, son, I have a feeling you might jist like what we are up to tonight. We come here most every Saturday night and it's about the most special place in the world."

I shot him a slight smile and didn't bother to answer. What in heaven's name could be so special about this rundown place? I hadn't a clue.

119

Dickie parked his old truck in a field next to an enormous garage that set in the back and to the side of the house. The garage wasn't in disrepair at all. As a matter of fact, the garage looked fairly new and was in tip top shape. When we got out, I followed him around to a side door that led us in. What I saw next shocked the hell out of me.

"Hey, Dickie, "a man shouted. "Thought you might not be comin' tonight what with your company and all. But glad you are here."

My eyes quickly scanned around a room the size of a barn. There were so many men milling around that I could hardly believe it. They all had beer or some form of adult beverages in their hands. It looked to me as if they had been there for some time already and were laughing and carrying on like they were teen-agers.

Dickie was in his glory and shouted for everyone to pay attention. "Before we commence to partying, I want you all to meet my young friend here. His name is Tug Alston. He's a young reporter down from Baltimore. He's a right good boy and he is here to try to help us get the message out to those bastards that are building up our waterfront. I want you to make him feel right to home here tonight. He's never been to a garage gathering before."

With that announcement over, I was suddenly swamped with company. Dickie left me and walked over to grab me a beer from a big old galvanized bucket that had tons of ice in it and flowed over with all kinds of drinks, most of them alcoholic. I knew that I was in for quite a night. These men were here to drink and have a good old time.

The first man to shake my hand told me his name was "Tater" Cummings. The next one introduced himself as "Tweet" Wheatley. And so it went for the next twenty minutes. My head was swimming in nicknames of all kinds and I could hardly take them all in. I was trying bravely to keep from bursting out loud in laughter at some of their nicknames and God only knew how they got them. I wasn't about to ask. I was afraid of the answers.

Finally Dickie rescued me and we went and sat down on an old torn sofa. I was glad for that. A lot of the men just stood around and spoke in that same Eastern Shore dialect that kept me sharp to even begin to know what they were saying. However, after the last few days down here, I was either glad or sad to say, I was beginning to understand a lot of it. God! What would my friends back in Baltimore say? For that matter, what would my dad think of all this? It didn't seem to matter at the moment. I was beginning to have the time of my life. After a short time, they began asking me all kinds of questions of what I thought of the shore and how I liked it down here. I felt as if they had taken me right in. Not so far beneath my surface I was feeling a bit distressed at having to leave in the morning.

An older man named "Rats" Everly shouted out to me. "Have you ever seen how we skin rats down here Tug?" I quickly figured out that his question had a great deal to do with his nickname.

I shook my head no and then Dickie poked me and said, "You'll have to come back here in the winter, son. It's a big thing down here. A lot of the watermen make good money from skinning rats and selling them to the fur market."

"Rats?" I questioned out loud. They all laughed at me. "Dickie, you go on and tell that boy what we are talkin' about. Dickie was only too happy to comply.

"Rats, son. That's what we call 'em. You might know them as muskrats. Ornery critters, they is. We trap 'em by the thousands and then skin 'em up and sell their hides. We have a big time in February with it. It's known as the National Outdoor Show. That how old Everly there got his name. He can skin one of them varmints faster than your eye can take it in."

I was aghast! I didn't know whether to puke at the thought or just run straight out of there and report them all to the insane asylum. They just had to be kidding. "You don't say," is all I could think of to reply to this tale.

"Honest, son," Dickie shouted. "Don't go getting' wimpy on us. It's a good part of how we make it through the winter. Between the rats and the arsters, we make enough to get us through until the crabs begin to run again."

I just had to remember all this. It wasn't just what they were telling me, but it was the way they told these stories and how much fun they all had in telling me all about it. The mere visual of the whole thing had me slightly nauseated, but by the time they were done telling me all about it; I had already become a seasoned fan. Then they went on to tell me how they cooked them and what seasonings they used to prepare their beloved beasts. It almost sounded good, but I hardly thought my mom would want to try it.

I got up and got another beer. I could tell that this was going to be a late night and yet it would be one that I would learn more about these folks than if I had read a thousand books about the watermen of the Eastern Shore.

More stories and tales flew but none were as wonderful as the ones that Dickie told. He was onstage and he knew it. He was the man of the hour and there wasn't a man in that garage who didn't love him. He sure is a character, but he was *their* character and they held on every word even if some of the tales were as old as dirt.

I saw the genuine quality of these men and how they loved life. They loved their lives on the water and wouldn't trade one day of it for all the money in the world.

"Where's yer head, son?" Dickie questioned to me as I seemed to have drifted off trying to remember every story that was being told. "Is you having a good time? I'll bet you are, even if you don't admit to it."

"Dickie," I said, "I am having the best time of my life." And it was the truth. I have never been so relaxed and accepted. These men were the real article and I loved being a part of them. I wondered if I could ever go back home and not have that gnawing feeling that I belonged somewhere else.

"I got one for ya, Dickie," shouted "Jitter" Evans. "The other night 'Nookie' told me that he and his wife, Josie, got to talkin' about their funeral arrangements. Seems she's been harpin' on him to make plans and stop procrastinating about the whole mess. Well 'Nookie' got to thinkin' real serious about it some and then told old Josie that when he dies, he wants her to take his old body down to the water and put him in his skiff. That she were to cover it with water bushes, light it afire and float his ass down the Honga."

Now could anyone not go hysterical with these men? The very picture of this man's wife doing exactly what he had told her to do caused me to laugh so hard I thought one of my ribs had broken. The tears streaked down my face as all of us snorted like there was no tomorrow.

"I kin jist picture old Josie doin' that to 'Noookie,'" Dickie shouted out as he about choked on his soda. He turned and looked at me while I convulsed in hysteria. It wasn't just the story; it was the way that these men could spin a yarn or two and enjoy it more than anything.

"You know, Tug, you liked that one so much, you might like to hear tell the story old 'Duck Egg' Martin tell the other night."

I grabbed hold of my left side, it hurt so much. "Oh, please, I don't think I can stand anymore." That only made them go on more.

Without hesitation, he kept on going.

"Well, old Duck Egg, he got to thinkin' he would go out huntin' the ducks one night. Well, he got himself positioned right and then he took aim at them birds. He was ready all right and when he commenced to firing, them ducks deeve under the water and when they come up, old Duck Egg cut nary a feather."

The conclusion to this tale found my beer running straight out my nose. I damned near did choked to death. In all the years at Harvard, with all the stories guys tell one another, I had never heard anything this funny in my life. I dropped my beer on the cement floor and held both my sides. They were splitting in half. The roar of the men could most likely be heard for miles. I didn't know if Duck Egg was in that room or not, but it wouldn't have mattered. These men adored making fun of one another. It was the way they lived and loved.

I finally caught my breath and told Dickie I couldn't stand anymore. We had been laughing for almost three hours straight and I could easily see that it wouldn't be hard to actually laugh myself to death in this garage.

"Why son, we do this most every week. It's early still."

"Early or not, Dickie, I have to leave in the morning and I am already half shit-faced."

A sly smile rolled across his face this time as he said, "Maybe you won't go home, son. Maybe you won't want to leave us. We are the best, you know."

"You have made me a believer, Dickie, but if I don't go back, who will write your tale?"

Dickie held his hand to his chin and answered, "Well, you do have a point there. You'll miss us, though. You'll wake up in the middle of the night up there in yer fancy home, and you'll miss us."

I had a feeling he wasn't just talking about himself and the men. He had Lindy on his mind and as he said it, I knew he was right. I would miss them all. Including Lindy- very much.

About that time, the side door flew open and a woman, the size of a small house, stood there with her hands on her hips. "'Sooty' Ward," she yelled. "You come on out here. It's time fer you to come home."

I leaned quietly across to Dickie and asked, "Who is she?"

Dickie didn't say a word. He sat as still as the leaves before a thunderstorm. All the men stopped talking and laughing when they saw here standing there. She was a towering presence and they seemed a bit scared of her. I decided to shut up too.

"I say Sooty; I know you're in here. You come on out now, you coward."

Momentarily a meek little man made his way out from another room in the garage. He looked like he was about to be skinned like one of those muskrats that they talked about. I didn't doubt that she could do it.

"You come on now, Sooty. You know how you git when you come down here." She then cast a very mean eye around at all of us. Not one man said one word.

"Shame on all of you for carrying on like a bunch of danged old fools. And I see you have dragged that young stranger man in here with you, Dickie Short. What in the world will he think of us folks?"

Dickie said nothing, but threw his hands up like he was saying "I don't know."

Sooty Ward staggered toward her and it looked to me as if this wasn't the first time his old lady had come down here to fetch him. He was pretty drunk and I shuddered to think of what was waiting for him when he got home.

The side door slammed as the charming couple departed. I couldn't wait to ask Dickie just what that was all about.

He guessed what I was about to say and before one word got out of my mouth, he said, "That Doris is really somethin' isn't she? Old Sooty comes down here every Saturday night and gets drunker than a skunk and every Saturday night Doris comes and fetches him up. I can tell you he looks right green in church the next day. But, they love each other. It's jist the way of things for them."

I could only imagine the tongue lashing that man was getting on his way home and how his head was probably throbbing as she lit into him. I did get a chuckle out of it though. Nobody seemed to care one wit about it. They just picked up where they left off.

"I hate to break up your party, Dickie, but I really must insist that you take me home. You can come on back if you like."

"I guess you're right. You really have had a lot goin' on while you've been down here. Come on; let's get on out of here."

I stood up and waved to all the men. "Thanks guys. This has sure been one of the best nights in my life. I won't forget you."

As they shouted their good byes, Dickie and I walked out the door and as it slammed shut, I felt that twinge of nostalgia wash over me again. There was something about this place that did that to me and I supposed it would take a long time for me to figure out why.

It was midnight when we climbed the front steps of Dickie's porch. It was still very warm out and though I was tired beyond reason, I didn't really want the night to end.

"Do you want something to drink, son?" Dickie said as if he could read my mind. But then again, he could, couldn't he?

"I really shouldn't, but thanks anyway. I still have some work to do before turning in."

"You'll work yerself to death one of these days, son."

"Maybe, but it has to get done. Besides, I love sitting in that front window upstairs and hearing all the night creatures calling to me from the willows out back. It's magical and it makes me feel as if they know me and are talking to me and telling me their stories."

"You are getting kind of weird on me, son. I know what you mean though. Those night sounds are a part of me as much as breathing. I couldn't live anywhere else in the world. I could never sleep if I didn't hear 'em."

I closed the door to my room behind me and stripped my shirt off. I sat down at a small desk that was in front of that window. I opened my laptop and began to write down more of the story of what was happening here. What was happening to this place that time had seemed to forget? As the words poured out of me, I realized that I had to return here to finish it. There were just too many things that were left unsaid…including how I felt about Lindy Short. And yes, it was all magical.

Good Bye for Now

T HE SMELL OF DICKIE'S COFFEE meant it was early morning. It was time for me to get up and get started. This wasn't going to be the happiest day in my life, and I really couldn't understand why it was bothering me so much to leave a place I had just come to know.

I had become used to all the rattling around and noises Dickie made every morning while trying to be quiet. Being quiet wasn't something Dickie Short could do if his life depended on it. Change at his age was not going to happen.

As the pipes clanked away, I jumped into the hot shower. I had pushed my body to the limit the last few days and it reminded me of how I felt at exam time in college. It was going to take me a week to get over this trip.

As usual, my coffee was handed to me when I walked into the kitchen. My head had stopped pounding slightly from the past evening's shenanigans, but it might take a few cups of "Joe" to get me passed the "I want to die" stage.

A chuckling voice said, "You look like this might be jist the thing, son."

"Very funny, Dickie. I guess you could say I went way passed my limit last night."

"But I'll bet you enjoyed yerself."

"I did indeed. I haven't had that much fun in years. My sides still ache from laughing so hard."

"They're a good bunch of guys. I have known most of them all their lives. We've been goin' down to that garage for longer than I can remember."

"To be honest with you, when we pulled into that driveway, I thought you had lost your mind. No one can possibly know how much fun you can have in an old garage with a lot of men."

I noticed he was busier than usual this morning. He fussed with things and didn't come over to the table and sit with me. He never even looked up from the sink when he said, "So, you have to leave us, do ya?"

"I'm afraid so. I want to thank you for all you've done for me. I couldn't have had a better host. Now, I have to get back and write all this down so that it makes sense."

Hooting out loud, he shot out, "If you kin do that, son, you will be Moses on the mountain."

I just shook my head and then drank the coffee. Moses on the mountain, I thought. Another one for the journal.

"You be sure to keep in touch, son. I will be looking for your articles in the paper."

"Oh, I'll just bet you will, Dickie. Do you think you could do me one more favor?"

"Sure, what's that, son?"

"Please don't send Max any more letters. I think I can explain it all to him without him getting any more of your animated correspondence."

Dickie placed some eggs and bacon in front of me and patted my shoulder. "I think you're right, son. I think Mr. Pierson there has had about enough of old Dickie Short for now. After all, he isn't such a bad guy. He *did* send you down here."

"That's right and please remember that. I'll do my best."

"I'll help you with your things when you tell me you're ready."

As I watched him go back to whatever it was he was doing, I thought of Lindy. I knew she would still be fast asleep. It was Sunday and she had told me she didn't work at Virgil's on Sundays. She slept in and then went on to church with her family. I would miss saying good bye to her and having one, last intimate kiss from her wonderful lips.

"Dickie?" I said quietly. "Please say good bye to Lindy for me. We said good bye last night, but I don't want her to think I wasn't thinking of her this morning."

Oddly enough, Dickie didn't turn around and look at me. He just kept washing dishes in the sink. "I'll tell her, son."

I got up and left the kitchen and headed upstairs to finish the few things that still needed packing. I was not looking forward to saying good bye to my host.

I didn't hear him in the house so I went outside to see where he was. It was time to leave whether I liked it or not. I found Dickie outside, wiping down my Cherokee with an old rag. I knew he didn't want to say good bye to me any more than I wanted to leave him and his home.

"Thanks for doing that. It was getting pretty dirty from riding all over the shore."

"She looks good now, son."

I decided to do something I rarely did. I put my bags and gear in my Cherokee and then turned, and hugged him tightly. He hugged me back.

"Now, what did ya go and do that fer?"

"I did it because I will not forget you and I wanted you to know how appreciative I am to you for all you have done for me."

He shoved me a little and then said, "Go on and git a goin'. The traffic will get right smart in a little while. It's always that way on Sundays when all the outlanders go on back home."

Only he would have said it that way and I as I waved good bye, I was already missing him.

THE TRAFFIC WAS THANKFULLY ALMOST non- existent at the hour I was on the road. It was great. It gave me time to think…time to remember…and time to ache for what I was already half in love with. My mind kept repeating some of the sayings that had become part of my new lexicon. I wondered how many times I would slip talking to my peers at work and how they would laugh at me for doing so. I frankly didn't care. They wouldn't understand one iota of what I had done these last few days and they wouldn't care either. All they would want to know was what kind of story I had dug up and when they heard or read it, they would wonder why Max wasn't firing me for not bringing something more headline-grabbing like serial murderers loose on the Eastern Shore. No, they would never understand what it meant to these people to have their land developed beyond reason and their waters over fished and polluted. They would never think that any of that was wrong. They would think these people ungrateful for what they saw as progress and a way to bring millions of dollars into their towns. They would have no care in the world that an entire way of life was passing before them to become extinct forever.

Before I knew it, I was past Salisbury and it wouldn't be but an hour or so before the Bay Bridge loomed into focus. Oh joy. I decided to call home and check in with my mom and dad. They would be up by now and my mom would love hearing about everything I had been doing for the past few days. I wasn't sure if the same would be true for my dad. He was such a tight-ass with me.

I was relieved when Mom picked up the phone.

"Tug, how are you? I have been thinking about you and your adventures down on the shore."

"Mom, it was a wonderful trip and I think I have found my story, even if it's a different one than what I came looking for. The people down here are wonderful. They are real Americana."

"You sound as if you have found heaven, Tug. I am so glad. There's something different in your voice. Are you sure there isn't more you want to tell me?"

She knew me so well. She knew that there really was more I wanted to say but I didn't want to go there just yet.

"Well, a lot happened in a few days. That girl I mentioned the other day is definitely different from any other girl I have met, but it's way too early to make something of it yet. I don't know if I will ever see her again, so don't go doing that Mom thing."

She laughed gently and said, "I won't bug you about that, Tug, You will tell me when it's time. Dad is in the other room. Should I tell him to pick up the phone? I told him where you were and what you were doing…"

"I'll just bet he was plussed about that," I interrupted.

"He was, Tug. You know him, he doesn't get all starry eyed over things."

That was my Mom's way of telling me that he thought my going down there was the end of my career. He was always ready for disappointment when it came to me.

"I suppose if he's within earshot, I really should speak to him. It's hard, you know Mom? It's always the same. His life revolves around Mikey and that's it for him. By the way, speaking of him, how is my kid brother?"

"He's just fine. He checks in with us occasionally, when he needs food. You know Mikey."

I sure did know Mikey. He was the apple of my father's eye and he could do no wrong. Even with all that; I loved him so much and I missed the hell out of him.

"Send him my love, Mom. Now, I think I am ready for Dad."

I immediately tensed up when he got on the phone. His first words did not surprise me at all. "So, Max sent you down to the Eastern Shore, huh? He called me the other night and at first, I thought it was curtains for you, but then he said that was a good thing."

I couldn't believe it. I knew he called Max, but would never tell me that so he just turned it around and said that his old buddy called him.

"Well that sure makes me feel better. So, it's a good thing, huh?"

"That's what he said. Those were his very words. I was pretty upset when Mother told me where you were. I thought he might be trying to ditch you on a dead-end story and then let you down gently. But quite the opposite is true. He tells me you are doing very well at the paper."

I could hear how relieved he was that I wasn't a failure, especially after the fight we had had about me not joining him at The Globe.

"Well, Dad, that makes me feel good. Actually, I found quite an interesting story down here. I hope to have some of it in print by week's end."

"That's great, Tug. Will you be coming home soon? I always have tickets to a Sox game. Just give me fair warning. You know how folks want to be my friend because they all know I am the man..."

Yes, you are that, aren't you Dad? You are the man for everyone else but your son who about killed himself to please you and do everything the way you wanted him to. I knew he really didn't mean he wanted me to go with him to a baseball game. That was always something he did with Mikey. But, it was the thought that counted, wasn't it?

"Thanks, Dad, but I don't think I will be coming home anytime soon. I have a lot to do right now. I met the neatest man. His names is Dickie Short. He's a bonafide waterman of the Eastern Shore. I stayed with him at his home."

"That's nice, Tug. Say, good talking to you. I have to run, but do keep in touch."

It's always the same. He gets on the phone and does his superficial dance of conversation with me. God, when will this bullshit end? When will he say he thinks I am doing a good job with anything? The answer to all of the above is never Tug!

I was glad that was over and it left me with such anger inside that I decided to stop at the next McDonalds and get a coke and try to shake it off. I just didn't understand how my loving and wonderful mother could have put up with that bastard for so many years. Different strokes for different folks, I guess.

The coke did the trick and I was back in the car and within a few miles of that heart stopping bridge. This time, however, I was determined I was not going to go and get all weak-kneed over it. I flew up the outside lane and continued on. This time I marveled at the ships on the Chesapeake and the sailboats that dotted all over the waters. It was beautiful. I had overcome my fear and was as proud of myself as ever, even though my body still felt tethered to the shore. It was then that I knew that I would go back. I would have to. Meeting Lindy had changed everything and then there was Dickie. Oh yes, there was Dickie. I would go back and I would write and keep writing until people listened and maybe we could get enough people to really change things.

Back on the Job

SOMEHOW MY TOWNHOUSE DIDN'T QUITE look the same to me. It's not that it was any bigger or smaller; it had just changed. Or was it me who had changed? I carted my bags and equipment into the house and as I passed through the kitchen, I noticed that the light was blinking like crazy on my message machine. Good God, I thought. I really don't want to answer whoever they are, but maybe Lindy called. I left her with my numbers, so I guess I better do that first.

After I listened to them all, Lindy was not one of them. Roger called to see if I survived and if I was coming in the next day. What did he think? That maybe I had been carried off by the watermen? Then Beth's voice giggled into the phone. She wanted to know if I had had my fill of crabs and the people down there. Good grief, Beth! Then, a surprise message was from the man himself. Max wanted to see me sometime the next morning. He wanted to know all about my trip. I was suspicious of that message especially knowing that my father had interfered.

I decided to throw some wash in and then go up and sit on the rooftop. I suddenly felt closed in and needed to get outside. I was beginning to understand what the watermen felt like when they had to be on land for too long. What was happening to me?

With a beer in my hand, I swung open the door and looked out on the harbor that was in the distance. I did love it up here and to be honest, I loved my whole place. This was my dream. To be able to be on my own, with a great job, and live in a super cool place. I had all three, and yet now, I didn't know if that was what I really wanted.

As I looked out onto the buildings beyond to the water, my heart skipped a beat and I closed my eyes and allowed the night specters to dance in front of my eyes. Come to join me were the watermen. Burger Boy laughing so hard his big belly shook like Santa. Poke, who was a little slower than everyone else, but that didn't keep them all from loving him. Sooty, who loved to drink it up with the guys on Saturday night until his adoring, and brash wife Doris came looking for him. And of course there was Dickie. There would always be Dickie. I had fallen in love with Dickie Short. He was the character to end them all in the small town that was just trying to say "hey, wait a minute fellas, can we talk about all this?" There couldn't be anyone else like him... anywhere. He was the persona of old America. America the way it used to be. America before money and objects took the place of good, old-fashioned fun. Oh Dickie, I thought. How in the world can I plead your case? I have a feeling Max may get a bit hot under the collar with it when I tell him just what you were talking about. I can hear his comments now. While he is a pretty nice guy, he's a man on the move and he knows what sells papers. I will have to do some fancy footwork to convince him that this story will sell.

In the middle of my thoughts about the watermen of the Eastern Shore, *she* popped out just like that. Lindy's sweet face was right in front of me. She was so pretty and I could taste those deep and loving kisses. I felt her small and tight body close to mine. I was losing it and I didn't care one bit. I picked up the phone and called her.

AFTER WAY TOO MANY RINGS, it was evident she, nor her parents, were home. I was terribly disappointed. I wanted to hear her voice and hear her laugh, and oh hell, I just wanted to talk to her so I could feel close to her and to the whole of Somerville.

I wanted to get Roger out of the way. Then, I had to get moving on this story. I needed to be prepared for the next day when I went to see Max.

When Roger answered the phone, I relaxed because hadn't Dickie taught me; there was always time for a friend?

"Hey there Tug, you came back to us. I thought you might stay there permanently."

"The thought did cross my mind, Rog."

"So you liked it. Did you find what you were looking for?"

"Yep, I like the place very much," I said knowing that he and I were talking about two different things. The people are outstanding down there."

Roger paused for a minute. Was this his old friend Tug Alston? The preppy, soft-spoken guy who was a bit of a snob from Harvard and Bean Town? Tug saying "yep?"

"I see. It would seem that you came back with a whole different impression than the one you left with."

"It took me a while to understand everything Roger, but once I did, the people that live down there are real folks, with real lives that they think are being threatened."

"So, the whole thing about murders going on turned out to be real?"

"In a manner of speaking yes. It's not quite what it seems though."

"Just how is that, Tug?"

I did not want to go into this with Roger right now. "I'm really tired, Rog. I wore myself out down there, so let's leave all the particulars until tomorrow. Is anything going on at the paper I should know about?"

Roger definitely picked up that he wasn't going to get anything else out of me, so he dropped the whole thing.

"Nothing that can't wait. Pretty much the same old same old, so I'll catch you in the morning. Get a good night's sleep buddy."

"Will do, Rog."

I was glad to have that over with so I could return to my thoughts about the past five days. I decided another beer was in order and as I reached for it in my small fridge upstairs, my phone rang. "Damn," I said out loud. "I just want to be left alone."

I took a swig of my beer and decided to answer it. "Hello?"

"I just wanted to know that you got home Okay."

Was I happy to hear her voice or what? There is a God. "Yes, I got home a short while ago and the trip was really good. There wasn't much traffic. I'm glad I left early."

"I take it the bridge wasn't so bad for you this time."

"As a matter of fact, Lindy, it didn't bother me much at all. The only thing that seemed to really bother me was that I was leaving instead of coming."

Lindy laughed and said, "Oh boy, Tug, you have made some real progress now. Do I detect that you might have come to really like us down here?"

She was fooling with me and I loved it. "Maybe a little, but please don't tell your Uncle Dickie."

"Well okay, I'll keep your little secret. Do you think you will be coming back again sometime soon?"

I was afraid she would ask me that and I didn't quite know how to answer her. If I said no, she might take that as a rejection, and if I said yes, she would be all over me about feelings and that sort of thing. Man, women weren't easy.

I hesitated to answer her, and I know she picked right up on it. I was trapped. I had to come up with something. Then, she helped me out. "I guess you'll be in Baltimore for a while writing your articles. It's just that I hoped you might want to come back before the summer was over."

Lindy had given me the out in case my feelings changed. I didn't think they would, but I had to be sure of exactly what my feelings for her were. "Yes, Lindy, you are correct about that. I loved the shore, but I do have a job here and I rarely take time off from it."

"I see," she answered soulfully. "I will miss seeing you around, but I did want you to know how much I enjoyed meeting you and being with you."

She was protecting herself. I didn't blame her. "I tell you what, Lindy, if I get some of these articles out and get some good feedback from them, I will come back as soon as I can. That's the best I can do."

That seemed to do the trick. Her spirits immediately soared. "That would be great Tug. Just let me know."

I knew she wanted more from me, but I just couldn't give it to her right now. After all, I had only just met her. I knew love could hit you fast like that, but this was the kind of gal that you didn't want to hurt. That thought right there told me that I was feeling more than just a passing fancy for her.

It became very strange between us. We didn't say a word to one another for a few moments. It wasn't really uncomfortable, but it was definitely time for me to end this conversation.

"I really have a lot to do tonight before hitting the bed, Lindy. I promise I will keep up with you. Remember, you gave me your e-mail and we can cyber-space it for a while. It was so good to hear your voice."

I could tell saying that lifted her spirits. She answered me with a much lighter voice. "Yes, Tug, we can do that." And then, she switched gears on me and her delightful humor took over. "You know what I will miss most about you?"

"Should I be afraid to answer that?"

She giggled and said, "I will miss you hanging out at Virgil's and listening to what all the guys say about you."

"What do they say about me?" I begged.

"Now, I can't tell you that. But if you come back soon, I will."

Got to hand it to her, she wasn't going to let me out of saying something that made her feel really close to me. Good girl, Lindy! "I will miss you too. Please give my best to Dickie and all the others. I am already wishing that I was going to have breakfast with you and the gang tomorrow morning at Virgil's."

"Bye Bye Tug."

The phone went dead and I was left sitting with the most nostalgic feelings that I have ever had. I had to make Max see the story and then I could go back.

THE NEXT MORNING, THE SUN hit my eyes like a beacon shining right at me. Apparently I was too stupid, or had had one too many beers to bother to pull the drapes closed. I glanced over at the clock and it was already seven thirty. I had to get a move on.

By the time I hit the office, it was buzzing already. A horrible murder had taken place in the wee hours of the morning and everyone was talking about it. It seemed that some real piece of shit had gunned down a husband and wife execution-style. I sure was glad that I didn't work those stories. Aside from the fact that they were gruesome to see; they were also so disheartening. No matter what the city tried to do to stop the violence, it still went on.

I slumped down in my chair and booted up my computer. I couldn't believe all the e-mails I had received. God! I was only gone from the office three days.

Ripping down through the list, I couldn't believe my eyes when I saw one from superwaterman.com. Now who else could it be? And where did he get a computer? I never saw one at his house. Good grief this man was so full of surprises. I clicked on and let 'er rip.

"Hi there son. I'll bet you are about as surprised as kin be. Didn't know old Dickie could use such things, did ya? Well I have to confess Lindy taught me how and then bought me one for my last birthday. I kept it under wraps while you was here.

Just wonderin' when I will read your first article about me and the folks down here? We sure are countin' on ya, son. Take care. I am off to Virgil's for my breakfast and then down to the pier. Beautiful day here.

Sincerely, Dickie

Reading his e-mail made me miss everyone and everything so much. It was so like him to say what he did and put it as only he could. I would start writing immediately. I wanted them all to see that I meant it when I said I would try to help.

Minutes into my story, I was interrupted by Beth who wanted me to come up and see Max as soon as I could. I told her I was on my way. I knew she was dying to hear all about my trip. She couldn't fool me. She might truly be interested, but she was the source for all gossip in the entire paper. I had to be extra careful around her and if she got even a whiff of a new girl in my life; I would rue the day. She would APB it everywhere.

Roger was making his way down to see me when I ran into him in the hallway. "Sorry, Rog, I'll have to talk to you over lunch. How about it?"

He didn't know what to say so he just yelled to me as I ran to catch the elevator. "Sure thing, old buddy. Meet you at noon at that deli down the street."

THE MINUTE I WALKED THROUGH the door, I could see I was about to get peppered with questions from "Lady Macbeth." I was right.

"So, I see you made it back from the war. How was your trip? You never called in to tell us what was going on."

"Whoa Beth, one question at a time. Yes, I made it back safe and sound, and I didn't see the need to phone into the office because, if you remember, I *was* away on an assignment. But if you must know, it was a great experience and I enjoyed it very much."

"That's it? That's all you are going to tell me? Come on, Tug, there has to be more to it than that. You do remember I read all those letters form that crazy man."

Max opened his door and I was rescued. "Well, there is more, but I see Max is ready for me. Bye." I knew she would be waiting to pounce on me the minute my meeting was over. God give me strength. She always wanted to be the first to know, but this time, she wouldn't get what she wanted.

"So Tug, did you find anything out that is of interest to the paper?"

"Yes sir, I did actually. I had a very interesting time down in Somerville."

"Did you meet that irascible bastard, Mr. Short?"

I couldn't help but laugh. Max had a way of getting right to the heart of the matter. Actually he reminded me a little of Dickie. "Yes, I did. He is some kind of character, but a wonderful human being."

Max sat back in his big old worn leather chair and played with a big fat cigar. He waited for me to continue.

"Well Max, he told me the whole story and it turned out to be a bit different than what he led you to believe."

"Now why am I not surprised at that? Crazy old coot."

"He isn't crazy Max. He is just an outspoken man who feels that he and the folks down there are being forced out."

Max sat up and leaned over his desk. "What do you mean- forced out? I thought this was all about murders. Tug, what is going on down there?"

"Mr. Short, or Dickie as I called him, wasn't really talking about literal murders. He was using that word to get your attention and his point across."

"Attention about what? I don't understand what the hell is going on here Tug."

"There's nothing going on Max. Well, there is but it's not like that."

"Will you please spit it out before I have you committed? You are jabbering like an idiot."

He was right. I was jabbering like an idiot, but he had me going in circles. I couldn't help it. I had to calm down and fast. There was so much to say and I knew Max wasn't going to sit still for much longer.

"Okay, Max. Here's the jist of it. Dickie and the other town's people are fighting mad about what the developers are doing to their town. They are building condos on their waterfront and it's just horrible. They see it as murder what these people are doing. And I agree with them."

Max sat back and looked at me with the most incredulous look on his face. I think he was thinking I had gone straight out of my mind. "Let me get this straight. I sent you down there to find out about people being murdered and you come back squawking about condos being built? Do I have this right?"

"Well, yes, in a way you do, but in a way you don't. Oh, this isn't coming out right at all."

Yanking the unlit cigar out of his mouth, he leaned across his desk and shouted, "You're damned right about that Tug. Don't you think we have run stories on what is going on over there? It's our playground too you know. But to link this development with the murder of the land is like trying to tell the story of *Wounded Knee* all over again. It doesn't wash, my boy. It doesn't wash at all."

I couldn't contain myself. I saw red for a reason that I don't even understand. I don't have a dog in this fight…or did I? It didn't matter, I went for it anyway.

"You are wrong Max. The generations of people who have been on that shore *do* see this as a massacre. They see it as a way of life disappearing one condo or retirement home at a time. It isn't reasonable what is going on and more than that; the waters are being compromised."

"Holy shit! I sent a nice young reporter out to find a story and he returns to me changed into a crusading moron."

I was in hot water now. I had to find a way to win back any respect he may have had for me. "I know I sound loony to you, but there are real problems with what's happening over there. I mean it's not just the buildings Max. It's the entire infrastructure that is being ignored. I saw it all with my own eyes. Dickie's great niece drove me all over the shore and I saw it everywhere. Roads insufficient for the amounts of traffic, ambulance and fire companies being stretched to their limits and God knows, in some places there aren't two feet between buildings. It's a maze of houses, condos, hotels, and stores. I know why they are angry. I tell you, Max, these people feel like they are at war in their own homes."

Max drew himself upright in his chair and his face showed no sign of a smile. He was all business and he suddenly became the man whom everyone feared when he got angry. I was sincerely nervous.

"Now listen here Tug. You seem to be all fired up here about something that seems quite real to you. I know what is going on over there. I told you the paper has written about this before, but you have to be careful about what you say and what you write. I am assuming you are going to tell me you want to write an article about what you saw while you were there. I'll give you the go ahead to write that piece but on one condition.

If you get off on some stupid tangent about comparing this to the last stand of mankind I will have to say good bye to you. Do you understand me?"

I did. I understood exactly what he was telling me and I knew he didn't usually give other reporters the heads up first before he fired them. I knew he was doing this because of his relationship with my dad.

"I get the message Max. I know very little can be done to correct what has already been done, but that doesn't mean that we can't get people to begin to take action about any future building over there."

I saw I had made a point with him.

"You might be right. You know Tug, I am sick over it too. I remember the shore as it used to be but you can't blame people for loving it so much that they want to live there. It's the way it is. For God's sake, you must have seen this happening on the Cape? It's all over. Anywhere there is water. People go nuts for water property. They can't get enough of it. They are drawn to it and then it drowns them."

"I know that Max and everything you have said is absolutely right, but that isn't the piece I want to do. I want to write a human interest story. I want our readers to have a real sense of the Eastern Shore watermen and their families. I lived right in the thick of it for five days and they took me in like one of their own. I really liked them. It took me a little time to understand them, but they are real Americans who are mad as hell. This story is from their point of view."

"Okay, Tug. You've convinced me. Write your story, but I warn you to be careful not to get too many of our advertisers pissed off. They pay our way and I am not about to throw them overboard for you."

"I will try to behave Max. By the way, you will be happy to hear that I don't think you will be getting anymore of those nifty letters from Dickie Short. If I write the piece the way I want to, he will be happy as a clam."

Max look at me totally relieved at that comment. He stood up and I knew we would be walking to his door. Our conversation was over and for the time being, I had won the day.

Putting his arm around my shoulder, he said, "You know your father called while you were away. He wanted to know how you were doing. I told him I was real pleased with you."

"I appreciate that very much Max, but Dad shouldn't have called you. It makes me feel like a kid in school when his parents want information and they have to call the teacher."

He loves you, you know. He is a tough man but he is brilliant at his job. I don't know anyone who doesn't respect Ted Alston. It's hard to live up to all that. That's why I jumped at the chance to have you come with us. "

Instantly my mind recalled what Dickie had said. *"It's not easy to be a son."*

"Well Dad and I don't always agree on things so this worked out for the best."

As he shook my hand, I knew I was back in his good graces. "Write a good story Tug. You only get one shot at this."

"I will Max and thanks."

I wasn't in the mood for Beth and her questions so I made a bee line for the door. I had a million things to do and I couldn't get caught up in her machinations. Besides, I wanted to put a good deal of work behind me before I met Roger at our favorite deli.

I was pleased that by the time noon rolled around, I had caught up on most of the work that had come in while I was gone. I was now free to get started on putting my story together. I just had to make this a powerful accounting of what was going on over there. I definitely wanted this piece to hit the Sunday edition so I had a lot of work ahead of me.

I hadn't realized how much I missed Roger's brand of humor until we had lunch. He was especially on top of his game when I told him about the scene in Virgil's with Burger Boy. He went wild and by the time lunch was over, I was shocked that neither of us had wet pants when we left.

Walking back to work, he was still laughing and said, "I can't believe the son of one of America's top sportswriters was actually getting down with the likes of those characters, Tug."

He was right of course, but a strange feeling crept over me because I know Roger and he was poking fun at the people I had come to like…and dare I say respect?

"Stop it, Rog," "They are great people. In fact, they are great Americans. They reminded me of the way people used to be. You know. Honest and to the point. No bullshitting from these folks."

He picked up on my annoyance about his joking about them. "Look, Tug, I don't mean to be a snob or anything. It's just that they grew up differently from us. When I used to go over there for summer vacations, I would always joke to my parents about the way they talked and their simple way of life. I guess it's kind of nice, actually. In a country kind of way."

Suddenly, we weren't laughing anymore. "You can't get out of this Roger. You are a snob and you know it. I suppose I am lucky in a lot of ways. My parents never taught us that we were better than anyone else. And the people down there have legitimate concerns about what is happening to their part of this country. They are miserable about it."

Roger stopped and stared at me. I don't think he could conceive that I might get this exercised about something. "Okay, Tug, I get it. They are good people, but you can't stop progress and you can't stop people from wanting to live over there. This is the baby boomer generation and there are millions of them and they have made lots of bucks and they are going to live where they want to."

He was right, but the way he put it sounded so… cold.

"Look Rog, I know I am pretty hot about this, but I saw the effects of all this building and expansion. It's hurting the water and the landscape, let alone the people who have lived there for generations. I really saw their pain and downright fear of what is coming."

Roger raised his hands in retreat. "I will back off, Tug. I can see nothing is going to stop you from this crusade. Just remember, even if you can get people to start paying attention to this, it isn't going to be a cake walk. A handful of angry folks aren't going to stop the bankers and developers where there are millions of dollars to be made."

"You are right about everything you have said, Roger, but it is time we take a long look at what we are doing to the land, the waters, the very culture of these people. They deserve to at least have a say in what is going on before they lose their identities."

"This one's on me Tug. Are you heading back or do you have something else to do?"

The truth was that I had gotten myself worked up pretty good about this. Here we were having a perfectly great lunch and now it had turned into this. I was unbalanced about this whole subject and if I didn't get some perspective on it, I could be out of a job. Maybe I should wait a day or two before I started writing this story. But then Dickie and the guys would be so disappointed, not to mention Lindy.

For Sure the Fur is Gonna Fly

For THE NEXT TWO DAYS I poured over every article that had been written about the development on the Eastern Shore. Just as Max had said, our paper had written a few about the future of the Chesapeake and the affect all this building was having on the waters that surround this vast estuary. As I dug further, I found great resources in the shore local papers. It seemed each week articles were being written about the frustrating circumstances that I saw with my own eyes.

With all this information swirling around I had to make this story about something different. It had to inspire our readers to see this from a different point of view. That being the view of the real Eastern Shore men and women. Those souls whose families had been a part of that land going back to the earliest days of this country.

I revisited my journal again and again, and there is where I found the roots for my article. It would be told through the people I had met and what they felt as their past became buried under the bulldozers and wrecking balls of today.

Making the deadline wasn't the only thing pulling me away from my friends. It was the honest truth that I wanted to be back over there, sitting at Virgil's, eating a sloppy burger with the guys. I wanted to hear more of their stories, and I sure wanted to be with Lindy.

The one or two times I had given in and gone for a quick beer after work, I found myself off someplace else. Roger kept trying to bring me back to the here and now, but the only here and now I wanted to be in was holding Lindy's hand, watching a sunset over the waters of Somerville.

Roger tried to understand what was happening to me, but he was in another place in his life. I thought I was right there with him…until I met Dickie Short.

I LEFT WORK EARLY TO go home and write. My eyes were a bit crossed going through the microfiche machine and reading all those articles. I knew I could get a whole lot more done there then I ever could in the office. Over the past year, it was my office that had become the gathering place and right now I needed solitude and no disturbances.

My first order of business was to get a beer and head upstairs. I could relax and unwind up there while putting my thoughts in order. I hadn't slept so well the night before and even though I had the best pillow top in the world, old Dickie's bed, with all the night noises, had seemed to comfort me more.

I called Mom. I wanted to let her know what I was going to be working on. I knew she would be so excited. I had to swear her to secrecy because if she said anything to Dad about this, he would blow his stack. He was a guy who played it safe. If he knew that this article could blow me out of the paper, it would kill him and I would never hear the end of it.

"Hey Tug. How are you? I assume you are back in Baltimore."

"Yes I am. I got back yesterday and I have been going a hundred miles an hour ever since. I hope you aren't mad at me for not calling."

"No, I have learned that no news is good news, but it is good to hear your voice."

"Mom, I have some exciting news, or at least it is to me. But you can't say anything to Dad, okay?"

"Oh…I guess so Tug. You know I don't keep things from your father, but I will promise not to say anything if that's what you want."

"It is Mom. Max has agreed to let me write a story about what I saw and learned while I was over on the Eastern Shore, but I will only have one shot at it."

"Why only one shot? I thought you wanted to do a series."

"I do. At least that is my hope but if this goes sour and he gets a lot of static about it, there will be consequences."

"I see. You have a lot on those shoulders of yours. Remember, you are a very good writer. Just think this through thoroughly before you submit it. I would hate to see you lose your job over it."

"Now you see why I don't want you to tell Dad. He would be all over me. He doesn't have the confidence in my writing that you do."

"Just make it an adventure story like the ones you used to write when you were a boy."

She hit it! That was exactly what I had to do. "God, Mom, you're right. You have just given me the piece of the puzzle I needed. I have to make people want to stop what is going on over on that shore and maybe all over."

"Sounds like a pretty tall order Tug. The water attracts everyone and for all different reasons. Some love it because it calms them down and others see it as a way to bring out their creativity and then others see it as their spirituality. How will you get them to stop all that? It's kind of like a human pilgrimage to them. It was to your Dad and me."

"I don't pretend that my story will stop much of anything, Mom, but if I can just get them to slow down and consider what the consequences are to the land and the people who have lived there forever. My God, most of them can't even afford to live in the towns that they are working in. The property values have gone through the roof."

"I see your point, Tug, and I can hear it in your voice how much this has affected you, but you can't always change things. I know you want to try, but don't get upset if people won't listen. Just go for it and let them know that everyone is responsible for the land they live on. I think it just may work."

I love you, Mom. Tell Dad I said hi and you can also let him know that I found out it was him who called Max and I'm not mad at him for it."

In truth, she didn't know that her husband had interfered with her son's career, but even if she had known, there was no use trying to do anything about it. He was the way he was and that was that. "I didn't know he did that, Tug. You probably were pretty hurt about it when you found out, but he must have felt strongly about something for him to call Max. He loves you deeply, even if he doesn't show it. Please believe that. I just wish the two of you could come to some understanding."

I doubted that would ever happen. There was always the hope that it might, but as it stood right now, that was a pretty distant hope. "Don't worry about it Mom. Who knows? Maybe some day I will be able to play that game of tug-of-war and pull the old man across the line."

"And maybe some day you won't care so much if you do."

And the Fur Flew

No MATTER HOW TIRED I was, I became obsessed with the article. When I was done, I read it like I was one of our readers.

Taking my mother's advice, I threw everyone into it. I had always loved to create my characters, but this time I didn't have to create a one of them. They were all real, if anyone could believe that. Dickie, Burger Boy, Poke, Tadpole and Rats. They all brought their own stories to life. I spun their story from the heart. This piece wasn't just them reaching out to grab hold of the readers; it was the truth and that always makes people sit up and take notice.

I had earned a solid reputation for the pieces I handed in every week. I picked the ones that would pull at the heartstrings and our readers would e-mail me, and better yet Max, and say how much they liked it. You got to have fans out there, or you don't make it in this business.

I had tinkered enough and handed it in. When the Sunday paper arrived, I held my breath.

Coffee in hand, I flopped down on my sofa and proceeded to read away. On the fourth or fifth time of reading and rereading, the phone rang. Naturally, it had to be a congratulatory call. Right?

"Hello?"

"You have to be kidding me," snickered Roger's voice on the other end of the phone."

I wasn't exactly sure what his tone of voice was telling me. "You read it, right? What do you think?" His response was not what I was expecting.

"I read it all right. And when Max reads it you may be moving out of your nice digs over there."

"What are you talking about? Didn't you like the piece? I think Max will be damned pleased when he gets all the rave reviews from the readers."

"Oh Max will be raving all right, but he will be raving mad as hell with you. You have started a revolution, my friend. Your bleeding-heart story was about hicks and farm folks who don't want change. I mean really, Tug, where did you get those names? I pray that they aren't real ones, although I don't know how a smart guy like you could make them up no matter how good a story-teller you are."

I instantly became so angry at him that if he had been standing in front of me I would have punched him in the nose. "For your information, Roger, I used the names that they go by over there. If you took the time to read the story 'en toto' you would see that that is the way they live their lives and they are fighting like hell to preserve it."

"God, I don't believe it, Tug. Did they drug you or something? You are a smart guy, but this time you have been had by a bunch of country bumpkins."

I couldn't say another word to him, I was so mad. He missed the point completely but what if everyone missed it? I couldn't have been that far off the mark, could I?

"I don't want to continue this conversation with you Roger. It's obvious that you don't understand anything about this."

"Oh yes I do, my friend. I understand that expansion makes money and if you think that the builders and developers are going to stop because of some people who are upset that their fifty year old drug store is being torn down, you have lost it altogether."

I slammed down the phone. I contemplated putting my fist through the wall, but the wall didn't piss me off. Roger did. I never realized what a snob he was and his sophomoric tone with me only served to make matters worse at the moment.

Could we ever be friends and co-workers again if he was this dense to see what I was saying? Then the thought struck me that maybe I was madder at myself thinking that I was like him too; until I met Dickie Short.

I needed a cold shower badly and then a brisk walk down to the harbor. Wasn't it Dickie who had told me that going to the water always made things right?

LISTENING TO THE WATER SLAP up around the dock did help. I thought long and hard about what Roger had said on the phone and how truly angry I was at him. We could not be close again. I may have to work with him but no matter what result came of this story, I would never be able to look at him the same again.

My answering machine was stacked full when I got back. I dreaded listening to the messages. Would there be more Rogers out there? Like it or not I needed to know.

Nervously I clicked the button down for the messages and the voice that began talking to me came as a welcome surprise. "Well son, you have 'em goin' now. Good story. I particularly liked you telling all about old Dickie here. The others like it too. I talked to most of the guys before they run off to church. They are proud of you, son. I wanted to give ya a call and say thanks. Hope they don't git too mad at ya over there in that paper of yours. You know you sure have stirred a hornet's nest up now. Call me when ya have the time. By the way, Lindy says hello to ya too."

Dickie's call put a smile on my face. It helped to take some of the sting out the call I got from Roger. But I was still pretty steamed at him. At least the people I cared most about liked what I wrote in my articles. That's really all that mattered, or was it? If I didn't touch all the readers then I had failed in what I was trying to accomplish.

The remaining messages were from fellow associates calling to say congrats on the piece. They said they really felt the admiration I felt for these people caught up in this dilemma.

The one obviously missing message on my machine was the one I wanted, or prayed, I would get. But Max didn't call and I knew this could spell trouble for me the next day. I would find that out immediately if Beth called and summoned me to his office. I had to remind myself that I went into this with both eyes opened and I knew the consequences.

I reread my story one more time and I loved it. As a matter of fact, I thought it was the best story I had ever written. It came from my heart. I tried to be fair and balanced with my examples and show a way that issues could be resolved without having to ruin it for everyone. However, with what I saw going on, some places had already gone so far that nothing could ever be the same again. I hoped that wouldn't happen in Somerville. While the citizens didn't like what had already happened, they still had time to stop it from swallowing their town forever.

Oh hell, let the chips fall where they may. I had written what I felt and Max couldn't change that…or could he?

THE NEXT DAY, I WAS a nervous wreck. I wondered what was coming and if there had been any fallout. It didn't take long for me to find out.

My heart sank when I saw a message had been left by Beth for me to call her when I got in. I knew this was not a good sign. To add to my worries, Roger was nowhere in sight. He always came down to my cubicle first thing in the morning and now he was plainly invisible anywhere in the office. I was still plenty mad at him, but sleep had made me a bit more open to his opinion, even if I thought he was a jerk about it. However, I knew he was going to be pissed with me. Roger had a quick temper that I had seen upon occasion when he had gotten into a disagreement with someone at the pub. I guess I would be pissed too if my best buddy had slammed the phone up in my ear. Oh well, first things first and that meant seeing Max.

I called Beth and she wasn't exactly her cheery self. I was in trouble. She told me to come up right away. My sweat glands began to work overtime. This wasn't going to be one of those 'nice job Tug' kinds of talks. This was going to be pure hell.

The elevator ride was excruciatingly painful. I knew what awaited me when I got to Max's office. It was clear that he wasn't as impressed with my story as Dickie and the Virgil's gang were. I was right on all counts.

Beth didn't even make small talk when I arrived. She said Max was waiting for me and then immediately went back to her work. I dreaded opening his door, but a man had to do what a man had to do.

Max was staring out the window with his back turned to me. I knew he knew I was in his office. Another bad sign.

"Max? I came as soon as I got Beth's message," I chirped as cheerfully as I could. "What's up?"

Turning slowly to face me, I saw the look that said it all. "Have a seat, Tug. We need to talk."

I swallowed hard and waited for the boom to be lowered.

He picked up a copy of the paper and slid it hard across his desk toward me. I caught it just before it went off the side. His message was coming in loud and clear.

His windup was short and to the point. "I read your story." Okay, I thought, that wasn't so bad. But then I looked at his eyebrows. Not good.

"You know, Tug, I made the decision after we talked the other day, not to interfere with you because I thought you and I had an *understanding* about things. Apparently I was wrong.

Oh I'll give it to you Tug; you can write and write well. In fact you write so well that my computer has been deluged with e-mails about what you wrote."

I couldn't think of anything else to say other than, "That's good, isn't it Max?"

"Depends on what good is Tug. You have our readers so worked up now that they are fuming at the developers over there. And you might be interested to know that I heard from some of those developers that you crucified and made in to the villains of the century. Those guys aren't happy one damned bit nor do they care one whit about Dickie Short and his posse of friends and how they feel about anything."

Not meaning to, an entirely spontaneous smile crossed my face. I had done exactly what I had wanted to do. I wanted to stir up a hornet's nest and now I was taking the heat for it. Oh well, Dickie told me that this was what was going to happen. He was a savvy man in a strange sort of way.

Max was not in the least amused and I could tell he thought I was appearing smug and confident when I heard his e-mail inbox was jammed full. "What the hell are you smiling at, Tug? I am really steamed about this. I told you that we get a ton of revenue from those men out there who you just put on a spit and cooked like hell. The paper can't afford to lose that kind of money."

He was steamed all right, but I stood my ground like any self- respecting reporter would do. I pulled myself upright and said, "I know that Max, but don't you see that there are a whole lot of people who obviously don't like what is happening over there? While they are making all kinds of money building away, they don't realize the damage it is doing to the folks who live there..."

Max wagged his finger in my face and yelled, "To hell with all of that, Tug. I have a real problem on my hands and it's all because of your blasted story. So why don't you wipe that stupid smile off your face and tell me how you are going to fix this. Huh?"

I couldn't believe my ears. I couldn't believe what he was asking me to do. He knew I understood him completely. He was going to ask me to apologize to the same people who were tearing the hell out of the shore. I wasn't gong to do it, but I knew he had no intention of dropping this.

"I have gone ahead and set up a meeting with two of our biggest advertisers. They are developers over there on that shore that, up until a week ago, you never knew existed."

He did have a point. Thinking quickly, I responded, "You are right on all counts, Max. I *didn't* know your shore up until a week ago, but now I do, and I was sent there by you, if you remember, to find a story. Well, I did, and this is the story I came back with." I knew I was sinking in quick sand but I hoped this might give him pause. It didn't.

Max slammed his fists down on the desk and shrieked, "I sent you to get a story on murders Tug, not a bleeding-heart *Wounded Knee* saga. Life goes on for people and if a bunch of fishermen can't accept that the days of old are passing, well then that's their problem."

"Watermen," I responded quietly.

"What?"

"Watermen, sir. They are watermen and not fishermen."

"Good God, they have taken your brain into the pod someplace. Watermen, fishermen, I don't give a damn. The truth is that their economies have never been so good. Now I'll bet they don't think all that extra money they are getting is so bad."

Max and I were coming from different planets. He didn't get it at all. "They would give it all up Max, if they could stop what is happening. Sooner or later all the crabs will be gone and the oyster beds will be destroyed forever. Their land will be swallowed up by thousands of homes and condos and all that they will have to show for hundreds of years of hard work will be a landscape that shouts vanilla pudding."

"Vanilla pudding? What the hell are you talking about? Vanilla pudding? What they will see is that they will have solid communities with lots of good people who have come there to live."

"I don't dispute the fact that good people are coming to the shore to live, but couldn't they slow it down? I mean couldn't they plan better rather than destroy everything around them? They don't have the road structures in place to handle this kind of development. And, they could use some more creative colors on the homes rather than the bland vanilla color they use. It's just plain wrong, Max."

I saw that he was thinking. That could be good or bad for me, but my ass was so far out now that I couldn't do a thing to change it.

"The meeting is tomorrow at two o'clock Tug. You be there to explain yourself. I understand your passion. It's not like this paper hasn't written about some of these issues before but we never personalized it the way you have. You made it too personal and when that happens, people get themselves all exercised."

"How couldn't I make it personal?" I snapped back in defense of myself. I lived with these folks. They trusted me to do a fair story about how they feel and I did. Now, you want me to water it down and make it seem as if they can live with this. Well, they can't, and more than that, they won't!"

If nothing more, I could see Max admired my grit. "You make it sound like some kind of war Tug. I hardly believe that. You and I know that if their own folks didn't sell the land; this couldn't happen. So now what do you say to that?"

He had me there. He was right and if this was to slow down any, I had to get Dickie and his people to make that point clear. "You're right, Max. I know that money talks and a lot of the watermen's kids don't want to go out on the water anymore and the farmers are facing the same situation, but something has to be done before it's all gobbled up and no Eastern Shore exists at all."

Max got up and walked around his desk, stopping just short of my personal space. He looked almost pained at this conversation and I felt the same. We both respected one another and I was truly sorry that I was the one who had made him so angry.

"Tell you what Tug, if you and I can pull this meeting off and make some of our advertisers go away somewhat relieved that you aren't going to pound them week after week, I think we, I mean you may have done something noble. I know you are a great reporter and I wouldn't want to have to make a decision that would be distasteful for either of us. But let me be clear here. I will if it comes to that. I think you know me well enough to know that I don't flinch from making tough decisions."

He was spot on with that comment. Max Pierson was known to be one tough bastard when it came to his business. I respected him for that and I imprinted his rant on the front of my brain.

Max was trying everything in his power not to fire me, even when he told me that was exactly what he would do if he got crap from his advertisers. He was going above and beyond and I had better be able to pull this off.

"I will do my very best to talk to these people Max. Maybe there is an answer for all this. I hope so with all my heart."

Shaking my hand, I saw the first glimmer of a smile cross his face as he said, "I pray that we can work this out Tug. See you tomorrow at two. We are meeting here in my office."

I marched out of Max's office with a slightly victorious look on my face. I knew that would get to Beth. She had to know what this meeting was about and how pissed off Max was. And to think that I thought she liked me. Well, she does work for him and no one could ever accuse her of not being a kiss ass.

The Meeting from Hell

NOW THAT I HAD GOTTEN a momentary reprieve, my biggest problem was how I was going to keep my job and make those advertisers happy. Piece of cake, right? I don't think so. The fact that they hated my guts at the moment, getting them to see reason may be unreasonable.

I cut out and went home. I snickered a little thinking that the divine Lady Macbeth would probably think I was on probation. Could someone please date this girl and give her a real life?

I could access my work computer from there and I could reread my inbox of e-mails and see if I could pick up on something that I could use the next day. Maybe somewhere in that stack of people's comments I could come up with a plan of action. Please, dear God, let it be.

My phone was ringing off the hook the minute I unlocked my door. I ran to catch it just before it went to message. I was shocked to hear the raspy voice of the man who got me into this mess in the first place.

"Dickie, how the hell are you? Is everything okay?"

"I'm fine son. I figured you might need a friend about now. I see, by the fact that you're home this early, that I was right."

"Well, yes and no Dickie. I wasn't fired if that was what you suspected. At least not outright. That may come tomorrow."

"What's tomorrow bringin' your way son?"

"The meeting from hell. I have been told to meet with some of our big advertisers. You and I know that they aren't going to exactly hand out kisses to me."

"Well, screw them son. That may sound kinda strong but that's what they have been doin' to us down here for a long time. They haven't given one witless thought to us or our lives." After a moment, he added, "How bad is it goin' to be?"

"Not good, I can tell you that. I came home early to reread some of the e-mails that people have written to me. I feel strongly that there may be a clue in one of them as to the direction I should take tomorrow."

There was a low chuckle coming over the phone. I braced myself.

"That direction might be to get out of Dodge fast son."

How could one person be so articulate? "You may have a point there Dickie."

"You know what I would do if I was you, son?"

"Trust me Dickie; I have no idea."

"I would tell them sons of bitches that they have no right to come over here and bust up what has always been ours. They don't see it that way, I know, but can't they stop building on every square inch? And can't they see what will happen if all the water gets polluted? That's what I would tell 'em."

For sure I couldn't call them sons of bitches, but the case I would have to make is precisely what Dickie had just told me. The future of the Eastern Shore would depend on what these people were doing now. Would they care? That was what I was going to try to make them see.

"I really love you, Dickie."

"What the deuce are you talking about son?"

"You know Dickie, sometimes you can be right as rain. I can't back away from this, and I have no intention of quitting writing stories about the effect all this development has on

163

a local culture. I would have to be a tad more sophisticated about it though."

"Well son, you be sophisticated all you want to, but the plain truth is the plain truth. Folks over here are mad as hell and they ain't goin' to sit back and jist loose everythin'."

"I know that Dickie, but you do have to make your point so that everyone feels like they come out a winner. I can't undo what's been done already, but maybe I can get them to see that there are other ways of doing this."

"Well if you kin do that, you're Jesus Christ. Remember one thing son; money is what talks down here and every other place in the world. And when it comes to land on water, Mabel hold on to yer hat.'"

"Yes, I know that. Remember I am a Boston boy and my summer vacations were on Cape Cod. They have done the same thing up there. Everyone in this world wants to live by water."

"And they don't care that there is jist so much water to go around," he added.

"You got it Dickie. I'll make it through and if they fire me, so be it."

The next thing he said stunned me. While I learned that anything could come out of his mouth, I was not prepared for this.

"You always have a place down here with me, son. You might like living here with real people who earn their living from the sea. Maybe you aren't meant to live in such a fancy place and have all that stress."

His words hit me like a ton of bricks. Up until a week ago, I would never have dreamed of such a thing, but then I met Dickie Short.

Now he had given me something to ponder. He had given me something I would never have thought about just two weeks ago. "You never know Dickie," I answered in a casual way. I didn't want him to think I might really go over there and live with him. And I certainly didn't want him running off at the mouth to Lindy. I still had to come face to face with that situation.

"Well you think some on it son. I ain't goin' anywhere and I want you to know that I don't make that offer to too many folks. As a matter of fact, I ain't never made it before, come to think about it. Hey listen to me here son. I almost forgot to say hi from Lindy. You know she is mighty lonely without you around."

My stomach twisted because I knew what he was up to. He was such a matchmaker and he was so obvious about it. I had thought about her a lot lately though. "I'm sorry that she is so lonely Dickie. We have talked a few times, but as you can see, I have my hands full right now."

"Now now son, women don't understand that sort of thing. After this meeting gets over, why don't you come on back here for a weekend?"

I could see through him as though he were clear glass. Nothing veiled about what Dickie Short was up to. No indeed. At least I knew he liked me a lot to want his favorite gal to see me. She meant the world to him.

"I will take that under consideration Dickie, but let's see what happens to my ass tomorrow."

"Take good care of it son. Then get the hell away and come see us. As much as I hate to admit it; I miss the heck out of ya."

"I miss the heck out of you too, Dickie. You tell Lindy I will call her tomorrow and please tell her what's going on so she won't be too upset with me."

"Upset with ya? Hell, that girl couldn't do that if she tried."

Laughing into the phone, I said good bye. I loved that man and it was then that I wished with all my heart that my father could be more like the Dickie Shorts of this world.

Anna Gill

NATURALLY I DIDN'T SLEEP MUCH. I finished up the last draft on my presentation around three and then needed an hour to unwind. If only I could be impassioned enough to make them understand. I was up against a hard argument. Progress was on their side and I knew that and I knew that development was good for everybody. The economy depended on it, but if they could just see the side of the people whose lives were being changed.

I grabbed coffee on the way out and settled into my Cherokee for the commute. My mind was full-steam ahead for this meeting. It was plain to me that my future at the paper hung on what I said and how I reacted, and I prayed I could hold my temper, no matter what came from this.

I was the last to arrive at the meeting, which didn't make Max too happy, but I had to go back through some of my journal to reinforce what I was preparing to say.

Glaring into my face, Max began. "Well, now that we are *all* here, I would like to introduce everyone. I couldn't wait for my introduction. I was sure that I would feel the nails being driven into my flesh.

Max started by explaining how I had been dispatched over to the shore in the first place. The part about Dickie's letters was amusing and I did hear the sound of a chuckle here and there which was a good sign. I was surprised that he set it up for me. I mean he wove this tapestry tight and by the time he handed it over to me, I felt like maybe there was some hope in the room. Max was actually trying to *save* my ass.

I looked around the room and there was one woman, in particular, that had a very attractive face and I thought she might be a good one to look at when I was speaking. However, looks can deceive and I was in no position to get in any further than I already was.

It was my time at up bat. I needed to choose my words carefully. After a few words of appreciation for them taking the time to hear me out, I began in earnest.

166

"I must admit the way I got down there was a ruse on the part of Mr. Short, but when I met him and we got to be good friends, and he came clean about the point he was driving home through the letters, I became interested in what was going on over there. They took me into their homes and hearts and I traveled around their part of that beautiful country and saw the affect of what all this expansion was doing to their world. To be truthful with you, I don't think any of us thinks about what price is paid when overdevelopment occurs. We concentrate on the jobs that it will bring, which is a good thing. We concentrate on the industries that will benefit, which is a good thing, but we don't think about the schools, the fire departments, the roads, the wetlands, the water, and we sure don't think about the lives of people who find themselves not being able to afford to live in towns where they work. What I am proposing to you is a sweeping vision to have what you want; but not destroy what they have."

Dead silence followed my opening statement. I didn't know whether to continue or bolt straight out of that door. The young woman was still smiling at me, so I couldn't have made too great an ass out of myself, right?

Max flicked his finger in my direction for me to keep on going.

"I know you came here today, more than a little upset with what I wrote, but I did it from the human point of view. That's how I write and that's really the job of a good reporter. If you don't get inside people's heads and find out what they are really thinking, you never get the full story. I don't want to believe that you don't feel one obligation to the population you are disturbing. I would rather believe that we can all reach our goals. I am afraid if we do not do something soon, there could be real trouble ahead. The people of the Eastern Shore, not those who are moving down there to retire, are going to revolt if something isn't done soon to protect them."

I knew it. Looks can deceive. The sweet, attractive woman wiped the sweet, attractive smile off her face and snapped at me. "Just what are you getting at, Mr. Alston?"

Ouch! She called me Mr. Alston. I definitely hit a nerve inside of her. Wasn't she the cool one?

"What I am getting at is that we can all work together for the common good. I understand full well that you have businesses to run and those businesses succeed when you are building properties and selling them. It's just that the entire infrastructure isn't ready for such enormous expansion over there. For instance, ambulances from towns that can't even accommodate their own, are being asked to do double duty in areas that aren't within their boundaries. The same holds true with fire departments and then there are the water and road concerns, let alone the matter of the wetlands that are being disturbed at an alarming rate."

I paused momentarily for a breath of air and noticed that the silence in the room was deafening. I wasn't sure what to think. Were they going to continue to sit there and listen, or where they going to skin me alive? Oh well, I had gone this far, I better say what I had to say and let the chips fall where they may. I bent down and yanked a pile of papers out of my briefcase. I put together fact sheets to show them just what effect their development was having on everything on the shore. So far, no one moved to leave the room or interrupt me. This was a tough crowd, but I held on to the hope that this was a good sign.

One by one they took the sheets and began to study them. It was now or never. "As you read over the factoid sheets I have given you, you can see we have a problem." I ask that you look at the sheet that is a report from one of the papers on the shore. I believe it hits right to the heart of the matter."

They found the sheet I referred to and began to read it. The story stated clearly what had happened to Delaware over the past few years. The statistic was staggering. "Over the first

300 years of Delaware's history, 125,000 acres were developed. Between 1984 & 2000, 118,000 acres were developed for urbanized uses." Tax payers were bearing the burden of the increased sprawl for new roads, school bus transportation and sewers. Pretty much the same was happening in Maryland, as well.

"As you can read for yourself, this is overwhelming for the people over there and some of them don't like it one bit. It's not that they don't understand that development brings revenue, but they can't withstand this onslaught at the rate it is happening. Even the people who are moving there are beginning to complain that the traffic and the crowding of where they came from is now here where they live."

Still no one ventured a word. I had said pretty much all I had to say. They could read the rest for themselves.

After an uncomfortable few moments, Mr. John Dawson decided to say what was on his mind. I was grateful that Beth had been amenable to giving me a list of those who would be coming today and I had had time to look each one up and find out who they were. Mr. John Dawson was the owner of one of the biggest developers in the east and from the look on his face, this was the moment I was about to be eaten alive.

Holding on to the sheets, he never looked up at me. He rather just began speaking. "I see you have done your homework, Mr. Alston." Now, I knew I was in trouble. Another snippy little Mr. Alston. "The facts are all there as some see them, but what I don't understand is how the *hell* do you propose we go about making a living? There are projects already in the works and many more to follow. Sure people get angry and want us to stop. It's the way it has always been with expansion, but if we listened to every upset local, we would never serve the needs of tens of thousands of other people who have every right to live where the hell they want to if they can afford it."

He was right and he had all the answers. This wasn't the first time a man like John Dawson had gone up against this kind of opposition. I knew what I was in for the minute Max told me that he called this meeting. But cast fate to the wind. If I was going to lose my job, at least I would give them a piece of my mind too.

"You can't stop what you are already doing Mr. Dawson, but I see this as a great opportunity for you as a leader in the industry."

Looking directly at me with a rather inquisitive stare on his face, he asked, "Just how is that?"

"I see this as a joint effort between you the builders and the people of the respective communities. It is obvious that many of the town leaders in those towns over there have no intention of stopping this, but you could become a role model in the nation to take on an issue that is deserving of your attention. You have to ask yourself the question, what is going to happen when you have developed every square inch of the place and there is nothing left? And what happens to the area when you are done and creeks and rivers are polluted? I refuse to believe that you don't give a damn about that. I also refuse to believe that you can't make significant strides to curtail some of the building in the wetland areas and still make a ton of money all at the same time."

There I had said it. I had dumped it in his lap for all to hear his answer. If he said he didn't give a damn then so be it. He would have a war on his hands and one he could have prevented.

Leaning forward in his chair was not a good sign. I wanted to duck to miss the blow, but I was supposed to be a man, right?

Shaking his finger toward me, he let loose. "Now you listen to me, Tug Alston." Ah, finally a first name recognition. I had gotten his attention. God help me.

"I know what goes into making developments work and I know what people want and my company gives it to them. It's not my problem or place to stop it. If I do, some other developer will go ahead and build it and then I lose money. Now what do you think about that fact?"

I held strong. There could be no retreat now. "I think it stinks frankly. And I think you are wrong. You and your company are big enough in the industry to change things. You can make things happen, John." I thought I would toss that in for good measure. What did I have to lose at this point? Max was sitting there like a lump of coal and God knows what was going through his mind. My death by a thousand cuts no doubt.

"You have the power behind you- and the money too. You could make a fortune just by sitting down with these towns and building their infrastructure. It's planning these folks want. They want an honest to goodness sensible plan of expansion and not what is happening over there right now. We all know it comes down to the ugly word called greed. And it's on both sides of the fence and it's as ugly as it gets. But when everyone has squeezed the last dime out of the land, all you will have left is a place that no longer resembles what everyone came there for in the first place. You could become a real modern-day hero, John. The ball is in your court."

Once again silence fell over the room. John Dawson sat and fumed, but I can't say that I didn't notice a slight ray of hope that he might have actually heard what I was saying. I didn't have the guts to look at Max. I knew he was about to throw me over. I had gone over the bridge and around the corner as far as he was concerned.

Then suddenly, as if an angel of light had entered the room and calmer heads would prevail, I couldn't believe what was said.

"I have to hand it to you Tug." Now I had a first name only. Maybe there *was* hope.

John continued. "I want to read over these stats and then I want to think about what we have discussed here. You may have hit on something. It's not that we are about to stop building over there. There's too much going on right now, but you may have inadvertently stumbled onto something. I am not a fool and I hear and see things too. We all may be at a point where we have to regroup for what's best for all of us. I'm not saying that it's a quick fix situation but I want to think this all through."

I couldn't believe what I was hearing. It was a miracle, but I knew that men like John Dawson were shrewd and they knew how to buy time. That's really what he was doing. But I would take what I could get. If he could talk to other developers and come up with something that was mutually satisfying to most of the people involved, then I had made a slight difference.

In the next breath he insisted that I lay off my writing about this for a while. That pissed me off. He was going to have his way about this and if I didn't comply. I was out on my ass for sure. But could I do it? How could I let Dickie and my new friends down?

Max saw what was happening and he also saw the look on my face. He knew me pretty well and he knew that I was a determined reporter, if nothing else. He spoke up and interjected this thought. "Perhaps this is a good time for a sort of cooling off period. I have to tell you John, that Tug here has caught the imagination of our readers and I have a computer full of fan mail to back up his point of view. You know I play a dicey game here between pleasing my readers and pleasing my advertisers. I will work this through with Tug and we will come up with a solution that will meet both our needs."

It was obvious the meeting was over and John gave a nod to Max's suggestion. I was saved for another day, I prayed.

When everyone left the room, Max asked me to stay. Not knowing which way his wind was blowing, I decided to stay on the offensive and exude an enthusiasm that maybe I had won the day.

"Sit down, Tug." Hmm, not quite where I had hoped we were heading.

"I want to tell you that I believe we got off the hook on this one but they will be back. They will never agree to stop what they are doing on the Eastern Shore and so this presents me with a new dilemma. You are one hell of a good reporter. You did do what I asked and then I blew when you came back and did it. I guess that old man Dickie Short sure has screwed us around. But having said all this, I have to tell you that I want you to stop writing about this now. Until we know just what way the wind is blowing, you have to go on to other crusades. Crusades that aren't as controversial as this one."

I knew I would hate myself forever for saying this, but a man had to do… With a genuine smile, I said, "You know I can't do that Max. You wouldn't do that in my position and I won't walk from a good story, It's what I am trained to do."

A sad expression came across his face. "I was afraid you were going to say that. I have a great respect for you and I have been a friend of your fathers since college, but I have to protect my own here. If you can't do as I ask, then we are going to have to part ways."

I knew deep down that this was coming all along.

"Before it gets to that point, Max, let me ask you a favor. I have been here at the Sun for a year now. I haven't taken one day of vacation time and now I think I would like to take it. Would that be all right with you? I think putting some distance between us for a short while may help give us some perspective."

The relief on Max's face was palpable. "I think you were reading my mind, Tug. I think it is more than all right. Maybe after a week or two away, you will come to the realization that there are some things in this world we just can't change no matter how desperately that pains us. I think the time away is a great idea. Give my best to your dad and give your mom a hug for me. She is quite a woman."

He had completely misread me or where I was headed to find myself those answers. "I…I am not going to Boston, Max. I am going over to the shore." The look on his face said it all. He knew that sooner rather than later we would have another conversation about this subject and it wouldn't turn out the way either of us had planned.

Always the consummate gentleman though, he patted my back and shook my hand. "Have a wonderful time away and we will talk when you return. Be careful not to get too sun burned. Not good for the skin you know."

"I'll keep that in mind and when I speak to Mom, I will send her that hug of yours over the phone."

I quickly walked away so I couldn't change my mind. Whatever fate had in store for me, I was heading right into it.

Sorting It All Out

Icouldn't just walk away from the office right then and there. I had too much work piled up, so I put my vacation time in starting the following Monday. There were two stories to cover and by the time I was finished writing them and getting the rest of my house in order, Monday would be the perfect time for my getaway.

I still had the issue with Roger to deal with. He had been my closest friend here at the paper for the last year, and maybe I had been too hasty with my anger toward him. I really liked him and didn't want to leave without trying to make it up to him. How could he possibly understand how I felt? I wasn't sure I understood exactly what I felt and yet I knew that I had found something in my life that wasn't ever there before. Sometimes things come along to change the direction a person is headed in and you can't expect even your closest friends to understand it all.

I did feel guilty about not going home to see my family. It isn't that I didn't want to; it was just that I couldn't. I had to seek whatever it was that was driving me back to the shore. For one thing, I had real feelings for Lindy. Feelings I had to sort out. I missed her terribly and that told me something. She wasn't the kind of girl I ever thought would turn my heart into mush, but she had.

I walked around my townhouse the entire evening. I played smooth jazz and headed up to my rooftop to think. I wanted to call Dickie and Lindy but thought better of it until I had concrete plans for my trip back.

Sitting outside, a warm breeze began to blow and when the phone rang, I almost had the urge not to answer it; but then I did.

"Hey man, it's Roger. I'm sitting down here at the pub with a bunch of the gang and we wondered if we could pry you loose and have you come on down to tip a few?"

Good old Roger. He was trying to make up to me in his own way. I welcomed the idea. "Sure I can, but maybe you and the gang would like to come on over here and we can party on the rooftop."

I could hear him asking if that's what everyone was in for and I heard them yell- "we'll be right over."

"See you in a while, Rog. By the way, thanks for calling."

"You are my best friend, you know. Let's forget about the fact that I shouldn't have said what I did. Okay?"

"You're the best, Rog. Be careful on your way over."

When I hung up, I was glad that they were all coming over. I hadn't partied in a while and it would be good for me to be around some of the crew. It was summer and to be enjoyed. Besides, it would take my mind off of all the other things I was tossing around in my head.

WHEN THEY GOT HERE, I had beer for everyone and loved the hustle and bustle of the conversation and the laughs going around my place. I didn't realize how much I missed doing this.

Roger and I were standing in the kitchen when the phone rang. I hesitated in answering it, but before I could make up my mind, Roger grabbed it. "Hey Tug, it might be a hot babe joining us for the evening. I know there were a few with us who looked like they really wanted to get inside the 'Tug's cave.'"

I never knew what was going to come out of that guy's mouth. He was simply something else. I grimaced when he answered, "Alston residence."

Lindy didn't know what to say. She could hear all the voices in the background and didn't know who was answering Tug's phone. It was obvious to her she had called at an inconvenient time. Her heart sank and she hung up.

"Who is it Rog? I am sure they appreciated the Alston residence thing."

"I don't know who it was. They hug up."

"Let me have the phone. I'll check the caller ID number."

I was sick when I saw it was Lindy's number. I knew what she was thinking and I had to call her back right away. I ran upstairs and grabbed the phone from my bedside table.

On the third ring, I heard her say "Hello?"

"Lindy? Did you just call me? One of my goofy friends picked up my phone and decided to play a joke."

"It sounds like you are having a party or something."

"Not a party exactly. Some of my friends from the paper are here and we're having a few beers." He desperately wanted to make her feel that she was the most important thing in his life, and he truly felt that way. He didn't want to hurt her or make her feel that her call had come at a bad time. There was no bad time when it came to Lindy. How are you? Nothing is wrong is it?"

The tone of her voice changed and became hard and cold. She was obviously in defense mode. "Does there need to be something wrong for me to call?"

I knew I had better handle this right or Lindy would be history. "No, it's just that your call is unexpected…but very welcome," he added quickly. "How are you?"

She realized that I was trying so she tried too. "I'm fine. I just wanted to hear your voice, but I don't want to interfere with your party."

"You could never interfere with anything. I am glad you called." I instantly decided to tell her I was coming. There was no need to wait. Besides I needed to say something more to make her feel like I truly did care for her. "I am coming to the shore next week."

"Get out!" she cried. "You are really coming here?"

"Yes I am. I will be there on Monday night. I have a lot to finish up here before I can come over."

"What on earth happened that you are coming back so soon? I mean I didn't think I would see you for a longer time than this."

"I know. I didn't either, but it seems that my article stirred up a hornet's nest and the boss thinks I should take some time away. I haven't had any vacation for a year, so we both agreed that this was the perfect time."

"Oh, I see. You got yourself in some real hot water over us down here, didn't you? I feel bad about that but it's wonderful news for me. I can't wait to tell Dickie; or does he know already?"

"No, I haven't told him. The decision was just made today after a rather tough meeting. If you want to be the one to tell him, by all means go ahead. And when you do, please ask him if I could stay in that wonderful room I stayed in on my last visit."

"He will be thrilled," Lindy shouted. "He misses you a lot. You sure made quite an impression on him and that's not an easy thing to do when it comes to my Uncle Dickie."

"Well he made quite an impression on me too."

A long silence interfered with the conversation. We both knew what we wanted to say but didn't have the nerve. I decided to take the bull by the horns. "I miss you Lindy. I miss you a lot."

"I miss you too Tug. I didn't know if you would feel freaked out if I said anything like that to you. I mean, I don't want you to run away from me because I said something stupid."

I knew what she meant. I was afraid of the same thing with her. We were both caught in the same place. Damned if we did and damned if we didn't. "I think you and I have a lot of talking to do."

"I agree," she said softly. "I'll let you go for now. I'll see you next Monday evening. I'll get some crabs and corn and we can have a reunion with Dickie. Won't he just love that?"

"Sounds heavenly. Take care Lindy."

"You too Tug."

I didn't want the conversation to end but it was the right time to wind it up. I was in love with the girl, no doubt about it. I suspected she felt the same.

Tug Takes A Time Out

WHAT ON EARTH AM I doing? Instead of driving straight home to Boston and seeking some real advice on my life from my parents, I am headed directly into the eye of the storm. Even though my dad and I don't see things quite the same, to say the least, he is on my side. My mom would tell me to go where my heart leads, but not dad. No, he would take me to the proverbial woodshed and beat some sense into me. And here I am, the always dependable, always predictable, Tug Alston. Harvard grad, racing like a fool to a girl I fancy myself in love with. What's gotten into me? What I am really doing is chasing moonbeams. And yet, I can't help myself.

My car was almost on auto pilot. It seemed to know the way without any help or direction from me. All I can do is sit here and make sure I don't crash into anything while my mind continues to argue with itself. I saw the look on Roger's face when I said adios! I knew he desperately wanted to tell me to take a cold shower and snap out of it. He had heard, just like the rest of them, all about the little *discussion* Max and I had had. Thanks to Lady Macbeth the whole staff at the paper probably knew that I wasn't leaving on holiday, but rather, I was given an indirect shove to take a time out. Well, God knows I need it. My head keeps spinning in twenty directions. I have the dream job I have always wanted and the neatest pad a guy could have and yet I am willing to risk it all for a cause and a girl. Let alone for an insane old man whose words rattle around my head as if he were living there. Maybe he is; who knows? Please God, help me see all things clearly.

I need to stop up ahead and get a soda before I go over the bridge. That extra sugar will go a long way to propel me across.

Tug's cell rang just as he was about to jump out of the Cherokee. To answer or not to answer, that was the question.

"Hello?"

"Tug? This is your father. I just spoke with Max and he said you were taking some vacation time. Are we to expect you in Boston sometime soon?"

Shit, I was busted.

"Hi Dad. Yes, I am taking some time away but I am afraid I won't be coming to Boston."

There was a slight pause and then he said, "You aren't coming home? Your Mother will be very upset. She misses you a great deal…and so do I."

Were my ears deceiving me? Did he really say that? He never said he missed me before. What was going on here?

"I appreciate your saying that dad. I really do, but I need to sort some things out."

"What kind of things Tug? Aren't you happy at the paper? Both you and Max seem pretty vague."

The hairs on the back of my neck bristled when he said that. It would appear that he and Max were having regular conversations about me and the job I was doing at the paper. I decided to set the record straight.

"You know Dad, I really wish you wouldn't discuss me or my job with Max. He is a great guy and I know you two have been friends for eons, but he does run the paper. It makes me look like a kid."

"Now Tug, you know I only have your best interest at heart. Max really likes you and wants you to concentrate on your career instead of…"

"Instead of what?" I interrupted.

"Well, you know; instead of running after causes for God's sake."

"Did you read my piece? Do you think it is a *cause*? "

"Well, let's say I have read other pieces you have written and liked them a lot better. You seemed to be way too involved with this one. You know it's a cardinal rule not to get personal."

He was absolutely right and I hated him for saying it. Well not hated him, but it sure did piss me off that he could see right through it.

After a moment, I said, "You're right, you know. I reread that article before I left and you and Max saw the same thing. I didn't see it at all when I was writing it, but you have a point. I guess I really did make it too personal. Well, I can't, and won't, retract it. That's why I am on this mutually agreed upon leave for two weeks."

"Look Tug, I know you and I know how sensitive you can get about things. It's one of the reasons I love you so much. But you are headed into troubled waters with this. Leave it alone. You can't stop progress and you can't stop the big guys from making millions and millions of dollars."

He said he loved me. I don't think I heard another word after that. The man himself actually said he loved me. Was this call for real, or had my mom told him he should make a bigger effort with me?

It was hard for me to know just what to say to him at this point. I was a bit uncomfortable, but he had said it and I wanted to make sure he knew I had caught it. Otherwise I might never hear it again.

"You know, Dad, you have never said you loved me. You have never said those exact words."

"For the love of Mike, Tug, are you suffering from some kind of childhood anxiety of not being loved enough? I think you better swing that Jeep of yours around and come home immediately."

We had never spoken to one another like this before. I wish we had, but men often don't relate with one another too well. While he was trying to get his point across to me in a very serious way, I remained stuck on the "I love you" part. I knew he loved me but why men don't say it to one another, I have no idea.

He was probably right on when he said I should turn my car around and head for Boston, but that wasn't going to happen. I had made my mind up and when that happens, I am like a bull charging into the ring. I began to laugh out loud at myself. Now I knew he wouldn't understand what was going on with me.

"You may be one hundred percent right Dad, but I can't do that. I know I should, but I am already committed."

"Oh you're committed all right and it should be straight to the insane asylum. Come home, Tug," he begged. "We'll take in a Sox game together and you can sit and have one of those marathon conversations with your Mother like you used to do all the time. God only knows what the two of you talked about, but you loved it and she did to. That wasn't the kind of thing I could do with you or Mikey. I found it easier to communicate with my sons through the contact sports. I guess it is kind of a guy thing, but that's how it is with me."

He was driving a hard bargain. I did miss talking with Mom and I sort of missed those insidious games of tug of war with him, but I was on my own mission here and I couldn't be distracted from it.

"How is Mom? She is the best you know."

"Yes she is and she is fine. Mikey is driving us both nuts looking for the perfect college. The perfect college for him is one that has a two to one ratio of women to men."

"That's my Mikey. Do you think he has made a decision yet? I tell you, he would like this college I saw on the Eastern Shore."

"That's not funny Tug. It's bad enough I have one son wandering around down there, but I won't have two of you running off and becoming watermen."

How odd that he said that. I had no idea he knew one thing about the Eastern Shore. He even knew to call them watermen, not fishermen.

"How do you know anything about the watermen?" I snapped back to him.

"I guess I never told you that I went down there a couple of times when I was a young man. A friend of mine's family had a home in Ocean City and all I can say is that we had quite the time. We even went out crabbing one day in one of their back water marshes in some place whose name escapes me now, but there were a lot of the old men coming back on their boats with their crab pots full. I know about the watermen Tug, and I know about the fishermen of Gloucester too but that doesn't mean I want to run off and become one of them."

"Is that what you think I am doing Dad?"

"Well, isn't it? And I hear you think you have fallen in love with one of the gals from one of those towns. Good grief, Tug, what is happening to you?"

Now he hit a nerve in me. He had no right to bring that up. "I don't want to talk about this anymore Dad. My life is my own. I appreciate your concern and all but I have to find out where I fit in and right now I am not sure."

That seemed to stop him from any further comments shot from the hip. Finally, in a tone of voice that screamed pleading with your son, he said, "Okay Tug. You go and find out where you fit in, but then come back to the real world. You are a Boston raised young man. You are descended from generations of Boston men who all, like you, went to Harvard. We are fortunate to have been blessed with a good deal of money and you have lived a very different life from any of these people you seem to be so enamored of, including the young lady you are so attracted to. You are worlds apart from these people and while you feel their pain with progress and change, you can't become one of them. All I am asking is that you please think on this. Can you promise me that much?"

I really thought he was completely overreacting to my situation. He already had me married and out on a boat, fishing all day and never thinking about anything else. This is what made me get so frustrated with him. I had proven my stripes in doing what every one of my male ancestors had done, and yet he still thought I needed direction and that could only come from him. Crap! When would he have some confidence in me and believe that I could figure things out on my own? Well, he did care enough about me to call and say what was on his mind. I respect him for that. Who knows if Mom put him up to it, thinking that the "come to Jesus talk" should come from him. I desperately wanted their approval with this, so I did the only thing a guy can do.

"I will Dad. I promise I will think about everything we have talked about. I better get off now and pay attention to the road here. Please give Mom a kiss for me and for whatever it's worth, thanks for caring enough to make this call."

I could hear him fiddling with papers in the background. He always did that when he didn't know what else to say or do. Clearing his throat, he said, "You're welcome, Tug. I hope it all works out for you. Call me and let me know where your head is at on your way back to Baltimore. Please be careful about what you do. You have years of love and energy poured into you. Don't make the wrong choice."

"I'll call you soon Dad. Hope the Sox beat the Yanks. I know how you love to write those stories."

He had given me the closest thing to love and freedom he could. I knew this had to be the toughest thing in the whole world for him. He cared and his call told me that. I just wish he hadn't waited so long. But I guess the old saying "better late than never" was truer than anyone can imagine. Now, my biggest problem was making the right choice.

EVERY YOUNG MAN HAS TO come to this place in the road. Some make it sooner; some make it later, but we all make it. I needed to be dead sure of which way I was heading or I was going to make the biggest mistake in my life.

As I got closer to Salisbury, I decided that I wanted to spend a day or two in this town on my way back. This truly was the hub of the entire peninsula and it warranted a closer look. I wanted to talk to some of the locals and wander around the waterfront and see what I could come up with. I instinctively liked this town. I made a mental note that I would contact the local newspaper down here and set a meeting up with some of the writers. That way I could pick their brains for what was the local reaction to all that was happening on the shore and their neck of the woods.

This time heading down Route 13, I paid way closer attention to the building that was going on surrounding the area. There was a lot of it but that didn't surprise me if this truly was the crossroads of the Eastern Shore. However, I wondered how all this was affecting the smaller towns not far away. I suspected they were seeing growth and maybe not all that happy about it. Any large development in any of these smaller towns could wreck havoc to it. Just plopping down homes wasn't the end of the story. I had seen the lengths some of the small towns on the Cape went through when they were going through their expansion times. It staggers one's mind.

One thing my conversation with Dad did bring into focus was my need to be more balanced with my approach to this subject. Max was right when he said I was losing my perspective and making this too personal.

Time would be my enemy. I might not have enough of it, but whether I did or not, I had to do the best with what I had. I knew that Lindy would want to spend every waking minute with me, and it wasn't that I minded that at all; it was just that I had to guard against another emotional situation that would cloud my better judgments. As for Dickie; well who knew what he would be up to?

I arrived just about the time I told Lindy I would and headed straight to the white two-story house that I had really missed. I knew they would be around back cooking up something wonderful. I decided to park a ways down the street and surprise them. I wanted to see the light shining in Lindy's eyes when I caught her by surprise.

As I snuck around the corner of the back of the house, the first thing I saw was Dickie's rear end bending over the huge pot that I knew held that day's crabs. I could smell it all over the place and my mouth began to water.

Lindy spotted me and let out an ear-piercing squeal, as she ran and jumped into my arms. She planted a big kiss on my lips and man…she tasted good. Dickie just stood there staring at the two of us, shaking his head. I began wondering if my face was covered in lipstick the way he looked at me and shot me that broad smile of his.

"What it is Dickie? What the hell are you smiling at?"

"You, son. I am smiling at you. It's so good to have you back. We've missed you."

"I missed you too." I stepped over to the pot and stuck my head right over it. "Crabs, huh? They smell heavenly."

"Nothin' but the best for you. These here were caught jist a few hours ago. Poke stopped by and give them to me. He got them from one of the guys who stopped by the drug store."

My head was swimming already. I hadn't been off the shore for two full weeks and already I had forgotten how they said things. I would need a refresher course, but with Dickie around; it wouldn't take long.

"You go on now and get settled. You know where things are. Lindy kin go and help ya. I have everything here under control. We'll eat directly, so go git washed up and settled in. These here crabs will wait. They ain't in no hurry to be eat up anyways."

Lindy slid her arm around my waist as we carried my bags inside. I could tell it would be more than a few minutes before we were back downstairs for supper. It was something about that look on her face that told me so.

Dickie finally gave up yelling for us and we heard him pounding up the stairs like a wild dog. "Can't you two hear anything? What's goin' on up here anyways," he grumbled as he walked into the room.

"Uncle Dickie, what's the fuss? We were just fixing to come on down and eat those crabs. They sure smell good."

"Now listen here, missy, I know what you two young folks be doin' up here and I run a right proper home here and don't fergit it." He was having such a good time with us. His "family" was together again.

Lindy walked across the floor and hugged him so tight he let out a shout. "Whooee girl. You sure are a strong one. Come on now let's go git them crabs before they run off on us."

The truth was that Dickie was mostly right. Neither Lindy nor I could break free of one another long enough to put anything away. If old Dickie hadn't come up those stairs when he did, heaven knows what would have gone on. I think he knew that.

The taste of the crabs, the corn, and the salt potatoes, washed down with a frosty Corona told me that I was glad to be back here. Life is good.

"Whatcha gonna do with all this time on your hands, son?"

"I am going to talk to a lot of people, see a lot more of the area and I want to go out on the water, if you can arrange that Dickie."

"You want to go out with the watermen? I mean I know your heart's in the right place, but do you have any idea of what you are in for?"

"No, not really. But I have to go out and see something for myself. Do you think they would mind if an outlander went out with them?"

"They go out to make money son. They don't go out to have a social time. That they do at the garage on Saturday nights."

I sensed some uneasiness in his voice when I asked him to fix me up. Was it that he didn't want to ask one of his fellow watermen or was it something else?

"I really *need* to do this Dickie. Please help me go out on the water. I know I don't know a lot about it but I want to learn. I know they are going out to make money and I won't get in their way. I just want a chance to see if what I feel is real."

"What is it you feel son?"

"I can't explain it really, but it's something that I have felt since I first came here."

Dickie took the measure of me and then said, "It kin git bad out there son. In the wink of an eye the weather kin change on a dime. Seen that all too many times in my years out there. One time it changed so fast that we all got washed overboard and dang near drowned. If it hadn't been for another boat nearby, we would have all been goners."

"You won't help me then will you?"

About this time Lindy cut in with her two sense worth. "You are a fool Tug, if you think you can go out with men who have been doing this all their lives and get the hang of it in a short time; you are crazy. These men have learned every trick of the trade and it took them since they were kids to learn it. You can't just expect them to take you out. This is the time of year they make most of their money."

I could tell this was going to be a hard sell to either or both of them. I was banging my head against the wall but I was determined to do this.

"Look, I understand how you both feel, but I am a lot tougher than you think. I can handle it and I won't get in anyone's way. Please, Dickie, talk to someone and see if they wouldn't take a chance. I think they owe me something for that article, don't you?"

"I see son. You think that you have something to bargain with, huh? Well maybe ya do at that. Lindy is jist worried about ya. It is a dangerous proposition out there and you have never seen hell until ya have seen a storm pull up quick. But I will ask around and let ya know."

"Thanks Dickie. This is real important to me."

"I can see that son. Well, I am off to bed. You and Lindy finish up here. I'll see ya in the morning."

"Why the early to bed, Dickie?"

"Cause if I want to talk to anyone about the young pup I have staying with me, who wants to go out on that water and pretend he is waterman; I have to git up mighty early."

"He was going to do it. I loved this man. And I can't say I minded having the rest of the evening to kiss the warm and delicious lips of Lindy Short.

Giving It The Old Harvard Try

IT WAS JUST AFTER SUN up when I awoke the next day. Dickie was nowhere to be seen, but that wonderful coffee of his was waiting for me. I found a note attached to the refrigerator that told me where he was. You got it. Virgil's. I knew he was on the mission to get me on one of those boats sometime soon.

Lindy and I had stayed up pretty late with me and when she left, all I could think about was how much I had missed her and how much I really wanted to be with her most of the time. I had a lot of other things to do while I was down here and telling her that I needed some time to myself was going to be mighty difficult. Those kisses were truly sweeter than wine.

I downed the coffee and decided to shower and get myself outside. The day was beautiful and time was a wasting. Dickie would be back soon and I had a thousand things to ask him. I wanted him to take me for a ride, although my body still hadn't fully recovered from those sunken seats of his and all the jiggling that went on up and down the streets. Maybe he would go in my Cherokee. I doubted that though. He was in love with that truck, not to mention how stubborn he could be about him doing all the driving.

I heard the back screen door slam. Ah, he was home. It was barely seven in the morning and hard for me to believe that I was up, dressed and ready to go exploring. This was the new me and I was ready for anything.

When I walked into the kitchen, Dickie was sitting at his big round oak kitchen table surrounded by newspapers and having a cup of coffee.

"Morning, Dickie. How was breakfast?"

"Breakfast was as it always is; good. Glad to see you're up and at it already."

"I was up not much after you left. Thanks for leaving the coffee." I knew he was holding out on me. I could see it in his face and prayed he was successful in talking someone into letting me go out with them.

"I know you like your coffee son, and it weren't no trouble for me, so glad you were pleased."

I couldn't stand it any longer. I had to know what he found out. "Did you talk to anyone this morning?"

He picked up the paper as if he were actually reading it. The shit-eating grin on his face told me that he was in the mood to tease, so this might take a while. "Sure, son, I always talk to the guys before they go out."

See? I knew what he was going to do. "I mean did you ask anyone if I could go out with them?"

Peering over the tip of the paper he stared at me intently and then said, "Yep."

"Well, yep what?"

"You sure are a pushy one, aren't ya feller?"

"Dickie, come on. What did they say?"

"Said they would be right pleased to have you go out with them. They figured if you had the balls to write that story; you had the balls to face the water."

"Really? Is that what they said or are you pulling my leg?"

"Nope, that's what they said word for word all right. They said you should meet them down to Virgil's tomorrow morning around three o'clock. In the morning."

"Funny, Dickie. What time do they really want me to meet them?"

Dickie sat up straight and laid the paper aside. I am *not* kidding. Three AM is when they want to see yer pretty face. Do you have it now?"

"Guess I do," I said woefully. "Why couldn't the crabs have a later start time?"

That one even amused Dickie. I shot up from the table and patted him on the arm. "That's fantastic. You are such a friend, Dickie. Thanks so much."

"Why don't you wait to thank me until after you have been out there for a whole day? You may not be so thankful when you git back here, tireder than a mule and aching all over yer body."

I hadn't thought about that part of this adventure, but it didn't matter. They were going to take me out and I was going to be an Eastern Shore waterman at least for one day of my life.

Dickie slid the paper across the table. "You might want to read this article in today's Sun before you take off somewhere. However, your blood might git to boilin' after you read it."

I picked up the section of the paper he was pointing to and the headline read: **Dawson Development to Build Huge Retirement Community on the Shore.** I thought I would throw up. As I read on down, John Dawson announced that his company planned a two thousand unit development on the Maryland shore outside of Berlin, Md. It was to contain single homes, townhouses, and apartment units that would sprawl over hundreds of acres. The project was set to begin next week.

"Why that sonofabitch! He sat there in that meeting and he played with me. He knew all along that he was going to do just what he wanted and he had no intention of holding on it until the infrastructure was built before going ahead."

"I told you that you were going to get your bowels in an uproar. Seems they messed with ya, son."

"They sure did, Dickie. And my boss must have known about this too. Even if he didn't know about this project, he knew that they weren't about to quit developing over here for even a short time. They just can't help themselves. I am so mad I could tear them all apart."

"It's no use son. They will keep it up until they have finished it all off. You tried your best, but where there's money involved; it's just no use."

"I don't know about that Dickie. I am not going to quit on this subject. But right now I want you to come with me. I want to ride around the area and ask you a million questions."

"That would be all right with me. Where are we going?"

"I want you to show me every part of this county. I want to see it all."

"Okay son. Let's git goin'. I will have to stop and git gas before we head out."

"I thought we could take my Cherokee."

"I wouldn't hear of it. The old truck is more used to these parts anyway. Wouldn't want anything to happen to that fancy vehicle of yours. Come on, let's go."

I knew I wouldn't win that battle but I had to try. I patted my butt and mumbled quietly, "here we go again pal."

I ASKED A THOUSAND QUESTIONS. I wanted to know about the old history of the area and Dickie was only too happy to tell me all about it. He told me about the native Indians that settled here along the Annemessex and how the first white settlers came in the early sixteen hundreds. He said some of his ancestors came a little later on but that the Shorts had been here pretty much from the time things got settled on the shore. He was so proud of the heritage of these parts. His eyes lit up when he told me about the days of the great harvest of crabs, fish, and oysters. Of course he called them "arsters," but it didn't matter. I loved the way he could spin the yarns and tell the tales. He was a part of those great years when Somerville yielded most of the crabs and oysters on the country. It was a happening place. Then came the decline and he and his fellow watermen had to really scrape along to make a living after the oyster beds had been dredged to near extinction and the crabs had been over harvested. The ducks were diminishing too and the men had to find work off the water.

"It was hard times, son. Ain't never been the same since, but yet the men go out and eek out a living the best they kin." Many have gone to land jobs for most of the year, but still crab some during the summer. It jist ain't like it used to be."

"I don't mean to be contrary Dickie but did you ever think that maybe trying to make your town a resort destination might be the salvation of it. I mean the town has gone through so much already. Maybe this is a way to make it come alive again."

He stopped his truck dead in the middle of the country road. He did not care who might be behind him. Thankfully no one was. I wished I hadn't opened my mouth.

"I see where you are going with that comment son, but Somerville is different than a lot of other places. It's a waterman's place. Always has been and always should be. "

"I know how you feel Dickie and they have gone overboard with how they have gone about it, but if we could get them to do it differently, couldn't it help to preserve what you have down here?"

"I don't see how ya kin do it son. It sounds like a good idea but you and me know that when they git to buildin' they build everywhere and then nothin' even looks the same as it did. They destroy; they don't build. There's a difference."

"There has to be an answer Dickie. If not, Somerville will either wither away or be lost forever, or it will stand and fight its way back to a place of prosperity."

"I don't know how someone like you, who doesn't know the first thing about us, can do that. I am willing to help you do it, if it's at all possible, but as you kin see from this morning's paper, they don't listen."

"You're right, but it's worth a try. I'll think about it and see if there is something else we can do to make the case. First I have to go out on the water."

"No first you have to finish my tour here. I want to drive you out to the neck and let you see all the shanties and tell ya about all those great days. Shantys lined these here waters and they were everywhere. There aren't near many left, but still, they are here and I want to take you to my old one. I still keep it up some. I think you will like it."

When we pulled up, I realized I was looking at what could be the closest thing to Eastern Shore history. I couldn't wait to see the inside. The tough part was navigating the wooden plank walk way to get out to it. I have been known to be fairly clumsy in my time, but walking carefully, I made it. The weathered gray boards on the small building reminded me of New England and the Cape. I instantly had a moment of yearning for that part of my youth that found me on the quiet beaches of the jewel of Massachusetts.

It smelled of all things seafood. He had an old pot-bellied stove in the corner and I could picture him warming his hands there on the cold days of winter after he came in from the water. All sorts of poles and repair tools for the nets were lined on the walls. Spools of all sizes sat on the big bench in the middle of the room. There was a short trough for culling at the opposite side of the room from where we were standing. As I looked at each piece of Dickie's life trade, he went into excruciating detail. I couldn't get enough of it. I was learning a whole history and one that all the watermen knew by heart. Then, he patiently handed me each item and gave me a crash course on what I would be handling the next day. It was so like him. He wanted me to see it as one of them when I went out with the men.

"Do you think I can learn to be a waterman, Dickie?"

"Don't know. But one thing I do know: You will feel it if it's in your bones. The water calls to ya, son. You'll know it if it does."

"I am a little scared, you know. I think you figured that out. But I have to do this Dickie."

"You'd be a fool if ya weren't son. This is a hard business, but you'll make it."

THE GOOD LORD WAS WITH me. It didn't call for rain and I was up and ready to take off to Virgil's before three o'clock. Dickie insisted on going down with me and I knew Lindy would already be there serving up breakfast to the men. I was glad because I really wanted to see her before I left. She would probably laugh her head off when she saw me in an old pair of Dickie's jeans, and an old shirt and a farmer's hat that had a feed insignia on it. Dickie had lent it all to me for the occasion. No one in my family would believe this was me or would they want to claim me for their relative.

"Morning Tug," Lindy smiled as I walked into Gordon's. "What do you want for breakfast or should I just bring you the special?"

"Why don't you just bring me the special? I am a waterman today."

"And you look just like one," she snickered and then shot me a wink. "The hat really sets the outfit off."

"Knew you would love it."

Dickie introduced me to the brave souls who had graciously consented to take me out. "These here are the men who will be takin' you out son. This here's Wally and over there is Clumpy. They'll show you what to do."

Wally shot me a grin that said he was ready for me. "First time out, huh? Well, nothin' to it. We'll have you a waterman by day's end."

"Thanks Wally. I really appreciate this. I promise I'll do my best."

"I know you will. Dickie speaks highly of you and that's enough for me and Clumpy."

I was dying to know how Clumpy got his name but I figured this wasn't the time to ask. There would be time later on when were out on the water.

"You eat now, Tug. We take off in a few minutes, so don't waste time talkin' to too many folks. Got to git out before the sun comes up if we gonna catch crabs."

"Yes sir. It won't take me long to eat and I'll be ready."

Lindy brought the food and put it down in front of my place. As she leaned down, I kissed her on the cheek. She blushed a bright red. "I'll see you tonight, Lindy."

"That's what you think, Tug. You have no idea of what you are in for today. You'll be sound asleep before night falls."

"I'll see you tonight." I insisted. She laughed at me and walked away.

The men were ready. There was another man who walked out with us and they introduced him as Hambone. He was a sturdy guy with massive hands. It was obvious he had been out on the water for ages. I was set and impatient to get going.

The boat was a fair sized skiff and they loaded her up with bait and there had to be a zillion other things in the boat that I had no idea of what they were. The motor started up and we were off. It was colder out on the water than I suspected and I was glad Dickie forced a jacket in my hand before I left the house. He said I would need it and he was right. Of course he was right. He had done this all his life.

Wally was the first man to engage me in conversation. "So, you think you might want to be a waterman do you?"

"I don't know but I will find out, won't I?"

"You sure will. We are heading out pretty far. I hope you don't get sea sick."

That thought had never occurred to me. As I had never felt sea sick before when I went out with my dad on the Cape, I dismissed that immediately.

You go on over to Clumpy and see what he wants you to do."

"As I moved over to where Clumpy was standing, the deck was still slick from the night's mist. I was almost to his side when my legs gave way and down I went right onto my ass. I fell so hard that I thought I had broken it, but then you can't actually break your ass.

"I wasn't only hurting; I was embarrassed right out of my ass, so I got up like nothing had happened. I heard them all laughing at me. I shrugged it off and asked Clumpy what he wanted me to do.

"Just start getting the poles ready. When we get out there we need to have everything in place. We can't waste time."

"I looked around and found the poles and a pile of gloves. I realized that this wasn't going to be easy but I was ready for it.

When Wally cut the engine, I knew that this was show time. It was now or never for me to learn what crabbing was all about. Hambone was already reaching for a pole and as I stood there watching him; Wally yelled out, "Grab a pole boy. You got to hook them pots."

Okay, I had to hook the pots. I reached over and grabbed a pole and then Clumpy yelled to me, "Get the gloves on boy or you will cut your hands to smithereens."

Smithereens, right. I didn't want that so I put a pair of gloves on. Just my luck; they were a tad too big.

"Don't worry about them being a little loose boy," said Wally. "They'll tighten some when the salt water gets onto them."

Salt water, right. That always does the trick. Now I had to hook the pot as we rocked on the sea. The first try-missed. The second try- missed again. I was determined to do this. It wasn't as easy as Clumpy and Hambone made it look but the third try was a charm. I had the line on my hook. Now what do I do?

"Haul it up boy," shouted Wally. "Just haul her up on the deck."

I grabbed the line and dropped the hook in back of me. I began to drag the damned thing up. It was the heaviest thing I had ever lifted. I remembered that water made things heavy.

"Got her boy?" shot Hambone. "Don't drop her. Just keep lifting her up."

As I lifted the heavy, wire pot out of the water, my eyes began to get those white dancing things in front of them. The next thing I knew I was back on my ass. My stomach didn't feel too good either. Then darkness fell over me.

When I came to, Wally was standing over me saying, "Are you all right boy?"

"I guess I am. What happened?"

"You passed out. I never seen anything like it. You went down like a tub of butter."

"How about the pot? What happened to that?"

"Clumpy came round and got it. Had a whole mess of crabs in it. It sure was a heavy mother."

"No shit," I said as I climbed back up.

"Good grief, how long was I out?"

"Long enough for us to pull up all our pots out here. We are on our way to the next group."

I was totally embarrassed now. "I didn't do so well, did I?" I asked looking at Wally.

"Don't worry about it son. Not everyone is cut out for this kind of work."

"Like hell I won't worry about it. I won't ever live it down when you tell Dickie what happened to me out here."

"We won't say a word," he winked to the guys. "You can have another try at it at the next stop."

When we got to the next place where Wally had traps; I was ready. I knew what to expect this time and I was definitely *not* going to fuck up this time.

"Here we go," yelled Hambone. "Give it another try Tug. You can do it."

"He definitely was the most supportive of the group.

I pulled on the gloves that had shrunken a bit just like Wally said. Then I grabbed a hook and on the first try, I nailed it. I was grooving now. I grabbed that pot and hauled for dear life. The pain in my arms hurt like a bitch but I was not going to drop this one. I hauled her up and then moved her around and dropped her on the deck. I was so proud of myself.

"Not one damned crab in there," said Clumpy. "What a shame son. All that work and you have nothing to show for it."

I couldn't believe my eyes. He was right. There was not one sea creature in there. The only thing that was clinging to the pot was a mass of sea grass.

"The crabs don't like that much. They won't come in the pot when the grass is all around it. Sorry son. Grab you another one. You're bound to do better next time.

My pride was shattered but I grabbed the pole and tried another. This time the pot was full and I yipped my head off. I have never seen men laugh so hard at one, clueless college kid trying so hard to please them.

"That's more like it," Wally yelled. Now we can tell Dickie that you brought in a mess of crabs."

"You make sure you tell him that and that only. He doesn't need to hear the rest of the story. Please?"

"Aw, don't you go worrying about Dickie none. You don't think he hasn't had himself a bad day or two?"

"I am sure not as bad as mine has been."

"It wasn't all that bad son," Wally remarked. You have learned about Sooks and Jimmies and what a peeler is. You have gotten a whole new degree out here."

He was right. I had learned more than I ever dreamed. I now knew that a female crab was a sook and a male was a jimmie. I think I had heard that before, but it was embedded in my brain now. Peelers were what they called crabs that were shedding their shells. And when they had no shell; they were soft shelled and how much money they brought to meet the demand of people who found that a delicacy.

"We are headed for home now," Wally said. "You've had a long day son. You'll sleep like the dead tonight."

He was right about that. I would think about the day and being out in the fresh air and the sound of the water slapping up around the boat. I would think back to the stories about pirates that were hidden in my desk drawer at home. This was as good an adventure as any I had written about. This was real and this was what life down here was all about.

On the way back in we started laughing about the day and all that had happened. I asked Clumpy and Hambone how they got their names and when they explained that Clumpy ate too many clumps of potatoes as a kid and Hambone liked to gnaw on the hambones his mother cooked, the laughter rose higher and higher. Then, naturally I had to account for Tug. We were all having a good time and enjoying life on the water. This was what it was all about. Camaraderie to the fullest extent of what men could know. They had the utmost trust in one another and they had to. Their very lives could depend on it at a moment's notice when they faced the waters of the Chesapeake.

We dropped the crabs off at one of the packing houses and then took the skiff back to Wally's shanty. Dickie was waiting there for me. He knew what time we would be back and he knew how tired I would be. Even his old truck was a welcome sight to my sore eyes.

"How'd he do." Yelled Dickie as we tied up the skiff.

Wally shot me a sheepish grin and then shouted, "Not bad for a first timer."

I knew Dickie knew exactly what that meant but he didn't make any further comments.

I helped them finish the work and then was definitely ready to go on home. I noticed the adoration for Dickie in their eyes. He was the master watermen and even though he no longer could go out; he was their leader. I saw that everywhere we went. Dickie Short was a legend in his time.

"You want to try it again tomorrow boy?" Wally asked.

"I wouldn't mind at all except I have to do other things tomorrow. But rest assured; I will do this again before I have to go back."

"That's great. You know where to find us when you're ready."

"See you around, Tug," called Hambone as he got in his truck and pulled away. Clumpy was leaving too and said his good byes. Wally had work to do in his shanty so we left him to do it. I couldn't thank him enough.

Dickie didn't waste any time. "So you survived, did ya son?"

"I loved it Dickie. I loved every minute of it."

"I knew you would. Somewhere deep down in that city boy of yours is a real Eastern Shore man. You jist have to find it."

"You may be right, but right now I need to eat."

"I have it all ready. Lindy is at home right this minute cooking up a mess of beans and a roast beef. She is some good cook, you know."

"Do you ever stop Dickie?"

"Stop what son?"

"Stop trying to be a matchmaker."

"You are in love with that girl of mine; I know you are. I can see it all over yer face. She feels the same. This is yer destiny son. Don't try to run from it."

"Okay Dickie. Have it your way. I'll let nature take its course and see what happens. However with you around I am sure you will be helping old Mother Nature along."

"Can't never tell son. You jist can't never tell."

Hurtin' For Certain

DICKIE AND I WERE NOT two tenths of a mile down the road when the jiggling of his old truck and the total lack of air conditioning hit me like a ton of bricks. My head began swimming and I had broken into a cold sweat.

"Stop the truck," I gurgled.

He took one look at me and pulled his old beauty to the side of the road. He hadn't even stopped completely when I swung the door open and puked my guts out. As wave after wave kept coming, all I could hear in the background was his hysterical laughter. God, I was in a world of shit. Here I was, with my body doubled over retching like a drunken sailor, and he was laughing. What was wrong with this picture? Didn't my old pal feel one bit of compassion for me?

"Here take this," he said as he passed over an old rag to wipe my face. My shaking hand took it and I couldn't believe my eyes. It was the filthiest piece of cloth I had ever seen, but I was grateful for it regardless of the oil and sundry other contaminants it had on it. It did the job and I wiped away the evidence of my day's adventure. When I was done, I straightened back up in my seat and realized that he was now laughing so hard he couldn't stop. I shot him a quizzical look and said, "What's so damned funny?"

"You are son. Look at your face."

I pulled down the visor and when I looked into the dirt encrusted mirror, I saw that my face looked like Al Jolson. Black all over. I was right on one score- oil was definitely one of the top ingredients on that rag.

"What the hell kind of rag did you hand me, Dickie? How am I supposed to get this shit off my face?"

"Calm down son. It's just a little dirt from under the seat. It's been under there for years, so how am I supposed to know what's on it. Handy I had though for such an occasion."

I grunted quietly under my breath as we took off again. I prayed my stomach would hold on until I could get to the shower.

Another mile and we pulled up in the driveway. Dickie jumped out and came around to help me. When he opened the door, I said, "Thanks Dickie but I can take it from here."

"Okay son, but I think you are going to need me."

What the hell did he mean? As I went to get out it became perfectly clear what he meant. We had been in that truck just long enough for my muscles to stiffen up and now the day's work was beginning to catch up with me. I grabbed on to the door handle as my legs felt like they were made of iron.

"Steady there son. I know how ya feel. You are going to be hurtin' for certain for a spell."

I let him help me around to the back of the house and through the door. I had forgotten all about the fact that Lindy was there, cooking her heart out. When she saw me, her eyes flew open wide and her mouth dropped open wide enough to catch flies.

"What the hell…"

"Help me Lindy," Dickie cried out. "He is one sorry puppy."

Lindy grabbed my other arm and they both pulled me up the stairs. I knew what I must look like and figured if Lindy could still like me after this display of wimpiness; we might have a chance together after all.

When they sat me on the bed, Lindy stood there and stared down at me. She broke into laughter and dashed down the hall to grab a camera Dickie kept on his dresser. Oh no, I thought. She wouldn't dare.

Racing back to my room, she aimed it and clicked away. She had captured my darkest hour for all eternity. "What did you do that for," I barked.

"I want to have this moment on film forever. You look like you were rode hard and put away wet." I didn't even want to answer that comment. I shrugged my shoulders and said, "Go ahead and laugh if you must, but I made it through the day, regardless of what condition I came home in."

"Yes you did Tug. I am so proud of you and I know that your Mama would be too. I think I will send her a copy of this picture."

"You do and I will kill you."

"Do you need any help to get in the shower?" she said in a provocative voice.

"No I don't," I snapped back. "You just go ahead and get that food on the table and I will be down in a few minutes."

"Okay, you take care of yourself and please try to get that gunk off of your face. It doesn't become you."

"If you don't get out of here right this minute, I will make sure you live to regret it."

"Okay, okay, we are going. Call us if you need us." With that the two, laughing magpies left my room. I truly had no idea how I was going to maneuver my aching body into the shower, but I was damned if I would call them to help me.

I NEVER MADE IT TO the dinner table. In fact, when I awoke, it was almost sunrise. I had to go to the bathroom really bad and I was starved out of my mind. All I could remember was standing under the hot shower for about a half hour and then returning to my room and resting my aching bones on the bed. I guess that's when my body said "that's enough boy. You need sleep."

The house was completely quiet. As I went to throw my legs over the bed and get out, that's when I felt the agony of being on the water. Every muscle reacted the same. They were in rebellion. I had to get to that bathroom or I would have another mess to clean up. I dragged myself step by step and finally reached my destination. As I stood over the toilet, I had to extend one arm to the wall to keep my legs from collapsing underneath me. This wasn't funny. The only answer was to get back into a hot shower no matter what. I managed to do just that and afterwards, I felt much better.

I heard a tapping on the bathroom door and then Dickie shouted, "Use the Ben Gay. It's in the medicine cabinet. I think you will be mighty glad you did. I didn't say a word but I opened the cabinet door and slathered the stuff all over me. It was the old kind of stuff. Smelled like hell and burned into your skin like you were roasting over a spit. It worked though. In minutes I was beginning to feel as if I were a human again.

The walk down the stairs was still tough, but I was not going to show it. I wasn't going to be laughed at again. No, not again.

Dickie was standing over the stove whipping up a batch of pancakes. I poured my coffee and as soon as he plunked them in front of me; I ate like there was no tomorrow.

"Missed dinner last night. Poor Lindy was so miserable, she went home half crying."

"I am sorry about that, Dickie, but I didn't know what hit me. I just sat down on the bed for a couple of minutes and I guess I was more tired than I realized."

"The water takes it out of a man. It's the sun, wind, and all that laboring. When you think about it, the crabs seek their revenge in a very serious way to us watermen."

"You can say that again. It's amazing how something that weighs so little can wreak so much havoc on a man's body. It's pack mentality. When they all get together, they weigh a ton and we fools have to pull that ton up and out of the water. Great play on their part, don't you think?"

"They ain't no fools. They figure they are goin' to make us work our tails off if we are goin' to eat them. What do you have planned for today son or have you changed your mind a bit?"

"No I haven't changed my mind. I can't waste time while I am here. First I suspect I am going to go down to Virgil's and apologize to Lindy, and then take a ride up shore. I will meet her later and we can spend the rest of the day together. I really feel bad about last night."

"She'll git over it son. Women always do if we men jist say we're sorry. Do you want some company on your drive?"

"Do you want to come? I have to tell you straight out though; I am driving."

"I won't argue with ya. You need to be in your Cherokee with the air conditioning and all. Of course I will freeze to death, but don't let that stop ya."

"I won't and you won't freeze to death. I want to check that new development out. I will be gone for a couple of hours, but if you want to come; I would love it."

"You go on down to Virgil's and talk to Lindy. I will be waitin' fer ya when ya get back."

MISSION ACCOMPLISHED. LINDY FORGAVE ME in an instant. I knew that we were getting closer all the time and I guessed that if she could still put up with me after yesterday, things were only going to get better between us. We made plans to go to the movies after I got back. I was already looking forward to that.

I made sure to have that newspaper article with me when we left. I was going to head straight north and go and check out this new development that John Dawson was going to build. I was still boiling over it and I was glad I was out on the water yesterday so I could physically work through my anger at it. That was another good thing about going crabbing. It didn't give you a minute to think about the aggravating things of this world.

"You sure are quiet this morning, son. Whatcha thinkin' about?"

"I am trying to figure out why some people are the way they are."

"What do ya' mean?"

"I don't know why on earth John Dawson even bothered to come to my boss's office and meet with me. I mean he knew all the time that he wasn't going to change one damned thing he was doing."

"It's a game, son. Folks with money like to play with people. It gives them a sense of power."

"I suppose you are right Dickie. The whole world is one, big fat game to those who are the players. It's not right though. They can sure mess things up and they don't give a damn who they are messing up."

"You're catching on to life son. It's the way of things and always will be. Take the Indians. They just wanted to live, have families, hunt their animals and go on the way they had for generations. Then the English came and things changed. Then the French came and things changed some more and then wars broke out and then the whole country went to war against the bigger countries and they won our independence and then years later, our country split up and went to war with itself. The Indians got caught in the whole mess and things really changed for them after all that. You know how that story ended. Now it's the money and greed for power that is at war with the rest of us. It's all over. It's not jist here. It's all up and down any coast where there's water. Even in the mountains people are getting' chased away from the peace and quiet they wanted to live with. It's called sprawl and expansion. But whatever name you put on it, it's ugly and there's nothin' we folks can do about it."

"I am not sure about that Dickie. We feel like we can't do anything but when people get stirred up about something; the politicians run for cover. They are all snakes who depend on our votes and when we get hot about a subject they tend to do something about it."

"You're thinkin' about something in particular son?"

"I guess. I have to think it all through. That's why I am down here. I need to think it all through."

Dickie didn't say another word. He knew that my mind was set on a whole bunch of things and he was a wise man to know to leave me alone to think.

WE ARRIVED IN BERLIN AND immediately found the site where the new project would be built. Berlin was a small, delightful shore town and the massive community was a mile or so outside of it. When we pulled up there, bulldozers were already doing their work. Pine tress by the thousands were being leveled and hauled to burning sites. Dozens of men were surveying and putting markers all over the place. The march to develop had begun.

Oddly enough, across the street, there were a group of protesters who were carrying signs telling the developers just what they thought of this new "planned community." It was going to be an over fifty five project, so that meant retirement. No young couples need apply.

"Lookey over yonder son," Dickie said. "I believe we have some company in our feelings with this."

"It sure looks that way, Dickie. I think I will swing on over and talk to them."

I decided to interview them right on the spot. They were only too happy to talk with me. They were mad all right.

Hotter than hornets, you might say. They knew that they couldn't stop this from happening, but they wanted to try to get the attention of the Dawson Company in hopes they might listen. Fat chance on that one.

Their point was exactly what I had tried to tell Dawson at the Baltimore meeting. The infrastructure couldn't handle this size project. More planning needed to be done before they proceeded.

They were happy to have me over there, joining in the fray. When I told them my name, they all smiled and told me they had read my article and loved it. At least someone loved me. They knew I was on their side. The sad fact of it all was that they were going to lose. Nothing they could do would stop this madness.

As I was interviewing the man who seemed to be their leader, a woman yelled out, "There he is now! There is Dawson, himself."

I turned when I heard what she was yelling about. There he was all right- John Dawson in the flesh. He had come down to oversee his new project.

"Why, I'll be damned," I mumbled.

Before I could say "Jack Sprat," Dickie was walking over to Dawson. I knew I better get in between the two of them or fireworks would start.

"Hey Dickie," I called out. "Wait for me."

Dickie waved me off and that was my cue that I had better step up my pace. For sure fur was about to fly at this meeting.

I didn't make it in time. Dickie beat me to John. He was letting him have it and if I didn't intervene, I knew that Dawson would have him removed by one of the workmen.

"John?" I yelled out. "It's me, Tug Alston.

I definitely startled him, but with Dickie screaming in his face, he looked glad to see me. "Tug, please come on over here and help me out."

I pushed my way through the crowd that had now gathered around the two men. "Hi John. I see you have already met my friend here."

Bewilderment appeared on John's face. "This is a friend of yours, Tug?"

"Yes, he is. He is a waterman from down at Somerville. I told you all about them when we last saw one another."

Dickie was smart enough to keep his mouth shut when Tug appeared. He knew that the boy could handle this one without his help. Or so he thought.

"What the hell is he doing here? For that matter, what the hell are you doing here?" John's tone of voice changed as he shot a glance over at Dickie. He wasn't at all amused by this man nor was he amused by the protesters screaming across the street.

"As it happens, I am on vacation down here for a couple of weeks. I read the article yesterday in the paper about this project, so I thought I would come and take a look. I see you just couldn't wait."

John caught my comment but let it go. He was already agitated by this whole scene. And I could see he quickly figured out what my "vacation" was all about and that Max must have been trying to cool things down.

"I see. I remember now. Wasn't he the man who wrote those letters to Max? With that he pointed his fingers right in Dickie's face. Things were going to another level fast.

"Yes, I see you do remember. I met Dickie Short a couple of weeks ago when I was down in Somerville. He is the real article here, John. You should listen to him. It is obvious that you didn't listen to anything I had to say in that meeting." The gloves were finally off.

"I don't have time to kick this around with you, Tug. I wish I did, but we all have work to do here and so I must say good bye."

I wasn't done yet with John Dawson. "I beg your pardon, John. I think you owe me an explanation of exactly what you meant when you said you would think about what we discussed. I see you had no intention of doing any thinking about anything."

"If you could get that Crusader Rabbit chip off your shoulders, you would remember that I told you I had pending projects. My *thinking* about anything wouldn't include those developments."

He had gotten my attention and I was pissed. "You aren't going to do anything, are you? You are going to build this community without any regard for any of the infrastructure concerns we discussed."

He turned and went to walk away. That was when Dickie grabbed him by the back of the neck and pinned him against one of the trucks standing behind them. I couldn't believe the strength or the speed with which Dickie nailed John's body against that truck. This was going to get ugly.

"Dickie!" I screamed out. "Let him go. We can't make him talk to us if he doesn't want to listen."

"Wanna bet?" Dickie replied in a none too pleasant tone of voice.

"Let go of him, Dickie. Nothing we say would change his mind anyway. The die is cast here. Come on."

Dickie dropped John's body so hard that it made a light thud on the ground. It was obvious to Dawson that he didn't understand how angry these people were down here.

Dusting himself off, he barked at me, as we walked away. "I guess I should thank you for that, Tug. That man is crazy."

To say that I had to hold Dickie back from assaulting the man again would be an understatement. Instead I chose to make it clear to John just how I was feeling at this moment. "You remember me, John. I am not done with this yet."

Dickie and I jumped into my Cherokee and peeled away from there, leaving nothing but dust trailing behind us. I was fuming and Dickie didn't feel much different himself. My little dust up with Dawson gave me a lot to think about and I sure knew I had a lot to think about. When Dickie finally did say something; it bordered on the prophetic.

"I know how mad you are at that man, son, but he isn't about to let anyone stand in his way. That is plain to see. You have to attack this from another place. Maybe you kin get the folks around here to go to war. You know, like a second revolution kind of thing. They will be on yer side if they know they have a chance to win."

A light bulb went off in my head. He might be right, but who was I to try to do this? Would they ever listen to a young, upstart reporter who was obviously going to be thrown out of his job if he wrote what he was hinting at? "Dickie; you just may have something at that, but I have a ways to go to figure this all out."

"You will, Son. It will all come to you."

Mr. Sophisticate

B Y THE TIME WE GOT back, it was getting to be late afternoon. I sure didn't want to make Lindy mad at me. Having one fight today was quite enough.

"Dickie? I think I will give Lindy a call and maybe we can go out for dinner before we take in a movie."

"She would like that. She really never goes out to dinner, being she works all day in a restaurant. It would do her good; and you too."

It dawned on me that I didn't see another restaurant in town. And where Lindy worked was definitely not where I wanted to take her for dinner. She would probably kill me for that. So I asked the answer man, "Where would one go out for dinner around here?"

"There aren't too many places left here. A real nice one closed a bit ago. You would have liked that one."

"Well, that sure helps me out, Dickie."

"Son, I have a better idea."

I was afraid to ask. "Oh? What might that be?"

"I think I will make up a picnic basket for the two of ya. Then, you kin go on out on the marsh. She loves it out there. Have yer dinner and then the two of you kin go to a movie. Or maybe you will be so interested in Lindy that ya won't want to be goin' to any old movie."

I shook my head. He was at it again. "You are too much, Dickie. But I have to say the picnic idea does sound wonderful. I'll call her and then I'll go and get a bottle of wine while you are packing up the basket."

"Sounds good to me, son. I'll have this here basket ready in no time."

I was in luck. Lindy loved the idea and when I asked her where exactly on the marsh we would go; she giggled and said, "You'll see." She and her Uncle certainly were cut from the same cloth.

We took off, leaving Dickie waving good bye to us. He was headed to Virgil's for dinner. We still had a few hours before sundown and it was still very warm, but a gentle breeze was blowing in off the water. I couldn't wait to see where she was taking me. Wherever it was, I was certain I knew I would love it. After the day I had had, most anything would be a blessing.

Even though I insisted on driving, Lindy directed me to somewhere I had already been. I didn't say a word, in case she was planning this to be a surprise. But Dickie said she would know where to take me. How odd. It appeared they were ganging up on me. Gee, was I surprised? I really didn't mind. I loved this place and a writer can never visit a potential scene for a future book too often.

When we got to where I already knew we were going, I waited for Lindy to tell me where to pull over. I was such a clever lad, no?

I slid my Cherokee to the side of the road right in front of the water and then gasped, "God, Lindy, this is beyond beautiful. I want to get some pictures of this place before it gets dark."

Gathering the basket and some things she had brought, she remarked, "I hope you haven't come down here with Uncle Dickie. I wanted this to be my surprise to you."

I had to tell her a white lie, didn't I? "No, I haven't been here with him. If I had, I would have suggested that we come here myself.

"I am so glad. I want you to share this special place with me and see it the way I do, and how the lighting changes at sunset. It is the most wonderful area around Somerville. I have been coming out here since I can remember. It's Uncle Dickie's favorite spot to be; even more than his house."

"You go on and take all the pictures you want. I will bring the basket and the wine. Be sure you look down into the marsh water. I think you may be surprised at what you see."

That was a pretty peculiar thing to say. What could possibly be in marsh water that she was so adamant about me seeing?

Wanting to please, I said, "Okay, Lindy, I will." I took my camera out and began to focus it. The marsh stretched out a ways before it ran into the big waters of Somerville. Being I had been here before, I remembered to be careful on the long, meandering, wooden walkway leading out to it. It could be a real nightmare if you didn't watch out for the broken planks. As I tip-toed along the old boards, I glanced down into the water like Lindy told me to do. I held a stare and saw the small fish skimming along in the water in-between the marsh grasses. There was such a rhythm to it all. I began to get that overwhelming feeling again that I belonged here. I was getting that a lot lately. I was at peace with the world and myself. Too bad I hadn't met up with John Dawson on the water today. The results of that meeting might have gone differently. I had no idea where all this emotion and feeling was coming from, but I figured it would be best to just go with it. In time, something would happen and tell me where all this was leading.

I looked down again and studied the way the grass moved ever so slowly to the ebb and flow of the water. It was like an aquatic symphony and I was being entertained by the dancing of the water and the sun's last rays of the day skimming across it. I knew why Lindy had made a point about this to me. She desperately wanted me to see what it was that she loved so much about living here.

Lindy glanced at me when she set the things down. She wanted to watch this guy she was falling for. He was so handsome, in a blondish kind of way. His blue eyes were gorgeous and she was more than a little enamored of him. She was setting her sights on him. That was for sure.

"Did you see it, Tug? Did you see what I wanted you to see?"

"I sure did, Lindy. I not only saw its beauty, but I felt something as I looked down into the water." I knew she would understand. We seemed to be of one mind and that scared me a little, but it also made me feel kind of good. "There aren't any ghosts down there, are there?"

I watched her as she laughed at me and then said, "You are too much, Tug Alston. If there were ghosts down there, I would have asked them to drag you under and talk sense to you."

"What do mean? I think I have a lot of sense. "

Lindy left the basket and all the other goodies and walked back to where I was standing. She looked down into the water and said, "All I see down there is the mystical beauty of the marsh. Perhaps it is haunted in a magical kind of way. Come on, let's go and open that wine. Be careful on these old planks. I have to fix some of them real soon before someone gets hurt."

She wasn't "Whistlin' Dixie" when she spoke those words.

"What do you mean *you* have to fix them?"

Lindy stopped and turned her head back to look at me. Her hair was blowing in the breeze and she looked simply lovely. Her eyes looked down on the walk and she answered in a sad sort of voice. "Dickie owns this shanty, Tug. He still comes out here some, but he can't do the work on it like he used to. So, I do it for him."

I couldn't let on that I knew who owned this shanty but I had no idea Lindy was doing all the work on it either. Her love for him was unending and I could feel that I was being drawn to her all the more.

"That's a nice thing to do. But then again, he is an easy man to love; even though he can drive you to distraction."

Lindy swung the door open and welcomed me in. She immediately took the bottle of wine and opened it. Offering me the plastic glass, she said, "You have to pay a toll first."

"What might that be?"

"A kiss, that's all. That's the toll for your wine. Take it or leave it."

Rubbing my chin as though in deep thought, I smiled and replied, "I think I'll take it."

One kiss led to another and by the time we finally stopped sucking one another's face, she gasped for air and told me to take a look around and ask her anything about everything. The second time around enchanted me even more. Maybe there were ghosts here after all. They were trying to tell me that I was home.

"This place is so neat, Lindy. It's like a little home that sets right on the water. I can understand why Dickie loves coming here."

"He sure does. He lets an old friend of his use it and as you can see, it gets all messed up this time of the year when the crabs are in. Then Uncle Dickie and I clean it up some in the fall, but when the winter comes it gets to looking like a mess again with all the arsters coming in."

The wine was finally in my hand and before I took one sip, Lindy offered up a toast. "Here's to Dickie and the watermen."

I took a sip and then held my glass up to make my own toast. "Here's to Lindy and Tug." Now I don't know why I said that. Maybe I was in the moment but it just seemed to slip out real easy and natural like.

SITTING ON TWO OLD, WOODEN chairs overlooking the water, we ate our dinner and finished the wine. Dickie had packed peanut butter and jelly sandwiches and chips galore. I don't think anything had ever tasted so good in my life. Maybe it was being out in the fresh air, or maybe it was being with someone I cared about very much. Lindy was comfortable and sweet and I couldn't ever remember any of the fancy, sophisticated girls I had met in Boston or at college, ever possessing the shear simplicity of the girl I was sitting next to now. Although I was supposed to be the sophisticate, Lindy kept up with me all the way. There was nothing she didn't understand and she was willing to learn about everything.

As the sun set, we held hands and then I leaned over and kissed her gently. She got up and sat on my lap and kissed me again. This time with such passion that I almost fell over and into the water. That wouldn't have been cool at all.

Out of nowhere, she said, "Tug? Tell me about your family. I mean I don't know anything about them."

I was dreading this. "Well, there's not much to tell really. They live in Boston. My Dad is a sport's editor for the Boston Globe and I have a younger brother, Mikey and my Mom is the greatest. I mean she puts up with all of us."

Lindy laughed and said, "Spoken like a true son."

"I guess so. Mom was a librarian for years, and even though she hasn't worked in a long time, she is the one I credit for my love for all things literary."

"Are you a close family?"

"Sort of, I guess you could say we are. Mikey is the athlete of the family, and much to the dismay of my Dad, he doesn't think about much else."

"We all can't be jocks you know. Does that make it tough between you and your Dad?"

"A little. He and I don't see eye to eye on a lot of things. He was real disappointed when I didn't stay in Boston after going to Harvard. He desperately wanted me to follow in his footsteps at The Globe."

Getting up and looking down at the water, Lindy said, "I see. I'll bet he doesn't much care for your being down here or the article you wrote about us annoying *hicks*."

I was horrified that she thought my parents might be thinking that. Actually, it never occurred to me what they might think if I took her home to meet them. It wouldn't matter because from the minute she said hi to them, they would love her.

"Now, I wouldn't say that, Lindy. He just doesn't understand what is happening to me."

"What is happening to you, Tug?"

"I am beginning to think that there is something special out there for me to do. Something that is far more important than running down stories about murders, and cats stranded in trees."

"Cats in trees?" she said furrowing her brow. "What are you talking about?"

"It's an expression that we use in the business. It means that you go out and cover stories that are really meaningless. They give those stories to the beginners to see what we are made of. It sucks."

"I see. There is so much I don't know about you yet and I want to know it all."

"There's plenty of time for that, Lindy. Let's just enjoy what we have right now."

She looked kind of sad and then said, "How do I know that you won't go back to Baltimore and forget all about us down here? And then you will forget about me?"

I had to do something. So I did the one thing that I knew would make her know that wasn't going to happen. I leaned into her and held her tightly and then kissed those sweet lips again and again. We were headed for trouble, but I didn't care. I liked this girl. I mean I liked this girl a lot.

"Do you believe me now?" I asked in a gentle voice. "Do you believe me when I say that I won't ever forget you?"

Holding on to me for dear life, she replied softly, "Yes, Tug, I do."

"Then trust me. I have things to think through, but that doesn't mean it's about you. It's just that I feel strongly that I have a destiny to fulfill. The problem is, it isn't the one that my Dad wants for me and all hell is going to break lose when I tell him. But I'm hopeful he will come around. It was something he said to me."

"Oh? What did he say that made you feel he might support your decision?"

"Well, after a tense few minutes on the phone discussing a lot of things, he paused and then said the words I thought he was not capable of saying. He actually said "I love you Tug. You know that. You have a good and independent mind so you will make the right decision. It blew my mind to hear him say that, but at the same time, he was letting me know he might come around to my way of thinking."

"That's great, Tug. So why are you worrying about anything?"

"Because making him proud of me is the most important thing in the world to me."

"You will Tug. You will."

The look in her eyes was soft and filled with urgency for me to calm down and just get over myself. She was right of course, but that's easier said than done. Her gentle support and the way she looked up at me was beginning to fill me with a desire that was a little too real for the moment. It was time to change the subject before…well before anything else got started.

Lindy broke away from me. She felt the moment too and knew that separation was the answer required here. She sure was one smart cookie.

"I think we had better get back. I have to get up early you know. What are you going to do tomorrow, Tug?"

"I think I am going back out on the water. That seems to be where I think best and this time, I don't intend to come back feeling so sore- or embarrassed."

Bursting out in laughter, Lindy made the funniest face. "Bet you do," she snickered. "It takes a long time to be able to go out on the water and crab and not come home feeling like you were just run over."

"Well, you just watch and see."

She couldn't contain herself. "I love you, Tug Alston. You know that. And I think you are falling for a country bumpkin yourself."

With that comment, she whisked up all the stuff and took off, headed toward for the car.

I followed in quick pursuit. I felt so good and kind of light-headed. It must have been the wine; or those kisses of hers. I guess I wasn't paying any attention at all as I crossed those boards,and then one split in two and my body dropped into that marshy water. Kerplunk!

Lindy heard the crack of the wood and when she turned to look back, I was waist deep in the marsh. Instead of rushing to help me, she stood there and laughed her fool head off at me.

"Stop laughing and come help me, Lindy. I am stuck."

She didn't move. She was going to stand there, laughing, and watch me pull myself out of the mucky water bringing God knows what up sucking at my legs.

"Okay then," I yelled to her. "You just stand there and watch me. " I tried to move my soaked feet slowly over to a part of the dock that was in better shape. I was able to pull myself up, but when I emerged, I looked like the *Swamp Creature*. All I could hear was the sound of her hysteria.

"This isn't so funny, you know, Lindy Short. I'll get you back for this."

"You look so funny, Tug. I can't help it. You look like a drowned rat."

I looked down at myself and she was right. I, Tug Alston, the sophisticated Harvard graduate, looked precisely like a drowned rat. I couldn't say anything, I was so mortified. And how was I going to get back home. I wasn't about to sit in my Cherokee, dripping with mud. And I would be damned if I was going to strip naked. Now, I could just hear Dickie going on about that.

Lindy finally took pity on me and ran back into Dickie's shanty. I hoped she was getting a rug or a blanket for me to use. I hobbled back down, praying that whatever she was going to find it wouldn't be like that rag Dickie gave me from his truck when I felt so sick.

"Here, Tug. Take this." She handed me an old wool blanket. "It's not great but it will get you home."

I looked at her and then broke out laughing myself. "I have no idea how we are going to explain this one to Dickie."

"We? I don't think that *we* are going to explain anything. I think you will be the one doing all the talking."

"That's nice, Lindy, real nice."

"Here, go and get out of those sopping clothes. I'll wait for you outside."

I took the blanket reluctantly. I had no choice here. "

When I emerged from the shanty, I must have looked a sight because as hard as Lindy tried not to laugh, she couldn't keep it in. I knew I looked like a fool, but hey, what's a guy supposed do?

She took my hand and led me back across the dock. She guided me gently and carefully. She knew where each and every weakness was on the old walk. She squeezed my hand and then, giggling again, she said, "You know, Tug, you have a real way of breaking the mood."

I shook my head and couldn't disagree with her on that score. You just had to love a girl like this.

Decision Time

MY FINAL DAYS OF VACATION were coming to an end. Lindy understood perfectly why I had to leave, even though she was terribly upset about it. Dickie, on the other hand, seemed to be somewhat less understanding. I saw a change in him. Something I couldn't put my fingers on, but it was there all the same. He looked a little older to me, but then again, Dickie was going on eighty. I couldn't figure it out but something was definitely different.

My last trips out on the water were very successful. I was becoming quite adept at crabbing and the guys didn't make so much fun of me. That was a welcome relief. They treated me like I was one of them and that was a triumph in and of itself. I loved being out on the water. It worked its magic on me. The sun and the salt helped to clear my head and put perspective on things like what I wanted and what I didn't. In the column of what I didn't want to do, was be a reporter any more. Oh yes, I wanted to write and do that more than anything in the world, but I didn't want to sit in my office and wait for the call to get right out to a fire or theft or even worse; a murder.

Dickie and I talked for hours when I would come home from the water. He always had something valuable to say to me. It's like he sat thinking about me while I was away from the house. I knew his attachment to me was becoming very intense. I felt the same about him. Our friendship was more than coincidence. It was destiny.

The night before I left, Lindy, Dickie and I had a wonderful, shore dinner. What else? Crabs naturally. We sat, talking afterwards and he started to tell me about an organization that he thought I would be interested in and might want to join.

"You know, son. I think it would be good for you to become involved in the Chesapeake Bay Foundation. They are a good organization and most of the members really care about the bay and what is happening to it."

"Tell me more about it, Dickie."

"Well, for one thing, they study the Chesapeake and what is going on in the water around these parts. They also check on the condition of the sea grasses and how they are being affected with all the changes. There are a number of watermen who belong and they have their say as to what they believe is causing all these shifts in the quality of the water and how it affects the crabs and the arsters. You might start there and then you'll see that there are folks from all around these parts who just need a little extra push to go further. We all need a leader, son."

Go further? What do you mean, Dickie?"

"The way I see it, and this is jist my opinion, is that you have what it takes to become a real advocate for us down here. For sure, you are one smart fella, and you have taken to us and our ways real fast. All that, combined with yer ability to write, could make a real difference. You could git people to start to fight all this. You know, son, all it takes is one, committed person to move mountains."

He was right on a couple of scores. One person can make a difference if their commitment is well placed and I definitely needed to belong to an organization where I could meet a lot of the people who wanted to get more involved in this battle to save the bay.

"Well, what do you think, son?"

"I think you are right…as usual. I need to start somewhere and I want to help. I want to do some other things too. But I really need to think this all through. That's why I have to leave, Dickie. I have to be absolutely certain of what I am doing or I won't be good at doing anything."

"You are going on home to Boston, aren't you son?"

"How did you know that? I didn't say a word to anyone, including Lindy, about that."

"Doesn't take a tree full of owls to figure that one out. I kin read you like a book. And I think you should go on home. You'll know what to do after you have seen your parents. A man needs to have his family behind him when he takes to doin' somethin' big and important."

I bit down hard on my lip. He was reading my mind again. He was good at that.

"It isn't going to be easy. They aren't going to understand all this and the fact that this has happened so fast isn't going to make it any better. They have a lot of years invested in me and I can see my Dad's face now when I tell him what I am thinking of doing."

"It ain't my business to stick my nose in, but they'll come around if they see that you are determined to do this. Parents have a way of doing that, ya know?"

"You don't know my dad, Dickie. He'll come unhinged over this. Come to think about it, Mom may not be so shot in the ass about it either. This will definitely not be what they expect of me as one of the long line of Alston men and…"

"Listen to me, son," he interrupted. "It's your life and it's what makes you happy that's all that counts in this world. If you continue to keep trying to please yer dad, you will eat yerself up alive inside. You will have spent yer life trying to be him and you will have missed all the joy that life can bring when you make yer own decisions and follow yer own dreams."

"I know you're right, Dickie, but my Dad is a force to be reckoned with."

"Just tell him from year heart. He can't fault you for that."

I had become so close to this man and he made me comfortable. I could say anything to him and he would just understand. He had more wisdom than a whole basket of Ivy League scholars.

"If I choose to leave the life I have made for myself, I just want to know I won't regret it later on. I mean I worked hard for the last year, to make a name for myself. It's not a big one yet but it's getting there. I am so confused, Dickie. Sometimes I wish I hadn't ever been sent down here."

"Then, we would never have met, son."

I realized I was being a jerk and I think I hurt his feelings.

"I know that Dickie. I wouldn't have missed meeting you for anything. What started out to be one kind of a story is ending up an entirely different proposition for me."

"That's how life goes. When you think you have life by the balls; it spins you around and kicks you in the ass."

I rubbed my head while laughing at him. "You do have a point there, Dickie. Maybe it's not quite the way I would have put it, but it gets to the heart of the matter really well."

"You think hard about all the things you have seen and heard. Then, you will make yer decision."

Think? Was he kidding? Think is all I was going to be doing on my trip home to Boston. "I will, Dickie, I will be doing nothing else. Thank you so much for everything."

Lindy had been outside doing some yard work. It was as if she sensed that I needed this time with Dickie alone. When she did come in, she noticed how quiet it was in the room. She walked over to me and sat down. I took her hand gently in mine. I needed that intimacy between us. We both knew that this was going to be our last time together for probably quite a while. Dickie looked at the two of us and knew it was time for him to make his exit.

"I am turnin' in fer the night. You two go along and go sit out on the porch or take a walk down to the pier. I'll see you in the morning, son."

I shot him a wink and he knew I was saying thank you. He understood everything so well.

SAYING GOOD BYE TO LINDY was tough enough, but when I stood in the driveway saying good bye to Dickie, he looked like a wounded pet whose master was leaving him. In such a short time, we had become very close. We just understood one another.

The three of us made the good byes quick and when I pulled away, I looked back to see Dickie cradling Lindy in his arms. It was so hard to say good bye.

The long hours ahead proved productive. I called in to the office to see what was going on. I was in luck that Roger was in his office.

"How's it going, Rog?"

"Well, another country heard from. Aren't I the one who should be asking you that question? Things here have been busy as hell since you left. Summer time brings all the crazies out and some of it hasn't been too pleasant."

"I'm sorry about that, Rog, but I have to tell you, I haven't paid attention to any of the news."

"Just as well," he mumbled back to me. "You sound like you are in your car. Are you heading back? I hope so. I have missed you one hell of a lot."

I must admit I felt guilty when I took off on good old Roger, but he would have to get used to it. Maybe sooner than later.

"I am in the car, but I am not heading to Baltimore yet."

I could hear him sigh. I knew he wasn't happy about that fact.

"So, where are you going?"

"I am on my way to Bean Town to see the folks."

"You're what? I thought you were down in that little town on the shore."

"I was, but I decided I better haul my ass home before they disowned me."

"I see. Guilt is an ugly thing," he chuckled.

"I just need to talk with my dad about a few things."

"Whoa, it must be something really big if you are driving all those hours. Not my business though. I hope it goes well. It's just that I know how you and your dad can get into it."

"Yeah. Well it's my hope that he and I can talk one on one, face to face. We need to come to an understanding this time."

"That would be nice. I will shoot up a quick prayer for you. When should we expect you?"

"I'll be back at work on Monday. I don't think I better stretch it out any longer or I may as well not come back at all."

"You've got that one straight. I think even Max misses you."

"Give me a break, Roger. I know Max likes me, but I wouldn't say he would lose any sleep if I decided to leave."

"Is that what you are thinking of doing, Tug?"

I sure didn't want to let on that that was exactly what I was thinking. Roger was my best buddy there, but his mouth worked like a sieve when he had a good piece of gossip to share with the gang. In that respect, he and Lady Macbeth got along perfectly. Hey, maybe she would be a good match for him. Perish that thought.

"No," I lied. "I am not thinking that. I just need to see my dad, that's all."

"Okay, good buddy. If there's nothing else pressing to discuss, I gotta run."

"I hear you, Rog. I'll see you on Monday. Behave yourself."

"Yeah, like that is going to happen."

After we hung up on one another I thought how much I would miss that guy if things worked out for me and I really did want to do what I was thinking of doing. Roger was a good friend and we sure had had a lot of fun together. He would go all the way to the top in his newspaper career. He wanted it. Now, I knew I did not.

Mikey was the first one to greet me. He was shooting hoops in the driveway when I pulled in. The look on his face was shear shock.

"What the hell…"

"Surprise, little brother. The Tugger is home."

"Did Mom or Dad know you were coming?"

"Nope. I thought I would just surprise you all, and I see I did."

"Mom will go nuts. She will be so happy though. I have been driving her crazy."

"Hmm," I growled. "Have you been a bad boy, Mikey?"

"Not bad really. I've just been being a guy. And this college thing is out of hand."

I grabbed the basketball away from him and shot it up in the air. As usual, I missed. "Can't decide, huh? Well, you are running out of time, so you better get your ass moving."

"I still have another year," he hissed as he shot one up and naturally it went in.

"It doesn't work like that when you are a jock, Mikey. You know that and shouldn't be taking it so nonchalantly."

"I know, I know, Tug. Don't you get on me about it. I think I have already figured it out anyway."

"Who's the lucky school?"

Mikey loved to tease me and this time was no exception. "The Peace Corps. Don't you think that's a great choice?"

I grabbed my bags and headed into the house, flipping him the finger. However, it would be like him to do just that. Now that really would be the end of Mom and Dad.

I threw my bags to the side of the door and walked into the kitchen. As always, Mom was standing over the sink getting dinner ready. I slinked quietly up behind her and put my hands over her eyes. "Guess who?" I asked in a deep and mysterious voice.

"Tug? Is that you?" she murmured in a soft and hopeful voice.

"How did you know?"

She swung around and hugged me so hard that my insides nearly burst.

"I don't understand…why are you here? Oh, it doesn't matter. You *are* here and that's all that matters."

I kissed her sweetly on her cheek and then picked up a carrot from the pile she was slicing. "What's for dinner?"

"I can't believe this. As we are speaking I am making your favorite dinner of pot roast. Could you smell it from your car?"

"That's funny, Mom. See? I guess I was meant to come home tonight."

"Are you staying for a while or is this an overnighter?"

"I am staying the weekend and then I really have to return to work on Monday."

"Your Dad will be so happy to see you."

I wasn't as sure as she was about that, especially given what I had to talk to him about. "I am eager to see Dad too. I want to talk with him. Do you think he will have time after dinner? Or do you two have plans?" They sometimes went to concerts on Friday nights. It was the one real cultural thing he did for her and she relished the nights they went.

"No, I think he will be home this evening. We don't have anything planned." She studied my face and then said, "Is there something special on your mind? I mean you drove a long way and I don't think you would have done that if it was just to shoot the bull."

"As always, you see right through me, Mom. I do want to talk with Dad about something. Something important. But I really don't want to go into it right now, if you don't mind. I think I will head upstairs and take a shower and rest until dinner, if that's all right with you?"

"Of course it's all right, Tug. You will find that I have kept your room exactly like you left it. I even put all your adventure stories in a bound notebook. It's by the bed. Maybe you can read some of them before you drift off for a nap."

I hugged her tightly again and said, "That's so like you, Mom. You and I have always understood one another so well. I really would like to go back through those old adventure stories."

"They were good, Tug. They were really good," she smiled and then turned back to continue slicing the carrots for the roast. "I'll call you when dinner is ready. And, Tug, I am so glad you are home."

I blew her a kiss as I left the room. I was glad to be home too.

THE SHOWER FELT SO GOOD. I settled onto my bed and reached for the leather bound notebook I had always kept my stories in. I began to go through them one by one until I found my favorite- *The Pirate with the Glass Eye*. It really was an amazing story given that I was thirteen when I wrote it. I wouldn't be at all surprised if I could sell it today and watch it land up on the teen best seller list. Maybe I could fall back on that if nothing else worked out for me, I chuckled to myself.

"Pirate Noble was his name and he cut a handsome, sturdy figure. He was young, when he took over his own boat called *The Sea Treasure*, and he was one of the most feared pirates of his time.

No matter what age the writer is, they say that we put a bit of ourselves into a particular character. Now, reading this tale of long ago, I wondered if Pirate Noble was really me.

Someone was poking at me in my dream and I wanted them to stop. They kept on doing it and when I opened my eyes, it wasn't a dream. It was my father.

"Hey, Tug. Wake up."

"Dad," I said sleepily as I jerked my body straight up.

"I couldn't believe my eyes when I pulled the car into the driveway and saw your Cherokee. Is everything Okay? I mean you told me you weren't coming home. Didn't things go so well down in that town?"

"No, everything went all right. I just decided that maybe you were right. I should come home and see everyone before heading back to work."

"Something's wrong, I know it. I know you, Tug, and I know when something isn't going right for you."

"I told you, Dad, everything is going fine. It's just that I wanted to talk with you. I hoped that we could go down to the wharf tonight and kick back a few drinks and talk."

I knew I hadn't fooled him. No one could fool Ted Alston. He was way ahead of the crowd. I could see him looking right through me and I would have to come clean sooner or later. But later would be after dinner. I was determined he wouldn't get a thing out of me until after I had eaten that roast.

"I...I think that would be nice," he stuttered. "We haven't done that in quite some time. We'll leave right after that wonderful dinner your mother has cooked for us. Speaking of that, we better get down there before she throws a fit."

"I'll wash up and be right down, Dad."

Turning to look at me before he left he room, he added, "I am glad to see you here. It means a lot to your mom, you know."

Well, I would have liked it if he could have thrown himself into that sentence too, but I suppose this was his way of telling me that.

Dinner was out of this world and we all kidded with one another just like old times. Speaking of old times, when we all cleared the plates and dishes from the table, Mikey grabbed the long rope from behind the kitchen door. "Anyone for a game of tug of war?" he shouted.

I thought I would die. "I can't believe we even have that thread bare rope around anymore. And that that red line is still on the kitchen floor."

"Want to take me on and earn that nickname, Tug?" Mikey yelled with a grin on his face.

"No thank you. If you remember, I passed that dumb game on to you and Dad ages ago. "

"Go on, Tug," My Dad encouraged. "With all those new muscles you have acquired this summer, you might win handily."

I *was* buff, wasn't I? All those days out on the water, hauling crab pots, had toned my tan body pretty tight. I probably could give Mikey or Dad a run for their money, but the truth was I hated that game. I never won and it made me feel physically diminished compared to all the other Alston jocks.

"No Dad, you go on and for God's sake yank that stupid grin off Mikey's face, will you?"

With that the two of them went at it. They huffed and puffed for a few minutes, looking as if their faces would explode from the intensity of the battle and then in two stiff yanks, Mikey had Dad across the line and down on the floor.

Looking up at me a bit sheepishly, the old master of the game knew his days as reigning champ were definitely over. "Are you ready for those drinks now Tug?"

I bent down and extended my hand to him and with a broad smile on my face I pulled him up and said, "I sure am, Dad. I think we both can handle that game."

Oops, He Said It Again

OUR HOME WASN'T ALL THAT far a walk down to the water. I hadn't realized how much I had missed doing this particularly since my brother and I used to complain like hell about it. As kids, Mom and Dad would do what Mikey and I called the "forced marches." You know the kind: when a stroll turns into an all-day event. Come to think about it, we didn't mind it all that much. We ate down at the dock and went to the aquarium and had some of that solid bonding time. I seemed to be closer to my Dad then. Oh well, times change and now I had to get some of those feeling back between us if I was ever going to get him to realize what I wanted to do with my life.

"A lovely evening, isn't it Tug?"   •

"Sure is. It's a real Boston summer's night." I took a deep breath and could smell the old familiar smells of the town I grew up in. But mostly, for some odd reason, it was the water that called to me. I instantly became a little homesick for the water I had left a few hours ago. And the beautiful girl who lived there.

"So, what's this all about, Tug? Not that I'm not enjoying this time with you, but something's on your mind."

"You know me so well, Dad. I do have a few things to kick around with you, but that can wait for a while. Let's enjoy our walk first, ok?"

"You're on. I can tell that it must be serious though because I can't remember you ever asking me to go for a walk."

"I never had to. Mom always was the one out the door and ready to go."

"She is something, isn't she? I wish I had the lust for the outdoors that she has."

"You might like it, Dad. You might find that the outdoors gives you a whole new perspective on life instead of being cooped up in your office writing sport's stories."

"Hang on there, Tug. I do have to go to those games, you know. That's as close to the outdoors as I want to get."

It was good to banter with him. I have to admit, he had a grand sense of humor, and while I am far more intense about life; Dad could always find something good about anything. I hoped that this would be the case when I told him why I had come home to visit.

Settled in at one of the bars along the wharf, Dad guzzled away at the beer he had ordered. I decided nothing less than a good, stiff martini would do for this occasion.

"So, are you going to get to it, Tug, or are you just going to fiddle around with that fancy glass your drink is in?"

My heart began to race. The time had come. "Well, it's like this Dad, and please hear me out before you say anything, all right?"

He looked at me with that stunned expression that said, good God, what's all this about?"

"I promise. Go ahead."

"It's obvious that you and Max have been talking on a regular basis. That pisses me off to a degree but you are old friends. I like him a lot and I know he is one of the best in the business. And I know that you had something to do with my job at *The Sun*, and that pissed me off at the time. But none of that really matters much anymore."

"Tug, where is all this heading?"

"I asked you to hear me out, Dad."

"You're right. Go on."

"You know I went down to the Eastern Shore to cover a story and you know that I came back and wrote that story, even if it wasn't at all what Max and I thought it was going to be about. He was great and let me run with the story I returned with. You told me that you read the story and that's where all this began."

He held his hand up and said, "Time out, Tug. You are going in circles with this. Just tell me what this is about."

"I'm getting to it, please?"

Dad sat back and now he was the one fiddling with his drink.

"That story stirred up a whole lot of dust. Mostly from the developers and a few other advertisers, but I didn't care. Max set up a meeting with all of them and I presented my case to them and gave them a lot to think about. Well, some of them took it pretty well, but I could tell, some were not of the same mind. After the meeting Max and I hashed it all out and that's when I took my vacation. It was to think things through clearly. Now I have."

He sat there; almost afraid to say a word, so I kept on going. I took a deep breath and went for it.

"I had a wonderful time down there in Somerville and I fished those waters several times with good watermen. I learned how to bait the crab pots and then bring them in. I loved it like I have never loved anything in my life. Those people are fighting for their lives, their homes, and their way of life…"

"Hold on, Tug," he interrupted. "You aren't about to tell me what I think you are, are you? This isn't like one of those fantasy stories you used to write about, is it? I read that piece you wrote, and I knew you were pretty exercised about something down there, but you can't take off and go fight some crusade for those people."

He had figured it out. I should have guessed he wasn't going to be too happy about it either. "Will you just listen, Dad? I have become very close to this man Dickie Short. He is the most amazing individual I have ever met and he is so sincere about this subject. And he is right."

I could tell the minute the words were out of my mouth about Dickie that Dad was going to unleash. He did.

"I don't give one shit about this man or what you *think* about what is happening down there. You might think he is right, but everything in life has two sides to the story. That's what you were trained to see, remember?"

"I do remember that. And I am damned good at what I do. Max thinks I am one of the best young reporters he has ever seen and…"

"And what?" he cut me off again. "And that he is going to put up with you even if you unintentionally begin to run his paper out of business by pissing off the people who pay for that paper? I don't think so, son."

Son, that was the word Dickie always called me. It hit me like a ton of bricks how much I wished Dickie were right here with me now telling Dad how he felt. Surely he would have to see the sincerity of the man and his desperate plea to stop what is going on.

"Look, Tug. I think I know what's coming next and don't think your mother is the only one that knows that there is some young gal attached to this crusade of yours. You think you're in love, and you think you can change things, and for God's sakes you think you can do it. Well, I am telling you life won't stop for you and whatever you are planning to do. Where there is money to be made, nothing stops it."

What could I say to him to make him understand? He was fired up now and when that happened not much calmed him down. I was in too deep to back out, so I did what I came home to do. Maybe not a wise choice, but a choice I had to make.

"I am leaving the paper, Dad," I said as calmly as I could muster. "I know you will never understand this decision, but I want to continue my writing; just not for the paper. I love it down there, and yes, there is a girl involved, but she has nothing to do with my decision. As a matter of fact, she would be the first one to say I better measure twice, cut once. I am going to do this and I was hoping you would at least give me your support."

I have never seen him sit so still. I could see the veins in his neck sticking out like a sore thumb. I braced for the attack, but was shocked when he finally answered me.

Drawing in a deep breath and then letting it out in one of those deadly sounds of desperation, he said, "I can see you are going to do what you are going to do, so my trying to talk you out of it appears useless. But you have to understand me clearly, Tug. I had dreams for you. Dreams that when you graduated from Harvard you would come on board *The Globe* and then someday maybe take my place. When that didn't happen, I hoped that your going outside for a while would eventually lead you back here to your home. In time I accepted that and was happy that Max took you into his paper. You earned that. I didn't ask Max for any favors like you think. You are brilliant and he knew that. He jumped at the opportunity to have you there. Now, you tell me that you want to turn in another direction all together. That's not so unusual for young people these days, but this? You want to go live in some jerk water town and fight for something that will never happen. How can I tell you that I am happy for you and give you any of my support? You have lost your mind."

I knew the shit would hit the fan and that he would never see what I was trying to accomplish on the shore. But I loved him. He was being totally honest with me and I had to respect his point of view. Perhaps he would come around and perhaps he wouldn't. Time would tell. He may be right. Maybe I have lost my mind...and my heart, but it's what I am going to do with his support or without it. I decided to make one more stab at it.

"You may be right, Dad. I may well have lost my mind. But I am certain on this. I can feel this one. It's the right place for me at the right time. You would know that if you came there with me." I thought I would throw that one out and see where it landed.

At least I noticed that the veins in his neck had sounded the retreat as he leaned across the small table and said quietly,

"I don't think I will ever come down there to see you. It would just be too painful for me to see you there and not in a big city, doing what you are so good at."

Ouch. He wasn't giving one inch. But hope springs eternal. "I will be good at this too, Dad. Please just tell me that you won't stop talking to me. I couldn't stand that. Please?"

It must have been the look on my face or maybe the shear begging in my voice. He relented some and then I saw it. Yes, I saw it. A slow half smile crossed that handsome face of his. Now, I really was nervous. I had no idea what game he would try this time to get me to come to his side.

"I will always love you, Tug and I will always talk to you, but you sure have grabbed me by the balls with this one. Does your *mother* know what you are planning to do?"

"No, I don't think so. She might intuit that something has happened to me and she sure was shocked when I came home. You know how she knows things."

He slid back in his chair and I saw a gentle light come into his eyes. Yes," he said slowly as if he were thinking of how much more in tune she was with her sons than he was. It always gratified him that she was the way she was. That's why they made such a good team all these years. Here he was able to communicate to everyone in the world, but not with his sons. She, on the other hand, had our number. She knew just about everything that was happening inside and out with us.

He was softening and I knew it. I sure was glad he said he wouldn't be angry at me. At least to my face. "So, Dad, that's about all I have to say." An understatement for sure.

"No, that's not all there is to say, Tug. Why don't you tell me about this girl and this man Dickie Short. They seem to have captured your fascination."

"The girl's name is Lindy Short. She is a grand niece of Dickie's and she's absolutely wonderful. You would love her. She has more sense than any of the girls I met at college. She has an education and when we met, I just knew she was the one."

"Like a thunder bolt hitting you, huh? I know that feeling. That's the way it was with your mom. Maybe we are more alike than we think."

I smiled at him and ordered us another round.

"Dickie is like no one I have ever met. He is part waterman, part philosopher, and has a keener mind than any professor at Harvard."

With a giant chuckle, he answered, "Now you are really stretching it, Tug."

"No I'm not. Talking with him is an inspiration. Oh, I'll grant you that he talks like nothing I have ever heard before, but he is funny, wise and very giving. He has extended his home to me, and I love it there. It's close by the marsh and the water he loves so much. He is now eighty years old and he can't go out on the water anymore. His legs gave out. His wife died a few years back and he misses her terribly. Then I came along and he took to me like a crab to a pot full of bait."

A look of horror dawned on his face. "I see you have picked up some of that Eastern Shore lingo yourself. I would never have believed that if I hadn't just heard it from your own lips.

"It's easy to do when you are around them for a while. I have to tell you, Dad, I have never laughed so hard at things until I began to see it all through their eyes and expressions. They are their own way of life. It's a life that is disappearing quickly and when it does it will be gone forever. I have to try to help them and make people see that they can't completely destroy what has been there for generations."

He stared at me and I knew he was beginning to see my passion. Finally, he was beginning to understand.

"You better hope that you don't make a bigger mess of this, Tug."

He was weakening; I could see it in his eyes.

"I will tell you this. I can hear it in your voice and feel it is in your heart. It's called compassion. There is nothing wrong with compassion but sometimes it can lead you to places you don't want to be. However, I see in you, my father. Grandpa was a man of great compassion and that's why he always favored you. He saw that keen intelligence and rare gift of loving what was inside of people. So, I am not really shocked. You have his genes. And you have your Mother's good looks."

A tear formed in my eyes, as a smile crossed my face.

"There is nothing more wonderful, I suppose, than a young man, with a good mind; with a cause."

I was so taken back, I didn't know what to say. So neither of us said anything. We just sat there, sipping our beers.

Finally I broke the silence. "Gee Dad, you are waxing poetic. I love it. Maybe I can make you as proud of me doing this than I ever could have in the newspaper business. I know it's going to be a tough fight and I know what money means to the big guys, but sometimes…just sometimes the little guy can win the game. The written word is a mighty weapon."

"You are right on all counts, but remember this: The big guys eat the little guys for breakfast and then spit them out. It's their game and they love it."

"Trust me on this. Please? I can do this."

Dad began to nod his head. I could tell he was digesting everything we had said to one another. He was beginning to believe in me.

"I am not very good at this father son thing sometimes, Tug, but you have been a man and come home to talk this out with me. I can't tell you how much I appreciate that. You are my son and I am proud of you and for whatever reason this moment in time has come to you; take it. Maybe I am a little jealous of your youth and maybe I am jealous of this man Dickie, who has made such an impression on you. I am ashamed of that fact, but that's the way I feel. Go after this dream and make it happen. I know it's going to be rough out there, but I want you to know that I will support you in this. Maybe your old man can even help you with it. Max will be losing a good reporter, but I think he may know he has already lost you. When will you tell him? I want to be prepared for that call."

You could have blown me over with a feather. Here was the great Ted Alston, descending from Mt. Olympus, to give me, a mere mortal his blessing. I choked up and now tears were streaking down my cheeks. We had finally told one another how we truly felt. Mom was right. He loved me. And I always loved him. I just couldn't see it through my own insecurity. He was choking too, but I knew his tears were never going to be seen. He was an Alston man. It was the way he was.

"As soon as I return. I am going to put my place up for sale and then head on out to Somerville."

"I see," he said pensively. "That soon, huh? Well I guess there is no use in waiting. A man has to seek his destiny and it appears you have found yours. It's kind of ironic and all, you know?"

"What's that, Dad?"

"That you should find your destiny in a place called Somerville."

"Wow, I never thought of that. I will have to save that one up and use it in a future novel."

"Just give me the credit," he laughed.

I didn't want this night to end. I had waited so long to have a closeness with him and now it was time to leave.

"You know, the shore is a beautiful place in the nice weather. Maybe Mom and I will have to come down there and check this place out when you get settled. Maybe we could even get her out on one of those fishing boats." He stood up and took the bill. I went to take it from him and he waved his hand at me and said, "No, this one is on me. You have my blessing, Tug. And maybe before you make a quick get away, you could sit down and tell your mother all about our conversation."

"I will, Dad. I promise. I will talk to her first thing tomorrow and then I think I should go back to Baltimore and face the music."

"I have a good hunch, my dear boy, knowing Max all these years, it won't be music you will be hearing."

I laughed and then followed him out of the bar. The night was even more beautiful on our way back home. But maybe it was because I was with my Dad. All was right with my world.

Walking along the narrow streets, the old streetlights shone down on the sparkling pavement as the wind rustled lightly through the trees. Boston is such a beautiful town. I love it. I always will. Heading up the steep hill toward our house, I looked back and saw the lights on the boats in the harbor. My mind returned to the stories I wrote long ago about pirates and the heroes of the American Revolution. Now, I was going to be one of them in a different time and place. I was both sad and exhilarated at the same time. How can that be? I was about to find out.

Just before we walked inside our house, I stopped my Dad and hugged him.

"Thank you for tonight, Dad. I think we crossed a big barrier and it was certainly about time. Please believe me that this is the right thing for me to do and it means everything to me to have you in my corner. I *will* change things."

Putting his arm around my shoulders, he opened the door and said, "Of course you will. You are an Alston. You are my son."

Shootout At The Ok Corral

"LOOK JOHN, LET'S BE REASONABLE. Calm down, for God's sake. I am sure it wasn't as bad as you are making it out to be."

"Like hell it wasn't, Max. I have a mess down here and then along comes your young *Crusader Rabbit* with some goddamn old man who tenpins me up against a truck. A fucking truck, for Christ's sake!"

"I am sure there is an explanation for all this, John. What did you say that got that old man so mad and who was he?"

"I didn't say anything. Tug and I were talking about this development project and he started to mumble something about infrastructure. You know the same shit *you* let him write about. That's when this old bastard, I think his name was Dickie Short, grabbed me and nailed me on the truck. I mean what the hell?"

Max shook his head. He couldn't believe this was happening. Dickie Short was back in his life and he wanted to puke.

"I'm sorry, John. I really am. I had no idea about any of this. Tug went on vacation and how the hell did I know that he was heading back down there? As for Dickie Short, I know this man…"

"You *know* this bastard? He blasted. "How on Gods' green earth could you possible know this kind of a being?"

"It's a long story. I think I mentioned him and his letters at that meeting, but I really don't want to go into it right now. Are you all right?"

"Yeah, I'm all right. It will take more than that asshole to take me down, but I tell you, I have a war down here. The last thing I need is to see that young stallion getting the folks any more exercised than they are right now. They cheered him on, Max. They cheered him on like he was their hero."

"Again, John, I'm sorry. I will take care of it when he comes back in."

"You're damned right you will take care of it. I have folks out here protesting with signs. With signs, do you hear me? I have never seen anything like this before. To add to that I have these Goddamn local yokel papers down here pounding the drum every week about how I am invading their homeland. Invading their homeland? I am helping their economy and bringing good people down here to live. You would think I was some kind of a criminal."

"To them, you are, John. You and I both know that this subject of over development has been boiling on the back burner for quite some time now. It appears that it has hit critical mass and is about to spill over."

"Max, let's understand something, shall we? I pay a lot of money to advertise in your paper. I even met with this kid Alston and I tried to keep this from getting out of hand. I thought I was buying some time with the kid. If you can't rein him in, I will pull my advertising. I want his ass on the carpet. I don't give a shit what you have to do. I want this to stop. Have I made myself perfectly clear?"

"Yes. Yes you have John. When he comes back I will take care of this once and for all."

"Then I have your word on this matter."

"You do."

"Good. Then I will get back to what I am doing down here. I don't want to see anymore stories, Max. I have millions invested in this project and if you can't deal with him; then I will and you and I know I can do that."

The phone went dead. Sweat was pouring down Max's armpits. The Dawson account brought in big money and now he had to figure out just how to deal with Tug.

"Beth? Come in here." He shouted from his office.

Beth had heard it all. She hadn't ever heard him this mad. She scurried her pretty, little body into his office at light speed.

"Yes, Max."

"When is Alston due back?"

"Why, I think he is coming back today."

"Good. When he dawns the door of his office, I want you to have him come see me immediately. I mean immediately. Before he even has time to get his coffee. Do I make myself clear on this?"

"Yes, Max. I will get right to it."

Beth always came in earlier than anyone else, except for the production folks. Max was an early riser and he hit his office before seven. It was now eight o'clock and Tug would come in around eight thirty. She had to make sure she got to him first thing. Max was on the warpath and from what she heard, which was everything, Tug was headed for a heap of big trouble.

It wasn't easy going back home. I wanted to stay longer and have some more time with Mikey and my mom. But duty called. I felt truly happy for the first time in my life. Dad and I had connected in a way I never thought possible. Mom was totally understanding. Wasn't she always? She wanted me happy and she was so eager to meet Lindy. When that would happen was anyone's guess. Maybe they would come down to visit.

When I opened the door to my townhouse she almost felt like she knew she was going to be sold. I loved the place but the time had come to move on with my life. Maybe Roger could buy it. He loved it so much and he made more money now that he too had been at the paper for a year. Oh, the parties he would throw. My poor home. I would call a real estate agent this morning and get on with it. I don't want any grass to grow under my feet. I miss the shore and I miss Dickie and damn it all; I miss Lindy. But first, I have to get up the nerve to talk with Max. That's not going to be easy. He will be so disappointed and he will try to talk me out of it, but a man's gotta do what a man's gotta do.

THE FIRST THING I SAW when I put my things down on my desk was a huge sign that read: Max wants to see you immediately. Don't stop for coffee. Immediately! Signed Beth.

"Oh boy, what now?" I said out loud. Better get right up there. Beth seems kind of agitated this morning. Oh well, I'll flash that old Alston smile at her and she will melt. I know she would give anything to be in Lindy's spot right now. Sorry Beth, you lost. But you never had a chance anyway.

I almost tripped over Roger as I left my cubicle. "Hey Rog. Good to see you, old buddy. I have to get upstairs right now, but how about lunch?"

Roger shot me a half smile and then said, "Hi Tug. Yeah, lunch will work."

"Gotta run. I'll catch you later. I have a lot to tell you."

"I'm sure you do," he said again with an odd look on his face.

What the hell was that all about? I thought. Roger looked as if he had seen a ghost or something.

As I walked through the door, Beth looked up and instantly turned a pale shade of white. What was going on?

She never even said hello. She pointed her overly long nails to the door. "Max is in there, waiting for you, Tug."

"What? No smile and funny jokes at my expense?"

"Not this morning."

Something was definitely wrong with this picture.

I tapped lightly on his door and walked in. I wasn't two steps into his office when he looked up at me from his desk and barked, "Sit down Tug. We have to talk."

"Good morning to you too Max. What's going on around here? Did something happen that I should know about?"

"You might say that," he shot, as he stood up and straightened his fairly fit middle aged body. He was what women would call distinguished, but right now, all he looked was angry.

"I had an interesting call this morning. Can you guess who it was?"

"No. No I can't. I just got back from vacation remember?"

"Yes, I do remember, Tug. I hope it was a good one for you."

"It was. It was very good, Max."

"That's nice," he said almost sarcastically. What was going on?

"John Dawson called me. Do you remember him?"

Shit! That old bastard called him and now I was beginning to get the picture.

"Why yes, I remember him. He was at our meeting."

"Yes he was. And he was on the shore working on his new project when he told me he ran into you. That is, he ran into you and that Goddamn Dickie Short."

The gloves were off. The cat was out of the bag and I was in deep doo doo.

"Yes, I did see him as I recall. Dickie and I went for a drive and happened to pass by his new development project."

"Did you now? Did you also speak with him and did you get into a fight with him and did your little old friend there throw him up against a fucking truck?"

Biting down hard on my lip, I said, "Why yes Max; all that occurred."

"All that occurred did it? Well you have managed to stir up a lot of crap, Tug, on that little vacation of yours." He emphasized the word vacation. "He has threatened to pull his advertising if we can't do something about all this. Now how do you propose we can fix this mess?"

I was sinking fast. I knew that I wasn't going to have to tell him my plans after all. No, I wouldn't need to muster up any guts here. It was already taken care of by John Dawson.

"Will you even listen to my side, Max, or was that a rhetorical question?"

Max sat down and said, "I'll let you have two minutes to tell me your side before I kick your ass."

Nope, I definitely didn't have to muster up any courage here.

"Yes, I was there. Dickie and I went for a ride along the coast and through the towns. It gave me a far more complete picture of the looming calamity that is about to happen to the Eastern Shore. It is already too late in some parts, but there is still hope for others. Then we saw these protestors and I stopped my car and got out. I interviewed some of them…"

"You what?" he yelled. "I hope to God you didn't tell them you wrote for us."

He used the word wrote, as in not present tense. "Well, I had to get their point of view."

"Jesus H. Christ! I don't believe this. Couldn't you just have gone home to Boston?"

"I did go home to Boston before my vacation was over."

Max grabbed his head and looked like he was going to scream. I think I caught most of the drift, but I knew this wasn't over.

"Let me get this straight. You left here and went to the shore. Then you got into your car with that insane old bastard, who has already caused me more pain than a human should have to bear, and then you got into a fight with one of our biggest advertisers, while all these crazies were watching, and then you went and played Mr. Big Shot reporter, and then you went home to Boston?"

I almost laughed watching poor, dear Max having a melt down, but knew that wouldn't be too smart. "That's about it. That's how it all went down," I croaked.

Max slumped down in his chair. I think he was trying to regroup, so I seized the moment. "If I get this straight, Max, I think you are trying to tell me that you got chewed out for what I did that you didn't even know I was doing, and that the next thing you are going to tell me is that I am fired. Is that about right?"

Max slowly turned his head and stared at me. He was simply stupefied.

"Yes, yes, Tug, that's about right. How do you feel about them apples?"

"Actually I feel pretty good about 'them apples'," I responded in a light tone. "I am sorry you had to go through this but I was coming in today to tell you I am leaving the paper anyway. I went to Boston to tell my folks and now here we are. Isn't it funny how it all turned out?"

"Funny? That's what your word is for this Goddamn mess is? Funny?" Max stammered out. "Frankly I can't believe it is only Monday and I feel like throwing up."

"Don't do that Max. I told you I am leaving. You can come out of this looking like a prince. Just tell John you fired me. He will love that action. I tell you, he isn't a nice man, Max. He is a bastard of another kind. You know him on a different level, but he is an out and out asshole."

Max was coming back to being somewhat coherent. He was thinking over that this might turn out all right after all.

John did want him gone and that is what was going to happen. So maybe he wouldn't have to kill himself at that.

"What did your Dad say? I can almost hear him now."

"Well, at first, I thought he was going to kill me, but then we talked it out and he said he was on my side. It was the best conversation I have ever had with him."

Max couldn't stay angry at me. He had known me all his life and this was a tough situation.

"That's a really good thing, Tug. Your Dad can be tough and I am beginning to see that you are a lot like him. I know you always felt differently about things and were sorry you weren't the jock he was, but I knew how much he loved you. He only wanted the very best for you. I am going to miss you. Do I even have to ask you where you are going?"

I smiled and said, "No, I imagine you know. I am headed down to Somerville. That's where my destiny lies for now."

"Do you have a job? Or are you going to make John Dawson's life miserable?"

"No, and yes," I laughed.

"When do you want to leave here? I have no intention of having you walked out. This will be a mutual decision. I kind of thought this might happen. You are very talented, Tug. No matter what you do, you will do it well. I won't even ask you about our little friend, Mr. Short. I just don't think I could take it."

"Come on, Max. You know he was your source of entertainment. He is quite a man. I love him. He is the real deal and they don't come like that much anymore."

"Keep in touch. I am sure I will see you around Boston when you go to visit your folks. I just hope I will be able to understand you. I can hear their sayings starting to slip into your lexicon already. Be careful, my boy. You might end up one of them in the end.

Max stood and came around his desk. I stood up too. It was time to say good bye. He patted me on the back and then slung one of his arms around my shoulder. "I will miss you. Roger will be happy because I am going to add to his responsibilities here. Please don't tell him until I have it all figured out. Good God, I will have to deal with that over inflated ego of his."

I broke out laughing. "I won't say a word. His life is beginning to look up though. I was planning lunch with him anyway. I wanted to tell him that my place down in Fells Point is going on the market. He has always loved it. I will miss that guy. Take good care of him."

"I will and remember to stay in touch."

"Oh, I will keep in touch, Max. You are an old friend of the family and besides, you *will* be hearing from me."

"I shudder to think of what that means. Go with God, Tug and please keep Dickie Short away from me."

"Will do, Max. He really loves you, you know."

"Get out of here, Tug, before I really do throw your ass out of here."

Wishes Do Come True

"Do you really think he will come back, Uncle Dickie?"

"Of course he will, Lindy girl. I suspect a team of wild horses couldn't keep him away from you."

Lindy sat on Dickie's worn out sofa, biting her fingers nails, as she pondered what her future would be like if Tug never did return. "I don't know what I would do if he changed his mind after seeing his family. I know that they are going to try to talk him into staying in Baltimore. I mean I would if I were them."

Dickie stared at her and saw the misery she was going through. He thought back on how he felt when he was so in love with his dear Shirley. How he would spend every waking minute he could with her. When he came back in from the water, he would run to her house and drive her parents crazy staying there until it was time for him to go. He smiled thinking of all the meals her mother made for him, until her father told him one day to marry her before they went broke. Those were the good old days; when love seemed to be so innocent and uncomplicated.

"Earth to Uncle Dickie. What are you thinking about?"

"How much I kin remember all the hurtin' when I was in love with your Aunt Shirley."

"Ah, come on. You didn't act like a love sick puppy, did you?"

"Sure did. Why, as a matter of fact, if I hadn't married her I think her parents would have skinned me alive. They couldn't wait fer us to get hitched. Now that was a wedding."

"Tell me about it, Uncle Dickie. I don't think I have ever heard about your wedding."

"Well it was quite the occasion. Near all the town turned out. My folks and hers were good friends and her daddy was a waterman too. Most all of us were watermen back then and thems that weren't had somethin' one way or another to do with the water. Some had land jobs by day and then went out on the water at night to get the crabs in summertime and in the winter, we all trapped the *rats*. Mighty good eatin' all year long."

"I'll bet Aunt Shirley was a beautiful bride."

"The purtiest, if I do say so myself. But all the men wanted Shirley and what she saw in me; only the good Lord knows. We had a real fancy wedding for those times. We were all purty poor, but her mama and daddy fixed us up nice. After the service, the food that was all around could have fed an army."

"I'll bet it was nice. Do you have any pictures of your wedding? I don't recall ever seeing any."

Dickie handed her some sweet tea and sat down beside her. "No, we don't have any pictures anymore. We had a fire in our first house and they all got burned up. Shirley like to die over that, but I told her it wasn't important. We had each other and we didn't need no pictures."

"That's awful, Uncle Dickie. I can imagine how sad she was about that."

"Well, you know how you women are about those things. Men don't care much, I suppose. When we moved into this house I kin tell you that I made darned sure that it was safe and wired right. That's important. The first place went up so fast we were lucky to git out alive."

"God!" Lindy exclaimed. "I don't even want to think about that. I can't imagine what my life would have been like without you and Aunt Shirley."

"Now, don't go thinkin' bout that. Can't help that things don't always go so good with yer folks. You have had a pritty good life in spite of them."

"I know they love me. That's really what's kept me going all these years. The fact that they couldn't show it was hard on me, but I had the two of you."

"Good thing. It bout broke Shirley's heart that she couldn't have kids, so see? It all works out in the end."

"Do you think Tug will come back here?"

"More important, do you think he will come back? I mean you two seemed purty tight. I see things you know. I may look dumb but I don't miss much. That boy is tore up about you and you feel the same. He will come back to us."

"You love him too, don't you, Uncle Dickie?"

"Now don't you go tellin' on me, but I couldn't have had a son I would have taken to any more than that boy. He is a real keeper. He's got the water in him and that's how I know he won't be able to stay away."

Lindy broke out laughing, thinking about how funny Tug looked when he fell into the marsh. And how all the water grass clung to him when she pulled him out. He was a sight she will never forget. He was so mad at her for laughing at him.

"Yes, he has the water in him, on him, and all around him."

"You won't ever let that boy fergit about that, will ya?"

"Nope."

The phone rang as they sat laughing at that humiliating experience for Tug. Dickie motioned to Lindy to sit tight and that he would get it.

"Why speak of the devil," Dickie shouted into the phone.

Lindy's heart jumped. Looking at her Uncle Dickie's face, she knew it was Tug.

"You what?" he yelled. "You did what?" he repeated. "Good Lord, son, you have done it now. At the word when, Lindy jumped up and grabbed the phone.

"Tug? What's going on?"

"I have quit my job and I am going to move down there, Lindy."

"I don't believe it. Dickie and I were just talking about you and I said I didn't know if you were ever going to come back here."

"Well, I guess you were wrong. Didn't you think I would keep my promise?"

"Yes. No. I don't know."

"Put Dickie back on and then I'll call you later."

Lindy's heart was racing a million miles an hour. She handed the phone to Dickie and she ran out of the house, yelling, "I'll see you later. I have so much to do."

"Well, you sure have our girl in a tizzy now, son. She ran out of here half-witted, and to do God knows what."

"I'm glad she's so happy…"

"Happy? Dickie interrupted. "She's somewhere between nuts and the moon."

Tug had never heard that one either, but he reckoned it meant that she was very glad he would be returning.

"Ah, Dickie, um, I have a favor to ask you."

"Ask away, son."

"Well um, I wanted to know if I could stay with you for a while. I mean just until I get a place of my own."

"A place of yer own? Won't hear bout that. You will stay with me fer as long as you like. I won't take no for an answer."

Tug breathed a sigh of relief. "You're the best, Dickie Short, regardless of what others might think."

"Others? What do others say any different bout old Dickie?"

"I'll tell you everything when I can sell my place and move down."

"How long will that be?"

"If everything goes right in an about an hour, it should be very soon."

The smile that crossed Dickie's face was indescribable. He too was somewhere between nuts and the moon.

TALKING TO DICKIE AND LINDY was a tonic. Now all I needed was to talk Roger into buying my place, and then I could get out of Dodge. I met him at our usual haunt and I ordered a beer the minute I sat down.

"Whoa tiger," Roger shot. "It's lunch time and you still have half the day ahead."

I leaned over to him and said, "Now Roger, you and I know that you know all about my morning meeting with Max. Lady Macbeth overheard all of it and I don't believe for one minute that she didn't haul her ass downstairs and dish to you."

Roger tried to cover the fact that Tug was right. Beth *had* spilled the beans.

"Well all right, Tug. She did say something to me about your meeting. I guess it was pretty hot between the two of you."

"Hot isn't the word, but we worked it all out in the end. I am leaving the paper, Roger, but you already know that."

"I almost called off lunch. I didn't know what to say. Are you okay about it?"

"I sure am. I haven't ever been so okay about anything in my life."

"Wow! You really have lost your mind."

"No I haven't, Rog. I have found my destiny and I have something to ask you."

Roger began to shrink away. I could see that he was afraid to ask what that something was.

I made it easy on him. I did all the talking. "I want to sell my place right away, but before I call a real estate agent, I want to know if you want to buy it from me."

Roger sat dazed. He loved Tug's place and would kill for it.

"I...I ...I would love to do that, Tug, but I am not quite sure I can afford it. You know I don't have the money you do."

I leaned over close to him and said, "I will make you an offer you can't refuse."

"What's that," Roger questioned, still stunned.

"I will rent it to you until you can buy it. I am sure good things will come your way after I have left." I didn't want to blow Max's little surprise to him.

"Do you know something I don't know? I mean did Max say something to you?"

"Absolutely not," I lied. "It's just that with my leaving, you are the natural one to pick up more work and more work means more money. So, what do you think?"

"I'll take a beer, Mac," Roger shouted down the bar.

"Well then, I guess that settles it. I will have all the papers drawn up by my attorney and you can move in as soon as you can square your place away."

"I don't believe this, Tug. I am sitting here, losing my best buddy, but at the same time, I am getting my dream. Your place is the absolute best. And as for my place; it's a dump compared to yours and I have a month to month, so that isn't going to be a problem."

"Splendid." Tug clanked his glass against Roger's and they toasted to good times.

Clearing The Decks

I INSISTED THAT WE EAT SOMETHING before going back to work. I didn't want Roger half shit-faced walking into the office. That wouldn't do if Max decided to move on this fast.

While Roger babbled on about his new digs, I sat and looked attentive while thinking about all that I wanted to do before the day was over. The first order of business would be to get my resignation to Max ASAP.

When we hit the door of our building, I told Roger that he should take one of my old faithful mints, being that he had had another beer over lunch. He accepted graciously.

I cranked out one of those short and sweet resignation letters and headed up to Lady Macbeth's office. I couldn't wait to see the look on her face when I walked in. She was such piece of work.

She didn't disappoint me. She sat there and looked at me with those big, round eyes of hers and tried to act like she was sympathetic. Good act Beth, I thought.

"Is Max in?" I asked.

"Actually he is not, Tug. Can I help you?"

Boy, she was good at this. Can she help me? Hadn't she done enough? By now, the whole building knew what went on in my meeting this morning with Max.

"Maybe you *can* be of assistance, Beth. Would you be so kind as to give this letter to Max?" I knew she was salivating to see what it was and couldn't wait for me to leave. That's why I didn't lick the envelope.

"I would be happy to do that." Now her voice was really sickeningly sweet. "Is it really important because Max won't be back for a couple of hours?"

"Yes, it's really important." I leaned over her desk and glared down at her. "I'll tell you what it is; if you can keep a secret," I taunted her.

"Oh, you don't have to do that, Tug. That's private between you and Max."

"Come on, Beth," I sneered. "You know damn well what's going on in every corner of this building. Don't take me for an idiot. It's my resignation letter. And it's effective immediately." There, that should get her. Now, if for some reason that bastard Dawson should happen to call back; she could be the first to tell him the good news; although that might be going too far even for this bitchy young lady.

"Oh," she said acting surprised. "I didn't realize that your conversation had gone *that* far this morning. I am so sorry."

"Always the professional, huh Beth? Well, it doesn't matter anymore. You see I am as happy as a clam about this and *so* is Max. It all works out in the end."

Her look changed considerably. Now that she had been *outed*, she returned to the cat she is. Grabbing the letter from my hand, she stated tartly, "I'll make sure Max gets it the minute he comes in.

"I sure do appreciate that, Beth. I'll be seein' you."

"Tug? Before you leave, I just want to tell you how much I have enjoyed working with you. I mean, I mean…"

"Cut the crap, Beth. I am sure you will all go right on without missing a step. But, thanks for the sentiments anyway." I flashed her my toothy grin and left promptly.

THREE BOXES WERE ALL IT took to clear me out of the newspaper business. It seemed so strange that your professional worth could be packed up in three boxes.

I dumped one of the boxes in the foyer of my townhouse when I got home. I would get the rest later. I wanted to call my attorney right away and get the ball rolling on the papers so Roger could move in as soon as he wanted to. My attorney was a few years older than me and a Harvard Law School grad. Had to keep it in the family, so to speak.

Derek Johnson's father was my Dad's attorney and he took his son into practice with him after Derek graduated. He was a pretty sharp guy and I really liked him. I had met him on and off through the years. The Johnsons were always invited to my parent's social gatherings at the holiday season and sometimes they would bring Derek. It was always assumed that he and I would be friends and then I would be Derek's client when he was all set up. It seemed to work out just the way the two older men had planned it.

"Derek? This is Tug Alston, calling from Baltimore."

"Well, what the hell is going on with you? I haven't heard from you in a while. Is everything ok?"

"Better than okay, Derek. I need you to do a little work for me."

"I'm there for you buddy. What gives?"

"It's kind of a long story, but I am moving away from Baltimore and need you to get some papers in order for me in regard to my townhouse."

"You just moved in there, didn't you?"

"A year ago, but I am making some changes in my life."

"I see. What paper is lucky to be getting you now?"

"I am not going to another paper, Derek. I am headed down to the Eastern Shore of Maryland."

"Oh boy. That's a pretty nice area. What are you going to be doing?"

"That's another conversation for another day. A good friend of mine down here wants my place, but can't really afford to buy it at the moment. I told him I would rent it to him until he gets things squared away to buy it."

"That's nice of you. Are you sure you want to do that?"

"Absolutely, Derek. I want you to draw up some letters for me stating that proposition and then FedEx them to me on the double. Can you do that?"

"Sure I can. You tell me the particulars and I'll get to it immediately. You should have them in a day or two."

"That's perfect. Here's what I want."

Derek and I finished the business part of our conversation and then shot some shit about past times at "Old Ivy." The memories were great and I told him that I would invite him down when I got settled on the shore. I thought I heard a bit of hesitation in his voice when I extended the invite, but it didn't matter one bit to me. Derek and his family were *Old Boston* and I knew that if he really knew where I was going and what I was going to attempt to do; he would be horrified. That's life.

I spent a lot of time mulling over my decision and found I had not one regret. Even my fabulous bachelor pad didn't appeal to me anymore. I would miss it some, but the call of the water was far more important to me now. I had things to do and I knew just where I wanted to start my new life in Somerville. It was definitely going to be a major change for me, but one that I was relishing more than anything I had ever done. Even being a reporter for a newspaper. Call me crazy, but something powerful was pulling at me.

A WEEK LATER, I HAD said all my good byes and even went to a party they had for me at the paper. Max came for a while and made a very grandiose speech and wished me well. That shut a lot of the gossipers up. Especially Lady Macbeth.

Max walked over to me and shook my hand and as he said *so long* I could see him well up. I told him that I would keep in touch and I could see he welcomed that.

Quietly, he leaned in to me and said, "You damn well better, Tug. I want to know how this story ends. But before you take off, I want to ask you one favor."

Lifting an eyebrow curiously, I said, "name it, Max."

"Please don't send my regards to that old man."

I wrapped my arms around him and hugged him hard, like men do at times like this. The smile was still on my face as Max disappeared out the door. I was going to miss that man but I knew our paths would cross again.

Max silently closed the door to his office. He truly felt sad. Tug wasn't just his best friend's son; he was the brightest young star he had ever seen. He was a quick-study and so very likeable. It was now going to take him more time than he wanted to spend to get Tug's friend Roger up to speed. But Roger was a team player. He always knew in his gut, that Tug was on another path to somewhere else

Glancing down, he saw the huge pile of mail that Beth had dropped on his desk before going on to Tug's party. As he sifted through it, casting most of it to the side, one letter stood out from the rest. He couldn't believe his eyes. He knew who sent this one.

"Jesus H. Christ," he yelled out loud. "Does this man ever stop?"

Ripping it open, he could feel the bile rising in his throat. What could this man possibly want now?

He leaned back in his chair and held on tight. With Dickie Short anything and everything was possible.

Dear Max,

I feel as if I know you now, so please forgive me for being less formal with ya. I was goin' to write this letter some time back, but you know how time gits away.

I ain't much good at sayin' things sometimes, but I had to let ya know how fond I am of that young boy, Tug. I mean it was you who sent him on down to take a look at what was goin' on down in these parts. He sure is a smart one. He saw it right off the bat and after a while he caught onto what needed to be done to stop these bastards from buildin' up every square inch of this here land of ours. Oh, by the way, speakin' of bastards, I suppose I owe you an apology of sorts for losin' my temper with that Mr. Dawson. Tug told me how mad you got when he called ya. I'm sorry 'bout that. I jist couldn't hep it. The man is an asshole.

Well, anyway, Tug told me that he is leavin' your paper and comin' down here to live. Jist wanted you to know that we'll take good care of him. He is a natural with gittin' on with the folks in these parts. They really like him, even if he is an outlander. It's what's in his heart and they can sense pretty good that he is one of us deep down inside.

You won't be hearin' from me anymore now that Tug is comin'. I'm sure you will be happy fer that. Jist wanted to say my thanks to ya.

Fondly,
Dickie Short

MAX WAS BLOWN AWAY. HE couldn't believe it. It was hard enough losing Tug, but losing him to this old coot was more than he could bear. And yet, he had to admit that Dickie Short had a sense of the right and wrong of things. After all, he did write to thank him and that's more than Max thought he was capable of. Maybe he had been off-base about Dickie. Maybe Tug saw through his rough exterior to the inside qualities of this old waterman. After all, those watermen were a tough breed, but they were real Americans and appreciated the values this country was founded on.

Folding the letter back up, he placed it in his desk drawer. He wanted to hold onto it as if it were a piece of Tug that he would have for a long time. He didn't realize until that moment, that Tug's departure meant more to him than he realized. Tug was his good friend's son and now he knew he wouldn't have that familiar communication with Ted Alston so much anymore either. Life was always changing, and as he slipped the letter away, he found himself choked with emotion. Maybe, just maybe, he thought, he would take Tug up on his offer and before too long he would find his way down to Somerville.

My Shore Now

THINGS GOT SETTLED QUICKLY WITH Roger and I was on my way. The only things I took were things that could be stored at Dickie's house until I could find my own place. I sure was glad I had the money to be able to make this change. Good old Grandpa. It sure was nice of him to remember me so well when he died.

This was certainly a different trip from the others. This time I was leaving for good and going to live with people I really liked and a gal I was head over heels about. The daunting task ahead of me would be retooling my life. I had a ton of notes to go over and reams of pictures to organize. My one hope was that Dickie and Lindy would give me some space. This wasn't a vacation for me. It was going to be long hours and hard work to establish some sort of routine to attack the subject at hand. I wasn't exactly sure of how I was going to do this, but I knew I had to do it.

Getting the right supplies was paramount, so as I approached Salisbury, I headed right up Route 13 and into strip mall country. The traffic here was almost as bad as around a big city. Stop lights at every intersection and I had to keep my eyes open for a Staples or Office Max. I spotted one and then had to figure out how to get to it. Naturally it was on the other side of the highway. This was going to take a feat of daring do. But I was up to the task.

I probably shouldn't have bought everything in sight, but hey, I wanted to get started, didn't I? After some tough juggling and cramming, my Cherokee now looked like a miniature version of a moving van. My last stop would be a gas station and then I would be on my way, for the last time, down to Somerville.

Lindy was on my mind something fierce. I picked up my cell and gave her a jingle. When she picked up on the second ring, my heart actually skipped a beat.

"Lindy? I am just out of Salisbury and on my way."

"Oh Tug, that's great news. I have been worried all day."

"You have?" I teased. "You shouldn't be worrying that pretty head of yours on my account."

"Stop it, Tug. I am so excited I can hardly stand it. I am going over to Uncle Dickie's and we'll have supper ready for you, when you get here."

"Boy that sounds good to me. Should I ask what we are having, or should I just let you surprise me?"

"Well, if you really have to know, I am making a meat loaf with mashed potatoes. Please don't tell me you don't like that."

"I love it. That's home cooking at its best. I am hungry as a bear and I can't wait to see you."

Lindy sighed into the phone. "Me to you. By the way, was it real hard leaving the paper?"

"Hurt like the devil, but I am sure about what I am doing and I am sure I want to be with you."

"Tug? Are you really certain about this move? I mean really certain in your heart and soul?"

Lindy's voice pulled up real serious and when a gal did that, a guy better come up with the right answer.

"Yes I am. For that matter, I better be. I have crossed the Rubicon and can't turn back now."

When she didn't answer me, I realized she might not know what I meant. "I mean that I have never been so certain about anything, Lindy."

She shot straight back at me. "I know what the Rubicon is, Tug. I 'ain't no idiot," she teased putting the emphasis on the word ain't.

I was the one feeling like an idiot. Lindy was smart and I felt like I may have hurt her feelings. I didn't want to start my new life out down there with her thinking that.

"I didn't mean to hurt your feelings, Lindy. Not everyone knows that expression, you know. You are one of the smartest babes I have ever met. That's why I like you so much."

"*Like* me?" she shrieked. "I thought you *loved* me."

Now I was in hot water for sure. "You know how I feel about you, Lindy. When I get there, I will show you." There, I thought, that should fix her.

Giggling into the phone, she said, "you've got that right, mister. You will pay for that comment, Tug Alston. You just wait."

I knew I was back in her good graces. "See you in a little while, baby. Make sure that meat loaf is ready."

"I will, Tug. Be careful. You are so close now."

"Over and out," I laughed into the phone and hung up. Lindy Short sure had taken my heart.

DINNER WAS THE BEST MEAT loaf I had ever eaten. Dickie sat there and listened while Lindy and I jawed on about a million things. He looked a bit tired to me, and that was the first time I had ever seen that in him. He was always the first one up in the morning and then spent his entire day on the go. I sensed something was out of whack when I looked at him.

"Are you all right, Dickie? You haven't said a word since we sat down."

"I'm fine, son. Jist a lot of excitement these last days. I am glad yer here. You two go on and old Dickie will clean up this mess of dishes. We kin have some ice cream later, if you like."

I still wasn't convinced it was just excitement that I saw in him. There was something else. But, at his age, he had a right to feel tired once in a while.

"Why don't you let Lindy and me clean up? You go on and read for a while."

Dickie gave me a look that said he knew that I knew he wasn't feeling up to par. Without too much of a fuss, he mumbled, "all right then. You two clean this up tonight, but tomorrow night, it's all mine."

As he walked out of the kitchen, Lindy looked at me with a strange sadness on her face. I decided not to say anything. If something was going on with Dickie, she would eventually tell me.

"I'm glad you liked dinner, Tug. I made it the way they do down at Virgil's. It's the best around here. It's their secret ingredient that makes it so special."

"I won't ask, Dickie. I think I will leave it Virgil's (and your) secret."

Lindy picked up on the look on Tug's face and couldn't resist. "You are too much, Tug Alston. I have no idea what you really think of us down here, but one thing's for sure. That meat loaf's secret ingredient sure is tasty. Yes siree. Genuine eel flesh."

I covered my mouth in horror. My eyes started to bug out and just before I could feel my dinner start to undulate like the eel, she broke down and started laughing.

"I'm teasing you, Tug. Really. I just wanted to see your face when I said that."

Almost gagging now, I muttered through my hands, "that's not funny, Lindy. That's not funny at all."

"I thought it was and I got to you, didn't I?"

With that, she ran out the back door. She ran for her life because when I caught her, I was going to…I was going to… kiss her so hard she would never forget it.

That little joke of hers would be the subject of much humor for years to come.

DICKIE WAS ALREADY IN BED when I came back from walking Lindy home. He left a note on the kitchen table telling me that he was pooped and would see me in the morning. This just wasn't like him.

I trailed upstairs and tried not to make a sound. Not that that would have made a big difference. Dickie was asleep and when he slept; he couldn't hear a thing. A hurricane could blow up and he wouldn't move a muscle. That's how it was with the watermen. They were used to going to bed fairly early and sleeping like the dead. They would be back up and at it in the wee hours of the morning. Some habits died hard.

I checked to see if I had had any phone messages. I had forgotten to take it with me when I left the house earlier. I saw that my Dad had called. God, I prayed nothing was wrong at home. I shut my door and called back. It was only ten o'clock and I knew they wouldn't be asleep.

"Dad? Is everything okay?"

"Everything is fine Tug, except for our son who didn't call to tell us he got down there all right. Your mother is frantic and so I told her to go on to bed and I would call you."

He was lying. Mom never worried much about where I was. It was him who was worried. I could hear it in his voice. And there was something else in voice, as well."

"I made it fine, Dad. When I got here, Lindy had dinner on the table and well, they eat earlier down here than you do in Boston."

"No excuse for not calling us, Tug."

"Okay, Dad, what's really on your mind? You have yourself upset about something."

I could hear him hesitate before answering. He let out one of those sighs people make when they are about to say something not quite that pleasant.

"All right, Tug. You caught me on this one. There are a few things that have me upset."

"And I assume I am one of the few things on that list?"

"Yes, you are. I am trying hard to understand what it is you are looking for. I know I told you that you had my blessing, but I am beginning to have second thoughts."

"We've been through this over and over, Dad. I have found something that excites me. It's something I can do to change things. I know you don't agree, but it's what I have to do right now. All I am asking is that you trust me on this."

He smacked his lips and when he did that, you always knew he was about to blow. "I am trying to see this from your point of view, Tug, but your mother and I think this has more to do with that young gal down there than anything else."

The real reason was out on the table and now he had genuinely pissed me off. "First of all, let's leave Mom out of this. It's you who thinks that; not Mom. While I am sure I am in love with Lindy, I consider this move to be about doing what I want to do with my life. I want to write stories and I want to try to stop the destruction of a land before it's too late. Is there something so wrong with that?"

I had hit him back, and the old man never liked that too much. "Yes, there is something wrong with that when it's a hopeless cause. You can't fight this, Tug. You weren't meant to do this. You were meant to be a reporter. If you remember, that's all you have wanted to do since you were a kid. Now, you have taken off on some dream quest that will only set you back and it could take years for you to get back into the swing of another paper."

"I don't want to work for another paper," I yelled. "While I was good at what I was doing, and I knew that opportunities for me were there for the taking, I didn't want to do that anymore. I thought you understood all this."

His quick temper didn't disappoint me. He screamed into the phone. "I understand that you are an Alston and you went to Harvard, and that you graduated top of your class. I understand that you got a damned good job because you're smart and my connections didn't hurt either. I accepted your not wanting to stay and work with me at The Globe, but for the love of God, I can't understand what is so almighty important about people building homes on land that would otherwise be worthless. You are giving all that up for what?"

I had to control myself. I didn't want this battle with him, but he had brought it on. I took a long, deep breath, and then answered him. "I don't want to fight with you, Dad. I did what I did and I don't regret it. I am staying here and I am going to help these people fight this sprawl. I am going to write articles and I am going to get them published. I am in love with Lindy Short and I will probably marry her someday. I love the water and I love to go out fishing with the men down here. Why can't you understand that sometimes, in life, things don't turn out the way you plan them to be? You taught me to go with my gut, and now I am doing that, and you beat me up for it. I can't discuss this with you again. I am here and if you want to see me, then here is where you have to come. I am sorry you feel like I have disappointed you. I haven't disappointed myself and that's the big thing here. I can use all that fancy education to do what I can to make a change. I would think you would be proud of me. I won't live a life that simply makes me money but holds nothing passionate in it. It's the way I am. It's the way I was raised…"

"It's the way Mikey was raised too, and you don't see him wanting to run off to some place in the middle of nowhere," he cut in.

"Mikey is just getting started. You have no idea where he is going to end up, unless you force him to do what *you* want

him to do and make him miserable for the rest of his life."
Cutting as that was; he deserved to hear it.

Silence fell between us until I couldn't stand it anymore.
"I have to get going, Dad. I want to be up early and start doing
my research."

I knew that he didn't want to end the conversation this
way, especially after we had come so far, but things were said
now, even if they were in temper.

"I said what I had to say, Tug. I know it hasn't gone down
well with you, but please think about what I have said. Max
would take you back. I know he would. He had high hopes
for you."

"I don't want to go back. I like Max, I even love Max,
but we said good bye and you can't go back after you say good
bye. Please don't talk to him about me anymore Dad." Then I
amazed myself. I couldn't end this conversation like this. Life
can be short sometimes, and then you have regrets. "I love
you, Dad. I know you think I am making a terrible mistake,
but I told you I will make you proud of me yet. Give Mom my
love and I promise you I'll call you as soon as I am underway
with my project here."

When he said good bye, I could hear that he was choking
up. He didn't want this conversation to end like this either.
"I love you too, Tug. Think long and hard and if this is where
your life is to be, then I guess we should put this subject to
bed. Please keep in touch."

I wanted to bury my head in my pillow and cry like I used
to do as a kid. But that wouldn't ever change him. He was an
intellectual snob and no matter how hard he tried to make me
one of his breed; I wouldn't buckle. I could at least say I loved
him and mean it. He said he loved me too and that would
have to be enough for me.

As I lay back on the bed and sleep drifted into my eyes, I
prayed hard that one day I would make him proud and that he

would see that when you want to do something badly enough, it really can change things.

Dickie hadn't been asleep; he was just dozing. He heard it all and he felt like a bolt of lightening had hit him. Maybe he had made a big mistake with this young man he loved so much. Maybe Tug was the son he never had and always wanted. Maybe he had been an old fool and put wild ideas into a young man's head. Could it be all of the above? Time would tell if he was wrong or not.

Closing his weary eyes, he too prayed. He prayed that Shirley could hear him and that she would show him if he had made all the mistakes he was beginning to think he had. Surely, his beloved Shirley would have loved this young boy as much as he did. And surely she would have seen the love that had sprouted up between her Lindy and him. And surely she was going to tell him that he was right in doing what he did. Dear God, he prayed over and over. Let me be right.

Getting Started Isn't So Easy

It was the clattering of noise from the kitchen that woke me up. Good grief, it was only six in the morning. I was beginning to believe Dickie did this on purpose to get me up and play with him. I wanted to pull the covers back over my head, but decided that maybe it was a good thing that I was awake. I could get a jump on the day.

Dickie was sitting at the kitchen table when I pattered in. He was doing his usual thing; reading the morning paper. He was talking to himself- something he did all the time. It had become amusing to me to hear him going on about the news of the day. I regretted not taping some of his personal editorials. They were a whole lot better than the pundits on TV.

"Morning, Dickie. You sure went off to bed early last night. Are you feeling ok?"

Dickie glanced up and shot me a look that said are you kidding? "I am just fine, son. I was just getting' out of your way so you and Lindy could have some private time, if you know what I mean?" He said with that sly wink of his.

Rolling my eyes, I said, "You didn't have to do that. This is your house and you can do whatever you want in it."

"Gee thanks, son, I needed you to remind me of that."

He was in a feisty little mood this morning. I grabbed my coffee and sat down beside him. "I have a lot to do today, Dickie. I have to get started on what I want to do."

"Just what is it you want to do down here, son?"

I thought his question was a bit odd being that if anyone should know exactly what I wanted to do; it would be Dickie.

"Well," I began, "I want to do some extensive research in the library and then go out and shoot some more pictures. It's going to take me some time to get on line with this story and how I want to write it."

He fooled around with his coffee cup and then said, "You will git the hang of it all, son. You already have a good start. By the way, there's a meeting of some of the townspeople tonight. You might jist want to go."

"What are they meeting about?"

"How to stop this damned building."

"Well that ought to be illuminating. What time?"

"Around six thirty, I spect. They like to git it all goin' before too late."

"I'll plan on it then. That should give me a good point of departure. In the meantime, I am heading down to Virgil's for breakfast and…"

"And see that purty little gal of ours too, eh?" he slid in before I could finish my thought.

"Yes, and see Lindy. I want to talk to her, if she has the time."

With a sarcastic smile on his face, he answered, "I am sure she will take the time, son."

"Do you want to come with me?"

"No, not really. I have a few things I want to git around to here. I need to fix that back door and there's some outside work to be done on the house before the weather gets colder."

"The weather won't get cold for a while Dickie. I can help you if you wait."

"Nope. No waitin'. I am stubborn that way. Shirley used to git all over me about not gittin' to things when they needed gittin' to, so now I jist go and do it. Besides, you need to be out and about on yer own for a while. That way, you kin git to know the folks better. When I am along, they always want to chatter on with me."

That was so true. Everyone loved Dickie and he was a sort of town character and they loved to swap stories with him. "Okay then, I'll be back later. Don't work too hard. Remember, I will help you. I don't want to stay here and do nothing. It's my way of paying my way, I guess, since you won't take any money for me staying here."

"Not a damned dime," he snarled in that stubborn voice of his.

"Just remember what I said." I grabbed my backpack and headed for the door.

As I walked away, I could hear him chuckling all the way from the kitchen. He loved to get the better of me.

Virgil's was always hopping. Lindy was whisking around the counter and then out to the floor to deliver the men all kinds of food. She looked so pretty with her blonde hair swept up on top of her head and those green eyes dancing with delight when she saw me come in and take a seat.

Pencil and paper in hand, she slid in next to me and asked, "What'll it be this morning?"

I leaned over and kissed her cheek and said jokingly, "Whatever you care to serve me."

She wiggled closer to me. "You've got it mister. Ham and eggs?"

I winked at her and muttered, "That wasn't exactly what I had in mind, but it will get me started."

Before she could make a quick exit out of the booth, Wally and Hambone blocked her way and stood looking down on us. "See you two are up and at it early this morning. Do you think we could take a seat with ya, Tug? And maybe git this pretty gal to bring us some coffee."

Lindy blushed, somewhat embarrassed. She pushed her way out of the booth and past them, and yelled back, "Two coffees coming up."

"We heard you were comin' back here to stay, Tug. Is that true?"

Picking up my mug full of freshly brewed coffee, I said, "Yes, it's true. I just couldn't live without you guys."

"Golly gee," Wally teased, "we couldn't live without you either. Are you going to be a waterman?"

I almost spit the coffee out of my mouth. "You, of all people Wally, ought to know that I would have a long ways to go before I could ever even call myself a waterman. No, I am going to be writing about the area."

"Writing, huh?" Hambone remarked. "Well, we are an interesting bunch. Writing about us should keep you purty busy."

Wally nudged his friend and said, "leave the boy alone, Hambone. We all know he is a great young reporter." He leaned in and looked at me straight in the eyes. "Gonna stir up some trouble, are ya?"

"Maybe. Maybe not. But one thing is for sure. There is a lot to be recorded down here and then write about it. My intention is to get people to take a second look at what is happening to not only the land, but the water. I should think that would get your attention, Wally."

"It sure will, boy. But I do hope you will save some time to come on out with us before the winter sets in. The fall is a beautiful time out on the bay. A man could live forever out there on fall days."

Wally had made me feel so wanted...and accepted. "I will save a few days for you guys. You can count on it."

They gobbled their breakfast down and headed out, while talking to the other men who were doing the same thing. I sat there and took pictures of them, which they naturally loved.

They were beginning to feel like I was going to make them Hollywood stars. Who knows, maybe I was.

Lindy wandered to the booth. "Where are you off to? If you wait a few minutes, I will be done and I could go with you."

"I am going to the library. I would love to have you tag along."

IT WAS A SMALL LIBRARY but one that had a good selection of books on the bay and the watermen and the history of the region. This would keep me going for a while.

"Tug? I really want to help you. I would like to be your assistant, if you would let me. I am a fairly good writer myself, you know."

"No, I didn't know that but I'll bet you are with your inquisitive nature and special way with words. By the way, how come you don't speak the same way Dickie or most of the folks down here do?"

"I guess I decided I wanted to be different from the rest. If I hadn't met you, I would probably have left here at some point. I want to see big cities and watch the people."

"Now that's funny, Lindy. You want to go to the cities and I want to run from them."

"That's because you have seen both. Will you take me to Boston someday?"

I knew what she was getting at. She wanted to know if I really loved her and wanted her to meet my folks. Better be careful here boy. "Most certainly. If you are a real good girl and we get a lot of work done, I will take you to Boston around Thanksgiving."

She shrieked so loud that some of the people in the library stared at us. "Really? Do you really mean that?"

"Shhhh," I mumbled. "Yes I really mean it. I think you will adore Boston…and if you're really a good girl, I'll take you to meet my family."

She saddled up next to me and squeezed my leg. That was the sign that I better get us moving before I embarrassed myself and couldn't stand up for fear of the bulge that was beginning to rise in my pants.

She giggled when she saw how abruptly I stood up. She knew exactly what she was doing and she was very proud of her powers over me.

As I began to gather up the papers on the desk, she grabbed my backpack and began to help. She grabbed it so fast that some of my files fell out onto the table. I stared down at one in particular and before I could snatch it away, her eyes caught the cover. I cringed seeing her reaction to it.

Her face turned pale and I thought tears would start to fall any minute.

In an angry voice, she yelled, "What's this, Tug? Is this what you think of Uncle Dickie? Do you see him as some fool who looks like a smiley face? Or for that matter, is this what you think of all of us?"

I quickly retrieved the file from her hands and snapped, "No, this is not what I think of Dickie or anyone else down here. This file was handed to me by Max when he sent me down here. The artistic work on the cover was done by his stupid secretary. That's all, Lindy, nothing else."

She wasn't about to drop the subject and by now, everyone who was within hearing range was staring straight at us.

"Oh really?" Now her decibel level had kicked up a few more notches. "You don't think we are hicks and taters?"

"Hicks and taters? What the hell does that mean?"

Frustrated by her own anger, she grabbed her purse and responded, "Oh, I don't know. It's just an expression," she snapped. "Maybe my background *does* come out once in a while especially when outlanders put us down."

She was red hot mad. Her use of the word outlander told me she was pretty steamed at me. Folks down here only use that word when they are describing those they don't particularly appreciate being here. She wasn't going to believe me no matter what I said. In the state she was in, I decided the best thing to do was to retreat. "I am leaving now, Lindy. Do you want a ride, or are you just going to stay mad at me all day?"

"I think maybe the all day option is the one I will take, she snarled."

"Suit yourself. I didn't draw that picture and I won't be blamed for it."

Silence was the only thing I could hear for a few moments. For some odd reason, I felt that perhaps humor was required here to end the argument, so I dove right in and took a chance. Putting on my best smile, I said, "When I first came down here, my dear, I did think you were all hicks and taters, as you would put it. But then it all changed when I got to know everyone." I couldn't tell if I was making headway with her, but I sure didn't want to spend my day wondering if she was still mad at me.

She turned her back to me, but I could tell she was breaking.

"You have to admit, it's kind of a cute smiley face. It really captures your Uncle." Had I gone too far?

I saw her back begin to move. She was trying to conceal her laughter, I could tell. "Come on, Lindy. Let's get out of here. We have already given these folks enough to talk about for today and this whole week, I suspect."

I had made the right decision. I had won the day. Turning to face me, she said quietly in a much sweeter voice, "It is kind of cute at that. I'm sorry, Tug. It just hit me the wrong way. I am very sensitive to people making fun of us down here."

I accept your apology then. Let's go."

Before she could hit me with the "accept my apology?" comment, I took her arm and lead her out of the library before there was another scene.

Safely seated in my Cherokee, she wiggled up to my face and then she let it out. "Accept *your* apology? I think not."

We were not going to go over this territory again. I put my arm around her and kissed her before she could utter one more word. When we came up for air, she laughed and said, "You think that will fix everything, don't you?"

"I hope so," I chuckled. "That was our first fight you know?"

"It won't be our last, Tug Alston, but the making up is so much fun. Want to try to calm me down again?"

I sure did and as I began to press my lips to hers, I croaked, "Women!"

Autumn On The Shore

THE SUMMER WAS GONE AND the first signs of fall were in the air. The crabbing season was just about over. The crabs were heading for cover and the watermen were turning to what comes next. It's all a wonderful cycle that has been played out for centuries on the water. One season ends and another begins.

I couldn't believe how fast time was passing. Lindy was an enormous help to me putting materials together that would have taken me months more to do. And she was correct when she told me that she had a real flair for writing. As a matter of fact she was darned good, if I do say so myself. She could see things I couldn't and put it all into wonderful dialogue. Our book was beginning to take shape.

I spent most of my time cranking out articles for the local papers down here. The local papers ate it up because they seemed to like having a former big city reporter down here trying to stop the onslaught of building in areas that were never meant to be built on. I was beginning to attain some celebrity status which Lindy loved. But it came at a price.

One evening, sitting in Dickie's living room, reading the papers that I collected each day from different places; the phone rang. It was my old boss, Max Pierson.

"Hey Max. How are you? It's been a while."

"Yes it has, Tug." I could tell this was business and not a pleasure call.

"What's going on in Baltimore these days?" I said hoping for the best.

"Well, to be honest with you, a lot is going on here. Not all of it is pleasant. That's the reason for my call. Your articles in your local papers down there are beginning to cause some trouble here."

"Oh?" I answered. "Why is that?"

"Along with John Dawson, your old friend, another one of the major developers is threatening to pull out of our paper."

"I don't understand, Max. I am out of there and we thought that would solve the problem. I don't see how my writing for these papers down here can possibly affect The Sun."

"As you know, Tug, a lot of people from the Baltimore area vacation over there. They retire there too and, lately, the letters to the Editor are pouring in commenting about the things you wrote about. Many of them have been there during the summer and they have seen it with their own eyes and they don't like it either. I can't ignore all the letters that come in to us and while I try to put the least controversial ones in, they are pretty rough too.

"I don't get it, Max. What do you want me to do about it?"

"I was hoping that maybe you and I could come to some agreement."

"Does John Dawson have anything to do with this?"

"You know very well that he did, Tug. The man holds a lot of our bottom line in his hands."

"Look Max, I can't stop writing about what I see. There is another side to this story and that's the one I am writing. If I stop then I lose all credibility with these folks. Besides, there are real environmental issues with all this. Doesn't anyone care about that?"

"You and I know that where money is to be made, environmental issues go out the window. They can only go so far with that and then they lose profits."

"It's the same old story over and over again, Max. Dawson runs to you and threatens you with advertising dollars so you will try to shut me up. Those days are gone. It's war down here for these folks. They have seen their farms bought up, houses being built everywhere on top of one another, traffic becoming a nightmare in strategic areas, and the wetlands shrinking because they are being filled in to build more homes and condos. I will be damned if I will stop writing about this."

I could hear Max's heavy breathing and that meant he was furious he couldn't get me to quit.

"What can I say to you, Tug? Couldn't you try to write other kinds of stories for a while?"

Now, I was the one doing the heavy breathing. I was beyond furious. "Just what kind of stories, Max? Cute, inane little pieces that say nothing? You must be kidding. If you have a problem with Dawson and the likes; then you have to solve it. I don't work for you anymore, remember?"

Maybe that was a little too strong, but I had said it and I would be damned if I would take it back.

"Yes, I do remember that, Tug. You just signed your death warrant, boy. You won't ever get a job in this industry again if you ever change your mind and decide to join the human race again."

He was pushing me and his inference of my friends not being part of the human race did not go unnoticed.

"So be it, Max. At least we have gotten one thing straight…"

"What's that?" he cut in.

"I am a damned good writer and people are beginning to pay attention."

"You are a fool, Tug. You can't stop progress and you can't stop the whole country from expanding and developing."

"Maybe I can't stop the entire fifty states, but, apparently, I am making pretty good progress in this area."

"I thought I could talk sense into you, Tug, but I see I am wasting my time."

"This is my home now and I love it here and I see what happens when people begin to stand up and fight. It can really change things."

"It can get you hurt too, Tug. Dawson and the others aren't going to be stopped by you or anyone else. Remember that and watch your back."

Max was still trying to reach out to me and I did feel a little sad about that. "Thanks for the warning, Max. I take it from our conversation here that I won't be seeing you anytime soon then."

"I don't think so, Tug. This is business, you know. I had to try. I didn't think I could get you to change your mind, but I had to take that chance."

"You are one, tough man, Max, and you have to do what you have to do and the same goes for me. I am truly sorry that Dawson can't join our fight down here and be a leader in his industry for real change over the way things are done."

"That will happen when pigs fly, Tug. He is all about the money. It's a sad tale these days, but the almighty dollar is king ."

"When it's all gone, one wonders what they will do then. Guess it doesn't matter. They will be dead and they won't have to look the next generation in the face."

I heard Max chuckle quietly into the phone. "That's about the size of it. I would like to ask you one favor, though."

Here it comes, I thought. He was going to make one last ditch effort to get me to bend. "What's that, Max? Or don't I want to hear what's coming?"

"I would like you to think very carefully about what you are writing. I know you are passionate about this and passion is a good thing and it can change the course of things, but don't be myopic. You really need to take a look on both sides of this argument. Development puts people in homes that they want. In areas they want to live. It employs a lot of people and that helps the economy of these areas. You might be Joan of Arc to a lot of people who want to return to yesterday but it's already too late for that. You can effect a change in the future of things, but you can't change what is already there and what is already in the works to come there. Be fair. That's a good writer and reporter's job."

Damn him! He always brought me back to center. There was a lot of truth to what he said but I was on a mission. However I still felt as if I owed him something for a reason I didn't exactly understand. Maybe it was his connection with my father; I don't know. I certainly worked hard at his paper and didn't ever ask for one favor. I didn't want to hurt this man so I had to choose my words carefully. If I had learned one thing, I had learned that age-old important lesson that you never burn your bridges. "I can promise you this, Max. I will take an honest look and approach to this situation and if I feel that there are two sides to this story; I will tell it. As always, your wisdom is welcome. I don't know how this will turn out, but one thing I am certain of and that is that all this taking away of land and destruction of the waters has to stop."

"Just think about it, Tug," Max pleaded. Changing the subject quickly, he added, "By the way, Roger is doing one; fine job here and I understand from my spies around here that he loves that townhouse of his."

"He sure is enjoying the spoils of war, isn't he, Max?" I desperately wanted to end this conversation. We had said all that needed to be said. It was time to go. "Well, I better shove off. I still have a lot to do today and I know you do too. Thanks for the call, Max and I'll think about what you said. In the meantime, good luck with those vultures."

I needed a walk after that conversation. I glanced over at Dickie, who had quite unbelievably sat stone still while I talked to Max. He must have felt my eyes drilling a hole through him and slid the paper down a bit and peered over it.

In a lame try to break the tension that had built up in the room, he said, "Max, huh? That man sure is determined to git you to quit. I don't think he has it straight yet."

"Has what straight yet, Dickie?" I snapped. I was suddenly exhausted and wasn't sure I wanted to go into this with him.

"The fact that there are some people who won't compromise their beliefs for the almighty dollar. That's all I will say on the subject. I kin see you are pritty agitated at the moment."

"Yeah, Dickie, I am. I think I will take a walk. Do you want to come with me?"

"Nah, it's bedtime for me, but a walk will do ya good. This time of the year is good for thinking things through in the cool evenings. It was Shirley's favorite time of the year. She would be getting' herself' all ready for the upcoming holidays and all. Go on now, son. Take yer walk. I am goin' to bed. I'll see ya in the mornin'."

"Good night, Dickie. Have a good night's sleep."

I left the house and walked toward town. I desperately wanted to go down to the pier and hear the water lapping up against the dock. Something about listening to the water calmed ones senses and cleared things from the mind.

The houses were almost all in darkness. It was the time of night when the watermen and their families went on down so they could be up early again in the morning. They still had lots to do, even though the crabs weren't running. Oysters were their next target and they had to make sure their boats were all ready for the cold, winter waters.

As I turned and walked down the main street, the scene wasn't much different. There were only a few men hanging around, drinking at the town bar. The peace and quiet was welcoming to me. Max's words rang in my ears over and over again. "Don't be myopic." I was being one-sided, damn it.

That's how I felt and that's what I was writing about, damn it, I chided myself.

The light breeze hit my face and I smelled the water. I hastened to it, knowing that I would find my answers somewhere in the waters that were ahead of me.

The dock was completely deserted when I arrived. I really didn't expect anyone to be down here, but it was a bit unnerving for the first few minutes. I sat on a long bench and just stared out. I let my mind wander freely and then tried to focus it. Exactly what was I trying to accomplish? To stop all building? To make it so that the people these folks call "outlanders" couldn't enjoy the beauty of nature and the waters of the bay? What right did I have to do that? So much swirled through my brain.

I jumped when I heard footsteps coming up from behind me. Who would be down here this late at night? Then I recognized the face.

"I didn't want you to be all alone down here, Tug."

"Dickie called you, didn't he?"

"Yes, and please don't be mad at him. He is worried about you. He said he saw something in your face after you got that call from Max tonight."

I took her hand as she snuggled next to me. "What did he see?"

"Confusion. Is he right?"

"Maybe a little. I needed to be down here by the water. I am not at all confused about being here, Lindy. And I am not confused about the writing you and I have been doing. But I am beginning to wonder if maybe we are taking all this too far."

"Taking it too far? We are beginning to win, Tug. People are beginning to get angry and are starting to fight back. Isn't that what we wanted?"

"Absolutely. But the fact remains that the shore is going to be developed one way or the other. I believe that it is our responsibility to make sure it's done correctly and in a manner that benefits the land."

Lindy snuggled closer, if that was possible. "I think that is what we are doing. The citizens are asking questions now like they never did before. They see it for themselves what has happened to the places that they love so much. They don't all like it. I don't think we are being stupid. We know that things will change. That things have changed. Change can be good, but not at the expense of others. There has to be a happy medium, if at all possible."

I hugged her gently. "You are right, you know. I think it's pretty amazing that you can see this, even when the place you love so much is rapidly changing in front of your eyes."

In the saddest voice, she said, "Uncle Dickie's world is coming to an end. Gone are all the wild spaces and the freedom and safety to roam them at all hours of the day and night. Gone are all the old ways of the people down here, who lived by a handshake and a promise of paying their bills in cash when their catch would be better the next day. Gone are most of their children who have left to find better money off the shore. Gone are many of the birds who once wintered here, and gone are the vast numbers of oysters who once were found in such abundance that they built this town on their shells. Gone too, is the railroad that once brought thousands of people here to work in the packing houses. It's a new time now. One where we all have to figure out how to make a living here and keep the town from going under. Development is one way to do that but then that got out of control when they tore up the whole waterfront. There are great problems to be addressed and we are giving people those options to learn and then decide for themselves, what they want this area to become." I bent down and kissed her gently. She saw it all so clearly. If I hadn't known better, I would have thought she was a much older woman. I loved her so much.

She gazed up at me, with the moon shining down on the water. "It isn't all bad you know. This mess brought you to me."

"And so it has, my dear. So it has. Your wisdom overwhelms me."

"Do you feel a little less confused now, Tug?"

"I suppose I do. After hearing the things you said, I think I know exactly which way to go."

"And that would be….?"

"And that would be for another day. I'll walk you back home. God, this weather is so lovely down here in the fall. It's almost as beautiful as Boston."

"Speaking of Boston…"

"I have it all under control, missy. We are going for Thanksgiving, if you can make sure Dickie is all right."

With both hands touching her mouth, Lindy said, "Maybe he will come with us. Oh, Tug, could he? Oh please, let's bring him with us. That way I won't worry about him while we are gone."

"Dear heaven, I don't know if I can handle my parents meeting you and Dickie all at the same time. That thought never crossed my mind." Then he shot a sly grin and began to giggle. "It would be fun though, wouldn't it?"

Holding tightly to my arm, Lindy giggled and said, "Now that would be a memory for a lifetime."

I rolled my eyes and said, "Darling, you just said a mouthful."

Dickie Does Boston

THERE WASN'T EVEN ONE TINY objection. Dickie leaped at the chance to come with us. Bags packed and in the car by five in the morning, the three Musketeers drove off for Boston.

It was very chilly when we left the shore, but that was nothing compared to what we were headed into. A nor' easter was headed up the coast and the Eastern Shore hadn't gotten it too bad, but they were expecting it to really slam in around Boston. At first, I thought maybe of canceling our trip, but then Dickie reminded me that we were watermen and this sort of thing was nothing to us men. Yeah, sure.

Lindy laughed when she saw all the extra provisions I had packed in case we got stranded somewhere along the way. "God Tug, it's a rain storm, not a hurricane. Half the time they are wrong about the weather anyway."

"You can laugh all you want at me now, but if we get stuck; you will be kissing my ass."

"Owee," she purred, "I would like that."

"I'll just bet you would," I shot with a leering smile on my face.

"Okay kids, it looks like we are more than set to go," yelled Dickie from his porch. "Now can we get this show on the road?"

"I don't see why not, my man. How would you like to be my co-pilot?"

The look on Lindy's face could have killed him dead right there. "I thought I would sit up front with you, Tug."

Dickie jumped in before the discussion of seating arrangements got heated. "Now don't you go getting' your pants in a bunch there girlie. You kin sit right up there with Tug. I am goin' to sit in the back and listen to this here old radio I am bringin' along."

Lindy knew she had been thoughtless and may have hurt her uncle's feelings, so she put her arms around him and said, "I didn't mean to be so uppity, Uncle Dickie. It's just that…"

"Think nothin' of it, my girl," he cut in. "I would much rather listen to my programs anyway than jab on with you two. Plenty of time fer that later on."

Giving him a tight hug, she jumped in the front seat and settled in. It would be her job to stay alert and tell Tug all the shortcut roads she and her uncle knew.

"That looks like it's it, so away we go and it's five after five AM. How about that?"

Dickie leaned over and tapped him on the shoulders. "Five after five in the morning is late, son. We had better git on it."

I couldn't argue with a man who spent most of his life up at two or three to eat breakfast and get on the water by sun up. In his eyes, we were definitely leaving in the middle of the day.

THE TRIP WAS A BREEZE really, that is until we hit New Jersey. Around the city was absolutely a mess and didn't promise to get any better. After all, what did I expect? It was the day before Thanksgiving when everyone and their brother was heading somewhere. The thought crossed my mind that Dickie had been right the night before when he suggested that we be on the road by three AM, Lindy and I shot his idea down with a bang, but now, looking at the traffic ahead of us, the old man was absolutely right…but I wasn't about to tell him that. I didn't have to say a word. I could feel what he was thinking all the way from his back seat perch.

I pulled off at the next rest stop and grabbed the maps from my case while Lindy and Dickie headed to the bathrooms and to grab something to eat. I looked frantically at the Jersey map to see if there was an alternate passage way to get to the Thruway and then to the Mass Pike. I found another way, although I knew it wouldn't be too much less of a pain, but it was worth whatever time we could save. I decided I better join the other two inside and take care of business. God knows when I would have the chance again.

Taking the route I found paid off and the traffic wasn't too bad yet. I could tell, from looking in my rear mirror that we were staying just ahead of the hungry wolf pack following us at speeds that were catching up. I pressed down on the accelerator and roared ahead.

Dickie began to tell some of his old shore stories to pass the time. There was no one who could spin a yarn like him. He was a master at it. With that Eastern Shore twang and slang, as I called it, he got me laughing so hard, I had to beg him to hold on for a few minutes while I caught my breath.

"I swear, Uncle Dickie, you will kill my Tug with your old stories," Lindy shrieked. "Where do you get them?"

Dickie was laughing at his own stories. That's what made it so damned funny. He would tell you the story and then at the punch line, he would get to laughing so hard that you were primed by the time he got to it. "That's what makes these tales so good, Lindy girl. They are all true. At one time or another, they happened jist like I am tellin' 'em. Honest. Cross my heart."

"You have to be kidding me, Uncle Dickie. No one could have lived these stories. You are funning on us."

I didn't bother to tell her that on the few Saturday night visits to the garage, I had met these men, and I could swear to the Pope that these men were not kidding. They had some tales to tell and when they did, there was nothing funnier on the face of this planet. You could die from the hurt in your stomach when they got going.

The sign up ahead alerted us that we were entering New York State. I had made it around the metro area and we were headed north. I saw Dickie gawking at the sign as we passed and there was an odd look on his face. "Something wrong, Dickie?"

"No, not really son. I was jist rememberin'"

"Remembering what, Uncle?"

"Reading that sign that we were in New York, I was thinking of the times way back when, when Hawkeye and me come up here to New York. We used to haul the arsters to the market. Then we would turn around and git right on back. I can't believe we did that. Bein' young you kin do anythin'."

"I didn't know you used to come to New York City, Uncle Dickie."

"How could ya? You weren't even born yet. Those were the days. Your daddy never wanted to make the trip. No siree bob. Travelin' off the shore wasn't for GD Short. He swore he would never go off shore land or fish off shore waters. And he never did. That's probably why you never heard nothin' about the good old days before you were born. Your daddy stayed put and thought I was crazy to be goin' up north. He had some notions that we might be taken or something. I think he was still fightin' the war or somethin'."

"Good grief, Dickie." I snorted.

"Go on and snicker about it, son. There are lots of folks, including myself I guess, that still think of the Eastern Shore as the south. It's below the Mason-Dixon you know."

Shaking my head, I said, "Are you sure of that, Dickie?"

"I know it to be the truth. I will take you there myself when we git back. Huh," he snapped. "You Harvard boys aren't as smart as you think you are."

"Maybe we aren't after all. I will take you up on that, Dickie. I would like to see it with my very own eyes."

"Don't you doubt me, son. You will see it fer sure." We sped along and by the time we reached Boston, Dickie was sitting up front with me and Lindy was fast asleep in the back.

"Wake up sleepy head," I shouted. We will be there in just a few minutes."

I looked in the mirror and saw Lindy's eyes widen as we wound up the big hill and turned into our driveway. I prayed she wouldn't be overwhelmed by the life I came from. I was a little nervous about that.

When my Cherokee came to a stop, I jumped out and opened her door. When she stepped out, she looked up at me and said, "This is beautiful, Tug. You sure came from a fairy-tale world."

I had to think quickly on my feet or she was going to bolt on me. I hugged her tightly and whispered, "Yes, I did Lindy, and now I have completed the picture with my own very own fairy-tale princess."

Smiling up at me, she said, "You are impossible, Tug Alston. I know you are trying to make me feel comfortable, but in an odd way, I do, even though this world is galaxies from mine. There is something about this home that makes me feel very welcome."

"Well good. Then let's go inside and you can meet my family." With my full attention on Lindy, I hadn't noticed that the one I was most nervous about was already knocking at the door. It appeared Dickie Short was in a hurry to begin the holiday.

ALL I CAN SAY IS that every calamity known to man happened over Thanksgiving in the Alston home. After the perfunctory introductions, all hell broke loose. The turkey went on fire in the oven. I still don't know what that was all about. My mother kept politely smiling at Dickie, although I knew she hadn't a clue at one thing he was saying. When my father came to the rescue and peeled off the charred skin from the turkey, he found that actually the bird, itself, was still rather raw. So while we waited for the microwave to do its magic, Lindy got into the mimosas with Mikey. I heard her begin to giggle uncontrollably and I didn't know how I was going to fix that little problem and then I caught my father staring at all of us in utter disbelief. I knew what was running through his mind. The man had paid a king's ransom to send his son to one of the best universities in America and to have him graduate and give up a very promising future for... for...for this?

Then the final touch came when the doorbell rang and my dad reluctantly opened the door, while trying to prevent any caller from seeing the scene going on in our home. I saw his mouth literally drop when he greeted his old friend, Max Pierson. It seemed Max was in Boston and decided to pay a surprise visit. Surprise wasn't the word for it. My only thought, in sheer panic mode, was how I could make myself evaporate in thin air?

I had to do something fast. My father was well aware of the feelings that Max harbored toward Dickie after I told him all about the letters and how I was sent off to find out what the man was writing to Max about. How could this be happening to me? Help! A thousand times help!

Mom jumped up from her chair and grabbed Max around the neck and hugged him. She was so happy to see their old friend. She obviously had no idea what was about to befall her Thanksgiving table.

"Oh Max, how wonderful to see you," she cried "You will stay for dinner, of course."

"Dear," my father said quietly, biting his lip and praying for a miracle, "maybe Max has other plans." But this was not the moment that Ted Alston would get a divine intervention.

Answering so quickly that one would think that this was planned by Max all along, he smiled and said, "I don't have any other plans and I would be delighted to share your table." Out of the corner of my eye, I saw my father reel a little to the side, and then I felt the gigantic hug Max was laying on me. "Tug, I am so glad to see you. I was hoping you would be here."

I was close to hurling now. "Why Max, what a surprise;" and it really was a surprise. Now there was nothing else I could do but to make the introductions and let the chips fall where they may.

I turned to Lindy with a sickening look on my face and said, "Max? This is Lindy Short. As Max took her hand I was relieved that he was not really listening to her last name. But who would be doing that when a gal this attractive and young was standing in front of you? Lindy, now really tipsy from Mikey's handiwork, shook Max's hand so hard that I could see she was beginning to go off balance. I took her by the elbow and helped her sit back down on the sofa. At least she was able to smile up at Max sweetly. Then, the ball buster of events was about to happen. Dickie stood up and waited for me to introduce him. His hand at the ready for a great big shake and a grin on his face that told me we were in for a kerfluffle, as he would put it. I stuttered so badly that even Dickie couldn't believe it and then took a deep breath and thought, what the hell? "Max Pierson, this is Lindy's uncle- Dickie Short."

The silence between the men was deafening. It hit them both at the same time. Dickie reacted like he was meeting royalty while Max's face turned the brightest color red I have ever seen. Dickie grabbed Max's hand and shook it until it damned near fell off. Max tried to conceal his utter contempt for the man who tried, and almost succeeded, in driving him crazy, not to mention the fact that this absolutely hideous man was the main reason he lost one of his best young reporters. I'll give it to Max; he was polite.

All would have been lost had Dad not handed Max a stiff Scotch and raised a toast. Thank God, dinner was ready!

The scene at the table was beyond description. Everyone sat glued to their seats watching my father try to carve up that miserable looking bird while my mother, sweet as ever, passed around the vegetables that were clearly way over cooked and dried out. I sat next to Lindy and made sure to keep a tight grip on her elbow to prevent any fall outs from the sidelines.

That wouldn't have gone down too well by anyone, including me. I glared at Mikey who was the instigator of her misery. He smiled back quite proud of himself. However, the one saving grace was that, much to my amazement, everyone was getting along. Dad started talking to Dickie and asking him a million questions about the shore and what I was getting myself into. With that, Max jumped in and before I knew it, we were all laughing at the outlandish tales of Dickie Short and his friends. Once again, Dickie came through like a thoroughbred, or at least, a prize mule. This was the man I came to love and now he was pouring out that Eastern Shore magic on my rather elitist Boston family.

After dinner, Mom took to the kitchen while Lindy had no choice but to excuse herself for a nap. Mikey grabbed a hold of Dickie and led him to the kitchen and said he had a game he wanted to play with him. Before I could stop Dickie, they were already down the hall. I looked at Dad and we knew what was going to happen next. We raced out to the kitchen and Mikey had handed Dickie the other end of the infamous Alston rope.

"Come on, Mikey," I barked. "Dickie is our guest. This is a family thing."

"Don't you go making excuses for me, son," yelled Dickie. "I kin take this young buck on in a heartbeat." Mikey stared at him and laughed. He had no idea how strong watermen could be. No idea at all.

"Give the go ahead, Dad," Mikey shouted.' We are ready."

With that, Ted Alston yelled "Go!"

Mikey pulled very hard and was beginning to move Dickie's feet toward the line. Dickie's face turned bright red and, for a minute, it looked as if he was going to be dragged across without any problem at all. Then, it all changed. Dickie stood up tall and yelled, "Geronimo." I knew right then Mikey was about to get a lesson.

Dickie tightened his grip on the rope until the veins in his hands popped out. The look on his face told me he was thinking he was back out on the water, pulling up the heavy crab pots. Indeed, Mikey was going to regret this.

Yanking hard on the rope, Mikey's feet began to give way. They slid slowly and torturously toward the dread line of defeat. Then, with one last hard yank, Mikey went flying over the line and onto his ass. It was over and Dickie let out a whoop that could be heard clear over to the Cape. In complete and utter amazement, Mikey shook Dickie's hand and went slinking away.

DAD INVITED MAX, DICKIE AND me into his den for a drink. I noticed that something was happening. It was a good thing too. Maybe it was the wink Max gave my Dad as we settled in.

"So, Dickie, I see you have taken my son away from reporting and have him onto a new adventure. Don't get me wrong, I was more than a little disappointed at first, but I can see how much he really wants to do this. And the fact that your pretty grand niece holds such sway over him, I knew I didn't have a chance to talk him out of doing this."

Your son is a good young feller, Ted. I know what you wanted for him, but it doesn't always turn out that way in life. In fact, sometimes it's the unexpected that makes our lives so darned exciting."

Max chimed in immediately. "I was really pissed at you, Dickie Short. I mean between those damned letters every day and then persuading Tug here to leave and try to help you folks down there...well, I thought he was out of his mind. But I can see now that he is starting to have a real life on the shore and that he is happy. The Eastern Shore is a beautiful and unique place."

"It was, once upon a time. But now the outlanders are over runnin' it. I know there are a lot of nice folks comin' on over, but it's what they are doin' to it that makes us so mad. I want you to know that I do feel bad that some of your advertisers are giving you holy hell over the commotion we are causing, but sometimes in a war, people git hurt."

Max scratched his head. I new that look on his face. It was one of exasperation. He wasn't going to get into a fight with Dickie and especially not here in our home, but I could see the thought had occurred to him. I was grateful that Max was appearing to be agreeable.

"Yes, Dickie, sometimes people do lose a lot, but I have told Tug to be careful that he doesn't lose sight of the two sides to this story."

Dickie looked over directly into my eyes. They penetrated me for a moment and then he said, "Are there two sides to this story, son?"

I was on the hot seat and couldn't escape. I had to tell him the truth and what I was truly beginning to believe.

"Yes, Dickie, there are always two sides to any dispute. However, right now, the outlanders have made this problem very lopsided and bad consequences have occurred because of it. My hope is to be able to write well enough to get people's thoughts and desires back in line with what is best for everyone-especially the land and waterways."

I saw the look on my Dad's and Max's face. Even Dickie sat back with a wistful and hopeful look glistening in his eyes. I had won this round quite surely and they were all convinced I wasn't about to run off in the night, half-cocked. I was hoping I could win the next round and then the next, but only time would tell. If this movement got big enough then we shore folks could even win this whole battle. This would be the greatest test of my writing skills. Thomas Paine called a nation to revolution, and while I would never dare to compare myself to him, still and all, this was my mission.

The Rallying Cry

THERE WASN'T A MINUTE TO waste once we all got back to the shore. I had so much to do that my head was spinning. Lindy was ready to go too. She loved my family, like I knew she would. The only problem was that I had to keep her mind focused on the project at hand and not on marrying me.

Dickie had had the time of his life in Boston. I don't think he had ever taken a trip like that. In his younger years, when he did travel, it was always delivering oysters or crabs and then rushing on back home. He told me that his alone time with my Dad down by the harbor was one of the best of his life. They talked about water things and he confided in me that my Dad told him how much the area had changed and how the over development had really changed the Cape and now it was even facing another problem. The Cape had out-priced itself for the younger people. They couldn't even afford to work out there in the summers and have a place to stay. It had gotten too expensive. Secretly Dickie thought that maybe my Dad truly hoped I would get something going for the shore before it was way too late and that maybe even ignite a spark of hope that would spread all over. I was enchanted by the notion, but was realistic to know that that was nearly impossible. It was all about money and not nostalgia. Nostalgia isn't good for the bottom line.

I noticed that Dickie was moving a bit slower these days. I guessed it had something to do with the coming of the winter. It had become increasingly apparent that the cold weather took its toll on these watermen. Their once limber joints swelled and the pain was almost unbearable. Dickie never complained. Never. It wasn't his style.

Lindy and I were at the library almost every day now. She researched and spoke to people there in a private room while I wrote, wrote, wrote. The local papers loved me and every week I had a deadline to make. The articles and stories were beginning to take on a life of their own. We could see that something was happening out there because every week there were dozens of letters coming into us and encouraging us to keep it up. Every time a new development was proposed, the meetings about it were packed in the city and town halls. The natives were restless and the developers were well aware of it from Delaware to Maryland and down to the Virginia coast.

I had taken quite a fancy to the tales and stories of the indigenous Indian tribes of the area and what had happened to them. In a series of weekly missives, I told some of the end results for what had been the colonization chapters of the shore. I compared them to the present and asked the question if this is where the shore was heading? If the development were to continue at this rate, the population would shift away from the settling families of the region to an entirely new group from all over. Not that this is a bad thing, but it would change the entire identity of the area. Gone will be the farmers, watermen, chicken producers, and everything that has made the Eastern shore what it is and what has attracted people to come and live here. Gone will be that unique and colorful vocabulary that makes this region so distinctive. Gone will be islands like James and Bingham where the King's English is still heard and a simpler way of life is enjoyed.

The people loved this series, and it became a basis to launch a rallying cry for reform and restraint on the shore. Up shore, down shore, east and west shore people were forming groups to take a second and third look at what was to be done about the constant building in all the towns. New restrictions were needed and a citizen revolt was in the air.

A rather interesting contingent of folks formed on Kent Island where they remembered what happened to their tiny island when the big boys across the Chesapeake decided it was time to build that bridge. Today the island is nothing like it was. The entire world that people knew has been swept away forever. It is totally built up with condos, restaurants, marinas and stores. Everyone wants to live on the marsh and overlook the Bay, but not everyone realizes that everyone in the world can't. There just is so much of that in the world and when it is gone. It's gone for good.

I made a point, when I could, to write the other point of view, so I couldn't be accused of not being fair and balanced. Because everyone knows there are two sides to everything. I think it's what gave me so much credibility. I wrote of how economies of towns need to grow and in order to do that you have to have expansion. Communities need new people and new ideas and new dreams. They just don't need to be overrun wall to wall. And they don't need to make infrastructure problems that will make matters worse for those who do come and live. And I stressed the strain on the environment and what all this development was doing to the wetlands and the species of beautiful birds and animals that are a main attraction for tourists each year. That money is significant to the shore economy and has to remain in the local and state coffers.

It was at supper one night that the really big idea came to us. Lindy and I were reading over the day's mail and letters from folks all over the shore. We even got one from a fellow in Jersey who had been down here and read my articles with keen interest. He was upset over what had happened to the Jersey shore over the years, but it was already too late for that to be saved to make any significant difference.

Dickie sat there and made his own comments and then he said, "Why don't we have a big convention. You know, invite everyone down here to talk it all out."

I didn't know what to say about that and then Lindy jumped up and planted a big kiss on his cheek. "That's a wonderful idea, Uncle Dickie. We could hold it down at the marina where the crab derby is every year."

"That's what I was a thinkin'."

"You know, it just might work. That way, we could get a real idea of what is going on out there. We could have literature printed up and a whole bunch of things."

"Yep, now yer comin' son. That's jist what I was thinkin'. And we could have a mess of crabs and some arsters jist so folks feel right at home."

"It would make a lot of money for us down here, you know."

"Money?" I asked, not even thinking of that aspect of it. "I don't know about that, Lindy. We don't want to make this a carnival. We are about serious business here, you know."

"I know that, Tug, but you do have to feed them and you do have to have a main speaker. And you, of course, would be the main speaker, Tug. You would have to do it."

"Good God, Lindy. I am just getting used to the idea of a gathering. I'll have to think about having speakers and who would do what. We may need someone of greater stature to do that."

Dickie smiled at the two of us. We were enjoying his idea and he was too, the sly devil. He was getting us to do exactly what he wanted us to do. It wasn't just for the land and water anymore. It was for him and all the decent watermen and their families. It was for the farmers and all the people of the shore. This was to be one of the largest, if not *the* largest gathering of Eastern Shore folk ever, and he was going to love every minute of it. Good God, could we pull it off? We had about six months to move heaven and earth. I needed a lot of help from a lot of people.

HELP BEGAN POURING IN ONCE we had set the date. June twentieth was going to be a day the Eastern Shore would never forget. If all went right, and God hope it would, the seeds of determination to begin to save what the people loved so much, would begin. It was going to take maximum effort, but hey, anything is possible, isn't it?

As country music rules on the shore, Lindy decided to strike out on her own without telling me and get some help on that score. I was still not convinced that you had to have entertainment and food concessions along with the speakers. She and Dickie disagreed with me vehemently and so I was over ruled. They were right of course. I needed to lighten up and go with the flow for this event. When Lindy bounded home one afternoon and had enlisted the help of a local, and well known DJ, she was out of her mind. "He is simply the best. Everyone knows him and they love him. We are guaranteed to have a huge crowd come if RC is spinnin' that country."

"He said he could get us a real big headliner to come on down here, if we wanted that. God, Tug, this is really exciting. Wouldn't it be the cat's pajamas if he brought Kenny Chesney down to our beloved shore?"

I didn't know who the hell she was talking about, but he must be good if she was this crazy about him. "Whatever you say, Lindy."

"You don't have a clue who I am talking about, do you?"

"No, no I don't but I'll take your word for it."

"I don't think you will have to worry about that, son," Dickie piped up from his chair in the living room. "I do believe this here git together is going to be something else."

"From your lips to God's ears, Dickie."

Dickie actually snorted out loud. "Now that is a new one on me, son. Where did you pick that saying up?"

"I don't know really. I heard it years ago. My mother used to say it all the time. My Dad has even used it in some of his sport's reporting. I guess it just says it like it is."

"By the way, Dickie did you get the food lined up?"

"I sure did. The town's folks are goin' to do it up right. Wally and Tadpole are takin' charge and Burger Boy is goin' to tend to the cheeseburgers and hots. Don't you worry none, it will all happen and folks won't go away hungry or if they do it will be their own fault."

"Wally? That's great. I am sure Clumpy will be right next to him along with Hambone. They are great men and will steam up those crabs by the ton."

"I can taste it all now," Lindy yelled in from the kitchen. "However, right now, you better get ready for my pot roast. I know it's not crabs, but it's pretty good."

Dickie leaned over from his big, old chair and said, "She really does have a way about her, doesn't she son?"

Tug chuckled. There was no need to even answer that comment.

They Do What?

WHILE IT WAS ONLY JANUARY, I knew that June would be coming faster than a speeding bullet, and there was a lot more to do than thinking about the food and format of the big day. I still had to convince my readers out there that this meeting was essential to show the developers and politicians that the people of the Eastern Shore meant business.

For the following couple of weeks I traveled around the whole shore as much as I could. One of the many beauties of the shore in winter is that it doesn't snow but for a few flurries at a time so one can move freely without worrying about whiteouts and nasty weather to postpone things. No matter where I went I saw bull dozers at the ready and fields being surveyed as if they were prime cuts of meat preparing to be devoured. I couldn't believe how fast land, cultures, and traditions could be swept away. All for the enchantment of hundreds of houses, shopping centers, condos and office buildings. There was the point that this was economic growth and a sign that good times may have returned to an area that had gone through a real downturn, but it still made me sad and more than a little angry.

Lindy and I scoured papers from all over the country. We wanted to see how other communities were handling this situation. Some areas were hit harder than others, but the coastal regions were being absolutely devoured. We were interested to find that in a couple of states, citizens were doing the same thing as we were. They were locked into battles over preservation. In every case, the local politicians always argued how good it was for the region. However, it struck us odd that while the bureaucrats were always quick to say build, the people that lived there weren't so enthusiastic.

One thing that always niggled me was that I wondered why people wanted to live all clustered together. Didn't anyone want to have a little space anymore?

Before I knew it February had arrived and with it Dickie had a whole new adventure for me to experience; one that would indelibly imprint itself on my mind forever. It was a cold Thursday in the second week when he and I sat at his kitchen table going through newspapers and weeding out the ones we needed from those that could hit the trash cans.

"I hope you and Lindy don't have any plans this weekend, son," Dickie said with a sneaky kind of look on his face.

"I don't think we do Dickie. Why?"

"There is somewhere I want to take you. Lindy won't want to go, so it'll be jist you and me."

"Sounds mysterious. Where is it, Dickie?"

"It's the National Outdoor Show. It's held in a small town not far from here."

"What do they do at this show?"

Dickie burst out laughing 'cause he knew what my reaction was going to be.

"Well, son, you see they skin rats..."

My eyes bugged right out of their sockets as I cut him off yelling, "They do what?"

"Now calm down, son," he begged. "It's a real big thing down here. I mean we have blue-ribbon champions right here from Somerville."

This was beyond belief. "People skin rats and they have shows and they have champions? Just where the hell did you say you are taking me?"

"It's called the National Outdoor Show and it isn't those sewer critters they skin. It's muskrats. We prefer to call 'em rats or sometimes marsh rabbits, but mostly they are rats to us."

In the time I had been down here, with all the twangs and slangs flying, I found this to be beyond the pale. My ears had to be deceiving me, but knowing Dickie; they were not.

I muttered out, "I suppose there is no use in saying I am not going. Let me guess. This is an Eastern Shore main event?"

"Not really for most folks, but to a lot of us it is. Why most folks that live in these here parts have been doin' this since they could walk. And I must tell ya, I am not jist goin' to watch, son. I am goin' to participate. Hell, I do pretty good with the skinnin' and most times come in first place, even at my age."

I couldn't say a word if I tried. I felt my stomach give a mighty heave at the very thought of what he was telling me. But I knew Dickie and I knew he was determined to drag me to this if it was the last thing he did and it certainly might just be the last thing I did, but I decided that the best policy was to go with the when in Rome thing...

"I take it this grand show is on Saturday?"

"Yep. We will need to git an early start son so don't go gettin' too involved tomorrow night with Lindy girl."

I waved him off with my hand and walked away. He had won yet again and I was more than a little apprehensive about this little trip with him. It certainly would be a whole new chapter of my new life on the Eastern Shore.

I WAS UP AT THE crack of dawn and made coffee before Dickie broke through the door to the kitchen.

"Well I see you are up and at 'em early, son." With a sly smile on his face he said, "You must really want to get to this event."

"I think maybe the operative thought here Dickie is that I want to get it over with."

Dickie's mouth curled at the corners and broke into a broad grin as he said, "You won't want to leave. I'll bet you a dollar."

That's all? I think we should bet a bit more, don't you?" I was sure this was going to be the easiest money I had ever taken from anyone. How could I lose this when I hated the very thought of what I was about to see?

"All righty then. Yer on. The most I will go is ten dollars and that's good cash money."

Leaning across the table, I extended my hand. "I'll take that bet, Mr. Short."

After a couple mugs of hot coffee and Dickie's fabulous scrambled eggs, we jumped into my Cherokee and took off an hour or so after sun up.

I must admit I think it might have been more appropriate if we had driven into this place in Dickie's old beaten up truck, but I had to make sure we would make it there (wherever there was) and back. With Dickie's "beauty" I couldn't be sure.

On the way to nowhere we talked and gabbed of all things shore. I loved it when we had time to do this. I never tired of Dickie's conversations and descriptions of this place he loved so much and all the rich memories he stored from his past. He was a master at finding interesting snippets to discuss, no matter what the topic. I marveled at how this simple man, educated just barely through high school and nothing thereafter, could turn philosopher at the drop of a hat. He put Washington insiders and elites to shame.

The time flew by as the two of us engaged in conversations about the things we love so much. He was heartened at how quickly I had come to love *his* shore as he would put it. With a turn here and a turn there, in an hour or so, give or take, we were there.

We drove into this small hamlet of a town. Many of the original buildings were now in disrepair or closed. A sign that there was once a more prosperous time. It reminded me of a scene out of the *Walton's* TV series. In this place I could imagine the hustle and bustle of days gone by with people sitting outside on the porch of the old grocery that had now all but fallen down. But there was still life here and an active high school. It was here we turned in and I parked my Cherokee along with dozens and dozens of other folks pouring in to stake their claim on a spot to view this bizarre tradition they had.

Dickie slowly opened his door and climbed down from the Cherokee. I had been noticing lately it was getting harder and harder for him to step down so far without help. Well, he was getting up there in years, but I would be damned if I would ever go near that conversation for fear of getting my head chopped off. As usual, he knew just about everyone who was there. Why was it that didn't surprise me? I remember thinking to myself one night that when he passed, the funeral would be huge. He was truly an Eastern Shore treasure.

"Isn't this excitin', son? Folks come from near everywhere to participate in this here event."

"I can't tell you how excited I am, Dickie," I sarcastically snarked at him.

Dickie kept one arm on mine and dragged me in every direction, introducing me to this one and that one over there. I felt like I was a spinning top. Then it dawned on me that he was doing this on purpose. He wanted everyone to meet me and put a face with the reporter who was going to need every one of them to be successful in the "new revolution" as he called it. The man didn't miss a trick and he knew very well that there was power in numbers.

I managed to finally break free and roam by myself for a while. Outside, there were tents set up with boiling pots of steaming water and men and women talking recipes. At this point, I couldn't imagine what was going to be boiled in those huge cauldrons. The scene looked like an artist's rendering of a witch's convention. All that was missing were a few incantations. In another group of tents was beer and booze. Now things were looking up. Even though it was pretty early yet, it didn't stop anyone from having a cold one before the show got going. Maybe they were on the right track.

From mere observation, I could see the anticipation was growing. I went back inside to find Dickie and just as I did a big, burly man the size of Burger Boy stood on a platform and began shouting. The whoops and hollers went up and soon everyone was in the spirit of what was about to begin. Then I saw them; the stacks of dead critters lying to the corner of the stage. I swallowed hard so not to get that feeling that I was going to puke. It wasn't easy, I can tell you. Dickie took one look at me and knew exactly what he needed to do to prevent the inevitable from happening to me. He left and went straight-way to get me a beer. When he got back, he didn't ask me. He told me to drink it fast. I didn't put up one argument and complied with gratefulness. Thank God, these folks were civilized on one level at least. The beer was a Corona. No lime however.

Now the man on the stage was yelling at the top of his lungs. He stepped forward and bellowed out, "Who will be the first to skin a few rats and git us started here?"

The beer was beginning to work and I felt a bit more relaxed. Grateful for another, I guzzled with gusto. I took a deep breath and braced myself for the man or woman (yes woman) who would step forward. I had noticed that Dickie had disappeared and then I went into a state of shock when I saw him step forward on the stage with a "rat" in his hand. God please give me strength.

"I will start 'er out," Dickie exclaimed. "Stand back and let a master show you how it's done." How was it, I thought, that he had never mentioned this little talent of his? Dear God, the man was not to be believed.

Dickie held up the limp lump of a critter and then in the flash of a moonbeam, before I could even really see what he was doing, the pelt fell to the ground and away from the beast's body. I stood there astonished and not at all as sick as I imagined I was going to be. As a matter of fact, when he did it again and again I found myself becoming a part of a collective kind of excitement that was hard to explain to any sane person alive.

"Did you see that, Chester?" yelled a man to his friend in back of me. "Dickie is the King. I mean he is the King of the two cut."

I realized I was standing in the middle of some kind of tradition that had obviously been going on for perhaps centuries. It had the feel of something old and mysterious but I couldn't put my finger on it. I had to admit I began to think it might be a cult-like thing where witches were about to dance naked before me. I mean I am not really kidding. Outside were the big cauldrons that were boiling over for something to be cooked… then it hit me. I now knew what was going to be cooked in those kettles. They were going to actually *eat* the muskrats. Good God!

Then man after man and a few women stepped to the stage and took their turns. But no one could touch Dickie. I turned and asked a man standing close to me what the two cut thing was all about. He was indeed proud to tell me exactly what it was and that Dickie Short was the master of it. In two cuts he could skin a muskrat and like a hot knife through butter the skin would fall right off. No one could do it as fast or as accurate as Dickie. I stood there, stone silent, realizing I was gaining a whole new education that Harvard had never heard of.

For over an hour I watched the skinning one after another until I had had enough. It no longer bothered me; which bothered me. I had joined them and prayed no one I knew from another life would ever find out about this. It would be my luck that some Jasper would snap a photo and it would end up online someday. That wouldn't be cool at all. When Dickie nudged me, he led me toward the door. It was time to eat and I wasn't at all sure I was ready for muskrat stew.

I sat down as Dickie insisted I do. He was going off to get my lunch. I was beginning to feel that queasiness return, but the beers had helped out a lot. I mean a lot.

I sat staring at these good people who were having the time of their lives. They loved coming here as, I suppose their parents and grandparents and as far back as they could remember their families coming to take part in this winter festival. I was particularly drawn to the faces of the old men like Dickie. They all looked to be watermen from all over the shore. Their skin was weathered and tough. I knew very well how hard these winters could be on them. Crabbing in the spring through early fall and then oystering in the winter. Now I knew they had another way to earn a living to make it through. They trapped the muskrats and a beast named Nutria and sold their pelts to several markets who bought for furriers. It was all beginning to make sense to me. The circle hadn't been broken. They knew how to feed their families and live off the land. This show would be too much for outlanders but for these shore men it was their winter gathering and a time to talk all things Eastern Shore. I was again learning.

On the way home, Dickie and I couldn't stop talking. He had won another blue ribbon for this year's show and I had learned lessons I could never have imagined. I even admitted that although I was slow to swallow the muskrat, when I did, I found it very tasty. In fact I confessed it was down right delicious. I even went so far as to tell Dickie that I had enjoyed myself immensely. And you might be interested to know that when we arrived home, Dickie's hand was out in a flash waiting for that ten spot I had bet him.

Nervous Nellie

WINTER WAS AT AN END and spring was already upon us. I had never seen such a beautiful place in the spring. Boston was good, but the shore was a show-stopper. Birds from all over were saying good bye and flying off to where they came from. The great migration north was wondrous to watch. The indigenous flocks were nesting all over the place and the giant osprey were perched on the many platforms that dotted the coastal stretches. There were eagles at the Blackwater Refuge and everyone was joyous about the return of the majestic bird to these parts. Everything was coming alive and that meant that there wasn't a lot of time left before June and this major event we were planning on having in Somerville. Could we do it? We had no choice, we had to. The building never stopped. Because of the milder winter weather, it continued in the winter and now that warmer days were here, it just accelerated the pace at which structure would go up. Some things needed to be resolved. Fast.

I was in my room doing work on my computer when I heard a crash downstairs. I ran like the wind and when I reached the kitchen I found Dickie lying on the floor and cussing like a sailor.

"Are you okay, Dickie?"

"Oh hell, son, I am fine. Jist a little shook up, that's all."

"Here let me help you up. Can you stand up all right?"

"Stop yer fussin' and all. I jist slipped, that's all and if you say one word of this to Lindy, there'll be hell to pay. You hear me?"

I knew what his hell to pay meant and I had seen it once with a man who was trying to tell Dickie he didn't know what he was talking about. Without hesitation, I said, "Yes sir."

"There, I am fine now. You go on about yer business now. I am goin' down to Virgils' and have me some lunch with the guys. Should you be at all inclined to want to eat, you kin consider that an invitation."

Ouch! He was really pissed off at me for helping him up, or was it that he was pissed at himself for falling and having me see him do it? Either way, even though I was very busy, I didn't want him to go down there by himself. The scary thing was that I just couldn't figure out how he had slipped, but damned if I was going to ask him again for fear of being beaten to death by those huge fists of his.

"You know, Dickie, I am a little hungry at that now that you mention it, so I think I will stop what I am in the middle of and accept your invitation."

"Well then git a move on. I am leavin' right now."

"Hold on there tiger," I said. "Let me just go back upstairs and shut down my computer and use the bathroom. I'll be back before you can say another word."

Dickie not saying another word was a truly ridiculous thing to say. The man lived to do nothing but talk. As I dashed and ran for the stairs, I smiled to myself hearing that crusty, old voice snarling out at me. Most people might have been offended by him, but to me, that was so Dickie Short and what made him so positively special to me.

When we did arrive at Virgil's Dickie took off and left me in the dust. He shot to his usual booth as I followed at a slower pace. I spied Lindy working behind the counter. I had totally forgotten that she was working the lunch shift in all the excitement of the day, but it didn't make one bit of difference. She didn't see me and was completely being overwhelmed by the huge number of watermen crushing the counter, trying to pay their bills or yelling out their take-out orders. I never knew how she did it. The place was always bedlam at this time of the day, but she did it like it was the most natural thing in the world. I would have socked half of them in their unprepossessing faces.

As soon as I sat down, she was right there. I gather she must have noticed me after all, but didn't let on. She did love to play games with me. "Hey there handsome, remember me?"

I blushed, winked and answered, "Why no I don't, but I would like to." I liked to tease her too.

Dickie let out a grunt that said "Come on kids, let's order and not flirt with one another, shall we?"

We both laughed at the same time, but I didn't think Lindy had caught on to the fact that her dear uncle was in one hell of a mood. I was wrong, as is oft the case down here with me, as I heard her ask, "What's got you going today, Uncle Dickie?" I immediately slid down on the slippery booth and shielded my eyes with a menu. Quietly I said to myself, "Here it comes."

"Nothing is wrong," he snapped at her. "Are you goin' to go git yer uncle a burger, fries and a coke or are you not?"

Lindy stared him down. Instead of hustling off to do what he ordered her to do, she shimmied herself right down next to him. Her next act was a gutsy one, but she knew him better than anyone, I guess. She planted a big old kiss on his cheek. She didn't stop sucking his face until she felt him start to smile. Her spell worked 'cause for the rest of lunch he acted like a tamed animal.

It wasn't long before almost every man in the joint came over and talked with us about the oncoming gathering that was about to take place faster than a speeding bullet. I was most heartened when Wally and crew stopped by our booth and gave us the thumbs up on the food. If all else went wrong, at the very least we could eat ourselves to death.

To say I had become a nervous Nellie would be an understatement. I was beginning to believe that we might be going a bit too far with this. Every time I voiced that concern, Dickie snapped my head off and Lindy looked at me like I was committing treason. The whole of Somerville and a good deal of Eastern Shore folks were now involved and invested in "the second revolution." I really wish they wouldn't call it that. But to them, this was a fight to the finish for their heritage to stay the way it always had been. They were acutely aware of what history's lessons taught on how a people could lose their land, their waters, and all the things around them that had given them a home for centuries. They were going to be damned if they wouldn't do something to stop it.

Dickie was so proud of himself and only wished that his dear Shirley could be at his side, fighting the good cause and watching her man go right into the fray, as he had been known to do many times. Oh, how he missed her and loved her.

Luck was with them as the fateful June day rolled around. There was no wind to speak of and the sun was shining down brightly by the time Dickie and Tug headed out to the fair grounds that lay just down the road and around the bend.

Lindy came running over to the Cherokee the minute she spotted us, yelling her damn fool head off.

"You won't believe your eyes, Tug. So many people have already pulled in and the food tents stretch for miles. It's so exciting."

"That sounds pretty terrific," I answered. "You did remember to pick up all the pamphlets, didn't you?"

"Of course I did, Tug," she said in an incredulous voice. "They are some of the most important weapons we have here today, so why would you think I would forget them?"

I knew I shouldn't have said it the way I did. A woman really doesn't like to be second-guessed. "Hey, I'm sorry, Lindy. I am just so nervous about all this."

"You better get a hold on yerself, son. You have to speak today in front of all these here folks and you have to be at yer best. So shape up."

I walked away from the two of them. I needed to go on down by the water's edge and stare out for a while. I knew the water would give me that sense of purpose I would need to have today to make it clear to all who had come, just how important this gathering was. Did I say important? Hell no- it was *key* to the whole project.

The sun's reflection off the water at the marina seemed to mesmerize me. I began thinking of how far this journey had taken me up to now. It seemed years and yet it was only months. I had fallen in love with an old waterman who had taught me more than anyone in my life. I had fallen in love with a fantastic gal, and I had fallen in love with a land that I desperately wanted to preserve…and yet something was bothering me; something that kept gnawing at my insides and I had to find out what it was before I spoke in a few hours. I knew it was something very important and yet, somehow, it just wouldn't reveal itself.

Seeing Tug down by the water, Dickie left Lindy to help out with the other vendors and told her he needed some time alone with the boy. She understood. Her uncle always seemed to know what was needed in times of great stress with people. He was an amazing man.

Dickie walked up slowly behind Tug and then said, "So, what ya thinkin', son? I kin see it all over ya."

I turned around and smiled at my dear friend. "How is it you know everything?"

"'Cause I am brilliant, and not at all modest."

I shook my head in a gentle way and said, "Not your style Dickie. But you are right. There is something tugging at my soul and I don't know what it is."

"Well, think it through, son. Usually when this happens it's because we aren't really certain of the situation at hand. Maybe you want to change things here, but you feel guilty that you might hurt the cause more than help it."

"Did you ever have that happen to you Dickie?"

He looked at me like I had just driven spikes through his hands.

After a moment, he answered my question. "Yes, yes, I have son. I never ran from a fight and one time I should have thought it through better. It was over the way we men were crabbin'. The government men were all over the waters, tryin' to catch us with them oversize crabs. We did it all the time and most times, I was lucky and never got caught. Then, once I did and they were goin' to take me in. That was a pretty tight year for Shirley and me with money and all, so there was no way I could pay what they were goin' to fine me. I had to think me up a plan to git out of it. So, I talked to them fer a while and explained that the crabs that I had hangin' onto my nets weren't goin' home with me. They were goin' to git thrown back. I said I was a God-fearin' man who would never do such a thing, and I jist kept talkin' and talkin' 'til one of them looked at the other and said, "Harry, let's git out of here. If we don't, this man will have us here all year talkin' us to death."

I couldn't say a word to him. This story was like all his stories. Once he got to telling it, you just held your breath until the punch line. I had no problem visualizing those poor bastards and how they probably were at the begging stage for him to shut up by the time they went on their way. Who is like Dickie? Absolutely no one. But his story helped to dislodge what it was that was bugging me. He had used the other side of the problem to solve it. I would have to do the same.

"That was a great story, Dickie. Believe it or not, you really helped me."

"I did?" he answered with a surprised look on his face. "Well, I sure am glad I could be of some help."

With a gentle pat on the back, he walked away. He had done it again. Without saying he was a know it all, he just told a story and there was no doubt in my mind that he knew exactly what story to pull out of his hat for this occasion.

The Time Has Come

I WALKED AROUND EVERY CORNER OF those fair grounds, watching people who had come from all over. I was stunned to see how many had made the trek down here to join us to show their solidarity for what we were doing; or at least trying to do.

I spotted Lindy across the field and smiled broadly. She was involved in all the kid's games and they were having a ball. In back of her were rows of white tents blowing in the gentle breeze off the water. The smell of all the crabs and oysters and corn on the cob, baked beans, and God knows what else, made me instantly hungry. I knew I had better get on over there and eat before I made my speech. It wouldn't be too cool if I fell off of the bandstand while trying to make some salient point. No, not cool at all.

Lindy waved to me and I pointed to her that I was headed to the chow line. She shot me a "thumbs up" and went back to the kids. As I stepped up to the steamed crab's line, I went into complete shock to see the two men who were walking straight for me. There was no time for me to make a quick bee line. I was trapped.

I stood my ground and extended my hand when none other than John Dawson and Max Pierson walked up to me and said, "Tug, how are you doing?"

"I am just fine. I must say I am shocked to see you two men here today."

Max shook my hand and said, "We wouldn't miss this for anything in the world."

"Hell no," John shot into my face. "It isn't every day that my colleagues and I get roasted over a spit."

"Hey, John, that's pretty rough. I don't think that was our intention here. It is, however, to educate folks on their rights and to try to form a large group of citizens who are interested in keeping their homeland from disappearing into a sea of nothing but houses and shopping centers."

"I know how you feel Tug, John snapped. Remember we have been through this before."

Max stepped in to try to calm the two of us down. " Look Tug, John and I came down here to hear what everyone has to say and to see what direction the wind is blowing in. That's just a good defensive play. That's all there is to it. There is no offense meant."

Tug shrugged his shoulders and said, "Then, there is no offense taken, Max."

Max desperately wanted to change the mood between the two of them. "Now, if you don't have any objections Tug, can John and I cut in here with you and get some of this food. I don't know about anyone else, but I am starving and the smell of these crabs is making me crazy."

Tug smiled at Max. He could always see reason when things got a bit heated. "Not at all. As a matter of fact, I would welcome it."

Even though Max had been able to avoid an all-out fight between the two, John was still boiling inside at this young upstart and what he was doing to his life. So onward he went to drive his point home.

"I see from your pamphlets that you are the main speaker, Tug. I also see that you have really given these people some pretty heavy duty ammunition by which to get them all riled up at those of us who make our livings constructing things over here."

Tug winced. There was just no way John was going to drop it, so naturally, I couldn't either. "As you have already noted before, John, we have gone through this. I trusted you when you said you would hold up on developments for a while until you could do more to insure the proper infrastructure and protection of the wetlands and wildlife. But you didn't. You kept right on going and as you are a builder, I am a writer/reporter. I call it like I see it."

Infuriated, John shot back. "And you see it only the way you want to."

Max shook his head and decided to let us go at it until we were finished.

"That's not true, John, I said, chomping at the bit to get my point across. "Apparently you have not read some of my articles that say that not all development is a bad thing. In fact, in some areas it is vital to the economy. But, for God's sake, you guys don't have to build on every square inch of land. It's not right and it's bad for both the natural and human world. I am trying to see both sides and offer some answers. That's a hell of a lot more than you are willing to do."

Max reached between them and grabbed a whole handful of crabs. He thought maybe by physically getting in the middle of us, he could prevent us from killing one another. "Come on guys. Grab some crabs and a beer and let's forget about this for now. There will be plenty of time later to fight this out."

He was right. I felt foolish having him stand between us like two kids in the school yard. "Good idea, Max." It was times like these that I knew why it was I liked this man so much.

No sooner had we sat down than John started in on me again. Thank the stars, Dickie saw my dilemma and walked on over. As relieved as I might've been at this moment, I was doomed because Dickie would certainly remember John Dawson and what happened the last time they were in each other's company. I was about to go from the frying pan into the fire.

"Hi son. Everything going okay?"

"Why just ducky, Dickie. I believe you know these men, don't you?"

Dickie extended his hand to Max and said, "Good to see you again, Max. Glad you could come on down to see how the people over here really feel about things that are going on down here. You kin hear it first hand."

Dickie's obvious snub of John Dawson hit its mark. John wanted to tear Dickie's head off. He remembered his last visit with Dickie Short. Shit!

I had to do something fast. I jumped up and grabbed Dickie by the arm and as I led him off, I yelled back to Max and John, "See you two later. Enjoy the food." It was kind of stupid, and Dickie knew he was being carted off, but I had to do something rather than create a scene that would have been totally unacceptable.

"Hold on, son. I git yer message. You don't want me near those men, but let me go. I won't do nothin' to embarrass ya."

"I know you won't, Dickie. I just had to get out of there and I am thankful you came over and bailed me out, but we have things to do and it's almost time for me to speak to the crowd. Where's Lindy?"

"She's fine. She's just fine, son. She's around here somewhere. She knows you have a million things to do, so she made herself scarce."

"I really would have liked to have seen her before I got up on that platform."

Dickie stopped short and stared directly into my eyes. I knew that look and I was about to get a talking to.

"Now, you listen here, son. You have come to like us all down here. Why you are one of us now as far as I kin see. People in these parts trust you and have come to hear you talk to them and tell them how we can change things and stop all this messin' with our shore. I know you are nervous and all, but seein' Lindy will only make you worse. I am goin' to git up on that stage and tell these folks to listen to you. You hear me, son?"

I was completely mortified. Dickie had put me in my place and I deserved it. He actually said I was one of them and that made me feel on top of the world. That's what I wanted more than anything in the world and here was the man that was one of the most revered old watermen on the Eastern Shore telling me I had made it into their closed society. I felt so happy inside.

"You are right, Dickie. I am being ridiculous and I have a lot to tell the folks. Lead on and make your introductions."

As he left my side, I yelled to him, "Thanks for telling me I am one of you. It means more than I can ever say." He never answered me. He just kept on walking.

Dickie stood at the podium and as all the loud speakers reverberated his craggy voice, as he yelled "How y'all doin' out there?" The masses went nuts. Many of them had no idea who this old man was, but those who did; went completely crazy. They loved him and I felt so proud that I had gotten to know him about as well as anyone could. I was also proud that soon, if everything worked out, I would be a part of his family. That is, if Lindy agreed to it.

He kept on going just like he was the main attraction. But then again, maybe he was. "I am here today to introduce you to a pretty smart young man. He came here to find out some things about our shore and after a little while with us, he decided to come on down for good." The cheers went up. It was obvious they all knew who he was talking about, but it still made me feel real good.

"Tug Alston has seen some things and gone some places. He has learned about our beloved shore and what we watermen and farmers have known forever. This here is the best land in the world and we love our lives and we want it to keep on going so our children and grandchildren kin have it for their futures."

At this point, I realized that perhaps Dickie and I might have some divergence of opinions. He just saw things in black and white while I saw them in gray. What he was saying was true enough about the shore, but he didn't want to see that the children of these watermen and farmers had different thoughts about their futures. Some wanted to leave for a while and take jobs elsewhere and some of them wanted to leave for good. The parents were left with no other choice but to sell their lands and retire. It wasn't what they wanted but this is the way it was. The Eastern Shore was being changed forever and it appeared no one, but the newcomers, liked it.

I felt sort of sick all of a sudden, but I had to tell it as it was, even if Dickie wasn't going to like it.

With that thought just leaving my mind, my name was called out and people were whooping it up and calling out to me. It was show time and the by the shear magnitude of folks who had come down here, I realized that there really was power in numbers. Now, if I can only get them to understand. The silence was deafening. They really wanted to hear what I was about to say and guess what? So did I.

"THANK YOU DICKIE," I SHOUTED as the crowd clapped non-stop for my dear old friend. I decided to seize the moment. "Isn't he something?" They really loved me now. I had to be the most conceited bastard in the world.

Finally they quieted down. Taking a deep breath, I began. "I am here today to share a dream. It's a dream of a shore that can have good water, good fishing, good living, and good planning."

With that, they exploded. I scanned quickly around the audience and my eyes picked up Max and John standing straight out in front of me. Now this is where it was going to get interesting.

"If we all work together to stop the massive expansions in these towns, and set forth a good plan of action, I believe we can save what is almost destroyed. We can no longer hope and pray that it will go away. It won't and if left to the developers, the shore and the Bay will be lost forever."

John was definitely not smiling now, but on the other hand, Max didn't seem to show much irritation.

"It is not my intention to get you against one another. The situation is this. It's not who's right or wrong, it's what is and we have to deal with that. That is why I have written my observations in your papers from two points of view. On the one hand, it is ruthless the pace at which the land is being gobbled up for homes and shopping centers, but on the other hand, in many areas, there is a need to do something to save the towns altogether. We need tighter restrictions and a more detailed look at what is to be built. So, we have to react in a reasonable way. It is too late in some areas, but we must save the Bay and water for the fishing industry and we must preserve a way of life that is quintessentially Eastern Shore."

I could tell they were listening to me because the applause was not coming so fast and furious now. At least I hoped it was that they were listening to me and not that they were going to rush the grandstand to tar and feather me. With Dickie's crowd, anything was possible.

"I ask all of you who have come here today, and there are more of you than I thought would ever be possible, to think about what it is you want more. Do you love your shore more than money? Do you love it more than a drug store on every corner? Do you love it more than anything else in the world? If so, then you are compelled to do something to work through this. You are no different than many other communities in this country who are struggling with the same dilemma. If you can do this now, then you can save what has been a part of you for over three hundred years and is part of the rich tapestry that is this country's early history. Some have compared this situation to what happened to the Native Americans. That may be close to the truth or maybe not. You have to make up your own mind what your future is going to be. But, plain and simple: it is wrong..."

Interrupting my train of thought, a few men started yelling out. "What kin we do? Where do we start?"

"You have already started just by being here today. There is a man among us who can be of enormous help. He might be willing to push our cause in his paper in Baltimore." With that, I pointed my finger out and landed on Max. I was definitely taking a chance and had no idea how Max might respond. He shot me one of those deer in the headlights looks.

"Will you help us, Mr. Pierson?" I really was losing my mind now to put Max in such a situation. And particularly with John Dawson standing right next to him.

Max squirmed for a moment and then looked straight at me and yelled, "Sure, why not, Tug. Let's win this battle for the Bay."

What happened next astounded me. John Dawson turned to Max and slugged him right in the face. The crowd around them reacted like it was a food fight and before long, everyone was into it. They cheered and yelled for Max and when Max slugged John in the face, the two of them went down and couldn't move. My eyes were glued to these refined men from the upper class, fighting like they were school bullies.

I leaped down from the stage and got to them before another blow could be struck. "Stop it you two. Remember it's me you are pissed at."

"I will get you, Alston," John screamed in my face. "I will get you for this if it's the last thing I do." I knew the threat was hollow. Dawson didn't want any more of this kind of street fighting. It was indeed not his way of handling this kind of situation. But he was checkmated now that Max had thrown in with us. Had Max gone mad?

Dawson stalked off as I helped Max up off the ground. Everyone cheered Max as he growled at the man, who was their sworn enemy, walked into the sunset so to speak.

I was done. No more needed to be said. The crowd broke up and milled around the marina taking boat rides with some of the watermen, eating all the food, and having a hell of a time. It was a success and how could I tell that? Hordes of people were signing petitions to our senators and congress folks. They were telling them it was high time they do something to protect the shore and the environment.

And what did Max say to me as he and I walked back to Dickie's house and then sat down on the porch? Yes, you're right. He told me he would be retiring sooner than expected because when John Dawson got done with him, he might be looking to come live with me right here on the shore.

I've Done It Now

THE OUTCOME OF THE GATHERING was very interesting. For one thing, Somerville had never been exposed to so many people. In the following days and weeks, the tourist trade picked up considerably, and, to some, this was not a very good thing. But on balance most of the townspeople were feeling quite pleased with themselves. Lindy had proven to be an excellent assistant and had observed the whole thing through the eyes of someone who really wanted to take it all in with a historical perspective. Her input was invaluable and we spent the next weeks getting it all down on the computer for future reference. She had also wandered through the crowd and leaned a keen ear to what all people were saying. It was exactly what I needed to continue writing my articles.

Every day Dickie's mailbox was chock full of articles people were sending us calling attention to a violation here and a violation there. Some went so far as to be descriptions and allegations of down right fraud going on in order for town officials to turn their heads while builders went forward with projects that clearly were in direct violation of state regulations.

Lindy and I could hardly get to it all and time was passing quickly. Fall was closing in on us and while we had support coming out our ears, we still had not gotten too many people's attention.

Max had written editorials of his own which had the outcome he suspected. He called to tell me he and his old leather chair were retiring to his lavish summer home on the Cape. He would spend his days thinking of what new mischief he could get into. I really felt bad that he took a beating with this, but he proved to be a man of great conviction and even more than that, he told me he was "damned proud" of what I was doing. Time had come to make adjustments in the way people thought about what they wanted and how they went about getting it. I was glad to have his support, but it was all getting to me. I needed to take a break. Boston wasn't the answer. The water was. The time had come to lay out a plan for my life.

When I announced that I was heading out on the mail boat the next day, Dickie just stared at me over his paper. He didn't say anything. I guessed he knew what I needed even more than I did. Lindy shot out of an old club chair that she had claimed long ago as her own.

"Is this trip just for you or can we go along too?"

Dickie plopped the paper down on his lap. "I don't have no intention of goin' out on that trip. I've done it more times than I kin count."

"Are you sure, Uncle Dickie?"

"I'm absolutely sure and while we are on the subject, don't you think that maybe this is meant to be a solo trip?"

A slight chill suddenly came over Lindy. She pulled her sweater up and around her shoulders. Casting a glance at Tug, she said, "That thought hadn't even crossed my mind."

I didn't know what to say. I was caught in one of those can't win situations. Think boy. No matter what you answer, you will be in deep shit here.

Lindy could see it written all over Tug's face. "All right then. I can see when I'm not wanted…"

"You are too," I snapped in quickly. "I always want you with me, but I do have a lot to think about these days."

Lindy looked at him straight in the eyes. "Then go out there without us."

"You're mad, aren't you?"

"I guess just a little."

"She'll git over it," Dickie chirped. "Women always do. They don't like it at first but then they git to thinkin' and well, then they fergit about it."

Lindy's eyes flew wide open and she yelled, "I don't believe you said that, Uncle Dickie. Why, for two cents, I'd just get up right now and leave you both sitting here without me. As a matter of fact, that's exactly what I am going to do."

I've done it now, I thought. In my rush for serenity to sort things out, I had gotten the one person I loved so much, mad at me. Good grief.

"Sit down, Lindy. Please. You aren't going anywhere. I'm sorry if I hurt your feelings, but I need to be alone and think. I have to come up with a plan for the next step we take. We have accomplished a lot with that gathering, but what we do from now on is key to our future. I have to make the people responsible realize we mean business."

Lindy removed the pout on her face and came over and sat on my lap. "I love you, Tug, and I wanted to be with you, but you are entitled to time off from both of us. I understand it is hard to think when you are in the middle of it every day. I forgive you."

"You forgive me? What did I do that you have to forgive me?"

"Hold on there, you two. Stop right in yer tracks or you will be fightin' all over again. Jist kiss and go on about yer business."

"I took Dickie's advice faster than a wink. I planted my lips right over that girl and sucked her breath away. The spat was concluded.

I FOUND A BASKET WITH snacks, soda and dessert sitting on the kitchen counter when I got up. A note lying beside it said that the sandwiches were in the fridge and that he had gone down to Virgil's for breakfast. I had a couple of hours until the boat would leave, so I decided to head on down there and grab breakfast with him.

I had been a bit worried about Dickie these days. The spring in his step seemed slower and he spent most of his time talking about Shirley and the old days. It reminded me of my grandfather. That's what he did after grandma had died and he got on in years. I thought that even though they were from different worlds altogether; the two men would have had enormous respect for one another.

When I opened the door, I spotted Dickie immediately and he was surrounded by all his buddies. Burger Boy was sitting to his right and Hambone was across from him. Poke was standing with a brimming mug of coffee in his hand and Tadpole was walking on over. Dickie was an icon in these parts and from what I had seen at the gathering, folks all over the shore seemed to know him or just respond to one of their senior citizens, who was so much like them all. He said it in their language and felt it in his bones. Their home was being invaded and he wanted desperately to be the one to save it.

As I sauntered on over, Dickie shot me that broad smile of his. He was glad I had joined them all.

"I see you finally got that lazy body out of bed, son," he teased.

Poke patted me on the back and then drew me up a chair. It was going to be one of those mornings when the stories flew every which way and the laughter would not end.

As all good things must come to an end, I checked my watch and saw that all of us had been laughing and going on for longer than I thought. I had just enough time to run home and get that basket full of food and then get on back over to the pier in time for the mail boat's departure. Saying good bye, I told Dickie to tell Lindy I would be back in time for supper and not to worry.

I made it by the skin of my teeth. Damn fool men had almost caused me to miss the boat. But then, it wouldn't have been the end of the world now would it? The boat went out every day and the honor to sit a while with those sages of the sea was probably the most wonderful thing in my life.

Once underway, I relaxed and opened one of the sodas in my basket. The sun was shining so brightly, even with sunglasses, my eyes were squinting. I loved the fall and couldn't believe this was my second one here already. Where did the time go? I thought about all that had happened over the months and I knew that progress had been made. At the very least, people were paying attention to things. They weren't just sitting back and watching the bulldozers tear up the land without a whole lot of questions being asked.

Nathan Tolliver, the boat captain snapped me away from my thoughts. He and I had become good friends over the past year. He was an old salt and a very wise man about all things water and sea and I respected him almost as much as Dickie. These old timers were a breed all their own and would be missed when they passed on. "How ya doin' there, Tug?"

"Just fine, Nathan. Sure is a pretty day."

"Don't git too many days like this here one. You sure picked a good day to come on out. Got business over there on James?"

"Monkey business, "I answered with a twinkle in my eyes. I figured that would let him know I was on vacation from my usual day's work.

"Good thing to do once and again. A man has to escape to the water to find himself and make some needed adjustments. So, just you sit back and relax, Tug. I'll do the rest."

"I'm counting on that." As I settled down into my seat, I turned and watched as we slowly left the pier. The town and the new high-rise condos began to drift off in the distance and I thought of how much anger had been stirred up by those buildings and those who built them. They were so out of place in this small town and at a dock that had looked pretty much the same forever. It seemed as if something else could have been planned. Perhaps fewer stories to the building, a design more in keeping with the old town and old ways, but no, these builders were in a hurry to get them up and the statement they made screamed out who was in control here. They dwarfed the natural look and made the vista look like a mini Miami Beach. I was so torn up about it all. I understood why some of the town's people hated them so, but I also knew why some of them tried valiantly to embrace the changes in hopes of a new future and direction for the town. The old ways were dying off and they were faced with letting it go forever or giving something else a try. There was no way to please them all. If I could just get them to work together then that would at least be something. After all, wasn't that what Dickie was trying to do when he wrote those ridiculous letters to Max? To him and a lot of old timers, this was murder, but to a younger group, this was salvation. The old fox had done what he set out to do. He wanted to bring his story and that of thousand like him, to light. He wanted to make his point in such a way that something would be done. Not just given lip service. I could never, in a million years, have known that it would be me who would be the one chosen for such a heart-felt crusade. I had to find the answer and unlock the mystery of how to go about this. For all the writing I had done, not much had changed except to make people choose sides. That was what was gnawing at me. It made me feel awful to know that neighbors were now divided on their feelings about things. It had to stop and a solution had to be found...fast.

A Day Alone Can Be Good

I DESPERATELY NEEDED THIS TIME TO myself. Everything was going at too fast a pace and I felt that nothing was getting accomplished. I mean really accomplished. I walked around for a couple of hours and then sat and stared out on the water, eating the basket full of food Dickie had put together for me. I thought everything through twice and then some, as Dickie would have told me to do. It was getting so that more and more I thought of what he would do in any given situation. He had become my dearest and closest friend and advisor and I don't think he knew how much I leaned on him.

I had spent days thinking through a solid plan that might get people to come together and really accomplish something, if only I could get the developers involved. All I needed was one, big fat cat, and the others would listen. Getting that one was the hard part. John Dawson was that man, but getting him was next to impossible. He wouldn't even answer my phone calls. How could I blame them? I was attacking their livelihoods on a weekly basis and to put it mildly, he and I had a rocky history. Nice, try Tug, I thought to myself. You better come up with another plan.

Next on my plate of "to think abouts" was this matter of Miss Lindy Short. I was so in love with her that she invaded my every thought. We made a damned good team and to my over-stuffed ego I had to admit she could out smart me at almost every turn. The time had come to tell my parents that a wedding was in the very near future. My mother would probably be okay with it, but old Ted Alston was never going to see eye to eye on this subject. Damn it to hell. Why did I care so much what he thought? But I did. Get it over with, I thought and seconds later, I was speaking to him on my cell.

Summoning up all the courage I had, I looked out onto the water and said, "Hi Dad. I'm glad I caught you."

Instead of answering me in his usual rushed way, he said, "Is everything okay down on that *shore of yours*?"

"I could hear the sarcasm in his voice when he said that shore of yours, but I had a mission to accomplish, so I had to stay focused.

"I am fine, Dad. I know I haven't been too good at calling home lately, but I really have been busy. I have been writing weekly articles for the local papers and running a column called Voice of the Shore. For the first time, actually, folks down here are really jazzed about the fact that maybe we can do something to stop, or at least slow down, the pace of overdevelopment down here. I think I told you about that huge gathering we had some months back in Somerville?"

"Yes you did and what you left out, Max Pierson told me. He stopped by to see me not long ago. He was in the process of moving to the Cape, but I guess you know that. He left the paper rather suddenly, but I guess you know about that too."

My stomach tightened. I was sorry I had called him. It was always the same with us. We had to go through this hideous stage in the beginning of our conversations and then, by the end, we somehow would be all right. But I was tired of that initial roustabout with him. I wanted, just once, for it to be a normal phone call. Why couldn't he have called me after he had seen Max and talked it out with me? No, he couldn't do that. It would be better to leave it until he could use it to get under my skin.

I had to stay focused on why I was calling him in the first place. So it was better to get this subject out of the way and then hit him with the reason for my call.

"Yes I know about Max. I felt bad about it, but you know, Dad, Max is a big boy and he did what he did because he made his own decision to stand for what he really believed in.

He knew he was walking into a field of dynamite, but Max is a tough man. I respect him more than I can say. He saw the reaction of the people when he came down to Somerville for that meeting. He saw their outrage and decided right then and there he was going to try to help. He did what he could and refused to play politics. He cared deeply and for that he got the crap beaten out of him. That takes guts."

There wasn't an answer, but rather a long, uncomfortable pause. Was he wishing I were talking about him that way? I would, oh God I would, if he could just stop his pretenses for one damned minute.

"Are you still there, Dad?"

I heard a sigh and then his answer. "Yes, Max told me what he did, and I have to say I was shocked. Max always played it safe when it came to the bread and butter of the paper. He went out on a limb this time, and he told me that he didn't give a shit. And that's a quote."

I let out with an uncontrollable belly laugh. "Gotta love that man, huh Dad?"

By his answer to me, I could tell that he didn't think this was quite as humorous as I did. "I don't know what to think anymore, Tug. You take off for that shore and live out in the middle of nowhere. You take off in boats to crab and write stories that make people miserable with themselves and where they live. What the hell has happened to you? You're acting like one of those pirates in those fairy tale stories you wrote when you were a child."

Now that pissed me off. "What's happened to me, Dad is that I have found what makes my life count for something. It may not be what you or your friends would want, but it is what I want. I am in a place I want to be, with a woman I love. And furthermore, I am going to marry Lindy Short. I wanted you to be the first to know and I had hoped you would be happy for me, but at the moment, it seems that you are hell-bent on disowning me."

I could hear his gasp. Not only wasn't he ready to hear this bit of news from me, but he wasn't prepared for the new and assertive me. His reaction was what I expected. Why, dear God, do we have to go round and round like this?

"God, Tug, have you gone crazy altogether? I mean Lindy is a pleasant, young girl, but you couldn't be serious about really marrying her?"

He was such a snob under it all. He played the good old boy with everyone, but he was an Alston through and through and his Harvard-bred son was not going to marry any country bumpkin. This was more than he could take.

I knew how he would react, didn't I? So fighting with him was just going to make things worse and I wasn't going to let anything ruin the love I felt for Lindy. I am a grown man now and I don't need to fight with my "Daddy" anymore.

"I am. I am one hundred percent dead serious about this Dad. I am going to ask Lindy to marry me and I am going to be a part of the Dickie Short family. They aren't Boston, but they are solid Eastern Shore."

I couldn't tell if he was going to slam the phone down outright or come back around for one more attack. He chose the second strategy.

"You said you haven't told anyone else yet?

"That's correct," I said.

"That includes you mother, I presume. I would think twice before you go off half-cocked and tell her. I don't believe this is the kind of news that she will welcome."

He pulled out the stops with this, but all his tricks in his magic hat weren't going to work. "You are dead wrong about that Dad. Mom understands me. She knows I am in love with Lindy. She will be happy for me…which I had hoped you would be. I see now that is never going to happen."

His voice, and anger, diminished a little. "You called me, Tug. You assumed you could just hit me with this information and that I would be dancing on the stars. You are an Alston, raised in Boston with all the privileges in the world. Lindy is a lovely, young woman, but she is from the opposite end of the world from you. I don't see how this is going to work. I was hoping…"

"They were your dreams, Dad. I have followed everything you ever wanted me to do, but fate led me elsewhere. I love where I am and the people I am with. Why can't you understand that?"

"Because none of this makes any sense, that's why."

"It doesn't make sense to *you*. But this is my life and I need to live it the way I want to."

I knew he was stunned at my response. I had never spoken to my father like this; until recently. I was spreading my wings in a lot of directions, and I knew that he resented it. He had positioned himself as the family patriarch after his father died. It was an unspoken rule that offspring were supposed to follow what they said without question. In the last year I had broken every one of those rules. I was at the moment every son comes to in his life. I had come of age completely and he wasn't really mad at me as much as he was sad. I belonged to myself now and not to him.

Exasperation took over in his voice. "I told you, Tug, that I don't know where you took this turn. I suppose I should be blaming Max. He sent you down there. You would never have gotten involved in all this if he hadn't wanted you to go after some cockamamie story."

"Don't blame Max, Dad. This was my destiny. You'll come around to see that one day. I know you like Lindy; she adores you. She can see right through that stubborn disposition of yours. She's a lot like Mom. I love her. Hey, I gotta run. I have a boat to catch to go back to the mainland."

"Catch a boat back? Where the hell are you, Tug? Just what is going on down there? Listen to me. This hasn't gone very well and I don't want us to hang up like this. You are my son…"

"Yes, I am and let's leave it at that. Be happy for me, Dad. I know you don't understand any of this, but you will someday."

"You may be right, Tug. It's time for me to stop telling you what you should and shouldn't do in your life. This news sort of hit me suddenly. I wasn't expecting it at all. I suppose I will get used to it and maybe even used to my son living down in…where?"

Kind of sudden? Is that what he said? I laughed to myself. This coming from a man who married my mother within six months of meeting her? From what I could see, that *sudden* decision had worked out just fine. They had been married forever and remarkably, they were still very much in love.

"Somerville, Dad. The whistle just blew again. I really do have to run, and I mean that literally. I'll talk to you soon and don't worry; Mom is my next call after I get onto the boat."

I SETTLED IN FOR THE ride back. Even though the call to my Dad started off pretty rough, I felt like we truly got somewhere today for the first time. Now, I had to deal with Mom. She would take this much better. Wouldn't she?

I was lucky not too many others were on the boat so I could have a lot of privacy with the call. "Hi Mom?"

"You had another fight with him, didn't you?"

He had called her and beaten me to it. "Yes, and no."

"Honestly, Tug, the two of you have to stop this. I told him the same thing, so don't think I am singling you out."

"Did he tell you what the fight was about?"

"Yes, he did."

She didn't add anything. Maybe she wasn't going to be the understanding mom I had always known. "And?"

"And what? You call your father and tell him you are going to marry Lindy, a girl you don't really know that well, and then expect him to jump for joy. This has been quite a year for you and I know you think you love it down there, and I know you think you love Lindy, but we think you need a time out for God's sake."

This wasn't going well either. Didn't he tell her that in the end, he agreed to let me do what I wanted? Apparently he left that little fact out altogether.

"Do you think that just maybe the two of you could just trust me? I hate to bring this up but you two got married pretty quick, didn't you? Can you honestly tell me that you knew Dad so well?" There, score one for me.

"That was different. My family knew the Alston family. Even though it was your Aunt Carol who dated your father, he was at our house a lot." Score one for her.

"You know as well as I do that when that happens, the kid sister is never treated like anyone. She is just there. You know; background noise." Two to one now.

"Oh Tug, don't be silly. Ted Alston was my heart throb and I set out to win him from Aunt Carol…and I did. Come to think of it, that did cause quite the situation inside our household, but I didn't care." Ought oh, she was a clever one and took that point and thought she had won this little discussion.

"But you only really dated him for six months. I mean think about that, Mom. I have known Lindy a lot longer than you and Dad and I know I love her and I am going to marry her."

My voice must have gotten above a loud whisper because that same woman started giggling at me. I was duly embarrassed, but hell, I had said so I may as well carry on.

"This is true, Tug. Well, you are a grown man now and I think that you have defended yourself so bravely, you should know that I told your father to mind his own business and wish you all the happiness in the world." Slam, dunk, game over.

"You did? Why you little minx Mom. You deliberately let me go on about this. How could you?"

"Because, if you really are in love with Lindy, I needed to hear how far you would go to defend this decision. So, my oldest son is gettin' hitched."

"Watch it there Mom, you are beginning to sound like these people down here."

"I liked Lindy a whole lot and if you are in love with her; then she's ok with me. One thing though…"

Here it comes. I knew I couldn't get away scott-free. "What?"

"I will never speak to you again if you don't bring that girl home first so you can put my mother's engagement ring on her finger."

"Mom? That's your ring. We can't do that."

"Oh yes you can. I have other rings and my Mother wanted you to have this one when you chose a bride. And don't worry about Mikey. He is getting the Alston diamond when his time comes."

I was blown away. She understood my heart completely. "Thanks. That's all I can say. I don't have any other words right now so if that's your only condition, I guess we will be seeing you soon."

"Please give me fair warning, Tug. I will have an engagement party and she can meet our friends. Would you be bringing her Uncle with you?"

"Now you really *are* trying to be a gracious mom. "I don't know. Lindy might want to leave him behind this time."

"Well, he is perfectly welcome as far as I'm concerned. He was the life of the party at Thanksgiving."

"That's one way of putting it, Mom. I'll call you soon. I love you and thanks so much…for everything."

"I suspect that your father's damned pride is wounded. I will help him get over himself. Let me know when you are coming."

Can a guy have a better Mom?

Can Peace Be Possible?

THE SUN WAS BEGINNING TO signal that it had had it for the day and would say good bye shortly. We were about a mile from the pier when I saw someone waving their hands toward us. I got my trusty binoculars and to my astonishment, it was Lindy. I scanned the glasses around and saw that Dickie's old truck was parked nearby and then I began to worry that something might be wrong. Never a perfect day I guess.

As the boat got closer, I could see that she didn't look upset, so what could it be? And where was Dickie?

"Thanks for the ride today," I yelled back to Nathan.

"Good to have you along, Tug. Come on out any day."

Lindy couldn't hold herself back any longer. She rushed to me and threw her arms around me. "I missed you so much."

"I was only gone for the afternoon, but I'll take all this loving."

"Oh, you haven't seen the half of it yet."

"What's that supposed to mean?"

With her eyes sparkling and her long hair blowing in the wind, she let go of me and stood erect and said, "You hold on there, Tug Alston. First, I have a surprise for you."

"Well before you give me my surprise, and I can't wait to see what that is, where is Dickie? Is he all right?"

"Yeah, why?" she answered with a puzzled look on her face. I turned her body around and pointed to the parking space behind her. "I see you drove that old truck of his."

"Why yes I did. Oh nothing is wrong, I was over to the house and I was running late so he told me to take his truck, rather than go home and get my car."

349

"He's such a peach."

"Come on, Tug. Let's go. The sunset is going to be gorgeous and I want to show you my surprise."

Now she really had me going. "You sure are being mysterious…and very sexy."

"Not hard when I'm, with the likes of you."

"I can tell you one thing, no matter where we are headed; we are going in my Cherokee and not "old beauty.""

"Whatever you say."

"Now, where to, or do I even have to ask?"

"Why the shanty, of course."

"Gee, what a surprise." I knew what that meant. Lindy was in one of her sexy moods and she wanted to watch the sunset and make love. Hey, how could I possibly object?

She kept fiddling with an envelope and it was driving me crazy. I figured whatever surprise she had for me, other than getting me all hot and bothered, that enveloped had something to do with it.

"What the hell is that envelope? I know it's something or you wouldn't keep doing that."

"Making you crazy, aren't I?"

Enough was enough. I wanted it and when I grabbed at it, the Cherokee careened off the right side of the road. I quickly recovered and began to straighten it out.

"Tug? Stop it right now," she screamed. That isn't funny. Any more to the right and we would have been in the water."

"Then give me that envelope and I'll behave."

She could tell I wasn't teasing. "I will give it to you when we get to the shanty. It's a surprise."

"Really? And here I thought your surprise was going to be my seduction."

"Honestly, Tug," she snorted. "You men are all alike." And then sounding like a purring kitten, she added, "However, that isn't a bad idea."

I rested my right hand on her leg and stroked it up and down. I knew that would get her engines started. "And you weren't thinking of that at all, were you?"

I pulled off the road and parked on a dirt path across from the shanty. I never lose my excitement about coming here. It's the epicenter of this world. I loved the weathered wood of the small little buildings and how each one of them was fashioned to reflect its owner. Their time had come and gone and now fewer and fewer of them were in use, but the one that I had come to love was the prize of them all. It was owned by the great waterman, Dickie Short.

Lindy noticed that as soon as I got out by the water and the shanty, my mind seemed to go a million miles away. This was my home now and I couldn't have felt any more like I belonged in a place more than the one I was in now

Lindy walked ahead silently. She knew where my head was at. That's what made us a matched pair. She understood the personality of a writer. We are dimensional and don't see the way others do. Ours is a world of observations and conclusions drawn from experiences had. I think it's what sets all these people apart from the outside world. They live their lives close to natural creatures of the land and sea. They are close to God.

She unlocked the shanty door and before I could go inside, she gently pressed the envelope in my hand, without saying a word, and then looked up at me and smiled.

I could see she had opened it and read it. I didn't care. We were a couple now. I decided to go around back and sit down on one of the old, wooden chairs, and read what was in this envelope that had her so excited.

I couldn't believe my eyes. None other than Mr. John Dawson, owner of Dawson Industries, was writing to ask me to meet with him. I mean a face to face- one on one. Could this mean a truce?

Excitedly I yelled into the shanty, "Lindy, stop fussing with that stuff and come on out here."

351

In the next minute, she wasn't only out on the deck, but she was sitting on my lap. "Don't you love it? He is asking for a meeting. I think you have him in a corner."

"Well, I don't know about that. John Dawson doesn't scare, my dear. But it is a start. I wonder what he wants from me."

"Does it have to be that he wants something from you, Tug? Do you always have to be so suspicious?"

"I am a reporter, Lindy, remember? We are always suspicious. He wants something all right and he wants it badly enough to meet face to face with me rather than make a phone call."

"I see your point. I just wish people could act like adults and stop this bickering. Do you think you will be safe? I mean he wouldn't kill you or anything, would he?"

I hugged her shoulder and said, "I don't think John Dawson wants to literally kill me, Lindy. Maybe he thinks it from time to time, but this is something else. I can feel it. He is a shrewd businessman and he needs something that only I can give him. It has to be about money. It always is."

"I know that, Tug, but there's more to life than money, you know."

"Not to John Dawson and friends. That's all there is and they don't give a damn about the little people."

"Then why should you have any hope for this meeting?"

"Because he is the one who asked for it."

Lindy went to get up from the chair, but I grabbed her. "Sit back down here. I am not done with you yet. I have a bone to pick with you. I see you opened this letter. It was addressed to me."

"I…I…I know that, but when I saw who sent it…"

"I kissed her before she could finish her sentence. With a tight hold on my arm, she led me inside.

Whispering to her, I said, "I thought you wanted to watch the sun set."

"We can do that any time."

I followed her inside with our hands locked together. She sure made me forget about anything else that was going on. And then it hit me...I was going to make love to this wonderful girl and then ask her to marry me.

DICKIE WAS OUT BACK WHEN we got home, chopping wood of all things.

Lindy grabbed the axe out of his hand and scolded him, wagging her finger in his face. "Uncle Dickie, what in Sam Hill are you doing? You know you shouldn't be doing anything like this."

"Now you give me back that axe, Lindy girl. This wood needs to be chopped and I aim to do it."

"Tug can do it."

My eyes flew open wide at the mere notion of my chopping wood. My god! The chances of my chopping my feet off would be one hundred percent. What was this girl thinking? "I am not sure about that, Lindy, but surely we could get someone around here to do it."

She stared at me in absolute shock. "You mean you wouldn't do this for Uncle Dickie?"

"Do you want to have a husband or chopped up pieces of one?"

Dickie pushed Lindy aside and shot straight to me and said, "Do you have somethin' to say to me, son?"

"What do you mean?"

"You said somethin' about Lindy havin' or not havin' a husband."

A smile began to form at the corners of my mouth. "I guess I did, didn't I?"

"Oh Uncle Dickie, the most wonderful thing has just happened. Tug asked me to marry him."

Dickie looked back at me. "Well, I see that goin' out to that island must have knocked some sense into you after all. So, you asked her, did ya?"

I swallowed hard. I had broken all the conventional rules. I didn't go to her father and ask for her hand and worse than that, I didn't ask Dickie, who was really the one who needed to give his approval. "I…I… hope you aren't mad at me, Dickie. It's just that it was the right time and all…"

"And all what, son?" he barked. He wasn't going to make this easy on me. The twinkle in his eye told me that.

"You know. I mean come on, Dickie, are you going to drag this out of us?"

"Maybe."

"Stop it, Uncle Dickie. This is private."

"It won't be when yer Mama hears tell of it. By the way, she called askin' fer ya."

"Oh, I better go call her. She will be ecstatic for me and you know it. Daddy will be too."

He let out a great big belly laugh and said, "I was jist teasin' you two. I am down right pleased as punch fer ya. I jist wish Shirley was here…"

He didn't finish the sentence. He walked off to stack what wood he had chopped before we seized that weapon from him. I could tell Lindy's news made him happy, but it also made him sad.

I heard Lindy screaming into the phone with her mother. Oh boy, I knew this was just the beginning. I began to help Dickie and told him about the letter. "What do you think about that, Dickie? We just may have scared him into doing something after all."

Throwing another log onto the enormous pile that stood beside his shed, he groused, "I don't trust that snake Dawson. He isn't goin' to give in this easy. He might feel some heat, but he ain't ready to yell uncle yet. Nope, he wants somethin', that's fer sure."

"You know, I am thinking the same thing. Max Pierson may be able to shed some light on this. I think I'll call him before I respond to Dawson."

"Why do ya think Pierson might be able to tell ya somethin'?"

"Instinct. He did come down here with John, and he is working on some of the same issues as we have up on the Cape, and so I figure he might be able to shed some light on this. I'll give him a call directly." Good Lord, did I say directly?

The Details Are In The Devil

WHAT I HADN'T TOLD DICKIE, was the back story of why I thought Max would know something. I had been faithful to keep up with my friends back in Baltimore; Roger mostly. I had enough sense to know that you never burn bridges or friends. He had told me that Max was plenty pissed when Dawson and friends put the heat on the board at the paper and forced Max into an untenable situation after writing some shore-friendly editorials. It was then that Max decided to retire gracefully. I had to admit I was stunned to see him with John at the meeting down here, but that was Max. He was always the diplomat, so that told me that he wanted to stay close to his enemy.

I was happy to hear his voice on the other end of the phone. "Hey Max, how is retirement treating you?"

"Wonderful. I am up at dawn and go fishing every day."

"And I believe I have a thousand acres of swampland to sell you."

"I can't fool you, can I, Tug?"

"Nope. How are things really?"

"Good. I am living the good life. I am doing a lot of research on the same issues you have down there. I go to a wonderful place near here and eat codfish sandwiches for lunch, and then cast fate to the wind for the rest of the day."

"That sounds pretty good to me."

He could tell I was making perfunctory niceties. "Why don't you cut to the chase and tell me the real reason for your call."

"You can always tell when something's on my mind, can't you? You're right. I got a letter from John Dawson and he wants to meet with me. He didn't say why, and before I get my hopes up, I wanted your take on it."

"Hmm, so Dawson wrote you and asked you to meet with him, eh? Something fishy about this. I can smell it a mile away."

"At first blush, I was excited, and then the reporter in me began to think the same thing. What could he be after?"

"Anything, that's my guess. He is not a nice man. I guess you know all the shit that went down surrounding my so called *retirement*. At least, the bastards on the board allowed me that much. Well, I wanted Dawson drawn and quartered, but I clearly knew what I was doing when I wrote those pieces. I want you to know that I didn't regret a one of them. The good news is that they got people mad and the bad news is that they got me fired. Oh, excuse me, they got me retired. Dawson got what he wanted and the heat was off of him for the moment so now he and his pals could carry on with their massive expansion on the Eastern Shore."

"Okay, so he is back to doing what comes naturally. So why meet with me?"

"Because you are fucking with his plans for Maryland. He already is more than well on his way in Delaware. He and his comrades have pretty much carte blanche in that state. The lower shore of Delaware is finding that there is money in that there land. Outside of Wilmington, where you have massive industry and banks, the rest of the state needed to find something that they could sell. The sweetness of low property taxes, combined with no sales tax and acres of land with old farms, made it the perfect target for a retirement destination. Now, they want Maryland in on the action. "

"But Maryland is different. They don't have the tax situation that Delaware has, so I don't get it."

"They have water and beaches. What is it that you fell in love with?"

"Good point, but I don't want to take land away or change things so much that you won't recognize it in the coming years."

"You may not want that but the good folks, with plenty of money in their pockets, don't give a damn about those quaint little ideals."

"I am not getting it, Max. Maybe I am not as smart as you all think I am."

"You just don't want to get it, Tug. You hold the notion that all people want to make things better. Well, think again. John Dawson sees you as his one, big obstacle to getting a sweetheart deal on the shore of Maryland. Just like he has in Delaware. Up until you went down there and got involved in all this, no one was squawking too loudly. Now, you and that Dickie Smart, have the locals marching off to war against the developers and being that he is the biggest one down there, that makes you his target. Are you getting it now?"

"Short, not Smart."

"What?"

"Dickie's last name is Short. You called him Dickie Smart."

"Are you listening to me, Tug? Who the hell cares what that old bastard's last name is?"

"I do and so do a lot of people down here. He is like a folk hero and I wouldn't be this far without his help."

"Well, that's true. I'll give you that."

"So, what should I do? Should I meet with him?"

"You bet you should. Always know what the enemy is thinking. And he is your enemy. He told me as much when I went down to that fair you all had. Why did you think I went? Because I liked him so much?"

"You went because of me?"

"Damn straight. Your father would kill me if I knew you were heading into the eye of the storm and I didn't help you."

"I appreciate that Max, but when were you going to tell me about all this?"

"I didn't have to, did I? You figured it out yourself."

I had so much to learn. Here I thought I was Mr. Big Shot and in one conversation, an old friend had put my feet back down on the ground. "Thanks, Max. You have advanced my learning curve. I will let you know what he wants, but you probably already know that."

"Be careful not to give anything away. Hold firm and don't give in."

"I will. Hey, I almost forgot the really big news in my life. I have asked Lindy to marry me. You remember her. She was at our house in Boston over Thanksgiving. She is Dickie's great niece or something like that."

"I am sure your parents are thrilled. She seemed to be a really swell gal."

After I hung up, it wasn't the tone in Max's voice about my marrying Lindy that bothered me. It was his less than subtle warning about John Dawson and how he played to win.

JOHN AND I NEVER DID speak on the phone. It seemed we were destined to set this meeting up playing phone tag. Finally, we accomplished that task and in one week, I would know what John Dawson had on his mind.

I felt really terrible asking Lindy to do this amount of work in such a short period of time. However, it didn't seem to bother her at all. She was on cloud nine these days thinking about us getting married. She didn't even complain once that she wouldn't be accompanying me. Truly amazing!

I wanted someone to be at home with Dickie. I didn't like leaving him alone for too long these days. It wasn't my imagination; his years were beginning to catch up with him.

The week flew by and all of us were pretty intense about things. Lindy was exhausted compiling everything I needed into a *Reader's Digest* format. I was spiraling out of control wondering what was coming, and Dickie was full of advice for me. To say that all three of us were beginning to get on one another's nerves, would be an understatement.

When Friday rolled around, I was up early and ready to go. The meeting was outside of Salisbury and I didn't want to be late for this. I said good bye to Lindy, while gathering all my stuff in my bedroom. When she kissed me, I could feel the fireworks going off. I put the brakes on immediately. "Not now, little girl. Save it for when I come home. I have to be at the top of my game today and this isn't going to get me there."

She shot me a coy and seductive look and said, "Well then, you better be ready to take up from where we left off when you get back."

I left her standing there as I walked down the stairs to say good bye to Dickie. It was my hope that I would have good news to tell him when I got back. His whole heart and soul were in this project and I desperately wanted to see something done before he… well, I didn't want to think about that right now. I wasn't at all surprised to see him waiting for me in that old rocker recliner of his when I walked in the living room.

Almost afraid to ask him, I said, "So, Dickie, do you have any words of wisdom for me before I shove off?" Naturally, I knew he would.

"You take care not to let that old snake charm you into anything," Dickie snapped, as he got up and helped me on with my jacket.

"You can be sure I will be all ears, Dickie. You take care of yourself too today. I'll be back by dinner."

"Don't you worry about me none. Lindy will make sure I am behavin' myself."

I could see that look in his eyes that said he wished he could just be left alone, but these days, that wasn't a good idea. He moved slower and the fact is that he had slipped a couple of times recently, out on the back porch. He brushed it off as nothing, but it was clear; Dickie was showing his age.

"Be nice for Lindy now. Give her an extra hug for me."

"Oh you can be sure of that. That's the easy part. It's all that fussin' and stuff she does over me. Why she doesn't think I kin do anythin' anymore. At least she lets me go to the bathroom by myself, and if I am a real good boy, she lets me go on down to Virgil's for lunch."

I hugged him hard and said, "That's because she can keep an eye on you while she is working."

In a polite shove, he moved me out the door. "You jist remember snakes can be deadly."

I waved to him as I hopped in my Cherokee. I loved that man so much.

Not Exactly What I Expected

Dawson and I agreed to meet at an old diner outside of Hebron, a suburb outside of Salisbury. I had to use a map to locate this small hamlet and then wondered how he would ever know of such a place. But when I pulled into the dirt parking lot, I understood. It was surrounded by hundreds of acres of vacant land; farm land. Just the kind of land John Dawson liked to buy. Did I even have to wonder if this would be the site of his new "within a short distance of the water" development? That really slayed me when these developers built out in the middle of nowhere and then advertised it as "a short distance from the water." I mean really...

He was already there, sipping coffee in a booth at the back of the room. He waved over to me flashing his beautiful set of white teeth and a smile that looked like Eden's most famous celebrity. I could feel Dickie's radar beaming down to me. "Watch out, son!"

Extending my hand for a polite shake, I said, "You beat me here, John. I made a couple of wrong turns. How the heck did you ever find this place?" Or should I even ask, I thought to myself.

He lied with impunity. "An old buddy of mine who lives down here told me about it. They have the best cheeseburgers around, if you eat meat."

"I do indeed. I love cheeseburgers, so that makes it easy."

When the server arrived moments later, ordering was not complicated. Two cheeseburgers, fries, and cokes summed it up in a hurry and then I could tell Dawson wanted to get down to business. He wasn't a man given to idle pleasantries.

Flashing that somewhat fake smile again, the one that said beware of the dog, he began our little meeting. Leaning in to me, he said, "I see that you are going to continue to write articles that make life hell for us developers down here. In a spirit of some kind of co-operation, until we can get a solid plan of how we are all going to get along, is there any way I could get a truce on that Tug?"

He was probing me to find out exactly what the ground rules were going to be. It was a hopeful sign, but he wasn't going to jump for joy with my response. "That depends. If you can show me we can reach some common ground on things, then I might be persuaded to let up for a while."

"What do you need, Tug? I told you I was working with the other builders and the towns. Things take time, you know." He was beginning to show that his anger with me was right there, close to the surface.

"I know," I replied, "but I don't see that there is real commitment yet. Perhaps a lot of shuffling around of papers and your own PR on the matter, but the truth is that I get reports every day that tell of some new violation here and another one over there. It never stops and neither does the expansion."

Looking perplexed, he offered, "I don't know what kind of reports you are getting Tug, nor do I know where and from whom, they are coming, but I do know that we are changing some of our policies to accommodate for new internal regulations and it was my hope that we could get together here talk this through and settle this in a manner that benefited everyone."

I knew he was lying and he was doing it outright. He really must think I am an idiot. Maybe I would too if I had some young kid in front of me, pricking me everytime I turned around and hurting my bottom line, but I knew the truth, and he wasn't giving it to me. It made me madder than hell.

"I'm not sure of that, John," I snapped at him. "You want me to cave in and go away. I have made things tough for you on a huge scale. You developers have never had any opposition like this before. You saw the number of people who showed up in Somerville and it scared you that this time, they mean business."

I could see the furrow deepen in his brow. A shadow of anger flashed underneath his face. I was getting to him and that's just what I wanted to do. After talking with Max, I gave a lot of thought to how I was going to play this and now; I am glad I did.

"You aren't going to give an inch, are you? It's war or nothing with you. I have no choice then but to hit you back. There are lots of folks who want to live here, Tug, and they aren't going to like what you and your good Eastern Shore friends are doing. I was willing to try to work this out amicably, but I see you aren't going to do that. So, let me explain a few things to you, laddie boy."

He really didn't say that, did he? I wanted to smash his face in with that obvious condescending comment. Dawson was mad now, and his pearly whites were bared and about to take a bite. He wasn't nearly finished with me. I was about to take the hit for every nasty thing he thought about me and everyone down here. This wasn't turning out to be exactly the hopeful news that I prayed it would be.

His eyes narrowed as he leaned across the table. I could almost smell his breath when he said, "Now let me tell you how this game is played, Tug Alston." And so he did.

"It's all about those who have the money and those who want it. I have the money and the states I build in want it. It's as simple as that. The beautiful part of all this is that what I am selling is what hundreds of thousands of people want too. Everyone wins, except for a handful of ungrateful farmers and watermen. Aside from the occasional dustup, nobody felt too bad about anything until you came down here and stuck your nose into it. You gave them hope that they could stop the sands of time and hope, my dear boy, is one thing you can't give them. Billions of dollars are riding on all this development and do you really think, for one moment, that you are going to stop that? You must be mad. I know you have fallen in love with the shore. Everybody does. That's the reason they want to live down here. And now that you have taken to one of theses shore girls, aren't you going to make this your home?"

Boy, was he egging for a fight or what? I was egging to give it to him. Why is it I couldn't stay away from falling down that proverbial "rabbit hole?" What I had hopefully mistaken for a break through was nothing more than a meeting in an out of the way place, to tell me off and run me out. Well, John Dawson, think again. You have made yourself clear, and now I will do the same to you.

Sitting back and away from him, I let him know exactly what was on my mind. "My love life has nothing to do with this, so you can leave that out of this conversation. You brought me here under false hopes today. That was a clever move but it won't work, John. You want me to fold my tent and walk away from all this mess. A blind eye is going to make this whole matter worse in a short period of years and then what is going to happen? Oh you will have made your billions and so will your friends, but you will have destroyed this place for good and it will never be able to go back to what it was. Doesn't that bother you, just a little?"

His eyes never left mine; his answer short and to the point. "Nope."

"You are one, cold sonofabitch, John Dawson. I guess some would say you were a brilliant businessman, but you have no heart. You have no sense of responsibility to the people here, the land, the water, the animals... you just don't care. You use others to do your dirty work and your lawyers clean up all the messes. You use arcane laws to get what you want, and you never lose one minute's sleep over it. It's bloody incredible. Are you sure you weren't here before when the white men decided that they wanted the land that belonged to others?"

Thank God the server wasn't intimidated enough not to bring us our food. However, given this heated discussion, I rather doubted I was going to taste this cheeseburger. Besides, it couldn't be half as good as the ones cooked at Virgil's. How I wished I was there right now.

Seizing this timely interruption, John took over. "Well now, you think you have it all wrapped up neatly, don't you now Tug? Well, you don't know shit. People are going to do what people are going to do. With all the baby boomers retiring, they want to come on down here. The weather is milder and the taxes are senior friendly. If they want to be here; I am going to build for them. That's how it goes, and furthermore, I would appreciate it if you would stop writing that corruption is flowing all over the place. You can't prove that and I can tell you, a man can end up going to court for saying those kinds of things. So knock it off."

I hated admitting to myself that he had a point. I knew that limb I was out on could break at any time and now I knew he was the one willing to do it. John Dawson was a tough man, with a pocketful of money and that was a deadly combination. I had to protect the innocent people who gave me that information. It would be awful if they ended up paying the price for my fervor. This argument had to take a turn for the better…immediately.

"Look, John, let's stop it right here. This wasn't what I was expecting to happen. We both have our own viewpoints. That's what makes this so hard for both of us. You have a buying public who wants to come here, and I have thousands of Eastern Shore folks who want this to go away. Now we have a problem. The question is can we fix it?"

He sat back in the booth and let out a sigh. I knew I might finally be striking a chord. He didn't want this to keep on going on. It wasn't productive for either of us and he was smart enough to know the power of the press. I could tell he wanted to come to a resolution. But how we did it was the nub of the whole thing.

"I don't know, Tug. I have to be honest with you. A lot of people are really mad on both sides. What's built is built and we can't change that. The truth is that many of the old timers aren't telling you exactly all of it. While they complain about the changes and all the people coming here, it's put money in their pockets. Their towns and they, themselves, have profited handsomely from a lot of this development. I don't hear them talking about that side of the coin, do you?"

He was spot on with that statement. There was a lot of money being made by the farmers and watermen who found now that their land was their fortune. They had lived the life that they loved, and now were willing to cash in on it. "I am big enough to admit what you say bears merit John, but there are points to be made for the overdevelopment of this land. The old timers, as you call them, don't all want to sell out. They want to see some sensible planning for the future of their homes and towns. They may die off, but a lot of their families aren't leaving and they want that protection. At the rate this is going, they know that in twenty years, it will all be gone, if they don't stop it now."

John nodded his head. He knew I was right and couldn't fight me on that point. With the thought that perhaps we were making some headway, I decided to chomp into the luscious cheeseburger that was in front of me. No use letting it go to waste, right?

The grease drooled down my chin and I didn't care. I was in heaven. "God, this *is* good. These out of the way places have the best road food around." Maybe Virgil's had competition after all.

"With a smile, he followed suit and bit into his, and then added with a full mouth, "I told you so."

After a few more bites, I looked around and said, "You know this old diner makes my case for me. If all this around here is torn up to build new homes and stores; this will disappear. It will no longer be what it is right now. Most likely it won't exist at all. Then one more chapter of life here will be gone forever. It's places like this that make people love it here so much. It's that down home feeling that they are leaving behind in the big cities. And then they will get here and it will look just like where they left."

Swallowing the last few bites of his cheeseburger, it was obvious he wasn't going to answer that statement. The anger between us was gone now. Who knows, maybe it was this damned cheeseburger and maybe it was the fact that here we sat. Two men of different ages and different perspectives and neither of us knew quite where to go at this point. One thing was abundantly clear - nothing was going to be completely settled today. Maybe that was good. We both might go our separate ways and decide that the next time we would meet it would be more hopeful news. The meeting was over and both of us knew it.

"Tug, I know your heart is in the right place, but you can't stop progress. I can tell you this. I don't always like change and at my age, I like it less and less. But change comes one way or the other. The Eastern Shore will survive, but it will survive in a different way. The memories I had as a young man coming down here will be different memories for my grandchildren. They won't know, or care, about what once was. That's how it is. You don't have to like it, but that doesn't change things."

I picked up my glass and twirled with it in my hands. Tragically he was right on so many levels. Unless the people here were willing to physically stand in front of every bulldozer, which they weren't going to do; the war here was over. Dawson's life was all about building communities and he would keep on doing that for as long as he lived.

When the waitress came with the check, John took it immediately. He didn't allow me to get near it. "This one's on me, Tug. I know this wasn't the meeting you hoped for, so please allow me to get this one."

I knew he was trying to say he was sorry, and I was grateful for that. We both let things get heated.

"You know if you could see your way clear to write some stories that were more positive about the good things going on down here, it might help a little."

In his way, he was asking for a moratorium. I agreed that might be a good idea.

"Okay, you've got it. I will do that, John. It will give us some time to think about solutions rather than keep on fighting like this."

He grinned at me, as we stood at the counter waiting to pay. "What's so funny?"

"The thought just occurred to me that we finally agreed on something. Guess you won't go home empty-handed after all."

I patted him on the back and said, "I'll be in touch."

That Nasty Thing Called Reality

I TOOK MY TIME ON THE way back to Somerville. My stomach was tied in knots and I was as unsettled as I could be. I, also, had a tinge of feeling like I was about to become a traitor to Dickie's cause. At least that's the way I thought he was going to view what I was about to tell him.

I played that meeting over and over again in my head and each time it came out the same. Both of us were right and both of us were wrong. Now, how do you explain that to a straight shooter like Dickie Short? Let alone, what I was going to have to go through with Lindy. While she was very much in love with me, she was a fierce defender of the shore and how it needed protecting from an outside world that threatened to tear it apart and leave it that way forever. No amount of love was going to spare me from what they were going to say to me about this meeting. They hated the John Dawsons of this world and would refuse to see anything they might say as having one iota of merit. Along with all that, I was beginning to get it through my think skull that while we had won battles, we were going to lose the war. It really did come down to money and the balance of power and we all knew what side we were on.

John said some pretty interesting, and thought-provoking things in his tirade with me. The fact that many of the Eastern Shore people themselves had given their homeland over to be developed any way the buyer wanted was a fact that niggled at me. I was an outlander and I was fighting as hard as anyone, and a good deal of the people whose families lived here for generations didn't think twice about selling out. And there was the fact that the Eastern Shore had seen some very bleak years that threatened to bury a history all on its own. Development brought it back to life, and yet it destroyed it at the same time. It was always the same story, everywhere you looked. If people want to live where you are; they will and nothing can stop them from coming. If you live near water, the chances go up a bazillion percent that you won't have an inch of land left before it's all gone. An added extra plus to that fact is that by the time it all gets developed, you won't be able to afford to live or work where your roots set down long ago.

So many things raced through my head. I drove from town to town down the coast and then cut over and inland heading home. I began to doubt myself and if I really wanted to live way out here. My parents may have had a point when they tried to talk what they called sense to me. I don't know. I do know that what I feel for Lindy is real and the admiration and love I feel for Dickie is absolute, but can I really fit in with folks who spend their lives on the water? I am a writer and need literary food to survive. Maybe, all along, I have mistaken adventure for reality and now meeting with John, the reality part is kicking in. I have deluded myself into believing that me, the great Tug Alston, can come to the rescue and save the fair princess in the burning castle. The fact is I am suffering from an over-inflated ego that could bring this whole situation down on these people like a house of cards. I would always be free to leave, but they live here and their lives are here and leaving for them, is not an option.

I HAD DRIVEN EVERY OUT of the way road I could find to make this trip home as long as possible. I had beaten myself up pretty good and now it was time to go home and face the music. And that music would come to the tune of a thousand questions Dickie and Lindy would ask. I had to be honest and they would have to try to understand. That was the hardest part of all. Who knows? If it went badly, I would be spending the night back in that lovely motel where I stayed when I first arrived over a year ago. God help me!

I didn't see either Lindy or Dickie when I first walked through the kitchen door. That seemed odd to me. Dropping my brief case down on the chair must have made sufficient noise to get Lindy's attention out on the back porch because she yelled to me immediately. "Tug, I am out here. I am so glad you are back home."

I heard the urgency in her voice. "Is something wrong? You sound kind of weird?"

The next thing I knew she was in my arms, shaking with tears in her eyes. "Oh Tug, I tried to reach you but you must have had your phone off. Uncle Dickie passed out in the bathroom and the ambulance came and took him to the hospital."

"What?" I shouted. "When did this happen and why aren't you there with him?"

She jerked her head back to look me in the face. "I was there all afternoon, but I wanted to be here and tell you myself, when you came home. Don't be mad at me…please."

My knees and hands began to shake. "I knew something like this was going to happen. I just knew it. Let's go right now." It didn't take two seconds for them to grab their jackets and jump into the Cherokee.

I was driving like a mad man and I didn't care at all if the police spotted me. I wasn't about to let them pull me over. They could race me to the hospital.

"Tell me again how it happened, and please don't leave out one detail. I can't believe this is happening. I should never have gone today."

"There isn't that much to tell. I was in the back yard, cleaning out some of Aunt Shirley's flower beds, when I heard him yell for me. By the time I got into the house and upstairs to the bathroom, he was lying on the floor, unconscious. I was scared to death, Tug."

I slipped my hand in hers and squeezed gently. "I know. Try to calm down. It will be all right. Dickie is a tough old bird."

"Yes he is, but lately, I have noticed him staring at pictures of Aunt Shirley and I swear he looks as if he is talking to them. He wants to be with her, Tug. They were together for so long and he is so lonely without her."

"I know Lindy, I know."

"Let's change the subject for a few minutes. How did the meeting go?"

"It went and I really don't want to go into it right now. I am too upset over Dickie." The truth of it was that the guilt I was feeling was palpable. I wasn't there when Dickie needed me, and on top of that I would eventually have to tell him and Lindy what really was said today. Dickie's "second revolution" was all but over and if whatever is wrong with him now doesn't do him in, this piece of news might.

"So, it didn't go well. You had high hopes but under it all, you knew that that might happen. Just tell me this; have we lost?"

She was so perceptive. For a gal raised in the sticks, so to speak, she knew more than half the college grads anywhere. "Let's just say that this meeting gave me a lot to think over. John Dawson is very persuasive and he makes his point very well. I know I do too, but that's the problem."

Lindy could tell it had been a rough meeting, but there was something else he was avoiding saying. Sometimes it's best to leave well enough alone; and sometimes you just can't help yourself. "Okay, Tug, I won't press you now, just tell me if one of those things you are thinking over is how you feel about me."

Oh…My…God, she completely took what I said the wrong way. "No, Lindy, no!" I reinforced quickly. That's probably the only thing that didn't change for me. I love you and that's for sure."

We pulled into the hospital parking lot and thankfully we could stop talking about the meeting between Dawson and me. We jumped out and tore inside to see how Dickie was doing.

We were both relieved and alarmed, at the same time, to find out he was still in the emergency room. But given how hospitals were these days, it wasn't that big a shock. They led us back right away. They didn't say a word about how he was doing.

He was hooked up to a million monitors with wires leading in every direction. It didn't look so good, and neither did he, as he lay there sleeping...or so we thought.

I heard a light rustle of the sheets and by heavens, Dickie's eyes met mine straight on. "What are you doing here, son? Why aren't you at that meeting with Dawson?"

Understandably, he was totally disoriented. I was beginning to join him on that score.

"I am here with you; that's why. No more questions or comments from you now. Just rest, Dickie. I brought your favorite gal to keep you company. I will be right back. I have to use the bathroom," I lied.

I headed straight for the nurse's station to find out what was going on. I wasn't in the mood to get jerked around. When I found the head nurse, I peppered her with a million questions and she went off to get the doctor. I guess she could see I wasn't about to let her off the hook without answers, so she took the path of least resistance.

In minutes, Doctor Hugh Tyler appeared and took me aside and introduced himself. "Mr. Alston, I am the doctor in charge of Mr. Short. You aren't a direct relative, so there really isn't much I can tell you. You know the confidentiality laws and all."

"I know that but Dickie doesn't have a wife and I am like a son to him."

"That may be but I need a close relative to share his information with."

I left him standing there and in minutes Lindy was with me. "Now, can you tell us?"

He looked a little uncomfortable with me standing there, but he went on anyway. "Your Uncle had a slight heart episode. It's called SVT- supraventricular tachacardia. It's when an irregular heart beat kicks out and the heart races very fast. In your uncle's case, it lasted longer than normal and he passed out. We have given him some medicine for the palpitations and he seems to be responding to it nicely. I suspect he has had these palpitations before, but never said anything to anyone."

"He will be all right then?" Lindy said, deeply concerned.

"He should be fine. In fact, if he continues to have a normal heart response for an hour more, he can go home with you."

Both Lindy and I looked at each other, shocked. "He could be in his own bed in a few hours. He was going to like that news.

"Thank you, Dr. Tyler, I said as Lindy made a bee line back to Dickie's cubicle. She couldn't wait to tell him. He wasn't exactly the sort of patient any hospital wanted to keep for too long.

Suddenly I felt drained. A coffee cart was nearby so I bought a cup of caffeine and drank. This day had been full of realities that I didn't want to face. I wanted to run back home to Boston and be that little boy again, writing about pirates and patriots, and adventures that happened to them. I didn't want to have to admit that I couldn't change life and make it go back in time. I couldn't change the fact that people got old and that time didn't wait for them either.

I looked down the hallway and saw Lindy waving for me to return. I knew that I loved her and I knew that I loved Dickie too. The only true reality for us was that whatever our future held; we would face it together.

What Goes Around Comes Around

WINTER WASN'T A PARTICULARLY A real good time to be near or on the water except if you were a waterman or Dickie Short. No amount of pleading was going to keep him from going to the pier and looking out to the water. Nor was he going to listen to you if you asked him not to go out to the shanty once in a while and spend hours in the damp air puttering around and remembering old memories. He was as stubborn and ornery as they come, but we loved him.

The medicine that the doctor put him on was working well and there was no evidence of any more spells. For that, Lindy and I were very grateful. It cut down on the worry factor.

There was no end to the research I was doing for my book. I was keeping my promise not to write any articles for the time being, that would provoke any further incidents with the builders and John Dawson kept his promise to stay in contact with the other developers and try to establish some guidelines. There were a few signs that something might be happening on that front. I was, at least, encouraged.

Deep in thought at my computer, I heard the tap of Lindy's nails on my bedroom door. "Hey handsome, gotta a minute?"

"Sure do," I answered, not looking up.

"What would you think if I asked you to take me to Boston for the weekend?"

"I would ask you what's in that pretty head of yours?"

"Nothing quite that bad, Tug. I just think we should head on up there before we get married."

Good God! I had completely forgotten all about going home. With all the craziness over Dickie, I had put our marriage out of my mind. Lindy had too. We were completely involved in taking care of him. And what were my parents thinking? Probably that I changed me mind and that I wasn't going to marry Lindy after all.

I stood up and stretched and then kissed her. "I think that's just what we need, but how about Dickie? We can't leave him here alone."

"We won't have to. My Mom and Dad are going to watch him."

"They were the ones who urged me to ask you."

"Are they still so excited about having a Harvard writer in the family?"

Lindy smiled and her eyes became mischievous as she said, "Well, they might have liked a waterman better."

I raised my eyebrows and looked at her with a fake hurt expression on my face. "I thought I was making pretty good progress at being one. I mean go ask the guys."

"The guys love you, Tug. They would lie like rats for you and you know that. You can't fool me any. You may like going out on the water some, but you aren't any waterman."

"Dickie says I am," I snapped in self defense.

"Well, good for Uncle Dickie. He would never lie for you now would he?"

We both laughed as I picked up my phone and called my folks. They were delighted and said that this called for a big party. Lindy was so happy that she cried.

I was so happy because I knew that they had accepted my life.

THE DAY WE LEFT, I could see that Dickie was trying to cover up his feelings of disappointment at not going. He just wasn't up to it and, while he knew that, it still didn't make it easier as we pulled out of the driveway and left him in his niece's care. He never got on well with her. It was her daughter he loved so much and she was with me.

The entire trip up, Lindy talked non-stop about our wedding, until I finally asked her to take a five minute break. "I guess I have been going at it pretty strong, haven't I?"

"Gee, I didn't notice," I laughed.

"Well, you pick a conversation then. Go ahead, anything."

"How about what we are going to do when we are married. I mean I am not working now and I think I better remedy that before I turn into a lazy slob."

"You will never be that Tug. Besides, you and I aren't nearly finished with our preservation work. I know how tough Uncle Dickie was on you when you told him how you had learned to look at things from different perspectives, but he didn't mean that you should quit and walk away. He would be devastated if you did. Then all his hopes and dreams for the future of the shore would be dashed for good. You couldn't live with that."

"No I couldn't. I love that old man, but for now, there is little I can do. That's why this book is so important. Words can move people, Lindy and this book will be a call to action to people who don't want to lose it all in a couple of decades. That is my hope anyway."

"Then you write, Tug. You write day and night until you are finished. People will pay attention to you. You have learned so much and if you can get them to think, even, about the consequences of what is happening then you will have carried on Uncle Dickie's dream."

"Do you think he can settle for that? I mean he really wanted a war, replete with cannons, I do believe."

The only war Uncle Dickie is going to see is if this wedding doesn't take place soon. I think he really wants to live to see us married…and maybe have a baby."

I blushed at the thought of a baby. I hadn't given that subject a moment's thought. Hesitantly I said, "Let's get married first and then see what happens from there."

"Your point is well taken. Let's just get married."

"You are a broken record on that subject Lindy."

"I can't help it. From the minute you asked me, all I wanted to do is to be Mrs. Theodore Alston the third."

"Sounds nice, doesn't it?"

"Yes it does, but I don't think we can go by that too often in Somerville."

"No indeed," I chuckled.

BEING WITH FAMILY CAN HAVE a wonderful way of cementing things. From the moment we walked through the door, I saw that Dad truly wanted to get to know Lindy. The look on his face when she gave him that first kiss on the cheek told me that that was not going to be a problem. He beamed.

Mom was mom, only this time she outdid herself. She gave me her mother's diamond ring and then made sure it was sized and given to Lindy for her party. She was in hog heaven whirling about the huge room, telling everyone how she loved Lindy and how proud she was of me, writing a book and all.

With the clinking of glass, the room grew quiet. Dad was front and center. Lindy walked to my side and held my hand. We knew what was coming. When he went to make a toast, his voice choked. He elegantly held his hand to his mouth and cleared his throat. Then he proceeded to give the most beautiful speech I had ever heard him make. He extolled the virtues of marriage through the love he had for my mother. He spoke with such tenderness and affection that I was stunned. Then he turned to Lindy and me and raised his glass to us and said:

"To my son, Tug, who has been the gentle giant of compassion that I never was and never could be; and to Lindy, his true soul mate. I wish them a lifetime of happiness and love."

Everyone clapped and I felt my Mom's hand slide through mine. Whispering in my ear, she said, "Sometimes he can surprise you in the most amazing ways." She moved away quickly and then went to Dad's side and gave him a kiss. For the first time in my life I understood him. I truly understood him. He was a man's man, given to few words outside his news column. And it wasn't until this moment that I clearly saw that he was full of love…for me.

As we left to return home, we all kissed and hugged like never before. We had all agreed on a spring wedding and it would be in Somerville. It was to be nothing fancy; just a good party for all. Mikey broke in that he was very excited about getting such a neat new sister-in-law and that he would be able to visit them a lot more now that he had chosen to go to the University of Maryland. I knew that he meant well, but a newbie jock wasn't going to have a lot of spare time on his hands. We had to get going and pulling Lindy away from my family was not easy. I have to say how it warmed me to see how much they had come around to love her. I knew they would.

Our return trip was even more taxing on my patience. Lindy was on the roof with excitement. I politely put on my earphones again and decided to smile at her once in a while so she might think I was trying to do both things at once. It worked for a while until she caught onto me.

"That's rude," she yelled. I was busted and realized if I wanted to make it home alive I better pay attention for real. I must say she took mercy on me and laughed at herself for being over charged about the whole thing. I loved that in her.

When she knew she was being irritating, she could laugh at herself and crack me up.

While we were gone we made sure to call home every day and talk to Dickie. We knew there would be hell to pay if we didn't. Sometimes Mom and Dad joined in the conversations and it became a fun and raucous time. Only Dickie could say things that could make you almost die from laughing. He was the biggest character my family had ever met and now he was going to be family, a point he drove home every chance he could.

I could see that Dad had gotten over his jealousy with Dickie. As a matter of fact, he would comment how much he actually liked Dickie and how it was men like Dickie that made our country so strong and great. I was shocked when he said that, but he could see right to the heart of liars and cheats. I wish I had studied that trait a little closer. It might have helped me out when it came to men like John Dawson.

I was beginning to see a lot of things lately. Maybe being in love pushed me to think about things that I had let fester for a very long time. I desperately wanted my new life with Lindy to start out fresh and new; not with tons of baggage that I had been carrying around. My father was trying to bridge the gap between us and it was up to me now to make the next move. Oft times people use the expression what goes around, comes around to mean that everyone gets theirs in the end, but I am beginning to see it a bit differently. Remember, I am a writer. It's all about when you go through the tough times and find out who these people, you call family, really are. When you do, it's the beginning of understanding what life is all about.

Quiet Time With Dickie

WE WEREN'T IN THE HOUSE two minutes and Lindy was babbling like a fool. Dickie sat in his big, old recliner and smiled while her parents listened to every word. Now it was too late for me to back out-not that I would.

"You're pritty quiet there son. I see this here news isn't quite as excitin' to you. Well, it never is to the men folk." He laughed and settled back into his chair.

"Well, with Lindy going on and all, no one could get a word in edgewise if they wanted to."

"So shout over her. What's on yer mind?"

"I was just thinking that things have turned out just the way you wanted them to, haven't they?"

That lovable grin crossed his face. "Jist about, 'ceptin' for the buildin' thing. That didn't go the way I wanted."

"It will; eventually."

"How do you say that?"

I smiled and sat down beside him. "Because, Dickie, the probability is that they will keep on developing and after a while, the eventuality is that they will run out of land."

Dickie swatted me on the leg and said, "You're bein' smart with me. Come on and let's git out of here and go out in the kitchen away from all this fussin' and squeelin'."

"Sounds good to me. I could use a beer anyway."

Lindy's dad left and went home. He wasn't much for conversation. The last words I actually heard her mom and she say is that they were headed upstairs to find some things that belonged to Aunt Shirley. I didn't have to guess that whatever they were looking for had something to do with the wedding.

Dickie popped open a beer for me and he poured himself a cup of coffee. "This would kill a bull, it's so strong, but I like it that way."

"What's on your mind, Dickie? Are you feeling ok?"

"I feel fine and all. Oh a palpitation here and there but nothin' like that last mess. I jist wanted to sit down a spell and talk; that's all."

"Well, where would you like to begin?"

"How 'bout we talk about what you intend to do now once you marry my Lindy. Things will change for her, you know. Have you thought about that?"

I was confused. I didn't have an idea of what he meant. "What exactly are you trying to say, Dickie?"

"Well, for one thing, I can't believe you will want to live down here anymore. Your kind of work will take you to big cities a lot of the time."

"Ah, I get it; you want to know if I am going to take Lindy away from you. I hadn't given that too much thought, but I don't think so. I love it here and I am writing this book and that will take me quite a while yet, so you don't have to worry about that."

I saw the relief rush into his eyes. He was scared to death that we were going to dash off someplace else once we were married. After being here for over a year now and coming to love these waters and the people who live here, it would be nearly impossible to move back to a city or anywhere else, for that matter. "What else is bothering you, Dickie?"

Pushing back in his chair, with his coffee mug in his hands, he looked at me and said, "Well, there is somethin' else, but I don't want you tellin' Lindy."

I was becoming very apprehensive. Dickie was about as serious about whatever he was going to tell me, than anything

I had ever talked to him about. "I won't say a word, I promise. What is it?"

"I went to my lawyer while you and Lindy were away. I wanted to add something to my will and I didn't want it to wait and then get all tangled up in the law and all."

"Dickie, I have a bad feeling about this..."

"Let me finish, dammit son. Now where was I? Oh, yes. When I pass on, I want you and Lindy to have this house. It's free and clear and it is a good, solid house that Shirley and I loved to pieces. It's close to the water and well, it's just what I want. I know my Shirley would have wanted it that way too."

I was stunned. This was the ultimate act of his love for both of us. It wasn't just his Lindy, but he was telling me this to let me know how much he loved me too.

"I am overwhelmed, Dickie. I don't know what to say other than thank you very much. I know when the time comes and Lindy finds out about this, she will be overjoyed. She loves this house and it has been her *real* home for years."

"That's the truth of it, son. Her parents and she get on okay, but not like she related to me and my Shirley."

I really didn't know what else to say. He had outdone himself this time. The only way I could show him how much I cared was to tease him.

"You aren't planning on moving out anytime soon, are you?"

That wonderful grin came across his face as he said, "That is not my plan, but you never know. Life has a funny way of ending jist when you git 'er started."

I laughed with him about that. He was unique and I knew that when his time came, no one ever again would replace him.

We must have sat there talking for over two hours. Lindy and her Mom went on home. They sensed that this time together for Dickie and me was a special one. And indeed it was.

WHEN I SAW LINDY IN the afternoon, she wasn't quite as chirpy as she had been at Dickie's house. However, there was no way she could keep on running her engines at that speed before she would collapse.

"Hey Tug, can we shelve the work this afternoon? I am kind of in a bad mood."

"Sure we can, Lindy. What's going on? I mean when you left here you were on cloud nine." Figuring I had done or said something, like men were always accused of, I said, "Does your bad mood have something to do with me?"

She swatted my arm and shot me a half smile. "No, you didn't do anything. It's my parents. While they are happier than clams that we are getting married, they just wish we would wait a while longer."

I couldn't believe it. Here we were, two kids in love, from different parts of the universe, and yet both sets of parents felt the same way. "Well, that is really amazing. What do you think? Don't get mad at me, but maybe they are right."

Lindy swung an arm around me. "Mom and Dad are worried about Uncle Dickie. They said he was acting really strange while we were away."

"What's so odd about that? He is always acting strange. That's his persona, Lindy."

"It's not funny, Tug. He is getting old and worn out."

"Are you all worried he is going to die on us?"

"I wouldn't be at all surprised. So, I think we should postpone our wedding for a while."

I was astonished. I knew how much she wanted to get married, but her Uncle Dickie came first. I hugged her and held her tight against my body. "Well, I think you are a very special gal. However, I got to tell you, Dickie will fight us all the way on this."

"Not when Mom tells him that she doesn't have enough time to plan a proper wedding. He will want me to have it just right."

"That's collusion, you know and he will figure it out."

"Well, if he does, he won't say anything to cause trouble."

"Boy that will be a first."

PUTTING OFF THE WEDDING TURNED out to be the best idea in the world. I dug into my book, *Reclaiming Our Lives*, and it was really beginning to gel. I had taken hundreds of interviews with watermen, farmers, businessmen and anyone else I could talk with. It took me forever to sort through my tapes and then come up with a story that reflected the spirit of the Eastern Shore.

Meanwhile I got a call from a group that was part of Dickie's "Short's Rebellion" in Delaware, and they told me that the most wonderful results of our push back game were happening. There was a huge development proposed by the John Dawson's company and the folks up there swung into action. They had all the information they needed about clean waters, sewers, schools and on and on with infrastructure issues and how they would adversely affect the area if this deal went through as proposed. Over a period of more than two months, the group protested and made quite a ruckus until John Dawson, himself, came down there and pulled back on the proposal. They decided to make it a much smaller project with more open spaces within the development. They brought their revised impact projections to the meeting and it met with approval from everyone. Finally, the victory everyone had been waiting for.

Dickie got so excited about this news that he was about to crank up Old Beauty and head on up there before I persuaded him to go in my Cherokee. As we traveled up there, he actually started whooping it up and telling me that he lived to see the day when the people of his beloved shore were really "goin' to do somethin'." But the really big moments for him were just ahead.

Lindy had her own victory going on. She had gone back to school and doubled up on the load and was determined to graduate by the end of the year. Uncle Dickie was so happy she was doing this. This was another one of those things he desperately wanted to see happen in his lifetime.

The mail had just been delivered when I heard Dickie yelling up to me to come on down. I left my book in mid-sentence and rushed down to the kitchen.

"What's up Dickie? You can hear you yelling for miles."

"This is what's up, son," he said, shoving an envelope in my hand.

"Gee, I don't know whether I should take that or not. The last time a Short handed me an envelope, I ended up having one hell of a meeting with John Dawson.

"Go on. Read it, son. Read it and then you kin kiss my ass."

My eyes flew open when he said that. This has to be really good.

And it was. Dickie Short had been named Man of the Year by the Chesapeake Bay Foundation and they were going to have a special recognition dinner for him.

"Well, I'll be damned," I said, plopping down into one of the chairs around the table.

"Well, you kin be damned, son, but kin you believe it? I am goin' to git an award. A bright, shiny one too, I'll reckon."

"Yes you are, Dickie. You do know you will have to get all dressed up for this, don't you?"

"I know that. I figure I kin wear one of my old church suits back when I used to go on with my Shirley."

The very image of what he was talking about wearing sent shivers down my spine. I had to talk him out of that in a hurry.

"You know, Dickie, this is such a great honor that nothing but a tuxedo will do. You will be the most handsome man on the shore."

He stood up and walked over to an old scratched up mirror that hung on the wall by the phone. He peered into it and said, "You know, son, you are absolutely right. I *will* be the most handsome bastard the shore has ever seen."

I left the kitchen, hysterically laughing all the way back upstairs. This night and Dickie's honor would most definitely have to make the book.

Dickie's Last Stand

EVERY SINGLE PERSON ON THE Eastern Shore heard about Dickie's "trophy," as he called it. I kept telling him it was an award, but he insisted it was a trophy.

"Danged, son, awards are tiny, little silver plates. This here is a bona fide trophy. It's tall and shiny. It's even autographed." I gave up and let him just tell people the way he wanted to. The man was completely out of control.

Lindy was just about to graduate and we were going to celebrate. That meant we were going to take a picnic basket to the shanty and eat and make love. Sounded good to me.

I had never given Lindy my Mother's engagement ring because we put the wedding off and then it just seemed like we all got so busy that there wasn't a good moment. I figured this would make quite a nice graduation gift and the moment would be perfect.

"I am stuffed, Tug. Did you have enough chicken?"

"Any more and my pants will burst open."

She shot me a devilish smile and said, "Well, let's not have that happen. I would much rather do that honor myself."

Lindy! I shouted, laughing. "What's got into you?"

"I hope you will."

"Good grief, woman. You are crude tonight. Besides, you are going to hang on there for a minute. I have something I want to show you."

"You do, do you? Well, get on with the show and tell then."

I reached for the small box that I had placed in an old cabinet that afternoon. Wasn't I the clever boy? Then, I gave it to her and threw in a kiss for good measure.

"What in the world...?"

"Just open it, Lindy. You don't need to have a running commentary."

Her eyes flew open wider than I have ever seen. I had her complete attention.

"Tug Alston. I don't believe this. It's so beautiful. Where did you--------"

I kissed her again while placing the ring on her finger. Then I whispered, "It's time we think about getting married."

"You're right. Holding her hand up, she said, "You are so right."

She popped up and said, "I have to go show this to Uncle Dickie. He will go bananas when he sees this rock."

I could only imagine what would come rolling out of his mouth when he saw my Mother's three carat diamond on his precious girl's hand.

WE LAUGHED OUR WAY BACK to Dickie's and began to think about dates for our wedding. When we hit the driveway, Lindy raced me up the steps and into the house. She won. She always did. We stopped short when we saw him.

Dickie was sitting upright in his old recliner, with his paper in his lap. His award was at his side and he had the most wonderful grin on his face; but he was not moving. In fact, he was not breathing. Lindy let out a scream and I called 911.

Dickie Short was gone. The ultimate waterman who was loved by all had now gone to his final reward. He must have known he was leaving because by his side, on that old, dilapidated TV table of his, he left me a letter.

After they took his body to the funeral home and Lindy went to be with her family, I laid down on my bed and read it.

Dear Tug,

I hate to run' off on you like this, but sometimes this is how it goes. I got to feelin' poorly and kinda figured what was goin' on and didn't want to leave without sayin' good bye. I love you, son. I think you know that. I expect you to take good care of my Lindy and give her a life as happy as me and my Shirley had. I am sorry I will be missin' the weddin' and all, but I can't tell The Man upstairs what I want. Fer the first time in my life, I have to behave. Kin you imagine? Before I go on now, there is somethin' I want you and Lindy to do fer me. Tell her Mom and Dad that I want a big party down to the garage after they plant me by the marsh. I want all my friends to have a heck of a time tellin' my old stories and laughin' their behinds off. You do that, son, and you make that book of yers go onto the best seller list. Don't ever let them fergit old Dicke.

Give that girl of mine a hug and kiss and good luck to you son.

Love,
Dickie

Could I be more blessed than to get this from this man? Lindy would cherish it for the rest of her life and I would never let anyone forget Dickie, although I think he never had to worry about that.

We did just what Dickie wanted. We buried him down by his old shanty and then all of us, men and women, went to the old garage. We had a hell of a time. Even Doris let Sooty come and I did notice she threw back a few beers herself.

It wasn't hard to laugh at all the stories. Lindy got into them really good. She added tales I had never heard before and, with each one, we all roared louder and louder. Then, Clumpy stood up and said, "Folks, we have to do somethin' before we all git to goin." He walked over to the side of the room and picked up two large, handmade, wooden boxes. I had never seen them before and I looked over to Lindy and whispered, "Do you know anything about these?"

"No, I don't. And Uncle Dickie never said anything about them neither. I don't have an idea of what is going on."

With that, Clumpy open the lids of both of them and yelled out, "It is my honor to be the one chosen to do this deed." With that, Clumpy took a picture out of one box and put it in the other. The circle is complete," he yelled out again. They held up a beer and drank. All the men seemed to know what was going on, but me. They all took a swig in, what was obviously, Dickie's honor.

Lindy shrugged her shoulders and said, "I am going to march right over there and see what all this is about." I followed in hot pursuit.

To my utter amazement, the boxes that were sitting on the table were marked Live Box, and Dead Box. I tapped Clumpy on the shoulder and asked, "Clumpy? What was going on here just now?"

"Awe, we have this tradition, Tug. When one of us dies, their pictures go from the live box into the dead box. Old Dickie would have haunted me forever if I hadn't done that.

My mouth was hanging open. Lindy was laughing her ass off.

"This is so like these old fools, Tug. They are too much." Then she added, "I love them all so much."

I did too and then I remember something that I had to tell Lindy. "Can we get out of here for a minute, Lindy?"

"Sure. Why?"

"Do you always have to ask me why?"

With a simpering little smile on that gorgeous face, she giggled, "yep."

We walked around the property. It was a really pretty late autumn day. I held her hand and she snuggled up to my side.

"I remembered something that Dickie told me a while ago."

"What, Tug?"

"You remember that night when you and your mom were upstairs, going through Aunt Shirley's things and you were all excited about the wedding?"

"Sure. You and Uncle Dickie seemed to be a million miles away downstairs, talking in the kitchen. I remember Mom and I sneaked out quietly so as not to disturb you."

"Well, he wanted to tell me something really important to him. You know, Lindy, I think he knew all along that it wouldn't be too long before he left us."

"I know what you mean. He had a sense about things. A lot of the watermen are like that, Tug."

"He told me not to say a word to you and that he wanted this to be a surprise when he died. Well, he is dead so I can share it with you."

"Will you get on with this?"

"He went to see a lawyer and he left his house to us."

Lindy stopped short and looked at me with tears in her eyes. He left us his house? Do you know how much he must have loved you to do that?"

"Not just me, Lindy. He wanted you to know how much he loved you."

Lindy's tears turned into laughter. She couldn't control herself. You might say she was getting down right hysterical.

"What's come over you? I don't think this is so funny."

"Don't you see, Tug? That clever old waterman planned this."

Knowing Dickie, she might have been on to something. I began laughing to myself at the thought.

"Well, if he did, he cut it kind of short, don't you think? We are getting married in two weeks."

"Even God couldn't resist Uncle Dickie. This was his wedding gift to us. Don't you see that?"

It would be so like him to do this, I thought. He would never want to give it to us and then have to listen to all the fussing over it. "You may be right after all."

I gave her a tight squeeze and kissed her cheek. Our life together held such promise. Suddenly, a gentle breeze blew up out of nowhere, but I had the feeling I knew who had sent it. I grabbed Lindy by the shoulders and said, "Do you hear that, Lindy? Do you hear that music? Why I do believe that's that old familiar tune being sung by a heavenly choir; led by none other than Dickie Short. *Dum Dum Da Dum…*"

A Final Comment

I DO HOPE YOU ENJOYED READING this book. It was a work of love for me. In the years of research and living part time on the Eastern Shore, I have come to fall more and more in love with this unique area. It is truly a national treasure and one that can easily be destroyed if we do not take seriously the real problems of over development and pollution that are occurring there. For certain, all who visit there dream that one day they would like to live there. Whether that becomes a reality for some or their visits are summertime pleasures only, it is urgent for us to make sure that it stays in good stead for our children and grandchildren and generations far beyond that.

If you would like to know more about the Chesapeake, the waterways that surround it and the life of its creatures, big and small, who call it their home, you can contact the Chesapeake Bay Foundation. Or, you can just mosey around the shore and, if you are real lucky, you can find some of those marvelous watermen of the Chesapeake. Sit and talk awhile and discover how many of them are just like Dickie Short.